大魚讀品
BIG FISH BOOKS

让日常阅读成为砍向我们内心冰封大海的斧头。

带上她的眼睛

刘慈欣 _ 著
[美] 周华 (Joel Martinsen) 等 _ 译

北京联合出版公司
Beijing United Publishing Co.,Ltd.

图书在版编目（CIP）数据

带上她的眼睛：汉英对照 / 刘慈欣著；（美）周华
（Joel Martinsen）等译. — 北京：北京联合出版公司，
2022.5

ISBN 978-7-5596-6072-5

Ⅰ . ①带… Ⅱ . ①刘… ②周… Ⅲ . ①幻想小说—小
说集—中国—当代—汉、英 Ⅳ . ① I247.7

中国版本图书馆CIP数据核字（2022）第046716号

带上她的眼睛：汉英对照

作　　者：刘慈欣
译　　者：［美］周华（Joel Martinsen）等
出　品　人：赵红仕
责任编辑：龚　将

北京联合出版公司出版
（北京市西城区德外大街 83 号楼 9 层　　100088）
北京世纪恒宇印刷有限公司印刷　新华书店经销
字数 390 千字　　　880 毫米 × 1230 毫米　1/32　　16.75 印张
2022 年 5 月第 1 版　　　2022 年 5 月第 1 次印刷
ISBN 978-7-5596-6072-5
定价：65.00 元

编者按

在翻开这本书之前，你或许已经浸淫在科幻故事中多年，或许只是匆匆过客，或许已经读过书中个别篇目，又或许与之素未谋面。前者也好，后者也罢，单纯从阅读的维度来看，这套书无疑会带你进入一场全新的旅途。

你即将读到的 21 篇经典中短篇小说的英译版出自两本科幻作品集：*To Hold Up the Sky* 和 *The Wandering Earth*。这两本沉甸甸的精装书于 2020 年到 2021 年相继面世，是由托尔出版公司对刘慈欣经典科幻中短篇小说进行全新选编而成的。

华语科幻的译介是一场漫漫征途，将英译版作品重新引入国内则是"照镜子"一般的历程。文字的意义是流动的，不同语言、不同译者的文本往往呈现出极具差异化的风貌。编辑过程中，编者在最大限度地保持英译本的独立性和完整性的基础上，对一些规范性的内容进行了统一，与此同时，也在有必要提示之处插入了简短的注释，尽可能减少困惑，消除阅读障碍。

值得注意的修订有：

其一，*To Hold Up the Sky* 和 *The Wandering Earth* 两本书在英文符号的使用上有所不同，为了方便中文读者阅读，在编辑过程中对个别篇目的标点符号进行了修订，做到了统一。

其二，如果你在中英文对照阅读的过程中，发现某些地方英文比中文描述得更详尽，请不必感到困惑，考虑到译者本身的文字风格以及英语表述习惯，对于不影响文意的润色和增减，编者在编辑稿件时尽可能地保留了。

其三，在《带上她的眼睛》一辑中，《吞食者》和《诗云》的故事存在交集，文字和人物也均有"串场"，两位译者对个别人物、段落的表述不同，编辑无意在两个版本中做取舍，于是在文内相应位置添加了脚注，供读者阅读赏析。

其四，对于英译稿存在明显误读的地方，编者进行了修订；除了技术性偏误之外，一些误读是文化传播中出现的认知偏差所致，一些则是顾及文化差异、"入乡随俗"的有心之举——如《梦之海》中改变了主人公的性别。对于上述两类情况，编者分别以直接修订和添加脚注的方式做了处理，尽可能将译介过程中微妙的文意变化呈现出来。

阅读是一场走进心灵的旅途，希望这套作品能够陪伴你探索认知的边界，聆听华语科幻在世界舞台上律动的音符。

公子政

2022.1.18

目录

梦之海
_1

诗云
_37

带上
她的眼睛
_105

吞食者
_189

欢乐颂
_73

地火
_123

思想者
_167

山
_227

梦之海 SEA OF DREAMS

上篇

低温艺术家

是冰雪艺术节把低温艺术家引来的。这想法虽然荒唐，但自海洋干涸以后，颜冬一直是这么想的，不管过去多少岁月，当时的情景仍然历历在目。

当时，颜冬站在自己刚刚完成的冰雕作品前，他的周围都是玲珑剔透的冰雕，向更远处望去，雪原上矗立着用冰建成的高大建筑，这些晶莹的高楼和城堡浸透了冬日的阳光。这是最短命的艺术品，不久之后，这个晶莹的世界将在春风中化作一汪清水，这过程除了带给人一种淡淡的忧伤外，还包含了更多说不清道不明的东西，这也许是颜冬迷恋冰雪艺术的真正原因。

颜冬把目光从自己的作品上移开，下定决心在评委会宣布获奖名次之前不再看它了。他长出一口气，抬头扫了一眼天空，就在这时，他第一次看到了低温艺术家。

最初他以为那是一架拖着白色尾迹的飞机，但那个飞行物的速度比飞机要快得多，它在空中转了一个大弯，那尾迹如同一支巨大的粉笔在蓝天上随意地画了个钩，在钩的末端，那个飞行物居然停住了，就停在颜冬正上方的高空中。尾迹从后向前渐渐消失，像是被它的释放者吸回去似的。

颜冬仔细地观察尾迹最后消失的那一点，发现那点不时地出现短暂的闪光。他很快确定，那闪光是一个物体被阳光反射所致。接着他看到了那个物体，它是一个小小的球体，呈灰白色；很快他又意识到那个球体并不小，它看上去小只是因为距离比较远，它这时正在飞快地扩大。颜冬很快明白了那个球体正在从高空向他站的地方掉下来，周围的人也意识到了这点，人们四散而逃。颜冬也低头跑起来，他在一座座冰雕间七拐八拐。突然间，地面被一个巨大的阴影所笼罩，颜冬的头皮一紧，一时间血液仿佛凝固了。但预料的打击并未出现，颜冬发现周围的人也都站住了脚，呆呆地向上仰望着，他也抬头看，看到那个巨大的球体就悬在距他们百米左右的上空。它并不是一个完全的球体，似乎在高速飞行中被气流冲击得变了形：向着飞行方向的一半是光滑的球面，另一半则出现了一束巨大的毛刺，使它看上去像一颗剪短了彗尾的彗星。它的体积很大，直径肯定超过了100米，像悬在半空中的一座小山，使地面上的人产生了一种巨大的压迫感。

急剧下坠的球体在半空中急刹住后，被它带动的空气仍在向下冲来，很快到达地面，激起了一圈飞快扩大的雪尘。据说，当非洲的土著首次触摸西方人带来的冰块时，都猛抽回手，惊叫：好烫！在颜冬接触到那团下坠的空气的一刹那，他也产生了这种感觉。而能使在东北的严寒露天的人产生这种感觉，这团空气的温度一定低得惊人。幸亏它很快扩散了，否则地面上的人都会被冻僵，但即使这样，很多人暴露在外的皮肤也都受到了不同程度的冻伤。

颜冬的脸因突然出现的严寒而麻木，他抬头仔细观察着那个球体表面，那半透明的灰白色物质是他再熟悉不过的东西——冰，这悬在半空中的是一个大冰球。

空气平静下来之后，颜冬吃惊地发现，那半空中巨大冰球的周围居然飘起了雪花，雪花很大，在蓝天的背景前显得异常洁白，并在阳光中闪闪发光。但这些雪花只在距球体表面一定距离内出现，飘出这段距离后立刻消失，以球体为中心形成了一个雪圈，仿佛是雪夜中的一盏街灯照亮了周围的雪花。

"我是一名低温艺术家！"一个清脆的男音从冰球中传出，"我是一名低温艺术家！"

"这个大冰球就是你吗？"颜冬仰头大声问。

"我的形象你们是看不到的，你们看到的冰球是我的冷冻场冻结空气中的水分形成的。"低温艺术家回答说。

"那些雪花是怎么回事？"颜冬又问。

"那是空气中氧和氮的结晶体，还有二氧化碳形成的干冰。"

"你的冷冻场真厉害！"

"当然，就像无数只小手攥紧无数颗小心脏一样，它使其作用范围内所有的分子和原子停止运动。"

"它还能把这个大冰团举在空中吗？"

"那是另一种场了，那是反引力场。你们每个人使用的那一套冰雕工具真有趣：有各种形状的小铲和小刀，还有喷水壶和喷灯，有趣！为了制作低温艺术品，我也拥有一套小小的工具，那就是几种力场，种类没有你们的这么多，但也很好使。"

"你也创作冰雕吗？"

"当然，我是低温艺术家，你们的世界很适合进行冰雪造型艺术，我惊讶地发现这个世界早已存在这门艺术，我很高兴地说，我们是同行。"

"你从哪里来？"颜冬旁边的另一位冰雕作者问。

"我来自一个遥远的、你们无法理解的世界，那个世界远不如你们的世界有趣。本来，我只从事艺术，一般不同其他世界交流的，但看到这样一个展览会，看到这么多的同行，我产生了交流的愿望。不过坦率地说，下面这些低温作品中真正称得上艺术品的并不多。"

"为什么？"有人问。

"过分写实，过分拘泥于形状和细节，当你们明白宇宙除了空间什么都没有，整个现实世界不过是一大堆曲率不同的空间时，就会觉得这些作品是何等可笑。不过，嗯，这一件还是有点儿感觉的。"

话音刚落，冰团周围的雪花伸下来细细的一缕，仿佛是沿着一条看不见的漏斗流下来的，这缕雪花从半空中一直伸到颜冬的冰雕作品顶部才消失。颜冬踮起脚尖，试探着向那缕雪花伸出戴着手套的手，在那缕雪花的附近，他的手指又有了那种灼热感，他急忙抽回来，手已经在手套里冻僵了。

"你是指我的作品吗？"颜冬用另一只手揉着冻僵的手说，

"我，我没有用传统的方法，也就是用现成的冰块雕刻作品，而是建造了一个由几大块薄膜构成的结构，在这个结构下面长时间地升腾起由沸水产生的蒸汽，蒸汽在薄膜表面冻结，形成一种复杂的结晶体，当这种结晶体达到一定的厚度后，去掉薄膜，就做成了你现在看到的造型。"

"很好，很有感觉，很能体现寒冷之美！这件作品的灵感是来自……"

"来自窗玻璃！不知你是否能理解我的描述：在严冬的凌晨醒来，你蒙眬的睡眼看到窗玻璃上布满了冰晶，它们映着清晨暗蓝色的天光，仿佛是你一夜梦的产物……"

"理解理解，我理解！"低温艺术家周围的雪花欢快地舞动起来，"我的灵感也被激发了，我要创作！我必须创作！！"

"那个方向就是松花江，你可以去取一块冰，或者……"

"什么？你以为我这样的低温艺术家，要从事的是你们这种细菌般可怜的艺术吗？这里没有我需要的冰材！"

地面上的冰雕艺术家们都茫然地看着来自星际的低温艺术家，颜冬呆呆地说："那么，你要去……"

"我要去海洋！"

取冰

一队庞大的机群在 5 千米高的空中向海岸线方向飞行，这是有史以来最混杂的一队机群，它由从体形庞大的波音巨无霸到蚊子似的轻型飞机在内的各种飞机组成，这是全球各大通讯社派出的采访飞机，还有研究机构和政府派出的观察监视飞机。这乱哄哄的机群紧跟着前面一条短粗的白色航迹飞行着，像一群追赶着牧羊人的羊群。那条航迹是低温艺术家飞行时留下的，它不停地催促后面的飞机快些，为了等它们，它不得不忍受这比爬行还慢的速度（对于可随意进行时空跃迁的它，光速已经是爬行了），它不停地抱怨说这会使自己的灵感消失的。

对于后面飞机上的记者们通过无线电喋喋不休的提问，低温艺术家一概懒得回答，它只有兴趣同坐在一架中央电视台租用的"运–12"上的颜冬谈话，于是到后来记者们都不吱声了，只是专心地听着这一对艺术家同行的对话。

"你的故乡是在银河系之内吗？"颜冬问，这架"运–12"距离低温艺术家最近，可以看到那个飞行中的冰球在白色航迹的头部时隐时现，这航迹是冰球周围的超低温冷凝了大气中的氧、氮和二氧化碳形成的，有时飞机不慎进入这滚滚掠过的白雾中，机窗上会立刻覆盖上厚厚的一层白霜。

"我的故乡不属于任何恒星系，它处于星系之间广漠的黑暗虚空中。"

"你们的星球一定很冷。"

"我们没有星球，低温文明起源于一团暗物质云中，那个世界确实很冷，生命从接近绝对零摄氏度的环境中艰难地取得微小的热量，吮吸着来自遥远星系的每一丝辐射。当低温文明学会走路时，我们便迫不及待地进入银河系这个最近的温暖世界。在这个世界中我们也必须保持低温状态才能生存，于是我们成了温暖世界的低温艺术家。"

"你指的低温艺术就是冰雪造型吗？"

"哦，不不，用远低于一个世界平均温度的低温与这个世界发生作用，以产生艺术效应，这都属于低温艺术。冰雪造型只是适合于你们世界的低温艺术，冰雪的温度在你们的世界属于低温，在暗物质世界就属于高温了；而在恒星世界，熔化的岩浆也属于低温材料。"

"我们之间对艺术美的感觉好像有共同之处。"

"不奇怪，所谓温暖，不过是宇宙诞生后一阵短暂的痉挛所产生的同样短暂的效应，它将像日落后的暮光一样转瞬即逝，能量将消失，只有寒冷永存，寒冷之美才是永恒的美。"

"这么说，宇宙最终将热寂？！"颜冬听到耳机中有人问，事后知道他是坐在后面飞机上的一位理论物理学家。

"不要离题，我们只谈艺术。"低温艺术家冷冷地说。

"下面是海了！"颜冬无意间从舷窗望下去，看到弯曲的海岸线正在下面缓缓移过。

"再向前，我们要到最深的海洋，那里便于取冰。"

"可哪儿有冰啊？"颜冬看着下面广阔的蓝色海面不解地问。

"低温艺术家到哪里，哪里就会有冰。"

低温艺术家又向前飞行了一个多小时，颜冬从飞机上向下看，下面早已是一片汪洋。这时，飞机突然拉升，超重使颜冬两眼一黑。

"天啊，我们差点儿撞上它！"飞行员大叫，原来低温艺术家突然停下了，后面的飞机都猝不及防地纷纷转向。"惯性定律对这家伙不起作用，它的速度好像是在瞬间减到零，按理说这样的减速早把冰球扯碎了！"飞行员对颜冬说，同时掉转机头，与别的飞机一起，浩浩荡荡地围绕着悬在空中的冰球盘旋着。静止的冰球又在空气中产生了大量的氧氮雪花，但由于高空中的强风，雪花都被吹向一个方向，像是冰球随风飘舞的白发。

"我要开始创作了！"低温艺术家说，没等颜冬回话，它突然垂直坠落下去，仿佛在空中举着它的那只无形的巨手突然放开了。飞机上的人们看着它以自由落体的方式越来越快地下落，很快便消失在海面蓝色的背景中，只能隐约看到它在空气中拉出的一道雾化痕迹。很快，海面上出现了一团白色的水花，水花消失后有一圈波纹在扩散。

"这个外星人投海自杀了。"飞行员对颜冬说。

"别瞎扯了！"颜冬拖着东北口音白了飞行员一眼，"飞低些，那个冰球很快就要浮起来了！"

但冰球并没有浮出来，在那个位置的海面上出现了一个白点，这白点很快扩大成一个白色的圆形区域。这时飞机的高度已经很低了，颜冬仔细观察，发现那白色区域其实是覆盖海面的一层白色雾气。白雾区域急剧扩大，加上飞机在继续降低，很快，可以看到的海面全部冒起了白雾。这时颜冬听到了一个声音，像连续的雷声，又像是大地和山脉在断裂，这声音来自海面，盖住了引擎的轰鸣声。飞机贴海飞行，颜冬向下仔细观察白雾下的海面，首先发现海面反射的阳光很完整、很柔和，不像刚才那样呈刺目的碎金状；他接着看到海的颜色变深了，海面的波浪变得平滑了，但真正震撼他的是下一个发现：那些波浪是凝固不动的。

"天啊，海冻了！"

"你没疯吧？"飞行员扭头扫了他一眼说。

"你自个儿仔细看看……嗨，我说你怎么还往下降啊？想往冰面上降落？！"

飞行员猛拉操纵杆，颜冬眼前又一黑，听到他说："啊，不，真邪门儿了……"再看看他，一副梦游的表情，"我没下降，那海面，哦不，那冰面，在自己上升！"

这时他们听到了低温艺术家的声音："你们的飞行器赶快让开，别挡住上升的路，哼，要不是有同行在一架飞行器里，我才不在乎撞着你们呢，我在创作中最讨厌干扰灵感的东西。向西飞向西飞，那面距边缘比较近！"

"边缘？什么的边缘？"颜冬不解地问。

"我采的冰块呀！"

所有的飞机像一群被惊飞的鸟，边爬高边向低温艺术家指引的方向飞去，在它们的下面，因温度突降产生的白雾已消失，深蓝色的冰原一望无际。尽管飞机在爬高，但冰原的上升速度更快，所以飞机与冰面的相对高度还是在不断降低。"天啊，地球在追着我们呢！"飞行员惊叫道。渐渐地，飞机又紧贴着冰面飞行了，凝固的暗蓝色波涛从机翼下滚滚而过，飞行员喊道："我们只好在冰面上降落了！我的天，边爬高边降落，这太奇怪了！"

就在这时，"运–12"飞到了冰块的尽头，一道笔直的边缘从机身下飞速掠过，下面重新出现了波光粼粼的海洋。这情形很像航空母舰上的战斗机起飞时，跃出甲板的瞬间所看到的，但后面这艘"航母"有几千米高！颜冬猛回头，看到一道巨大的暗蓝色悬崖正在向后退去，这道悬崖表面极其平整，向两端延伸出去，一时还望不到尽头；悬崖下部与海面相接，可以看到海浪拍打在上面形成的一条白边。但这道白边在颜冬看到它几秒钟后就突然消失了，代之以另一条笔直的边缘——大冰块的底部已离开了海面。

大冰块以更快的速度上升，"运-12"同时在下降，它的高度很快位于海面和空中的冰块之间。这时颜冬看到了另一个广阔的冰原，与刚才不同的是它在上方，形成了一个极具压抑感的阴暗的天空。

随着大冰块的继续上升，颜冬终于在视觉上证实了低温艺术家的话：这确实是一个大冰块，一大块呈规则长方体的冰，现在，它在空中已经可以被完整地看到，这暗蓝色的长方体占据了三分之二的天空，它那平整的表面不时反射着阳光，如同高空的一道道刺目的闪电。在由它构成的巨大的背景前有几架飞机在缓缓爬行，如同在一座摩天大楼边盘旋的小鸟，只有仔细看才能看到。事后雷达观测数据表明，这个冰块长 60 千米，宽 20 千米，高 5 千米，呈一个扁平的长方体。

大冰块继续上升，它在空中的体积渐渐缩小，终于在心理上可以让人接受了。与此同时，它投在海面上巨大的阴影也在移动，露出了海洋上有史以来最恐怖的景象。

颜冬看到，他们飞行在一个狭长的盆地上空，这盆地就是大冰块离开后在海中留下的空间。盆地四周是高达 5 千米的海水的高山，人类从未见过水能形成这样的结构：它形成了几千米高的悬崖！这液态的悬崖底部翻起百米高的巨浪，上部在不停地崩塌着，悬崖就在崩塌中向前推进，它的表面起伏不定，但总体与海底保持着垂直。随着海水悬崖的推进，盆地在缩小。

这是摩西劈开红海的反演。

最让颜冬震撼的是，整个过程居然很慢！这显然是尺度的缘故，他见过黄果树瀑布，觉得那水流下落得也很慢，而眼前的这海水悬崖，尺度要比那瀑布大两个数量级，这使他可以有充足的时间欣赏这旷世奇观。

这时，冰块投下的阴影已完全消失，颜冬抬头一看，冰块看上去只有两个满月大小，在天空中已不太显眼。

随着海水悬崖的推进，盆地已缩成了一道峡谷，紧接着，两道几十千米长、5千米高的海水悬崖迎面相撞，一声沉闷的巨响在海天间久久回荡，冰块在海洋中留下的空间完全消失了。

"我们不是在做梦吧？"颜冬自语道。

"是梦就好了，你看！"飞行员指指下面，在两道悬崖相撞之处，海面并未平静，而是出现了两道与悬崖同样长的波带，仿佛是已经消失的两道海水悬崖在海面的化身，它们分别向着相反的方向分离开来。从高空看去波带并没有惊人之处，但仔细目测可知它们的高度都超过了200米，如果近看，肯定像两道移动的山脉。

"海啸？"颜冬问。

"是的，可能是有史以来最大的，海岸要遭殃了。"

颜冬再抬头看，蓝天上，冰块已看不到了，据雷达观测，它已成为地球的一颗冰卫星。

在这一天，低温艺术家以同样的方式又从太平洋中取走了上百块同样大小的冰块，把它们送入绕地球运行的轨道。

这天，在处于夜晚的半球，每隔两三个小时就可以看到一群闪烁的亮点横贯夜空飞过，与背景上的星星不同的是，如果仔细看，每个亮点都可以看出形状，那是一个个小长方体，它们都在以不同的姿势自转着，使它们反射的阳光以不同的频率闪动。人们想了很久也不知如何形容这些太空中的小东西，最后还是一名记者的比喻得到了认可：

"这是宇宙巨人撒出的一把水晶骨牌。"

两名艺术家的对话

"我们应该好好谈谈了。"颜冬说。

"我约你来就是为了谈谈，但我们只谈艺术。"低温艺术家说。

颜冬此时正站在一个悬浮于 5 千米空中的大冰块上，是低温艺术家请他到这里来的。现在，送他上来的直升机就停在旁边的冰面上，旋翼还转动着，随时准备起飞。四周是一望无际的冰原，冰面反射着耀眼的阳光，向脚下看看，蓝色的冰层深不见底。在这个高度上晴空万里，风很大。

这是低温艺术家已从海洋中取走的 5000 块大冰中的一块，在这之前的 5 天里，它以平均每天 1000 块的速度从海洋中取冰，并把冰块送到地球轨道上去。在太平洋和大西洋的不同位置，一块块巨冰在海中被冻结后升上天空，成为夜空中那越来越多的亮闪闪的"宇宙骨牌"中的一块。世界沿海的各大城市都受到了海啸的袭击，但随着时间的推移，这种灾难渐渐减少了，原因很简单：海面在降低。

地球的海洋，正在变成围绕它运行的冰块。

颜冬用脚跺了跺坚硬的冰面说："这么大的冰块，你是如何在瞬间把它冻结，如何使它成为一个整体而不破碎，又用什么力量把它送到太空轨道上去？这一切远超出了我们的理解和想象。"

低温艺术家说："这有什么，我们在创作中还常常熄灭恒星呢！不是说好了只谈艺术吗？我这样制作艺术品，与你用小刀铲制作冰雕，从艺术角度看没什么太大的区别。"

"那些轨道中的冰块暴露在太空强烈的阳光中时，为什么不融化呢？"

"我在每个冰块的表面覆盖了一层极薄的透明滤光膜，这种膜只允许不发热频段的冷光进入冰块，发热频段的光线都被反射，所以冰块保持不化。这是我最后一次回答你这类问题了，我停下工作来，不是为了谈这些无聊的事，下面我们只谈艺术，要不你就走吧，我们不再是同行和朋友了。"

"那么，你最后打算从海洋中取多少冰呢？这总和艺术创作有关吧！"

"当然是有多少取多少，我向你谈过自己的构思，要完美地表达这个构思，地球上的海洋还是不够的，我曾打算从木星的卫星上取冰，但太麻烦了，就这么将就吧。"

颜冬整理了一下被风吹乱的头发，高空的寒冷使他有些颤抖，他问："艺术对你很重要吗？"

"是一切。"

"可……生活中还有别的东西，比如，我们还需为生存而劳作，我就是长春光机所的一名工程师，业余时间才能从事艺术。"

低温艺术家的声音从冰原深处传了上来，冰面的振动使颜冬的脚心有些痒痒："生存，它只是文明的婴儿时期要换的尿布，以后，它就像呼吸一样轻而易举了，以至于我们忘了有那么一个时代竟需要花精力去维持生存。"

"那社会生活和政治呢？"

"个体的存在也是婴儿文明的麻烦事，以后个体将融入主体，也就没有什么社会和政治了。"

"那科学呢，总有科学吧？文明不需要认识宇宙吗？"

"那也是婴儿文明的课程，当探索进行到一定程度，一切将毫发毕现，你会发现宇宙是那么简单，科学也就没必要了。"

"只剩下艺术？"

"只剩艺术，艺术是文明存在的唯一理由。"

"可我们还有其他的理由，我们要生存，下面这颗行星上有几十亿人和更多的其他物种要生存，而你要把我们的海洋弄干，让这颗生命行星变成死亡的沙漠，让我们全渴死！"

从冰原深处传出一阵笑声，这又让颜冬的脚痒起来："同行，你看，我在创作灵感汹涌澎湃的时候停下来同你谈艺术，可每次，你都和我扯这些鸡毛蒜皮的事，真让我失望，你应该感到羞耻！你走吧，我要工作了。"

"日你祖宗！"颜冬终于失去了耐心，用东北话破口大骂起来。

"是句脏话吗？"低温艺术家平静地问，"我们的物种是同一个体一直成长进化下去的，没有祖宗。再说你对同行怎么这样，嘻嘻，我知道，你嫉妒我，你没有我的力量，你只能搞细菌的艺术。"

"可你刚才说过，我们的艺术只是工具不同，没有本质的区别。"

"可我现在改变看法了，我原以为自己遇到了一位真正的艺术家，可原来是一个平庸的可怜虫，成天喋喋不休地谈论诸如海洋干了呀、生态灭绝呀之类与艺术无关的小事，太琐碎太琐碎，我告诉你，艺术家不能这样。"

"还是日你祖宗！！"

"随你便吧，我要工作了，你走吧。"

这时，颜冬感到一阵超重，使他一屁股跌坐在光滑的冰面上，同时，一股强风从头顶上吹下来，他知道冰块又上升了。他连滚带爬地钻进直升机，直升机艰难地起飞，从最近的边缘飞离冰块，险些在冰块上升时产生的龙卷风中坠毁。

人类与低温艺术家的交流彻底失败了。

梦之海

颜冬站在一个白色的世界中，脚下的土地和周围的山脉都披上了银装，那些山脉高大险峻，使他感到仿佛置身于冰雪覆盖的喜马拉雅山中。事实上，这里与那里相反，是地球上最低的地方，这是马里亚纳海沟，昔日太平洋最深的海底。覆盖这里的白色物质并非积雪，而是以盐为主的海水中的矿物质，当海水被冻结后，这些矿物质就析出并沉积在海底，这些白色的沉积盐层最厚的地方可达百米。

在过去的 200 天中，地球上的海洋已被低温艺术家用光了，连南极和格陵兰的冰川都被洗劫一空。

现在，低温艺术家邀请颜冬来参加他的艺术品最后完成的仪式。

前方的山谷中有一片蓝色的水面，那蓝色很纯很深，在雪白的群峰间显得格外动人。这就是地球上最后的海洋了，它的面积相当于滇池大小，早已没有了海洋那广阔的万顷波涛，表面只是荡起静静的微波，像深山中一个幽静的湖泊。有三条河流汇入了这最后的海洋，这是在干涸的辽阔海底长途跋涉后幸存下来的大河，是地球上有史以来最长的河，到达这里时已变成细细的小溪了。

颜冬走到海边，在白色的海滩上把手伸进轻轻波动着的海水中，由于水中的盐分已经饱和，海面上的波浪显得有些沉重，而颜冬的手在被微风吹干后，析出了一层白色的盐末。

空中传来一阵颜冬熟悉的尖啸声，这声音是低温艺术家向下滑落时冲击空气发出的。颜冬很快在空中看到了它，它的外形仍是一个冰球，但由于直接从太空返回这里，在大气中飞行的距离不长，球的体积比第一次出现时小了许多。这之前，在冰块进入轨道后，人们总是用各种手段观察离开冰块时的低温艺术家，但什么也没看到，只有它进入大气层后，那个不断增大的冰球才能让人知道它的存在和位置。

低温艺术家没有向颜冬打招呼，冰球在这最后海洋的中心垂直坠入水面，激起了高高的水柱。然后又出现了那熟悉的一幕：一圈冒出白雾的区域从坠落点飞快扩散，很快，白雾盖住了整个海面；然后是海水快速冻结时发出的那种像断裂声的巨响；再往后白雾消散，露出了凝固的海面。与以往不同的是，这次整个海洋都被冻结了，没有留下一滴液态的水；海面也没有凝固的波浪，而是平滑如镜。在整个冻结过程中，颜冬都感到寒气扑面。

接着，已冻结的最后的海洋被整体提离了地面，开始只是小心地升到距地面几厘米处，颜冬看到前面冰面的边缘与白色盐滩之间出现了一条黑色的长缝，空气涌进长缝，去填补这刚刚出现的空间，形成一股紧贴地面的疾风，被吹动的盐尘埋住了颜冬的脚。提升速度加快，最后的海洋转眼间升到半空中，如此巨大体积物体的快速上升在地面产生了强烈的气流扰动，一股股旋风卷起盐尘，在峡谷中形成一道道白色的尘柱。颜冬吐出飞进嘴里的盐末，那味道不是他想象的咸，而是一种难言的苦涩，正如人类所面临的现实。

最后的海洋不再是规则的长方体，它的底部精确地模印着昔日海洋最深处的地形。颜冬注视着最后的海洋上升，直到它变成一个小亮点融入浩荡的冰环中。

冰环大约相当于银河的宽度，由东向西横贯长空。与天王星和海王星的环不同，冰环的表面不是垂直而是平行于地球球面，这使它在空中呈现为一条宽阔的光带。这光带由 20 万块巨冰组成，环绕地球一周。在地面可以清楚地分辨出每个冰块，并能看出它的形状，这些冰块有的自转、有的静止，这 20 万个闪动或不闪动的光点构成了一条壮丽的天河，这天河在地球的天空中庄严地流动着。

在一天的不同时段，冰环的光和色都进行着丰富的变幻。

清晨和黄昏是它色彩最丰富的时段，这时冰环的色彩由地平线处的橘红渐变为深红，再变为碧绿和深蓝，如一条宇宙彩虹。

在白天，冰环在蓝天上呈耀眼的银色，像一条流过蓝色平原的钻石大河。白天冰环最壮观的景象是环食，即冰环挡住太阳的时刻，这时大量的冰块折射着阳光，天空中会出现奇伟瑰丽的焰火表演。依太阳被冰环挡住的时间长短，分为交叉食和平行食，所谓平行食，是太阳沿着冰环走过一段距离，每年还有一次全平行食，这天太阳从升起到落下，沿着冰环走完它在天空中的全部路程。这一天，冰环仿佛是一条撒在太空中的银色火药带，在日出时被点燃，那璀璨的火球疯狂燃烧着越过长空，在西边落下，壮丽至极，已很难用语言表达。正如有人惊叹："这一天，上帝从空中蹚过。"

然而冰环最迷人的时刻是在夜晚，它发出的光芒比满月还要亮一倍，这银色的光芒洒满大地。这时，仿佛全宇宙的星星都排成密集的队列，在夜空中庄严地行进。与银河不同，在这条浩荡的星河中可以清楚地分辨出每个长方体的星星。这密密麻麻的星星中有一半在闪耀，这 10 万颗闪动的星星在星河中构成涌动的波纹，仿佛宇宙的大风吹拂着河面，使整条星河变成了一个有灵性的整体……

在一阵尖啸声中，低温艺术家最后一次从太空返回地面，悬在颜冬上空，一圈纷飞的雪花立刻裹住了它。

"我完成了，你觉得怎么样？"它问。

颜冬沉默良久，只说出了两个字："服了。"

他真的服了。这之前，他曾连续三天三夜仰望着冰环，不吃不喝，直到虚脱。能起床后他又到外面去仰望冰环，他觉得永远也看不够。在冰环下，他时而迷乱，时而沉浸于一种莫名的幸福之中，这是艺术家找到终极之美时的幸福，他被这宏大的美完全征服了，整个灵魂都融化其中。

"作为一个艺术家，能看到这样的创造，你还有他求吗？"低温艺术家又问。

"我真无他求了。"颜冬由衷地回答。

"不过嘛，你也就是看看，你肯定创造不出这种美，你太琐碎。"

"是啊，我太琐碎，我们太琐碎，有啥法子？都有自己和老婆孩子要养活啊。"

颜冬坐到盐地上，把头埋在双臂间，沉浸在悲哀之中。这是一个艺术家在看到自己永远无法创造的美时，在感觉到自己永远无法超越的界限时，产生的最深的悲哀。

"那么，我们一起给这件作品起个名字吧，叫——梦之环，如何？"

颜冬想了一会儿，缓缓地摇了摇头："不好，它来自海洋，或者说是海洋的升华，我们做梦也想不到海洋还具有这种形态的美，就叫——梦之海吧。"

"梦之海……很好很好，就叫这个名字，梦之海。"

这时颜冬想起了自己的使命："我想问，你在离开前，能不能把梦之海再恢复成我们的现实之海呢？"

"让我亲自毁掉自己的作品，笑话！"

"那么，你走后，我们是否能自己恢复呢？"

"当然可以，把这些冰块送回去不就行了？"

"怎么送呢？"颜冬抬头问，全人类都在竖起耳朵听。

"我怎么知道。"低温艺术家淡淡地说。

"最后一个问题：作为同行，我们都知道冰雪艺术品是短命的，那么梦之海……"

"梦之海也是短命的，冰块表面的滤光膜会老化，不再能够阻拦热光。但它消失的过程与你的冰雕完全不同，这过程要剧烈和壮观得多：冰块汽化，压力使薄膜炸开，每个冰块变成一个小彗星，整个冰环将弥漫着银色的雾气，然后梦之海将消失在银雾中，然后银雾也扩散到太空消失了，宇宙只能期待着我在遥远的另一个世界的下一个作品。"

"这将在多长时间后发生？"颜冬的声音有些发颤。

"滤光膜失效，用你们的计时，嗯，大约20年吧。嗨，怎么又谈起艺术之外的事了？琐碎琐碎！好了同行，永别了，好好欣赏我留给你们的美吧！"

冰球急速上升，很快消失在空中。据世界各大天文机构观测，冰球沿垂直于黄道面的方向急速飞去，在其加速到光速的一半时，突然消失在距太阳13个天文单位的太空中，好像钻进了一个看不见的洞，以后它再也没有回来。

下篇

纪念碑和导光管

干旱已持续了5年。

焦黄的大地从车窗外掠过，时值盛夏，大地上没有一点儿绿色，树木全部枯死，裂纹如黑色的蛛网覆盖着大地，干热风扬起的黄沙不时遮盖了这一切。有好几次，颜冬确信他看到了铁路边被渴死的人的尸体，但那些尸体看上去像是旁边枯死的大树上掉下的一根根干树枝，倒没什么恐怖感。这严酷的干旱世界与天空中银色的梦之海形成了鲜明的对比。

颜冬舔了舔干裂的嘴唇，一直舍不得喝自己带的那壶水，那是他全家四天的配给，是妻子在火车站硬让他带上的。昨天单位里的职工闹事，坚决要求用水来发工资，市场上非配给的水越来越少，有钱也买不到了……这时有人拍了拍他的肩膀，扭头一看是邻座。

"你就是那个外星人的同行吧？"

自从成为人类与低温艺术家沟通的信使，颜冬就成了名人，开始他是一位正面角色和英雄，可是低温艺术家走后情况就发生了变化，有种说法，说是他在冰雪艺术节上激发了低温艺术家的灵感，否则什么事都不会发生。大多数人都知道这是无稽之谈，但有个发泄怨气的对象总是好事，所以到现在，他在人们的眼中简直成了外星人的同谋。好在后来有更多的事要操心，人们渐渐把他忘了。但这次他虽戴着墨镜，还是被认了出来。

"你请我喝水！"那人沙哑地说，嘴唇上有两小片干皮屑掉了下来。

"干什么，你想抢劫？"

"放聪明点儿，不然我要喊了！"

颜冬只好把水壶递给他，这家伙一口气喝了个底朝天，旁边的人惊异地看着他，从过道上路过的列车员也站住呆呆地看了他半天，他们不敢相信竟有人这么奢侈，这就像有海时（人们对低温艺术家到来之前的时代的称呼）看着一个富豪一人吃一顿价值10万元的盛宴一样。

那人把空水壶还给颜冬，又拍拍他的肩膀低声说："没关系的，很快就都结束了。"

颜冬明白他这话的含意。

首都的街道上已很少有汽车，罕见的汽车也是改装后的气冷式，传统的水冷式汽车已经严格禁止使用了。幸亏世界危机组织中国分部派了辆车来接他，否则他绝对到不了危机组织的办公大楼。一路上，他看到街道都被沙尘暴带来的黄尘所覆盖，见不到几个行人——缺水的人在这干热风中行走是十分危险的。

世界像一条离开水的鱼，已经奄奄一息了。

到了危机组织办公大楼后，颜冬首先去找组织的负责人报到，负责人带着他来到了一间很大的办公室，告诉他这就是他将要工作的机构。颜冬看看办公室的门，与其他的办公室不同，这扇门上没有标牌，负责人说：

"这是一个秘密机构，这里所有的工作严格保密，以免引起社会动乱，这个机构的名称叫纪念碑部。"

走进办公室，颜冬发现这里的人都有些古怪：有的人头发太长，有的人没有头发；有的人的穿着在这个艰难时代显得过分整洁，有的人除了短裤外什么都没穿；有的人神色忧郁，有的人兴奋异常……中间的长桌上放着许多奇形怪状的模型，看不出是干什么用的。

"欢迎您，冰雕艺术家先生！"在听完负责人的介绍后，纪念碑部的部长热情地向颜冬伸出手来，"您终于有机会把您从外星人那里得到的灵感发挥出来，当然，这次不能以冰为材料，我们要创作的，是一件需要永久保存的作品。"

"这是在干什么？"颜冬不解地问。

部长看看负责人又看看颜冬，说："您还不知道？我们要建立人类纪念碑！"

颜冬显得更加茫然了。

"就是人类的墓碑。"旁边一位艺术家说。这人头发很长，衣衫破烂，一副颓废模样，一只手拿着一瓶二锅头喝得颇有些醉意，这东西是有海时剩下的，现在比水便宜多了。

颜冬向四周看看说："可……我们还没死啊。"

"等死了就晚了，"负责人说，"我们应该做最坏的打算，现在是考虑这事的时候了。"

部长点点头说："这是人类最后的艺术创作，也是最伟大的创作，作为一名艺术家，还有什么比参加这一创作更幸福的呢？"

"其实都多……多余！"长发艺术家挥着酒瓶说，"墓碑是供后人凭吊的，没有后人了，还立个鸟碑？"

"注意名称，是纪念碑！"部长严肃地更正道，然后笑着对颜冬说："虽这么说，可他提出的创意还是不错的：他提议全世界每人拿出一颗牙齿，用这些牙齿建造一座巨碑，每个牙齿上刻一个字，足以把人类文明最详细的历史都刻上了。"他指指一个看上去像白色金字塔的模型。

"这是对人类的亵渎！"另一位光头艺术家喊道，"人类的价值在于其大脑，他却要用牙齿来纪念！"

长发艺术家又抢起瓶子灌了一口："牙……牙齿容易保存！"

"可大部分人都还活着！"颜冬又严肃地重复一遍。

"但还能活多久呢？"长发艺术家说，一谈到这个话题，他的口齿又利落了，"天上滴水不下，江河干涸，农业全面绝收已经三年了，90%的工业已经停产，剩下的粮食和水，还能维持多长时间？"

"这群废物，"秃头艺术家指着负责人说，"忙活了5年，到现在一块冰也没能从天上弄下来！"

对秃头艺术家的指责，负责人只是付之一笑："事情没有那么简单。以人类现有的技术，从轨道上迫降一块冰并不难，迫降100块甚至上千块冰也能做到，但要把在太空中绕地球运行的20万块冰全部迫降，那完全是另一回事了。如果用传统手段，用火箭发动机使冰块减速并使其返回大气层，就需制造大量可重复使用的超大功率发动机，并将它们送入太空，这是一项巨大的技术工程，以人类目前的技术水平和资源贮备，有许多不可克服的障碍。比如说，要想拯救地球的生态系统，如果从现在开始，需要在四年的时间里迫降一半冰块，这样平均每年就要迫降2.5万块冰，它所需要的火箭燃料在重量上比有海时人类一年消耗的汽油还多！可那不是汽油，那是液氢液氧和四氧化二氮、偏二甲肼之类，制造它们所消耗的能量和资源，是生产汽油的上百倍，仅此一项，就使整个计划成为不可能。"

长发艺术家点点头："所以说末日不远了。"

负责人说："不，不是这样，我们还可以采取许多非传统、非常规方法，希望还是有的，但在我们努力的同时，也要做最坏的打算。"

"我就是为这个来的。"颜冬说。

"为最坏的打算？"长发艺术家问。

"不，为希望。"他转向负责人说，"不管你们召我来干什么，我来有自己的目的。"他说着指了指自己带的那体积很大的行囊，"请带我到海洋回收部去。"

"你去回收部能干什么？那里可都是科学家和工程师！"秃头艺术家惊奇地问。

"我从事应用光学研究，职称是研究员，除了与你们一样做梦外，我还能干些更实际的事。"颜冬扫了一眼周围的艺术家说。

在颜冬的坚持下，负责人带他来到了海洋回收部。这里的气氛与纪念碑部截然不同，每个人都在电脑前紧张地工作着。办公室的正中央放着一台可以随意取水的饮水机，这简直是国王的待遇，不过想想这些人身上寄托着人类的全部希望，也就不奇怪了。

见到海洋回收部的总工程师后，颜冬对他说："我带来了一个回收冰块的方案。"说着他打开背包，拿出了一根白色的长管子，管子有手臂粗，接着他又拿出一个约一米长的圆筒。颜冬走到一个向阳的窗前，把圆筒伸到窗外摆弄着，那圆筒像伞一样撑开了，"伞"的凹面镀着镜面膜，使它成为一个类似于太阳灶的抛物面反射镜。接着，颜冬把那根管子从反射镜底部的一个小圆洞中穿过去，然后调节镜面的方向，使它把阳光聚焦到伸出的管子的端部。立刻，管子的另一端把一个刺眼的光斑投到室内的地板上，由于管子平放在地上，那个光斑呈长椭圆形。

颜冬说："这是用最新的光导纤维做成的导光管，在导光时衰减很小。当然，实际系统的尺寸比这要大得多，在太空中，只要用一面直径 20 米左右的抛物面反射镜，就可以在导光管的另一端得到一个温度达 3000 摄氏度以上的光斑。"

颜冬向周围看看，他的演示并没有产生预期的效果，那些工程师们扭头朝这边看看，又都继续专注于自己的电脑屏幕不再理会他。直到那光斑使防静电地板冒出了一股青烟，才有最近的一个人走了过来，说："干什么，还嫌这儿不热？"同时把导光管轻轻向后一拉，使采光的一端脱离了反射镜的焦距，地板上的光斑虽然还在，但立刻变暗了许多，失去了热度。颜冬惊奇地发现，这人摆弄这东西很在行。

总工程师指指导光管说："把这些东西收起来，喝点儿水吧。听说你是坐火车来的，从长春到这儿的火车居然还开？你一定渴坏了。"

颜冬急着想解释自己的发明，但他确实渴坏了，冒烟的嗓子已经说不出话来。

"不错，这确实是目前最可行的方案。"总工程师递给颜冬一杯水。

颜冬一口气喝光了那杯水，呆呆地望着总工程师问："您是说，已经有人想到了？"

总工程师笑着说："与外星人相处，使你低估人类的智力了。其实，在低温艺术家把第一块冰送到轨道上时，这个方案就已经有很多人想到了。后来又有了许多变种，比如用太阳能电池板代替反射镜，用电线和电热丝代替导光管，其优点是设备容易制造和运送，缺点是效率不如导光管方案高。现在，对它的研究已进行了 5 年，技术上已经成熟，所需的设备也大部分被制造出来了。"

"那为什么还不实施？"

旁边的一名工程师说："这个方案，将使地球海洋失去 21%的水，这部分水或变成推进蒸气散失了，或在再入大气时被高温离解。"

总工程师扭头对那名工程师说："你们可能还不知道，美国人最新的计算机模拟表明，在电离层之下，再入时高温离解产生的氢气会立刻同周围的氧再化合形成水，所以高温离解的损失以前被高估了，总损失率估计为 18%，"他又转向颜冬："但这个比例也够高的了。"

"那你们有把太空中的水全部取回来的方案吗？"

总工程师摇摇头，说："唯一的可能是用核聚变发动机，但目前我们在地面上都得不到可控的核聚变。"

"那为什么还不快些行动呢？要知道，犹豫不决的话地球会失去百分之百的水的。"

总工程师坚定地点点头："所以，在长时间的犹豫之后我们决定行动了，很快，地球将为生存决一死战。"

回收海洋

颜冬加入了海洋回收部，负责对已生产出的导光管进行验收的工作，这虽不是核心岗位，但也使他感到很充实。

在颜冬到达首都一个月后，人类回收海洋的工程开始了。

在短短的一个星期内，从全球各大发射基地，有 800 枚大型运载火箭发射升空，把 5 万吨荷载送入地球轨道。然后，从北美的发射基地，20 架航天飞机向太空运送了 300 名宇航员。由于沿同一航线频繁发射，在各基地上空形成了一道经久不散的火箭尾迹，从轨道上看，仿佛是从各大陆向太空牵了几根蛛丝。

这批发射，把人类在太空的活动规模提高了一个数量级，但所使用的技术仍是 20 世纪初的，这使人们意识到，在现有的条件下，如果全世界齐心协力孤注一掷干一件事，会取得怎样的成就。

在直播的电视中，颜冬同所有人一起目睹了在第一个冰块上安装减速推进系统的过程。

为了降低难度，首批迫降的冰块都是不自转的。三名宇航员降落在这样一个冰块上，他们携带着如下装备：一辆形状如炮弹，能够在冰块中钻进的钻孔车、三根导光管、一根喷射管、三个折叠起来的抛物面反射镜。只有这时才能感觉到冰块的巨大——他们三人仿佛是降落在一个小小的水晶星球上，在太空中强烈的阳光下，脚下的冰的大地似乎深不可测。在黑色的天空上，远远近近悬浮着无数个这样的水晶星球，有些还在自转着。周围那些自转或不自转的冰块反射和折射着阳光，在三名宇宙员站立的冰面上，不停地进行着令人目眩的光与影的变幻。向远处看，冰环中的冰块看上去越来越小，密度却越来越大，渐渐缩成一条致密的银带弯向地球的另一面。距离最近的一个冰块与他们所在的这块间距只有 3000 米，以它的短轴为轴自转着，在他们眼中，这种自转有一种摄人心魄的气势，仿佛三只小蚂蚁看着一幢水晶摩天大楼一次次倒塌下来。这两个冰块在一段时间后将会因引力而相撞，结果将使滤光膜破裂，冰块解体，破碎后的冰块将很快在阳光的照射下蒸发消失。这种相撞在冰环中已发生了两次，这也是首先迫降这块冰的原因。

操作开始后，一名宇航员启动了那辆钻孔车，钻头车首旋转起来，冰屑呈锥状向外飞溅，在阳光下闪闪发光。钻孔车钻破了冰面那层看不见的滤光膜，像一枚被拧进去的螺丝一样钻进了冰面，在身后留下了一个圆形的钻洞。随着钻洞向冰层深处延伸，在冰层中隐约可以看到一条不断延长的白线。到达预定深度后，钻孔车转向，沿另一个方向驶出冰面，这就形成了另一条钻洞。最后，共向冰块深处打了四条钻洞，它们相交于冰层深处的一点。接下来，宇航员们把三根导光管插入三个钻洞，再把一根喷射管插入直径较大的第四条钻洞，喷射管的喷口正对着冰块运行的方向。然后，宇航员用一根细管向导光管、喷射管与洞壁之间填充某种速凝液体，使其形成良好的密封。最后，他们张开了抛物面反射镜。如果说回收海洋的最初阶段采用了什么最新技术的话，那就是这些反射镜了。它们是纳米科技创造的奇迹，在折叠起来时只有一立方米大小，但张开后形成了一面直径达500米的巨型反射镜。这三面反射镜，像冰块上生长的三片银色的荷叶。宇航员们调整导光管的伸出端，使其受光端头与反射镜的焦点重合。

在冰层深处三条钻洞的交点处，出现了一个明亮的光点，它像一个小太阳，照亮了大冰块中神话般的奇景：银色的鱼群、随波浪舞动的海草……这一切在瞬间冻结时都保持着栩栩如生的姿态，甚至连鱼嘴中吐出的串串小气泡都清晰可见。在距此100多千米的另一个也在回收中的冰块里，导光管导入冰层深处的阳光照出了一个巨大的黑影，那是一条长达20多米的蓝鲸！这就是人类昔日的海洋。

蒸汽使冰层深处的光点很快模糊了，在蒸汽散射下，光点变成了一个白色光球，随着被融化的冰体积的增加，光球渐渐膨胀。当压力达到预定值后，喷射管喷嘴上的盖板被冲开了，一股汹涌的蒸气流急速喷出，由于没有阻力，它呈一个尖尖的锥形向远方扩散，最后在阳光中淡化消失了；还有一部分蒸汽进入了另一个冰块的阴影，被冷凝成冰晶，仿佛是一大群在阴影中闪闪发光的萤火虫。

首批100个冰块上的减速推进系统启动了，由于冰块质量巨大，系统产生的推力相对来说很小，所以它们须运行少则 15 天多则一个月的时间，才能使冰块减速到坠入大气层的速度。在坠落之前，宇航员们将再次登上冰块，取回导光管和反射镜。要全部迫降 12 万个冰块，这些设备应尽可能地重复使用。

以后对自转的冰块的回收操作要复杂许多，推进系统将首先刹住其自转，再进行减速。

冰流星

颜冬与危机委员会的人们一起来到太平洋中部的平原上，观看第一批冰流星坠落。

昔日的洋底平原一片雪白，反射着强烈的阳光，不戴墨镜是睁不开眼的。但这并没有使颜冬想起自己的东北故乡的雪原，因为这里如地狱般炎热，地面气温接近 50 摄氏度，热风吹起盐尘，打得脸生疼。在远处，有一艘 10 万吨油轮，那巨大的船体斜立在地面，有几层楼高的螺旋桨和舵上覆满了盐层。再看看更远处连绵的白色群山，那是人类从未见过的海底山脉，颜冬的脑海中顿时涌出两句诗：

大海是船儿的陆地，黑夜是爱情的白天。

他苦笑了一下，经历了这样的灾难，还摆脱不了艺术家的思维。

一阵欢呼声响起，颜冬抬头向人们所指的方向望去，看到在横贯长空的银色冰环中，出现了一个红色的亮点，这亮点飘出了冰环，膨胀成一个火球，火球的后面拖着一条白色的尾迹，这水蒸气尾迹越来越长、越来越粗，其色彩也越浓、越白。很快，火球分裂成了数十块，每一块又继续分裂，每一小块都拖着长长的白尾，这一片白色的尾迹覆盖了半个天空，似乎是一棵白色的圣诞树，每根树枝的枝头都挂着一盏亮闪闪的小灯……

更多的冰流星出现了，超声速音爆传到地面，像滚滚的春雷。天空中旧的水蒸气尾迹在渐渐淡化，新的尾迹不断出现，使天空被一张错综复杂的白色巨网所覆盖，现在，已有几万亿吨的水重新属于地球了。

大部分冰流星都在空中分裂汽化了，但是也有一个较大的碎冰块直接坠落到地面，坠落点距离颜冬所在的地方约 40 千米，海底平原在一声巨响中震动不已，在远处的山脉间腾起一团顶天立地的白色蘑菇云，这大团的水蒸气在阳光下发出耀眼的白光，并随风渐渐扩散，变为天空中的第一片云层。后来，云多了起来，第一次挡住了炙烤大地 5 年的烈日，并盖满了整个天空，颜冬感到一阵沁人心脾的凉爽。

后来，云层变黑变厚，其中红光闪闪，不知是闪电，还是仍在不断坠落的冰流星的光芒。

下雨了！这是即使在有海时也罕见的大暴雨，颜冬和其他人在雨中欢呼狂奔，他们觉得灵魂都在这雨中融化了。但后来大家只好都躲回车内或直升机里，因为这时人在雨中会窒息。

雨一直下到黄昏才停，海底平原上出现了许多水洼，在从云缝中露出的夕阳下闪着金光，仿佛大地的一只只刚睁开的眼睛。

颜冬随着人群，踏着黏稠的盐浆，跑到最近的水洼前。他捧起一捧水，把那沉甸甸的饱和盐水洒到自己的脸上，任它和泪水一同流下，哽咽着说：

"海啊，我们的海啊……"

尾声

10 年以后。

颜冬走上了冰封的松花江江面，他裹着一件破大衣，旅行袋中放着那套保存了 15 年的工具：几把形状各异的刀铲、一个锤子、一只喷水壶。他跺跺脚，证实江面确实冻住了。松花江早在 5 年前就有了水，但这是第一次封冻，而且是在夏天封冻。由于干旱少雨，同时大量的冰流星把其引力势能在大气层中转化为热能，全球气候一直炎热无比。但在海洋回收的最后阶段，最大体积的冰块被迫降，这些冰块分裂后的碎块也较大，大多直接撞击地面。除了几座城市被摧毁外，撞击激起的尘埃挡住了太阳的热量，使全球气温骤降，地球进入了新的冰期。

颜冬抬头看看夜空，这是他童年时看到的星空，冰环已经消失，只有从太空中残余的少量小冰块的快速的运动中才能把它们与群星的背景区分开来。梦之海又变回现实的海，这件宏伟的艺术品，其绝美与噩梦一起永远铭刻在人类的记忆中。

虽然回收海洋的工程已经结束，但以后的全球气候肯定仍是极其恶劣的，生态还要很长时间才能恢复。在可以看到的未来，人类的生活将是十分艰难的。但至少可以活下去了，这使所有的人感到了满足。确实，冰环时代使人类学会了满足，但人类还学会了更重要的东西。现在，世界危机组织会改名为太空取水组织，另一个宏大的工程正在计划中：人类打算飞向遥远的类木行星，把木星卫星上和土星光环中的水取回地球，以弥补地球在海洋回收过程中失去的18%的水。人们首先打算用已经掌握的冰块驱动技术，驱动土星光环中的冰块驶向地球，当然，在那样遥远的距离上，阳光已很微弱，只有用核聚变来汽化冰块核心以得到所需的推力了。至于木星、卫星上的水，要用更复杂和庞大的技术才能取得，已经有人提出把整个木卫二从木星的引力巨掌中拉出来，使其驶向地球，成为地球的第二个卫星。这样，地球上能得到的水便多于18%，这可以使地球的生态系统变得天堂般美好。当然，这都是遥远未来的事，活着的人谁都没有希望看到它的实现，但这希望使人们在艰难的生活中感到了前所未有的幸福，这是人类从冰环时代得到的最大财富：回收梦之海使人类看到了自己的力量，教会了他们做以前从不敢做的梦。

颜冬看到远处的冰面上聚着一小堆人，他一滑一滑地走了过去，那些人看到他后都向他跑来，有人摔了一跤后爬起来接着跑。

"哈哈，老伙计！！"跑在最前面的人同颜冬热情拥抱，颜冬认出来了，他就是冰环时代之前好几届冰雪艺术节的冰雕组评委之一。颜冬曾对天发誓不再同这些评委说话，因为上一届艺术节上的冰雕特等奖，显然是基于那个妙龄女作者的脸蛋和身段而不是基于她的作品。接着，他又认出了其他几个人，大都是冰环时代之前的冰雕作者，同这个时代的所有人一样，他们穿着破烂，苦难和岁月已把他们中许多人的双鬓染白。现在，颜冬有流浪多年后回家的感觉。

"听说，冰雪艺术节又恢复了？"他问。

"当然，要不咱们到这儿来干什么？"

"我寻思着，日子这么难……"颜冬裹紧了破大衣，在寒风中发抖，不停地跺着冻得麻木的脚，其他人也同他一样，哆嗦着，跺着脚，像一群乞丐难民。

"日子难怎么了，日子难不能不要艺术啊，对不对？"一位老冰雕家上下牙打着战说。

"艺术是文明存在的唯一理由！"另一个人说。

"去他的，老子存在的理由多了！"颜冬大声说，众人都大笑起来。

然后大家都沉默了，他们回顾着这十几年的艰难岁月，挨个数着自己存在的理由。最后，他们重新把自己从一群大灾难的幸存者变回为艺术家。

颜冬掏出了一瓶二锅头，大家你一口我一口地传着喝了暖暖身子，然后他们在空旷的江岸上生起一堆火，在火上烘烤一把油锯，直到它能在严寒中启动。大家走到江面上，油锯哗哗作响地切入冰面，雪白的冰屑四下飞溅。很快，他们从松花江上取出了第一块晶莹的方冰。

诗云

CLOUD
OF
POEMS

伊依一行三人乘一艘游艇在南太平洋上做吟诗航行，他们的目的地是南极，如果几天后能顺利地到达那里，他们将钻出地壳去看诗云。

　　今天，天空和海水都很清澈，对于作诗来说，世界显得太透明了。抬头望去，平时难得一见的美洲大陆清晰地出现在天空中；在东半球构成的覆盖世界的巨大穹顶上，大陆好像是墙皮脱落的区域……

　　哦，现在人类生活在地球里面，更准确地说，人类生活在气球里面——地球已变成了气球。地球被掏空了，只剩下厚约100千米的一层薄壳，但大陆和海洋还原封不动地存在着，只不过都跑到里面了——球壳的里面。大气层也还存在，也跑到球壳里面了，所以地球变成了气球，一个内壁贴着海洋和大陆的气球。空心地球仍在自转，但自转的意义与以前已大不相同：它产生重力，构成薄薄地壳的那点质量产生的引力是微不足道的，地球重力现在主要由自转的离心力来产生了。但这样的重力在世界各个区域是不均匀的：赤道上最强，约为 1.5 个原地球重力，随着纬度增高，重力也渐渐减小，两极地区的重力为零。现在吟诗游艇航行的纬度正好是原地球的标准重力处，但很难令伊依找到已经消失的实心地球上旧世界的感觉。

空心地球的球心处悬浮着一个小太阳，现在正以正午的阳光照耀着世界。这个太阳的光度在 24 小时内不停地变化，由最亮渐变至熄灭，给空心地球里面带来昼夜更替。在适当的夜里，它还会发出月亮的冷光，但只是从一个点发出的，看不到圆月。

游艇上的三个人中有两个其实不是人，他们中的一个是一头名叫大牙的恐龙，它高达 10 米的身躯一移动，游艇就跟着摇晃倾斜，这令站在船头的吟诗者很烦。吟诗者是一个干瘦的老头儿，同样雪白的长发和胡须混在一起飘动，他身着唐朝的宽大古装，仙风道骨，仿佛是在海天之间挥洒写就的一个狂草字。

他就是新世界的创造者，伟大的——李白。

礼物

事情是从 10 年前开始的，当时，吞食帝国刚刚完成了对太阳系长达两个世纪的掠夺，来自远古的恐龙驾驶着那个直径 5 万千米的环形世界飞离太阳，航向天鹅座方向。吞食帝国还带走了被恐龙掠去当作小家禽饲养的 12 亿人类，但就在接近土星轨道时，环形世界突然开始减速，最后竟沿原轨道返回，重新驶向太阳系内层空间。

在吞食帝国开始它的返程后的一个大环星期，使者大牙乘着它那艘如古老锅炉般的飞船飞离大环，它的衣袋中装着一个叫伊依的人类。

"你是一件礼物！"大牙对伊依说，眼睛看着舷窗外黑暗的太空，它那粗放的嗓音震得衣袋中的伊依浑身发麻。

"送给谁？"伊依在衣袋中仰头大声问，他能从袋口看到恐龙的下颚，那像是一大块悬崖顶上凸出的岩石。

"送给神！神来到了太阳系，这就是帝国返回的原因。"

"是真的神吗？"

"它们掌握了不可思议的技术，已经纯能化，并且能在瞬间从银河系的一端跃迁到另一端，这不就是神了？如果我们能得到那些超级技术的百分之一，吞食帝国的前景就很光明了。我们正在完成一项伟大的使命，你要学会讨神喜欢！"

"为什么选中了我，我的肉质是很次的。"伊依说。他 30 多岁，与吞食帝国精心饲养的那些肌肤白嫩的人类相比，他的外貌有些沧桑感。

"神不吃虫虫，只是收集，我听饲养员说你很特别，你好像还有很多学生？"

"我是一名诗人，现在在饲养场的家禽人中教授人类的古典文学。"伊依很吃力地念出了"诗""文学"这类在吞食语中很生僻的词。

"无用又无聊的学问。你那里的饲养员默许你授课，是因为其中的一些内容在精神上有助于改善虫虫们的肉质……我观察过，你自视清高、目空一切，对于一个被饲养的小家禽来说，这应该是很有趣的。"

"诗人都是这样的！"伊依在衣袋中站直，虽然知道大牙看不见，但还是骄傲地昂起了头。

"你的先辈参加过地球保卫战吗？"

伊依摇摇头："我在那个时代的先辈也是诗人。"

"一种最无用的虫虫，在当时的地球上也十分稀少了。"

"他生活在自己的内心世界里，对外部世界的变化并不在意。"

"没出息……呵，我们快到了。"

听到大牙的话，伊依把头从衣袋中伸出来，透过宽大的舷窗向外看，看到了飞船前方那两个发出白光的物体，那是悬浮在太空中的一个正方形平面和一个球体，当飞船移动到与平面齐平时，它在星空的背景上短暂地消失了一下，这说明它几乎没有厚度；那个完美的球体悬浮在平面正上方，两者都发出柔和的白光，表面均匀得看不出任何特征。这两个东西仿佛是从计算机图库中取出的两个元素，是这纷乱的宇宙中两个简明而抽象的概念。

"神呢？"伊依问。

"就是这两个几何体啊，神喜欢简洁。"

距离拉近，伊依发现平面为足球场大小，飞船在向平面上降落，它的发动机喷出的火流首先接触到平面，仿佛只是接触到一个幻影，没有在上面留下任何痕迹，但伊依感到了重力和飞船接触平面时的震动，说明它不是幻影。大牙显然以前来过这里，没有犹豫就拉开舱门走了出去，伊依看到它同时打开了气密过渡舱的两道舱门，心一下抽紧了，但他并没有听到舱内空气涌出时的呼啸声,当大牙走出舱门后,衣袋中的伊依嗅到了清新的空气,伸在外面的脸上感受到了习习的凉风……这是人和恐龙都无法理解的超级技术,它温柔和漫不经心的展示震撼了伊依,与人类第一次见到吞食者时相比,这震撼更加深入灵魂。他抬头望望,以灿烂的银河为背景,球体悬浮在他们上方。

"使者,这次你又给我带来了什么小礼物?"神问。他说的是吞食语,声音不大,仿佛从无限远的太空深渊中传来,让伊依第一次感觉到这种粗陋的恐龙语言听起来很悦耳。

大牙把一只爪子伸进衣袋,抓出伊依放到平面上,伊依的脚底感受到了平面的弹性。大牙说:"尊敬的神,得知您喜欢收集各个星系的小生物,我带来了这个很有趣的小东西:地球人类。"

"我只喜欢完美的小生物,你把这么肮脏的虫子拿来干什么?"神说。球体和平面发出的白光微微地闪动了两下,可能是表示厌恶。

"您知道这种虫虫?!"大牙惊奇地抬起头。

"只是听这个旋臂的一些航行者提到过,不是太了解。在这种虫子不算长的进化史中,这些航行者曾频繁地光顾地球,这种生物的思想之猥琐,行为之低劣,其历史之混乱和肮脏,都很让他们恶心,直到地球世界毁灭之前,也没有一个航行者屑于同它们建立联系……快把它扔掉。"

大牙抓起伊依,转动着硕大的脑袋看看可往哪儿扔,"垃圾焚化口在你后面。"神说。大牙一转身,看到身后的平面上突然出现了一个小圆口,里面闪着蓝幽幽的光……

"你不要这样说!人类建立了伟大的文明!"伊依用吞食语声嘶力竭地大喊。

球体和平面的白光又颤动了两次，神冷笑了两声："文明？使者，告诉这个虫子什么是文明。"

大牙把伊依举到眼前，伊依甚至听到了恐龙的两个大眼球转动时骨碌碌的声音："虫虫，在这个宇宙中，对一个种族文明程度的统一度量是这个种族所进入的空间的维度，只有进入六维以上空间的种族才具备加入文明大家庭的起码条件，我们尊敬的神的一族已能够进入十一维空间。吞食帝国已能在实验室中小规模地进入四维空间，只能算是银河系中一个未开化的原始群落，而你们，在神的眼里也就是杂草和青苔一类的。"

"快扔了，脏死了。"神不耐烦地催促道。

大牙举着伊依向垃圾焚化口走去，伊依拼命挣扎，从衣服中掉出了许多白色的纸片。当那些纸片飘荡着下落时，从球体中射出一条极细的光线，当那束光线射到其中一张纸上时，它便在半空中悬住了，光线飞快地在上面扫描了一遍。

"哟，等等，这是什么东西？"

大牙把伊依悬在焚化口上方，扭头看着球体。

"那是……是我的学生们的作业！"伊依在恐龙的巨掌中挣扎着说。

"这种方形的符号很有趣，它们组成的小矩阵也很好玩。"神说，从球体中射出的光束又飞快地扫描了已落在平面上的另外几张纸。

"那是汉……汉字，这些是用汉字写的古诗！"

"诗？"神惊奇地问，收回了光束，"使者，你应该懂一些这种虫子的文字吧？"

"当然，尊敬的神，在吞食帝国吃掉地球前，我在它们的世界生活了很长时间。"大牙把伊依放到焚化口旁边的平面上，弯腰拾起一张纸，举到眼前吃力地辨认着上面的小字，"它的大意是……"

"算了吧，你会曲解它的！"伊依挥手制止大牙说下去。

"为什么？"神很感兴趣地问。

"因为这是一种只能用古汉语表达的艺术，即使被翻译成人类的其他语言，也会失去大部分内涵和魅力，变成另一种东西。"

"使者，你的计算机中有这种语言的数据库吗？还有有关地球历史的一切知识，好的，给我传过来吧，就用我们上次见面时建立的那个信道。"

大牙急忙返回飞船上，在舱内的电脑上鼓捣了一阵儿，嘴里嘟囔着："古汉语部分没有，还要从帝国的网络上传过来，可能有些时滞。"伊依从敞开的舱门中看到，恐龙的大眼球中映射着电脑屏幕上变幻的彩光。当大牙从飞船上走出来时，神已经能用标准的汉语读出一张纸上的中国古诗了：

白日依山尽，黄河入海流。

欲穷千里目，更上一层楼。

"您学得真快！"伊依惊叹道。

神没有理他，只是沉默着。

大牙解释说："它的意思是：恒星已在行星的山后面落下，一条叫黄河的河流向着大海的方向流去，哦，这河和海都是由那种由一个氧原子和两个氢原子构成的化合物组成的，要想看得更远，就应该在建筑物上登得更高些。"

神仍然沉默着。

"尊敬的神，您不久前曾君临吞食帝国，那里的景色与写这首诗的虫虫的世界十分相似，有山有河也有海，所以……"

"所以我明白诗的意思，"神说，球体突然移动到大牙头顶上，伊依感觉它就像一只盯着大牙看的没有眸子的大眼睛，"但，你，没有感觉到些什么？"

大牙茫然地摇摇头。

"我是说，隐含在这个简洁的方块符号矩阵的表面含义后面的一些东西。"

大牙显得更茫然了，于是神又吟诵了一首古诗：

前不见古人，后不见来者。
念天地之悠悠，独怆然而涕下。

大牙赶紧殷勤地解释道："这首诗的意思是：向前看，看不到在遥远过去曾经在这颗行星上生活过的虫虫；向后看，看不到未来将要在这行星上生活的虫虫，于是感到时空太广大了，于是哭了。"

神沉默。

"呵，哭是地球虫虫表达悲哀的一种方式，这是它们的视觉器官……"

"你仍没感觉到什么？"神打断了大牙的话问，球体又向下降了一些，几乎贴到大牙的鼻子上。

大牙这次坚定地摇摇头："尊敬的神，我想里面没有什么的，一首很简单的小诗。"

接下来，神又连续吟诵了几首古诗，都很简短，且属于题材空灵超脱的一类，有李白的《下江陵》《静夜思》和《黄鹤楼送孟浩然之广陵》，柳宗元的《江雪》，崔颢的《黄鹤楼》，孟浩然的《春晓》等。

大牙说："在吞食帝国，有许多长达百万行的史诗，尊敬的神，我愿意把它们全部献给您！相比之下，人类虫虫的诗是这么短小简单，就像他们的技术……"

球体忽地从大牙头顶飘开去，在半空中沿着随意的曲线飘行着："使者，我知道你们最大的愿望就是希望我回答一个问题：吞食帝国已经存在了8000万年，为什么其技术仍徘徊在原子时代？我现在有答案了。"

大牙热切地望着球体说："尊敬的神，这个答案对我们很重要！求您……"

"尊敬的神，"伊依举起一只手大声说，"我也有一个问题，不知能不能问？！"

大牙恼怒地瞪着伊依，像要把他一口吃了似的，但神说："我仍然讨厌地球虫子，但那些小矩阵为你赢得了这个权利。"

"艺术在宇宙中普遍存在吗？"

球体在空中微微颤动，似乎在点头："是的，我就是一名宇宙艺术的收集和研究者，我穿行于星云间，接触过众多文明的各种艺术，它们大多是庞杂而晦涩的体系，用如此少的符号，在如此小巧的矩阵中蕴含着如此丰富的感觉层次和含义分支，而且这种表达还要在严酷得有些变态的诗律和音韵的约束下进行，这，我确实是第一次见到……使者，现在可以把这虫子扔了。"

大牙再次把伊依抓在爪子里："对，该扔了它，尊敬的神，吞食帝国中心网络中存贮的人类文化资料是相当丰富的，现在您的记忆中已经拥有了所有资料，而这个虫虫，大概就记得那么几首小诗。"说着，它拿着伊依向焚化口走去。"把这些纸片也扔了。"神说，大牙又赶紧反身去用另一只爪子收拾纸片，这时伊依在大爪中高喊：

"神啊，把这些写着人类古诗的纸片留作纪念吧！您收集到了一种不可超越的艺术，在宇宙中传播它吧！"

"等等，"神再次制止了大牙，伊依已经悬到了焚化口上方，他感到了下面蓝色火焰的热力。球体飘过来，在距伊依的额头几厘米处悬定，他同刚才的大牙一样受到了那只没有眸子的巨眼的逼视。

"不可超越？"

"哈哈哈……"大牙举着伊依大笑起来，"这个可怜的虫虫居然在伟大的神面前说这样的话，滑稽！人类还剩下什么？你们失去了地球上的一切，即便能带走的科学知识也忘得差不多了。有一次在晚餐桌上，我在吃一个人之前问他：地球保卫战争中的人类的原子弹是用什么做的？他说是原子做的！"

"哈哈哈哈……"神也让大牙逗得大笑起来，球体颤动成了椭圆，"不可能有比这更正确的回答了，哈哈哈……"

"尊敬的神，这些脏虫虫就剩下那几首小诗了！哈哈哈……"

"但它们是不可超越的！"伊依在大爪中挺起胸膛庄严地说。

球体停止了颤动，用近似耳语的声音说："技术能超越一切。"

"这与技术无关，这是人类心灵世界的精华，不可超越！"

"那是因为你不知道技术最终能具有什么样的力量，小虫子，小小的虫子，你不知道。"神的语气变得父亲般温柔，但潜藏在深处阴冷的杀气让伊依不寒而栗，神说，"看着太阳。"

伊依按神的话做了，这是位于地球和火星轨道之间的太空，太阳的光芒使他眯起了双眼。

"你最喜欢的颜色是什么？"神问。

"绿色。"

话音刚落，太阳变成了绿色，那绿色妖艳无比，太阳仿佛是一只突然浮现在太空深渊中的猫眼，在它的凝视下，整个宇宙都变得诡异无比。

大牙爪子一颤，把伊依掉在了平面上。当理智稍稍恢复后，他们都意识到另一个比太阳变绿更加震撼的事实：从这里到太阳，光需行走十几分钟，但这一切都发生在一瞬间！

半分钟后，太阳恢复原状，又发出耀眼的白光。

"看到了吗？这就是技术，是这种力量使我们的种族从海底淤泥中的鼻涕虫变为神。其实技术本身才是真正的神，我们都真诚地崇拜它。"

伊依眨着昏花的双眼说："但神并不能超越那样的艺术，我们也有神，想象中的神，我们崇拜它们，但并不认为它们能写出李白和杜甫那样的诗。"

神冷笑了两声，对伊依说："真是一只无比固执的虫子，这使你更让人厌恶。不过，为了消遣，就让我来超越一下你们的矩阵艺术。"

伊依也冷笑了两声："不可能的，首先你不是人，不可能有人的心灵感受，人类艺术在你那里只是石板上的花朵，技术并不能使你超越这个障碍。"

"技术超越这个障碍易如反掌，给我你的基因！"

伊依不知所措。"给神一根头发！"大牙提醒说，伊依伸手拔下一根头发，一股无形的吸力将头发吸向球体，后来那根头发又从球体中飘落到平面上，神只是提取了发根上带着的一点皮屑。

球体中的白光涌动起来，渐渐变得透明了，里面充满了清澈的液体，浮起串串水泡。接着，伊依在液体中看到了一个蛋黄大小的球，它在射入液球的阳光中呈淡红色，仿佛自己会发光。小球很快长大，伊依认出了那是一个蜷曲着的胎儿，他肿胀的双眼紧闭着，大大的脑袋上交错着红色的血管。胎儿继续成长，小身体终于伸展开来，像青蛙似的在液球中游动着。液体渐渐变得混浊了，透过液球的阳光只映出一个模糊的影子，看得出那个影子仍在飞速成长，最后变成了一个游动着的成人的身影。这时液球又恢复成原来那样完全不透明的白色光球，一个赤裸的人从球中掉出来，落到平面上。伊依的克隆体摇摇晃晃地站了起来，阳光在他湿漉漉的身体上闪亮，他的头发和胡子老长，但看得出来只有三四十岁，除了一样精瘦外，一点也不像伊依本人。克隆体僵站着，呆滞的目光看着无限远方，似乎对这个他刚刚进入的宇宙浑然不知。在他的上方，球体的白光逐渐暗下来，最后完全熄灭了，球体本身也像蒸发似的消失了。但这时，伊依感觉什么东西又亮了起来，很快发现那是克隆体的眼睛，它们由呆滞突然充满了智慧的灵光。后来伊依知道，神的记忆这时已全部转移到克隆体中了。

"冷，这就是冷？！"一阵轻风吹来，克隆体双手抱住湿乎乎的双肩，浑身打战，但声音中充满了惊喜，"这就是冷，这就是痛苦，精致的、完美的痛苦，我在星际间苦苦寻觅的感觉，尖锐如洞穿时空的十维弦，晶莹如类星体中心的纯能钻石，啊——"他伸开皮包骨头的双臂仰望银河，"前不见古人，后不见来者，念天地之……"一阵冷战使克隆体的牙齿咯咯作响，他赶紧停止了出生演说，跑到焚化口边烤火去了。

克隆体把两只手放到焚化口的蓝色火焰上烤着，哆哆嗦嗦地对伊依说："其实，我现在进行的是一项很普通的操作，当我研究和收集一种文明的艺术时，总是将自己的记忆借宿于该文明的一个个体中，这样才能保证对该艺术的完全理解。"

这时，焚化口中的火焰亮度剧增，周围的平面上也涌动着各色的光晕，使得伊依感觉整个平面像是一块漂浮在火海上的毛玻璃。

大牙低声对伊依说："焚化口已转换为制造口了，神正在进行能—质转换。"看到伊依不太明白，他又解释说，"傻瓜，就是用纯能制造物品，上帝的活计！"

制造口突然喷出了一团白色的东西，那东西在空中展开并落了下来，原来是一件衣服，克隆体接住衣服穿了起来，伊依看到那竟是一件宽大的唐朝古装，用雪白的丝绸做成，有宽大的黑色镶边，刚才还一副可怜相的克隆体穿上它后立刻显得飘飘欲仙，伊依实在想象不出它是如何从蓝色火焰中被制造出来的。

又有物品被制造出来，从制造口飞出一块黑色的东西，像一块石头一样"咚"地砸在平面上，伊依跑过去拾起来，不管他是否相信自己的眼睛，他手中拿着的分明是一块沉重的石砚，而且还是冰凉的。接着又有什么"啪"地掉下来，伊依拾起那个黑色的条状物，他没猜错，这是一块墨！接着被制造出来的是几支毛笔、一个笔架、一张雪白的宣纸，（从火里飞出的纸！）还有几件古色古香的案头小饰品，最后制造出来的也是最大的一件东西：一张样式古老的书案！伊依和大牙忙着把书案扶正，把那些小东西在案头摆放好。

"转化成这些东西的能量，足以把一颗行星炸成碎末。"大牙对伊依耳语，声音有些发颤。

克隆体走到书案旁，看着上面的摆设满意地点点头，一只手捋着刚刚干了的胡子，说：

"我，李白。"

伊依审视着克隆体问："你是说想成为李白呢，还是真把自己当成了李白？"

"我就是李白，超越李白的李白！"

伊依笑着摇摇头。

"怎么，到现在你还怀疑吗？"

伊依点点头说："不错，你们的技术远远超过了我的理解力，已与人类想象中的神力和魔法无异，即使是在诗歌艺术方面也有让我惊叹的东西：跨越如此巨大的文化和时空的鸿沟，你竟能感觉到中国古诗的内涵……但理解李白是一回事，超越他又是另一回事，我仍然认为你面对的是不可超越的艺术。"

克隆体——李白的脸上浮现出高深莫测的笑容，但转瞬即逝，他手指书案，对伊依大喝一声："研墨！"然后径自走去，在几乎走到平面边缘时站住，捋着胡须遥望星河沉思起来。

伊依从书案上的一个紫砂壶中向砚上倒了一点清水，拿起那条墨研了起来，笨拙地斜着墨条磨边角——他是第一次干这个。看着砚中渐渐浓起来的墨汁，伊依想到自己正身处距太阳1.5个天文单位的茫茫太空中，这个无限薄的平面（即使在刚才由纯能制造物品时，从远处看它仍没有厚度）仿佛是一个飘浮在宇宙深渊中的舞台，在它上面，一头恐龙、一个被恐龙当作肉食家禽饲养的人类、一个穿着唐朝古装准备超越李白的技术之神，正在演出一场怪诞到极点的话剧，想到这里，伊依摇头苦笑起来。

　　当觉得墨研得差不多了时，伊依站起来，同大牙一起等待着，这时平面上的轻风已经停止，太阳和星河静静地发着光，仿佛整个宇宙都在期待。李白静立在平面边缘，由于平面上的空气层几乎没有散射，他在阳光中的明暗部分极其分明，除了捋胡须的手不时动一下外，简直就是一尊石像。伊依和大牙等啊等，时间在默默地流逝，书案上蘸满了墨的毛笔渐渐有些发干了，不知不觉，太阳的位置已移动了很多，把他们和书案、飞船的影子长长地投在平面上，书案上平铺的白纸仿佛变成了平面的一部分。终于，李白转过身来，慢步走回书案前，伊依赶紧把毛笔重新蘸了墨，用双手递了过去，但李白抬起一只手回绝了，只是看着书案上的白纸继续沉思着，他的目光中有了些新的东西。

　　伊依得意地看出，那是困惑和不安。

　　"我还要制造一些东西，那都是……易碎品，你们去小心接着。"李白指了指制造口说，那里面本来已暗淡下去的蓝焰又明亮起来，伊依和大牙刚跑过去，就有一股蓝色的火舌把一个球形物推出来，大牙手疾眼快地接住了它，细看是一个大坛子。接着又从蓝焰中飞出了三只大碗，伊依接住了其中的两只，有一只摔碎了。大牙把坛子抱到书案上，小心地打开封盖，一股浓烈的酒味溢了出来，它与伊依惊奇地对视了一眼。

　　"在我从吞食帝国接收到的地球信息中，有关人类酿造业的资料不多，所以这东西造得不一定准确。"李白说，同时指着酒坛示意伊依尝尝。

伊依拿碗从中舀了一点儿抿了一口，一股火辣从嗓子眼流到肚子里，他点点头："是酒，但是与我们为改善肉质喝的那些相比太烈了。"

"满上。"李白指着书案上的另一个空碗说。待大牙倒满烈酒后，李白端起来咕咚咚一饮而尽，然后转身再次向远处走去，不时走出几个不太稳的舞步。到达平面边缘后又站在那里对着星海深思，但与上次不同的是，他的身体有节奏地左右摆动，像在和着某首听不见的曲子。这次李白沉思了不久就走回到书案前，回来的一路上全是舞步了，他一把抓过伊依递过来的笔扔到远处。

"满上。"李白眼睛直勾勾地盯着空碗说。

......

一小时后，大牙用两个大爪小心翼翼地把烂醉如泥的李白放到已清空的书案上，但他一翻身又骨碌下来，嘴里嘀咕着恐龙和人都听不懂的语言。他已经红红绿绿地吐了一大摊（真不知他是什么时候吃进的这些食物），宽大的古服上也吐得脏污一片，那一摊呕吐物被平面发出的白光透过，形成了一幅很抽象的图形。李白的嘴上黑乎乎的全是墨，这是因为在喝光第四碗后，他曾试图在纸上写什么，但只是把蘸饱墨的毛笔重重地戳到桌面上了，接着，李白就像初学书法的小孩子那样，试图用嘴把笔理顺......

"尊敬的神？"大牙伏下身来小心翼翼地问。

"哇咦卡啊......卡啊咦唉哇。"李白大着舌头说。

大牙站起身，摇摇头叹了一口气，对伊依说："我们走吧。"

另一条路

伊依所在的饲养场位于吞食者的赤道上，当吞食者处于太阳系内层空间时，这里曾是一片夹在两条大河之间的美丽草原。吞食者航出木星轨道后，严冬降临了，草原消失，大河封冻，被饲养的人类都转到地下城中。当吞食者受到神的召唤而返回后，随着太阳的临近，大地回春，两条大河很快解冻了，草原也开始变绿。

当气候好的时候，伊依总是独自住在河边自己搭的一间简陋的草棚中，自己种地过日子。对于一般人来说这是不被允许的，但由于伊依在饲养场中讲授的古典文学课程有陶冶的功能，他的学生的肉有一种很特别的风味，所以恐龙饲养员也就不干涉他了。

这是伊依与李白初次见面两个月后的一个黄昏，太阳刚刚从吞食帝国平直的地平线上落下，两条映着晚霞的大河在天边交汇。在河边的草棚外，微风把远处草原上欢舞的歌声隐隐送来，伊依独自一人在下围棋，抬头看到李白和大牙沿着河岸向这里走来。这时的李白已有了很大的变化，他头发蓬乱，胡子老长，脸晒得很黑，左肩背着一个粗布包，右手提着一个大葫芦，身上那件古装已破烂不堪，脚上穿着一双已磨得不像样子的草鞋，伊依觉得这时的他倒更像一个人了。

李白走到围棋桌前，像前几次来一样，不看伊依一眼就把葫芦重重地向桌上一放，说："碗！"待伊依拿来两个木碗后，李白打开葫芦盖，把两个碗里倒满酒，然后又从布包中拿出一个纸包。打开来，伊依发现里面竟放着切好的熟肉，并闻到扑鼻的香味，不由得拿起一块嚼了起来。

大牙只是站在两三米远处静静地看着他们，有前几次的经验，它知道他们俩又要谈诗了，这种谈话它既无兴趣也没资格参与。

"好吃，"伊依赞许地点点头，"这牛肉也是纯能转化的？"

"不，我早就回归自然了。你可能没听说过，在距这里很遥远的一个牧场，饲养着来自地球的牛群。这牛肉是我亲自做的，是用山西平遥牛肉的做法，关键是在炖的时候放——"李白凑到伊依耳边神秘地说，"尿碱。"

伊依迷惑不解地看着他。

"哦，就是人类的小便蒸干以后析出的那种白色的东西，能使炖好的肉外观红润，肉质鲜嫩，肥而不腻，瘦而不柴。"

"这尿碱……也不是纯能做出来的？"伊依恐惧地问。

"我说过我已经回归自然了！尿碱是我费了好大劲儿从几个人类饲养场收集来的，这是很正宗的民间烹饪技艺，早在地球毁灭前就已失传。"

伊依已经把嘴里的牛肉咽下去了，为了抑制呕吐，他端起了酒碗。

李白指指葫芦说："在我的指导下，吞食帝国已经建起了几个酒厂，并且能够生产出地球上的大部分名酒，这是它们酿制的正宗的竹叶青，是用汾酒浸泡竹叶而成。"

伊依这才发现碗里的酒与前几次李白带来的不同，呈翠绿色，入口后有甜甜的药草味。

"看来，你对人类文化已了如指掌了。"伊依对李白感慨道。

"不仅如此，我还花了大量的时间亲身体验。你知道，吞食帝国很多地区的风景与李白所在的地球极为相似。这两个月来，我浪迹于山水之间，饱览美景，月下饮酒，山巅吟诗，还在遍布各地的人类饲养场中有过几次艳遇……"

"那么，现在总能让我看看你的诗作了吧。"

李白呼地放下酒碗，站起身不安地踱起步来："是作了一些诗，而且是些肯定让你吃惊的诗，你会看到，我已经是一个很出色的诗人了，甚至比你和你的祖爷爷都出色，但我不想让你看，因为我同样肯定你会认为那些诗没有超越李白，而我……"他抬起头遥望天边落日的余晖，目光中充满了迷离和痛苦，"也这么认为。"

远处的草原上，舞会已经结束，快乐的人们开始享用丰盛的晚餐。有一群少女向河边跑来，在岸边的浅水中嬉戏。她们头戴花环，身上披着薄雾一样的轻纱，在暮色中构成一幅醉人的画面。伊依指着距草棚较近的一个少女问李白："她美吗？"

"当然。"李白不解地看着伊依说。

"想象一下，用一把利刃把她切开，取出她的每一个脏器，剜出她的眼球，挖出她的大脑，剔出每一根骨头，把肌肉和脂肪按其不同部位和功能分割开来，再把所有的血管和神经分别理成两束，最后在这里铺上一大块白布，把这些东西按解剖学原理分门别类地放好，你还觉得美吗？"

"你怎么在喝酒的时候想这些？恶心。"李白皱起眉头说。

"怎么会恶心呢？这不正是你所崇拜的技术吗？"

"你到底想说什么？"

"李白眼中的大自然就是你现在看到的河边少女，而同样的大自然在技术的眼睛中呢，就是白布上那些井然有序但血淋淋的部件，所以，技术是反诗意的。"

"你好像对我有什么建议。"李白捋着胡子若有所思地说。

"我仍然不认为你有超越李白的可能，但可以为你的努力指出一个正确的方向：技术的迷雾蒙住了你的双眼，使你看不到自然之美。所以，你首先要做的是把那些超级技术全部忘掉，你既然能够把自己的全部记忆移植到你现在的大脑中，当然也可以删除其中的一部分。"

李白抬头和大牙对视了一下，两者都哈哈大笑起来，大牙对李白说："尊敬的神，我早就告诉过您，这是一种多么狡诈的虫虫，您稍不小心就会跌入它们设下的陷阱。"

"哈哈哈哈，是狡诈，但也有趣。"李白对大牙说，然后转向伊依，冷笑着说："你真的认为我是来认输的？"

"你没能超越人类诗词艺术的巅峰，这是事实。"

李白突然抬起一只手指着大河，问："到河边去有几种走法？"

伊依不解地看了李白几秒钟："好像……只有一种。"

"不，是两种，我还可以向这个方向走，"李白指着与河相反的方向说，"这样一直走，绕吞食帝国的大环一周，再从对岸过河，也能走到这个岸边，我甚至还可以绕银河系一周再回来，对于我们的技术来说，这也易如反掌。技术可以超越一切！我现在已经被逼得要走另一条路了！"

伊依努力想了好半天，终于困惑地摇摇头："就算是你有神一般的技术，我还是想不出超越李白的另一条路在哪儿。"

李白站起来说："很简单，超越李白的两条路是：一、把超越他的那些诗写出来；二、把所有的诗都写出来！"

伊依显得更困惑了，但站在一旁的大牙却似有所悟。

"我要写出所有的五言和七言诗，这是李白所擅长的；另外我还要写出常见词牌的所有的词！你怎么还不明白？！我要在符合这些格律的诗词中，试遍所有汉字的所有组合！"

"啊，伟大！伟大的工程！！"大牙忘形地欢呼起来。

"这很难吗？"伊依傻傻地问。

"当然难，难极了！如果用吞食帝国最大的计算机来进行这样的计算，可能到宇宙末日也完成不了！"

"没那么多吧？"伊依充满疑问地说。

"当然有那么多！"李白得意地点点头，"但使用你们还远未掌握的量子计算技术，就能在可以接受的时间内完成这样的计算。到那时，我就写出了所有的诗词，包括所有以前写过的和所有以后可能写的，特别注意，所有以后可能写的！超越李白的巅峰之作自然包括在内。事实上我终结了诗词艺术，直到宇宙毁灭，其间所出现的任何一个诗人，不管他们达到了怎样的高度，都不过是个抄袭者，他的作品肯定能在我那巨大的存储器中检索出来。"

大牙突然发出了一声低沉的惊叫，看着李白的目光由兴奋变为震惊："巨大的……存储器？！尊敬的神，您该不是说，要把量子计算机写出的诗都……都存起来吧？"

"写出来就删除有什么意思呢？当然要存起来！这将是我的种族留在这个宇宙中的艺术丰碑之一！"

大牙的目光由震惊变为恐惧，把粗大的双爪向前伸着，两腿打弯，像要给李白跪下，声音也像要哭出来似的："使不得，尊敬的神，这使不得啊！！"

"是什么把你吓成这样？"伊依抬头惊奇地看着大牙问。

"你个白痴！你不是知道原子弹是原子做的吗？那存储器也是原子做的，它的存贮精度最高只能达到原子级别！知道什么是原子级别的存贮吗？就是说，一个针尖大小的地方，就能存下人类所有的书！不是你们现在那点儿书，是地球被吃掉前上面所有的书！"

"啊，这好像是有可能的，听说一杯水中的原子数比地球上海洋中水的杯数都多。那，他写完那些诗后带根针走就行了。"伊依指指李白说。

大牙恼怒至极，来回急走几步总算挤出了一点儿耐性："好，好，你说，按神说的那些五言、七言诗，还有那些常见的词牌，各写一首，总共有多少字？"

"不多，也就两三千字吧，古曲诗词是最精练的艺术。"

"那好，我就让你这个白痴虫虫看看它有多么精练！"大牙说着走到桌前，用爪指着上面的棋盘说，"你们管这种无聊的游戏叫什么，哦，围棋，这上面有多少个交叉点？"

"纵横各 19 行，共 361 点。"

"很好，每点上可以放黑子、白子或空着，共三种状态。这样，每一个棋局，就可以看作由三个汉字写成的一首 19 行 361个字的诗。"

"这比喻很妙。"

"那么，穷尽这三个汉字在这种诗上的所有组合，总共能写出多少首诗呢？让我告诉你：3 的 361 次方首，或者说，嗯……我想想，10 的 172 次方首！"

"这……很多吗？"

"白痴！"大牙第三次骂出这个词，"宇宙中的全部原子只有……啊——"它气恼得说不下去了。

"有多少？"伊依仍是那副傻样。

"只有 10 的 80 次方个！你个白痴虫虫啊——"

直到这时，伊依才表现出一点儿惊奇："你是说，如果一个原子存贮一首诗，用光宇宙中的所有原子，还存不完量子计算机写出的那些诗？"

"差得远呢！差 10 的 92 次方倍呢！再说，一个原子哪能存下一首诗？人类虫虫的存储器，存一首诗用的原子数可能比你们的人口都多，至于我们，用单个原子存贮一位二进制还仅处于实验室阶段……唉！"

"使者，在这一点上是你目光短浅了，想象力不足，是吞食帝国技术进步缓慢的原因之一。"李白笑着说，"使用基于量子多态叠加原理的量子存储器，只用很少量的物质就可以存下那些诗，当然，量子存贮不太稳定，为了永久保存那些诗作，还需要与更传统的存贮技术结合使用，即使这样，制造存储器需要的物质量也是很少的。"

"是多少？"大牙问，看那样子显然心已提到了嗓子眼儿。

"大约为 10 的 57 次方个原子，微不足道，微不足道。"

"这……这正好是整个太阳系的物质量！"

"是的，包括所有的太阳行星，当然也包括吞食帝国。"

李白最后这句话是轻描淡写地随口而出的，但在伊依听来却像晴天霹雳，不过大牙反倒平静下来，当长时间受到灾难预感的折磨后，灾难真正来临时反而有一种解脱感。

"您不是能把纯能转换成物质吗？"大牙问。

"得到如此巨量的物质需要多少能量你不会不清楚，这对我们也是不可想象的，还是用现成的吧。"

"这么说，皇帝的忧虑不无道理。"大牙自语道。

"是的是的，"李白欢快地说，"我前天已向吞食皇帝说明，这个伟大的环形帝国将被用于一个更伟大的目的，所有的恐龙应该为此感到自豪。"

"尊敬的神，您会看到吞食帝国的感受的。"大牙阴沉地说，"还有一个问题：与太阳相比，吞食帝国的质量实在是微不足道，为了得到这九牛之一毛的物质，有必要毁灭一个进化了几千万年的文明吗？"

"你的这个疑问我完全理解，但要知道，熄灭、冷却和拆解太阳是需要很长时间的，在这之前对诗的量子计算应已经开始，我们需要及时地把结果存起来，清空量子计算机的内存以继续计算，这样，可以立即用于制造存储器的行星和吞食帝国的物质就是必不可少的了。"

"明白了，尊敬的神，最后一个问题：有必要把所有的组合结果都存起来吗？为什么不能在输出端加一个判断程序，把那些不值得存贮的诗作剔除掉。据我所知，中国古诗是要遵从严格的格律的，如果把不符合格律的诗去掉，那最后结果的总量将大为减少。"

"格律？哼，"李白不屑地摇摇头，"那不过是对灵感的束缚，中国南北朝以前的古体诗并不受格律的限制，即使是在唐代以后严格的近体诗中，也有许多古典诗词大师不遵从格律，却写出了许多卓越的变体诗，所以，在这次终极吟诗中我将不考虑格律。"

"那，您总该考虑诗的内容吧？最后的计算结果中肯定有99%的诗是毫无意义的，存下这些随机的汉字矩阵有什么用？"

"意义？"李白耸耸肩说，"使者，诗的意义并不取决于你的认可，也不取决于我或其他任何人，它取决于时间。许多在当时无意义的诗后来成了旷世杰作，而现今和以后的许多杰作在遥远的过去肯定也曾是无意义的。我要作出所有的诗，亿万年之后，谁知道伟大的时间会把其中的哪首选为巅峰之作呢？"

"这简直荒唐！"大牙大叫起来，它那粗放的嗓音惊起了远处草丛中的几只鸟，"如果按现有的人类虫虫的汉字字库，您的量子计算机写出的第一首诗应该是这样的：

啊 啊 啊 啊 啊
啊 啊 啊 啊 啊
啊 啊 啊 啊 啊
啊 啊 啊 啊 唉

"请问，伟大的时间会把这首选为杰作？！"

一直不说话的伊依这时欢叫起来："哇！还用什么伟大的时间来选？！它现在就是一首巅峰之作耶！！前三行和第四行的前四个字都是表达生命对宏伟宇宙的惊叹，最后一个字是诗眼，它是诗人在领略了宇宙之浩渺后，对生命在无限时空中的渺小发出的一声无奈的叹息。"

"哈哈哈哈哈，"李白抚着胡须乐得合不拢嘴，"好诗，伊依虫虫，真的是好诗，哈哈哈……"说着拿起葫芦给伊依倒酒。

大牙挥起巨爪一巴掌把伊依打得老远："混账虫虫，我知道你现在高兴了，可不要忘记，吞食帝国一旦毁灭，你们也活不了！"

伊依一直滚到河边，好半天才能爬起来，他满脸沙土，咧大了嘴，既是痛得也是在笑，他确实很高兴，"哈哈，有趣，这个宇宙真他妈的不可思议！"他忘形地喊道。

"使者，还有问题吗？"看到大牙摇头，李白接着说，"那么，我在明天就要离去，后天，量子计算机将启动作诗软件，终极吟诗将开始，同时熄灭太阳、拆解行星和吞食帝国的工程也将启动。"

"尊敬的神，吞食帝国在今天夜里就能做好战斗准备！"大牙立正后庄严地说。

"好好，真是很好，往后的日子会很有趣的，但这一切发生之前，还是让我们喝完这一壶吧。"李白快乐地点点头说，同时拿起了酒葫芦，倒完酒，他看着已笼罩在夜幕中的大河，意犹未尽地回味着，"真是一首好诗，第一首，呵呵，第一首就是好诗。"

终极吟诗

吟诗软件其实十分简单，用人类的 C 语言表达可能不超过2000 行代码，另外再加一个存贮所有汉字字符的不大的数据库。当这个软件在位于海王星轨道上的那台量子计算机（一个飘浮在太空中的巨大透明锥体）上启动时，终极吟诗就开始了。

这时吞食帝国才知道，李白只是那个超级文明种族中的一个个体，这与以前预想的不同，当时恐龙们都认为进化到这样技术级别的社会在意识上早就融为一个整体了，吞食帝国在过去 1000万年中遇到的五个超级文明都是这种形态。李白一族保持了个体的存在，也部分解释了他们对艺术超常的理解力。当吟诗开始时，李白一族又有大量的个体从外太空的各个方位跃迁到太阳系，开始了制造存储器的工程。

吞食帝国上的人类看不到太空中的量子计算机，也看不到新来的神族，在他们看来，终极吟诗的过程，就是太空中太阳数目的增减过程。

在吟诗软件启动一个星期后，神族成功地熄灭了太阳，这时太空中太阳的数目减到零，但太阳内部核聚变的停止使恒星的外壳失去了支撑，使它很快坍缩成一颗新星，于是暗夜很快又被照亮，只是这颗太阳的亮度是以前的上百倍，使吞食者表面草木生烟。新星又被熄灭了，但过一段时间后又爆发了，就这样亮了又灭、灭了又亮，仿佛太阳是一只九条命的猫，在没完没了地挣扎。但神族对于杀死恒星其实很熟练，他们从容不迫地一次次熄灭新星，使它的物质最大比例地聚变为制造存储器所需的重元素，在第 11 次新星熄灭后，太阳才真正咽了气，这时，终极吟诗已经开始了三个地球月。早在这之前，在第三次新星出现时，太空中就有其他的太阳出现，这些太阳此起彼伏地在太空中的不同位置亮起或熄灭，最多时天空中出现过九个新太阳。这些太阳是神族在拆解行星时的能量释放，由于后来恒星太阳的闪烁已变得暗弱，人们就分不清这些太阳的真假了。

对吞食帝国的拆解是在吟诗开始后的第五个星期进行的，这之前，李白曾向帝国提出了一个建议：由神族将所有恐龙跃迁到银河系另一端的一个世界，那里有一个文明，比神族落后许多，仍未纯能化，但比吞食文明要先进得多。恐龙们到那里后，将作为一种小家禽被饲养，过着衣食无忧的快乐生活，但恐龙们宁为玉碎，不为瓦全，愤怒地拒绝了这个提议。

李白接着提出了另一个要求：让人类返回他们的母亲星球。其实，地球也被拆解了，它的大部分用于制造存储器，但神族还是剩下了其中的一小部分物质为人类建造了一个空心地球。空心地球的大小与原地球差不多，但其质量仅为后者的百分之一。说地球被掏空了是不确切的，因为原地球表面那层脆弱的岩石根本不可能用来做球壳，球壳的材料可能取自地核，另外球壳上像经纬线般交错的、虽然很细但强度极高的加固圈，是用太阳坍缩时产生的简并态中子物质制造的。

令人感动的是：吞食帝国不但立即答应了李白的要求，允许所有人类离开大环世界，还把从地球掠夺来的海水和空气全部还给了地球，神族借此在空心地球内部恢复了原地球所有的大陆、海洋和大气层。

接着，惨烈的大环保卫战开始了。吞食帝国向太空中的神族目标大量发射核弹和伽马射线激光，但这些对敌人毫无作用。在神族发射的一个无形的强大力场推动下，吞食者大环越转越快，最后在超速自转产生的离心力下解体了。这时，伊依正在飞向空心地球的途中，他从 1200 万千米的距离上目睹了吞食帝国毁灭的全过程：

> 大环解体的过程很慢，如梦似幻，在漆黑太空的背景上，这个巨大的世界如同一团浮在咖啡上的奶沫一样散开来，边缘的碎块渐渐隐没于黑暗之中，仿佛被太空溶解了，只有不时出现的爆炸的闪光才使它们重新现形。(选自《吞食者》)

这个来自古老地球的充满阳刚之气的伟大文明就这样被毁灭了，伊依悲哀万分。只有一小部分恐龙活了下来，与人类一起回归地球，其中包括使者大牙。

在返回地球的途中，人类普遍都很沮丧，但原因与伊依不同：回到地球后是要开荒种地才有饭吃的，这对于已在长期被饲养的生活中变得四肢不勤、五谷不分的人们来说，确实像一场噩梦。

但伊依对地球世界的前途充满信心，不管前面有多少磨难，人将重新成为人。

诗云

吟诗航行的游艇到达了南极海岸。

这里的重力已经很小，海浪的运行很缓慢，像是一种描述梦幻的舞蹈。在低重力下，拍岸浪把水花送上十几米高处，飞上半空的海水由于表面张力而形成无数水球，大的像足球，小的如雨滴，这些水球在缓慢地下落，慢到可以用手在它们周围画圈，它们折射着小太阳的光芒，使上岸后的伊依、李白和大牙置身于一片晶莹灿烂之中。由于自转，地球的南北极地轴有轻微的拉长，这就使得空心地球的两极地区保持了过去的寒冷状态。低重力下的雪很奇特，呈一种蓬松的泡沫状，浅处齐腰深，深处能把他们都淹没，但在被淹没后，他们竟然能在雪沫中正常呼吸！整个南极大陆就覆盖在这雪沫之下，起伏不平，一片雪白。

伊依一行乘一辆雪地车前往南极点，雪地车像是一艘掠过雪沫表面的快艇，在两侧激起片片雪浪。

第二天他们到达了南极点。南极点的标志是一座高大的水晶金字塔，这是为纪念两个世纪前的地球保卫战而建立的纪念碑，上面没有任何文字和图形，只有晶莹的碑体在地球顶端的雪沫之上默默地折射着阳光。

从这里看去，整个地球世界尽收眼底，光芒四射的小太阳周围，围绕着大陆和海洋，使它看上去仿佛是从北冰洋中浮出来的似的。

"这个小太阳真的能够永远亮着吗？"伊依问李白。

"至少能亮到新的地球文明进化到具有制造新太阳的能力的时候，它是一个微型白洞。"

"白洞？是黑洞的反演吗？"大牙问。

"是的，它通过空间蛀洞与200万光年外的一个黑洞相连，那个黑洞围绕着一颗恒星运行，它吸入的恒星的光从这里被释放出来，可以把它看作一根超时空光纤的出口。"

纪念碑的塔尖是拉格朗日轴线的南起点，这是指连接空心地球南北两极的轴线，因战前地月之间的零重力拉格朗日点而得名，这是一条长13000千米的零重力轴线。以后，人类肯定要在拉格朗日轴线上发射各种卫星，比起战前的地球来，这种发射易如反掌：只需把卫星运到南极或北极点，愿意的话用驴车运都行，然后用脚把它向空中踹出去就行了。

就在他们观看纪念碑时，又有一辆较大的雪地车载来了一群年轻的旅行者，这些人下车后双腿一弹，径直跃向空中，沿拉格朗日轴线高高飞去，把自己变成了卫星。从这里看去，有许多小黑点在空中标出了轴线的位置，那都是在零重力轴线上飘浮的游客和各种车辆。本来，从这里可以直接飞到北极，但小太阳位于拉格朗日轴线中部，最初有些沿轴线飞行的游客因随身携带的小型喷气推进器坏了，无法减速而一直飞到太阳里，其实在距小太阳很远的距离上他们就被蒸发了。

在空心地球，进入太空也是一件很容易的事，只需要跳进赤道上的 5 口深井（名叫地门）中的一口，向下坠落 100 千米穿过地壳，就会被空心地球自转的离心力抛进太空。

现在，伊依一行为了看诗云也要穿过地壳，但他们走的是南极的地门，在这里地球自转的离心力为零，所以不会被抛入太空，只能到达空心地球的外表面。他们在南极地门控制站穿好轻便太空服后，就进入了那条长 100 千米的深井，由于没有重力，叫它"隧道"更合适一些。在失重状态下，他们借助于太空服上的喷气推进器前进，这比在赤道的地门中坠落要慢得多，他们用了半个小时才来到外表面。

空心地球外表面十分荒凉，只有纵横的中子材料加固圈，这些加固圈把地球外表面按经纬线划分成了许多个方格，南极点正是所有经向加固圈的交点，当伊依一行走出地门后，看到自己身处一个面积不大的高原上，地球加固圈像一道道漫长的山脉，以高原为中心放射状向各个方向延伸。

抬头，他们看到了诗云。

诗云处于已消失的太阳系所在的位置，是一片直径为 100 个天文单位的旋涡状星云，形状很像银河系。空心地球处于诗云边缘，与原来太阳在银河系中的位置也很相似，不同的是地球的轨道与诗云不在同一平面，这就使得从地球上可以看到诗云的一面，而不是像银河系那样只能看到截面。但地球到诗云平面的距离还远不足以使这里的人们观察到诗云的完整形状，事实上，南半球的整个天空都被诗云所覆盖。

诗云发出银色的光芒，能在地上照出人影。据说诗云本身是不发光的，这银光是宇宙射线激发出来的。由于空间的宇宙射线密度不均，诗云中常涌动着大团的光晕，那些色彩各异的光晕滚过长空，好像是潜行在诗云中的发光巨鲸。也有很少的时候，宇宙射线的强度急剧增加，在诗云中激发出粼粼的光斑，这时的诗云已完全不像云了，整个天空仿佛是一个月夜从水下看到的海面。地球与诗云的运行并不是同步的，所以有时地球会处于旋臂间的空隙上，这时透过空隙可以看到夜空和星星，最为激动人心的是，在旋臂的边缘还可以看到诗云的断面形状，它很像地球大气中的积雨云，变幻出各种宏伟的让人浮想联翩的形体，这些巨大的形体高高地升出诗云的旋转平面，发出幽幽的银光，仿佛是一个超级意识没完没了的梦境。

伊依把目光从诗云收回，从地上拾起一块晶片，这种晶片散布在他们周围的地面上，像严冬的碎冰般闪闪发亮。伊依举起晶片对着诗云密布的天空，晶片很薄，有半个手掌大小，从正面看全透明，但把它稍倾斜一下，就能看到诗云的亮光在它表面映出的霓彩光晕。这就是量子存储器，人类历史上产生的全部文字信息，也只能占它们每一片存贮量的几亿分之一。诗云就是由 10 的 40 次方片这样的存储器组成的，它们存贮了终极吟诗的全部结果。这片诗云，是用原来构成太阳和它的九大行星的全部物质所制造的，当然还包括吞食帝国。

"真是伟大的艺术品！"大牙由衷地赞叹道。

"是的，它的美在于其内涵：一片直径 100 亿千米的，包含着全部可能的诗词的星云，这太伟大了！"伊依仰望着星云激动地说，"我，也开始崇拜技术了。"

一直情绪低落的李白长叹一声："唉！看来我们都在走向对方，我看到了技术在艺术上的极限，我……"他抽泣起来，"我是个失败者，呜呜……"

"你怎么能这样讲呢？！"伊依指着上空的诗云说，"这里面包含了所有可能的诗，当然也包括那些超越李白的诗！"

"可我却得不到它们！"李白一跺脚，飞起了几米高，在半空中蜷缩成一团，悲伤地把脸埋在两膝之间呈胎儿状，在地壳那十分微小的重力下缓缓下落，"在终极吟诗开始时，我就着手编制诗词识别软件，这时，技术在艺术中再次遇到了那道不可逾越的障碍，到现在，具备古诗鉴赏力的软件也没能编出来。"他在半空中指指诗云，"不错，借助伟大的技术，我写出了诗词的巅峰之作，却不可能把它们从诗云中检索出来，唉……"

"智慧生命的精华和本质，真的是技术所无法触及的吗？"大牙仰头对着诗云大声问，经历过这一切，它变得越来越哲学了。

"既然诗云中包含了所有可能的诗，那其中自然有一部分诗，是描写我们全部的过去和所有可能与不可能的未来的，伊依虫虫肯定能找到一首诗，描述他在 30 年前的一天晚上剪指甲时的感受，或 12 年后的一顿午餐的菜谱；大牙使者也可以找到一首诗，描述它的腿上的某一块鳞片在 5 年后的颜色……"说着，已重新落回地面的李白拿出了两块晶片，它们在诗云的照耀下闪闪发光，"这是我临走前送给二位的礼物，这是量子计算机以你们的名字为关键词，在诗云中检索出来的与二位有关的几亿亿首诗，描述了你们在未来各种可能的生活，当然，在诗云中，这也只占描写你们的诗作里极小的一部分。我只看过其中的几十首，最喜欢的是关于伊依虫虫的一首七律，描写了他与一位美丽的乡下姑娘在江边相爱的情景……我走后，希望人类和剩下的恐龙好好相处，人类之间更要好好相处，要是空心地球的球壳被核弹炸个洞，可就麻烦了……诗云中的那些好诗目前还不属于任何人，希望人类今后能写出其中的一部分。"

"我和那位姑娘后来怎样了？"伊依好奇地问。

在诗云的银光下，李白嘻嘻一笑："你们幸福地生活在一起。"

欢乐颂 ODE TO JOY

音乐会

为最后一届联合国大会闭幕举行的音乐会是一场阴郁的音乐会。

自本世纪初某些恶劣的先例之后，各国都对联合国采取了一种更加实用的态度，认为将它作为实现自己利益的工具是理所当然的，进而对联合国宪章都有了自己的更为实用的理解。中小国家纷纷挑战常任理事国的权威，而每一个常任理事国都认为自己在这个组织中应该有更大的权威，结果是联合国丧失了一切权威……当这种趋势发展了10年后，所有的拯救努力都已失败，人们一致认为，联合国和它所代表的理想主义都不再适用于今天的世界，是摆脱它们的时候了。

最后一届联大是各国首脑到得最齐的一届，他们要为联合国举行一场最隆重的葬礼，这场在大厦外的草坪上举行的音乐会是这场葬礼的最后一项活动。

太阳已落下去好一会儿了，这是昼与夜最后交接的时候，也是一天中最迷人的时候，这时，让人疲倦的现实的细节已被渐浓的暮色掩盖，夕阳的余晖把世界最美的一面映照出来，草坪上充满了嫩芽的气息。

联合国秘书长最后一个到，在走进草坪时，他遇到了今晚音乐会的主要演奏者之一克莱德曼，并很高兴地与他攀谈起来。

"您的琴声使我陶醉。"他微笑着对钢琴王子说。

克莱德曼穿着他喜欢的那身雪白的西装，看上去很不安："如果真是这样，我万分欣喜，但据我所知，对请我来参加这样的音乐会，人们有些看法……"

其实不仅仅是看法，教科文组织的总干事，同时是一名艺术理论家，公开说克莱德曼顶多是一名街头艺人的水平，他的演奏是对钢琴艺术的亵渎。

秘书长抬起一只手制止他说下去："联合国不能像古典音乐那样高高在上，如同您架起古典音乐通向大众的桥梁一样，它应把人类最崇高的理想播撒到每个普通人身边，这是今晚请您来的原因。请相信，我曾在非洲炎热肮脏的贫民窟中听到过您的琴声，那时我有种在阴沟里仰望星空的感觉，它真的使我陶醉。"

克莱德曼指了指草坪上的元首们："我觉得这里充满了家庭的气氛。"

秘书长也向那边看了一眼："至少在今夜的这块草坪上，乌托邦还是现实的。"

秘书长走进草坪，来到了观众席的前排。本来，在这个美好的夜晚，他打算把自己作为政治家的第六感关闭，做一个普通的听众，但这不可能做到。在走向这里时，他的第六感注意到了一件事：正在同美国总统交谈的中国领导人抬头看了一眼天空。这本来是一个十分平常的动作，但秘书长注意到他仰头观看的时间稍长了一些，也许只长了一两秒钟，但他注意到了。当秘书长同前排的国家元首依次握手致意后坐下时，旁边的中国领导人又抬头看了一眼天空，这证实了刚才的猜测，国家元首的举止看似随意，实际上都十分精确，在正常情况下，后面这个动作是绝对不会出现的，美国总统也注意到了这一点。

"纽约的灯火使星空暗淡了许多，华盛顿的星空比这里更灿烂。"美国总统说。

中国领导人点点头，没有说话。

美国总统接着说："我也喜欢仰望星空，在变幻不定的历史进程中，我们这样的职业最需要一个永恒稳固的参照物。"

"这种稳固只是一种幻觉。"中国领导人说。

"为什么这么说呢？"

中国领导人没有回答，指着空中刚刚出现的群星说："您看，那是南十字座，那是大犬座。"

美国总统笑着说："您刚刚证明了星空的稳固，在一万年前，如果这里站着一位原始人，他看到的南十字座和大犬座的形状一定与我们现在看到的完全一样，这形象的名字可能就是他们首先想出来的。"

"不，总统先生，事实上，昨天这里的星空都可能与今天不同。"中国领导人第三次仰望星空，他脸色平静，但眼中严峻的目光使秘书长和美国总统都暗暗紧张起来，他们也抬头看天，这是他们见过无数次的宁静的星空，没有什么异样，他们都疑惑地看着他。

"我刚才指出的那两个星座，应该只能在南半球看到。"中国领导人说，他没有再次向他们指出那些星座，也没有再看星空，双眼沉思着平视前方。

秘书长和美国总统疑惑地看着他。

"我们现在看到的，是地球另一面的星空。"中国领导人平静地说。

"您……开玩笑？！"美国总统差点儿失声惊叫起来，但他控制住了自己，声音反而比刚才更低了。

"看，那是什么？"秘书长指指天顶说，为了不惊动其他人，他的手只举到与眼睛平齐。

"当然是月亮。"美国总统向正上方看了一眼说，看到旁边的中国领导人缓缓地摇了摇头，他又抬头看，这次对自己的判断产生了怀疑：初看去，天空正中那个半圆形的东西很像半盈的月亮，但它呈蔚蓝色，仿佛是白昼的蓝天退去时被粘下了一小片。总统仰头仔细观察太空中的那个蓝色半圆，一旦集中注意力，他那敏锐的观察力就表现出来，他伸出一根手指，用它作为一把尺子量着这个蓝月亮，说："它在扩大。"

他们三人都仰头目不转睛地盯着看，不再顾及是否惊动了别人。两边和后面的国家元首们都注意到了他们的动作，有更多的人抬头向那个方向看，露天舞台上乐队调试乐器的声音戛然而止。

这时已经可以肯定那个蓝色的半球不是月亮，因为它的直径已膨胀到月亮的一倍左右，它的另一个处在黑暗中的半球也显现出来，呈暗蓝色。在明亮的半球上可以看清一些细节，人们发现它的表面并非全部是蓝色，还有一些黄褐色的区域。

"天啊，那不是北美洲吗？！"有人惊叫。他是对的，人们看到了那熟悉的大陆形状，它此时正处在球体明亮与黑暗的交界处，不知是否有人想到，这与他们现在所处的位置是一致的。接着，人们又认出了亚洲大陆，认出了北冰洋和白令海峡……

"那是……是地球！"

美国总统收回了手指，这时太空中蓝色球体的膨胀不借助参照物也能看出来，它的直径现在至少达到了月球的三倍！开始，人们都觉得它像太空中被很快吹胀的一个气球，但人群中的又一声惊呼立刻改变了人们的这个想象。

"它在掉下来！！"

这话给人们看到的景象提供了一个合理的解释，不管是否正确，他们都立刻对眼前发生的事有了新的感觉：太空中的另一个地球正在向他们砸下来！那个蓝色球体在逼近，它已占据了三分之一的天空，其表面的细节可以看得更清楚了：褐色的陆地上布满了山脉的皱纹，一片片云层好像是紧贴着大陆的残雪，云层在大地上投下的影子给它们镶上了一圈黑边；北极也有一层白色，它们的某些部分闪闪发光，那不是云，是冰层；在蔚蓝色的海面上，有一个旋涡状物体，懒洋洋地转动着，雪白雪白的，看上去柔弱而美丽，像一朵贴在晶莹蓝玻璃瓶壁上的白绒花，那是一处刚刚形成的台风……当那蓝色的巨球占据了一半天空时，几乎在同一时刻，人们的视觉再次发生了奇妙的变化。

"天啊，我们在掉下去！"

这感觉的颠倒是在一瞬间发生的，这个占据半个天空的巨球表面突然产生了一种高度感，人们感觉到脚下的大地已不存在，自己处于高空中，正向那个地球掉下去、掉下去……那个地球表面可以看得更细了，在明暗交界线黑暗一侧的不远处，视力好的人可以看到一条微弱的荧光带，那是美国东海岸城市的灯光，其中较为明亮的一小团荧光就是纽约，是他们所在的地方。来自太空的地球迎面扑来，很快占据了三分之二的天空，两个地球似乎转眼间就要相撞了，人群中传出一两声惊叫，许多人恐惧地闭上了双眼。

就在这时，一切突然静止，天空中的地球不再下落，或者脚下的地球不再向它下坠。这个占据三分之二天空的巨球静静地悬在上方，大地笼罩在它那蓝色的光芒中。

这时，市区传来喧闹声，骚乱开始出现了。但草坪上的人们毕竟是人类中在意外事变面前神经最坚强的一群，面对这噩梦般的景象，他们很快控制住自己的惊慌，默默思考着。

"这是一个幻象。"联合国秘书长说。

"是的，"中国领导人说，"如果它是实体，应该能感觉到它的引力效应，我们离海这么近，这里早就被潮汐淹没了。"

"远不是潮汐的问题了，"俄罗斯总统说，"两个地球的引力足以互相撕碎对方了。"

"事实上，物理定律不允许两个地球这么待着！"日本首相说，他接着转向中国领导人："那个地球出现前，你谈到了我们上方出现了南半球的星空，这与现在发生的事有什么联系吗？"他这么说，等于承认刚才偷听了别人的谈话，但现在也顾不了这么多了。

"也许我们马上就能得到答案！"美国总统说。他这时正拿着一部移动电话说着什么，旁边的国务卿告诉大家，总统正在与国际空间站联系。于是，所有的人都把期待的目光聚焦到他身上。总统专心地听着手机，几乎不说话，草坪陷入一片寂静之中，在天空中另一个地球的蓝光里，人们像一群虚幻的幽灵。就这么等了约两分钟，总统在众人的注视下放下手机，登上一把椅子，大声说："各位，事情很简单，地球的旁边出现了一面大镜子！"

镜子

它就是一面大镜子，很难再被看成别的什么东西。它的表面不仅能对可见光进行毫不衰减、毫不失真的全反射，也能反射雷达波；这面宇宙巨镜的面积约 100 亿平方千米，如果拉开足够的距离看，镜子和地球，就像一个棋盘正中放着一枚棋子。

本来，对于"奋进号"上的宇航员来说，得到这些初步的信息并不难，他们中有一名天文学家和一名空间物理学家，他们还可借助包括国际空间站在内的所有太空设施进行观测，但航天飞机险些因他们暂时的精神崩溃而坠毁。国际空间站是最完备的观测平台，但它的轨道位置不利于对镜子的观测，因为镜子悬于地球北极上空约 450 千米的高度，其镜面与地球的自转轴几乎垂直。而此时，"奋进号"航天飞机已变轨至一条通过南北极上空的轨道，以完成一项对极地上空臭氧空洞的观测，它的轨道高度为 280 千米，正从镜子与地球之间飞过。

那情形真是一场噩梦，航天飞机在两个地球之间爬行，仿佛飞行在由两道蓝色的悬崖构成的大峡谷中。驾驶员坚持认为这是幻觉，是他在 3000 小时的歼击机飞行时间中遇到过两次的倒飞幻觉[1]，但指令长坚持认为确实有两个地球，并命令根据另一个地球的引力参数调整飞行轨道，那名天文学家及时制止了他。当他们初步控制了自己的恐慌后，通过观测航天飞机的飞行轨道得知，两个地球中有一个没有质量，大家都倒吸了一口冷气：如果按两个地球质量相等来调整轨道，"奋进号"此时已变成北极冰原上空的一颗火流星了。

宇航员们仔细观察那个没有质量的地球，目测可知，航天飞机距那个地球要远许多，但它的北极与这个地球的北极好像没有什么不同，事实上它们太相像了。宇航员们看到，在两个地球的北极点上空都有一道极光，这两道长长的暗红色火蛇在两个地球的同一位置以完全相同的形状缓缓扭动着。后来他们终于发现了一件这个地球没有的东西：那个零质量地球的上空有一个飞行物。通过目测，他们判断那个飞行物是在零质量地球上空约 300千米的轨道上运行，他们用机载雷达探测它，想得到它精确的轨道参数，但雷达波在 100 多千米处像遇到一堵墙一样被弹了回来，零质量地球和那个飞行物都在墙的另一面。指令长透过驾驶舱的舷窗用高倍望远镜观察那个飞行物，看到那也是一架航天飞机，它正沿低轨道越过北极的冰海，看上去像一只在蓝白相间的大墙上爬行的蛾子。他注意到，在那架航天飞机的前部舷窗里有一个身影，看得出那人正举着望远镜向这里看，指令长挥挥手，那人也同时挥挥手。

于是，他们得知了镜子的存在。

1　一种飞行幻觉，飞行员在幻觉中误认为飞机在倒飞。

航天飞机改变轨道，向上沿一条斜线向镜子靠近，一直飞到距镜子 3 千米处，在视距 6 千米远处宇航员们可以清楚看到"奋进号"在镜子中的映像，尾部发动机喷出的火光使它像一只缓缓移动的萤火虫。

一名宇航员进入太空，去进行人类同镜子的第一次接触。太空服上的推进器拉出一道长长的白烟，宇航员很快越过了这 3 千米的距离，他小心翼翼地调整着推进器的喷口，最后悬浮在与镜子相距 10 米左右的位置。在镜子中，他的映像异常清晰，毫不失真；由于宇航员是在轨道上运行，而镜子与在地球处于相对静止状态，所以宇航员与镜子之间有高达每秒近 10 千米的相对速度，他实际上是在闪电般掠过镜子表面，但从镜子上丝毫看不出这种运动。

这是宇宙中最平滑、最光洁的表面了。

宇航员在减速时，曾把推进器的喷口长时间对着镜子，苯化物推进剂形成的白雾向镜子飘去。以前在太空行走中，当这种白雾接触航天飞机或空间站的外壁时，会立刻在上面留下一片由霜构成的明显的污痕，他由此断定，白雾也会在镜子上留下痕迹。由于相互间的高速运动，这痕迹将是长长的一道，就像他童年时常用肥皂在浴室的镜子上划出的一样。但航天飞机上的人没有看到任何痕迹，那白雾接触镜面后就消失了，镜面仍是那样令人难以置信的光洁。

由于轨道的形状，航天飞机和这名宇航员能与镜子这样近距离接触的时间不多，这就使宇航员焦急地做了一件事。得知白雾在镜面上消失，几乎是下意识地，他从工具袋中掏出一把空心扳手，向镜子掷过去。扳手刚出手，他和航天飞机上的人都惊呆了，他们这时才意识到扳手与镜面之间的相对速度，这速度将使扳手具有一颗重磅炸弹的威力。他们恐惧地看着扳手翻滚着向镜面飞去，恐惧地想象着在接触的一瞬间，蛛网状致密的裂纹从接触点放射状地在镜面平原上闪电般扩散，巨镜化为亿万片在阳光中闪烁的小碎片，在漆黑的太空中形成一片耀眼的银色云海……但扳手接触镜面后立刻消失了，没留下一丝痕迹，镜面仍光洁如初。

其实，很容易得知镜子不是实体，没有质量，否则它不可能以与地球相对静止的状态悬浮在北半球上空（按它们的大小比例，更准确的说法应该是地球悬浮在镜面的正中）。镜子不是实体，而是一种力场类的东西，刚才与其接触的白雾和扳手证明了这一点。

宇航员小心地开动推进器，喷口的微调装置频繁地动作，最后使他与镜面的距离缩短为半米。他与镜子中的自己面对面地对视着，再次惊叹映像的精确，那是对现实的完美拷贝，给人的感觉甚至比现实更精细。他抬起一只手，伸向前去，与镜面中的手相距不到 1 厘米的距离，几乎合到一起。耳机中一片寂静，指令长并没有制止他，他把手向前推去，手在镜面下消失了，他与镜中人的两条胳膊从手腕连在一起，他的手在这接触过程中没有任何感觉。他把手抽回来，举在眼前仔细看，太空服手套完好无损，也没有任何痕迹。

宇航员和下面的航天飞机正在飘离镜面，他们只能不断地开动发动机和推进器保持与镜面的近距离，但由于飞行轨道的形状，飘离越来越快，很快将使这种修正成为不可能。再次近距离接触只能等绕地球一周转回来时，那时谁知道镜子还在不在？想到这里，他下定决心，启动推进器，径直向镜面冲去。

宇航员看到镜中自己的映像迎面扑来，最后，映像的太空服头盔上那个像大水银泡似的单向反射面罩充满了视野。在与镜面相撞的瞬间，他努力使自己没有闭上双眼。相撞时没有任何感觉，这一瞬间后，眼前的一切消失了，空间黑了下来，他看到了熟悉的银河星海。他猛地回头，在下面也是完全一样的银河景象，但有一样上面没有的东西：渐渐远去的他自己的映像。映像是从下向上看，只能看到他的鞋底，他和映像身上的两个推进器喷出的两条白雾平滑地连接在一起。

他已穿过了镜子，镜子的另一面仍然是镜子。

在他冲向镜子时，耳机中响着指令长的声音，但穿过镜面后，这声音像被一把利刃切断了，这是镜子挡住了电波。更可怕的是，镜子的这一面看不到地球，周围全是无际的星空，宇航员感到自己被隔离在另一个世界，心中一阵恐慌。他掉转喷口，刹住车后向回飞去。这一次，他不像来时那样使身体与镜面平行，而是与镜面垂直，头朝前像跳水那样向镜面飘去。在即将接触镜面前，他把速度降到了很低，与镜中的映像头顶头地连在一起。在他的头部穿过镜子后，他欣慰地看到了下方蓝色的地球，耳机中也响起了指令长熟悉的声音。

他把飘行的速度降到零，这时，他只有胸部以上的部分穿过了镜子，身体的其余部分仍在镜子的另一面。他调整推进器的喷口方向，开始后退，这使得仍在镜子另一面的喷口喷出的白雾溢到了镜子这一面，白雾从他周围的镜面冒出，他仿佛是在沉入一个白雾缭绕的平静湖面。当镜面升到鼻子的高度时，他又发现了一件令人吃惊的事：镜面穿过了太空服头盔的面罩，充满了他的脸和面罩间的这个月牙形的空间，他向下看，这个月牙形的镜面映着他那惊恐的瞳仁。镜面一定整个切穿了他的头颅，但他什么也感觉不到。他把飘行速度减到最低，比钟表的秒针快不了多少，一毫米一毫米地移动，终于使镜面升到自己的瞳仁正中。这时，镜子从视野中完全消失了，周围的一切都恢复了原状：一边是蓝色的地球，另一边是灿烂的银河。但这个他熟悉的世界只存在了两三秒钟，飘行的速度不可能完全降到零，镜面很快移到了他双眼的上方，一边的地球消失了，只剩下另一边的银河。在眼睛的上方，是挡住地球的镜面，一望无际，伸向十几万千米的远方。由于角度极偏，镜面反射的星空图像在他眼中变了形，成了这镜面平原上的一片银色光晕。他将推进器反向，向相反的方向飘去，使镜面向眼睛降下来，在镜面通过瞳仁的瞬间，镜子再次消失，地球和银河再次同时出现，这之后，银河消失了，地球出现了，镜子移到了眼睛的下方，镜面平原上的光晕变成了蓝色的。他就这样以极慢的速度来回飘移着，使瞳仁在镜面的两侧浮动，感到自己仿佛穿行于隔开两个世界的一张薄膜间。经过反复努力，他终于使镜面较长时间地停留在瞳仁的正中，镜子消失了。他睁大双眼，想从镜面所在的位置看到一条细细的直线，但什么也没看出来。

"这东西没有厚度！"他惊叫。

"也许它只有几个原子那么厚，你看不到而已。这也是它的到来没有被地球觉察的原因，如果它以边缘对着地球飞来，就不可能被发现。"航天飞机上的人评论说，他们在看着传回的图像。

但最让他们震惊的是：这面可能只有几个原子的厚度，但面积有上百个太平洋的镜子，竟绝对平坦，以至于镜面与视线平行时完全看不到它，这是古典几何学世界中的理想平面。

由绝对的平坦可以解释它绝对的光洁，这是一面理想的镜子。

在宇航员们心中，孤独感开始压倒了震惊和恐惧，镜子使宇宙变得陌生了，他们仿佛是一群刚出生就被抛在旷野的婴儿，无力地面对着这不可思议的世界。

这时，镜子说话了。

音乐家

"我是一名音乐家，"镜子说，"我是一名音乐家。"

这是一个悦耳的男音，在地球的整个天空响起，所有的人都能听到。一时间，地球上熟睡的人都被惊醒，醒着的人则都如塑像般呆住了。

镜子接着说："我看到了下面在举行一场音乐会，观众是能够代表这颗星球文明的人，你们想与我对话吗？"

元首们都看着秘书长，他一时茫然不知所措。

"我有事情要告诉你们。"镜子又说。

"你能听到我们说话吗？"秘书长试探着说。

镜子立即回答："当然能，如果愿意，我可以分辨出下面的世界里每个细菌发出的声音，我感知世界的方式与你们不同，我能同时观察每个原子的旋转，我的观察还包括时间维，可以同时看到事物的历史，而不像你们，只能看到时间的一个断面，我对一切明察秋毫。"

"那我们是如何听到你的声音的呢？"美国总统问。

"我在向你们的大气发射超弦波。"

"超弦波是什么？"

"一种从原子核中解放出来的强互作用力，它振动着你们的大气，如同一只大手拍动着鼓膜，于是你们听到了我的声音。"

"你从哪里来？"秘书长问。

"我是一面在宇宙中流浪的镜子，我的起源地在时间和空间上都太遥远，谈它已无意义。"

"你是如何学会英语的？"秘书长问。

"我说过，我对一切明察秋毫。这里需要声明，我讲英语，是因为听到这个音乐会上的人们在交谈中大都用这种语言，这并不代表我认为下面的世界里某些种族比其他种族更优越，这个世界没有通用语言，我只能这样。"

"我们有世界语，只是很少使用。"

"你们的世界语，与其说是为世界大同进行的努力，不如说是沙文主义的典型表现：凭什么世界语要以拉丁语系而不是这个世界的其他语系为基础？"

最后这句话在元首们中引起了极大的震动，他们紧张地窃窃私语起来。

"你对地球文明的了解让我们震惊。"秘书长由衷地说。

"我对一切明察秋毫，再说，透彻地了解一粒灰尘并不困难。"

美国总统看着天空说："你是指地球吗？你确实比地球大很多，但从宇宙尺度来说，你的大小与地球是同一个数量级的，你也是一粒灰尘。"

"我连灰尘都不是，"镜子说，"很久很久以前我曾是灰尘，但现在我只是一面镜子。"

"你是一个个体呢，还是一个群体？"中国领导人问。

"这个问题无意义，文明在时空中走过足够长的路时，个体和群体将同时消失。"

"镜子是你固有的形象呢，还是你许多形象中的一种？"英国首相问，秘书长把问题接下去："就是说，你是否有意对我们显示出这样一个形象呢？"

"这个问题也无意义，文明在时空中走过足够长的路时，形式和内容将同时消失。"

"你对最后两个问题的回答我们无法理解。"美国总统说。

镜子没说话。

"你到太阳系来有目的吗？"秘书长问出了最关键的问题。

"我是一个音乐家，要在这里举行音乐会。"

"这很好！"秘书长点点头说，"人类是听众吗？"

"听众是整个宇宙，虽然最近的文明世界也要在百年后才能听到我的琴声。"

"琴声？琴在哪里？！"克莱德曼在舞台上问。

这时，人们发现，占据了大部分天空的地球映像突然向东方滑去，速度很快。天空的这种变幻看上去很恐怖，给人一种天要塌下来的感觉，草坪上有几个人不由自主地捂住了脑袋。很快，地球映像的边缘已接触了东方的地平线，几乎与此同时，一片光明突然出现，使所有人的眼睛一片晕花，什么都看不清了。当他们的视力恢复后，看到太阳突然出现在刚才地球映像腾出来的天空中，灿烂的阳光瞬间洒满大地，周围的世界毫发毕现，天空在瞬间由漆黑变成明亮的蔚蓝。地球的映像仍然占据东半部天空，但上面的海洋已与蓝天融为一体，大陆像是天空中一片片褐色的云层。这突然的变化使所有的人目瞪口呆。过了好一阵儿，秘书长的一句话才使大家对这不可思议的现实多少有了一些把握。

"镜子倾斜了。"

是的，太空中的巨镜倾斜了一个角度，使太阳也进入了映像，把它的光芒反射到地球这黑夜的一侧。

"它转动的速度真快！"中国领导人说。

秘书长点点头："是的，想想它的大小，以这样的速度转动，它的边缘可能已接近光速了！"

"任何实体物质都不可能经受这样的转动所产生的应力，它只是一个力场，这已被我们的宇航员证明了，作为力场，接近光速的运动是很正常的。"美国总统说。

这时，镜子说话了："这就是我的琴，我是一名恒星演奏家，我将弹奏太阳！"

这句气势磅礴的话把所有的人都镇住了，元首们呆呆地看着天空中太阳的映像，好一阵儿才有人敬畏地问怎样弹奏。

"各位一定知道，你们使用的乐器大多有一个音腔，它们是由薄壁所包围的空间区域，薄壁将声波来回反射，这样就将声波禁锢在音腔内，形成共振，发出动听的声音。对电磁波来说，恒星也是一个音腔，它虽没有有形的薄壁，但存在对电磁波的传输速度梯度，这种梯度将折射和反射电磁波，将其禁锢在恒星内部，产生电磁共振，奏出美妙的音乐。"

"那这种琴声听起来是什么样子的呢？"克莱德曼向往地看着天空问。

"在九分钟前，我在太阳上试了试音，现在，琴声正以光速传来，当然，它是以电磁形式传播的，但我可以用超弦波在你们的大气中把它转换成声波，请听……"

长空中响起了几声空灵悠长的声音，很像钢琴的声音，这声音有一种魔力，一时攫住了所有的人。

"从这声音中，您感到了什么？"秘书长问中国领导人。

中国领导人感慨地说："我感到整个宇宙变成了一座大宫殿，一座有 200 亿光年高的宫殿，这声音在宫殿中缭绕不止。"

"听到这声音，您还否认上帝的存在吗？"美国总统问。

主席看了总统一眼说："这声音来自现实世界，如果这个世界就能够产生出这样的声音，上帝就变得更无必要了。"

节拍

"演奏马上就要开始了吗？"秘书长问。

"是的，我在等待节拍。"镜子回答。

"节拍？"

"节拍在四年前就已启动，它正以光速向这里传来。"

这时，天空发生了惊人的变化，地球和太阳的映像消失了，代之以一片明亮的银色波纹，这波纹跃动着，盖满了天空，地球仿佛沉于一个超级海洋中，天空就是从水下看到的阳光照耀下的海面。

镜子解释说："我现在正在阻挡着来自外太空的巨大辐射，我没有完全反射这些辐射，你们看到有一小部分透了过去，这辐射来自一颗四年前爆发的超新星。"

"四年前？那就是人马座了。"有人说。

"是的，人马座比邻星。"

"可是据我所知，那颗恒星完全不具备成为超新星的条件。"中国领导人说。

"我使它具备了。"镜子淡淡地说。

人们这时想起了镜子说过的话，它说它为这场音乐会进行了四年多的准备，那指的就是这件事了，镜子选定太阳为乐器后立刻引爆了比邻星。从镜子刚才对太阳试音的情形看，它显然具有超空间的作用能力，这种能力使它能在一个天文单位的距离之外弹振太阳，但对四光年之遥的恒星，它是否仍具有这种能力还不得而知。镜子引爆比邻星可能通过两种途径：在太阳系通过超空间作用，或者通过空间跳跃在短时间内到达比邻星附近引爆它，然后再次跳跃回到太阳系。不管通过哪种方式，对人类来说这都是神的力量。但不管怎样，超新星爆发的光线仍然要经过四年的时间才能到达太阳系。镜子说过演奏太阳的乐声是以电磁形式传向宇宙的，那么对于这个超级文明来说，光速就相当于人类的声速，光波就是它们的声波，那它们的光是什么呢？人类永远不得而知。

"对你操纵物质世界的能力，我们深感震惊。"美国总统敬畏地说。

"恒星是宇宙荒漠的石块，是我的世界中最多最普通的东西。我使用恒星，有时把它当作一件工具，有时是一件武器，有时是一件乐器……现在我把比邻星做成了节拍器，这与你们的祖先使用石块没什么本质的区别，都是用自己世界中最普通的东西来扩大和延伸自己的能力。"

然而草坪上的人们看不出这两者有什么共同点，他们放弃与镜子在技术上进行沟通的尝试，人类离理解这些还差得很远，就像蚂蚁离理解国际空间站还差得很远一样。

天空中的光波开始暗下来，渐渐地，人们觉得照着上面这个巨大海面的不是阳光而是月光了，超新星正在熄灭。

秘书长说："如果不是镜子挡住了超新星的能量，地球现在可能已经是一个没有生命的世界了。"

这时天空中的波纹已经完全消失了，巨大的地球映像重现，仍占据着大部分夜空。

"镜子说的节拍在哪里？"克莱德曼问。这时他已从舞台上下来，与元首们站在一起。

"看东面！"这时有人喊了一声，人们发现东方的天空中出现了一条笔直的分界线，这条线横贯整个天空，分界线两侧的天空是两个不同的景象：分界线西面仍是地球的映像，但它已被这条线切去了一部分；分界线东面则是灿烂的星空，有很多人都看出来了，这是北半球应有的星空，不是南半球星空的映像。分界线在由东向西庄严地移动，星空部分渐渐扩大，地球的映像正在由东向西被抹去。

"镜子在飞走！"秘书长喊道。人们很快知道他是对的，镜子在离开地球上空，它的边缘很快就消失在西方地平线下，人们又站在了他们见过无数次的正常的星空下。这以后人们再也没有见到镜子，它也许飞到它的琴——太阳附近了。

草坪上的人们带着一丝欣慰看着周围他们熟悉的世界，星空依旧，城市的灯火依旧，甚至草坪上嫩芽的芳香仍飘散在空气中。

节拍出现。

白昼在瞬间降临，蓝天突现，灿烂的阳光洒满大地，周围的一切都明亮地凸现出来；但这白昼只持续了一秒钟就熄灭了，刚才的夜又恢复了，星空和城市的灯火再次浮现；这夜也只持续了一秒钟，白昼再次出现，一秒钟后又是夜；然后，白昼、夜、白昼、夜、白昼、夜……以与脉搏相当的频率交替出现，仿佛世界是两片不断切换的幻灯片映出的图像。

这是由白昼与黑夜构成的节拍。

人们仰望天空，立刻看到了那颗闪动的太阳，它没有大小，只是太空中一个刺目的光点。"脉冲星。"中国领导人说。

这是超新星的残骸，一颗旋转的中子星。中子星那致密的表面有一个裸露的热斑，随着星体的旋转，中子星成为一座宇宙灯塔，热斑射出的光柱旋转着扫过广漠的太空，当这光柱扫过太阳系时，地球的白昼就短暂地出现了。

秘书长说："我记得脉冲星的频率比这快得多，它好像也不发出可见光。"

美国总统用手半遮着眼睛，艰难地适应着这疯狂的节拍世界："频率快是因为中子星聚集了原恒星的角动量，镜子可以通过某种途径把这些角动量消耗掉；至于可见光嘛……你们真认为镜子还有什么做不到的事？"

"但有一点，"中国领导人说，"没有理由认为宇宙中所有生物的生命节奏都与人类一样，它们的音乐节拍的频率肯定各不相同，比如镜子，它的正常节拍频率可能比我们最快的电脑主频都快……"

"是的，"总统点点头，"也没有理由认为它们可视的电磁波段都与我们的可见光相同。"

"你们是说，镜子是以人类的感觉为基准来演奏音乐的？"秘书长吃惊地问。

中国领导人摇摇头说："我不知道，但肯定要有一个基准的。"

脉冲星强劲的光柱庄严地扫过冷寂的太空，像一根长达40万亿千米，还在以光速不断延长的指挥棒。在这一端，太阳在镜子无形手指的弹拨下发出浑厚的、以光速向宇宙传播的电磁乐音，太阳音乐会开始了。

太阳音乐

一阵沙沙声，像是电磁噪声干扰，又像是无规则的海浪冲刷沙滩的声音，从这声音中有时能听出一丝荒凉和广漠，但更多的是混沌和无序。这声音一直持续了10多分钟，毫无变化。

"我说过，我们无法理解它们的音乐。"俄罗斯总统打破沉默说。

"听！"克莱德曼用一根手指指着天空说，其他人过了好一会儿才听出了他那经过训练的耳朵听到的旋律，那是结构最简单的旋律，只由两个音符组成，好像是钟表的一声嘀嗒。这两个音符不断出现，但有很长的间隔。后来，又出现了另一个双音符小节，然后出现了第三个、第四个……这些双音符小节在混沌的背景上不断浮现，像一群暗夜中的萤火虫。

一种新的旋律出现了，它有四个音符。人们都把目光转向克

莱德曼，他在注意地听着，好像感觉到了些什么，这时四音符小
节的数量也增加了。

"这样吧，"他对元首们说，"我们每个人记住一个双音符小
节。"于是大家注意听着，每人努力记住一个双音符小节，然后
凝神等着它再次出现以巩固自己的记忆。过了一会儿，克莱德曼
又说："好啦，现在注意听一个四音符小节，得快些，不然乐曲
越来越复杂，我们就什么也听不出来了……好，就这个，有人听
出什么来了吗？"

"它的前两个一半是我记住的那一对音符！"巴西元首高
声说。

"后一半是我记住的那一对！"加拿大元首说。

人们接着发现，每个四音符小节都是由前面两个双音符小节
组成的，随着四音符小节数量的增多，双音符小节的数量也在减
少，似乎前者在消耗后者。再后来，八音符小节出现了，结构与
前面一样，是由已有的两个四音符小节合并而成的。

"你们都听出了什么？"秘书长问周围的元首们。

"在闪电和火山熔岩照耀下的原始海洋中，一些小分子正在聚
合成大分子……当然，这只是我完全个人化的想象。"中国领导
人说。

"想象请不要拘泥于地球，"美国总统说，"这种分子的聚集也
许是发生在一片映射着恒星光芒的星云中，也许正在聚集组合的
不是分子，而是恒星内部的一些核能旋涡……"

这时，一个多音符旋律以高音凸现出来，它反复出现，仿佛
是这昏暗的混沌世界中一道明亮的小电弧，"这好像是在描述一
个质变。"中国领导人说。

一个新的乐器的声音出现了，这连续的弦音很像小提琴发出的。它用另一种柔美的方式重复着那个凸现的旋律，仿佛是后者的影子。

"这似乎在表现某种复制。"俄罗斯总统说。

连续的旋律出现了，是那种类似小提琴的乐音，它平滑地变幻着，好像是追踪着某种曲线运动的目光。英国首相对中国领导人说："如果按照您刚才的思路，现在已经有某种东西在海中游动了。"

不知不觉中，背景音乐开始变化了，这时人们几乎忘记了它的存在，它从海浪声变幻为起伏的沙沙声，仿佛是暴雨在击打着裸露的岩石；接着又变了，变成一种与风声类似的空旷的声音。美国总统说："海中的游动者在进入新环境，也许是陆上，也许是空中。"

所有的乐器突然变为短暂的齐奏，形成了一声恐怖的巨响，好像是什么巨大的实体轰然坍塌，一切戛然而止，只剩下开始那种海浪似的背景声在荒凉地响着。然后，那简单的双音节旋律又出现了，又开始了缓慢而艰难的组合，一切重新开始……

"我敢肯定，这描述了一场大灭绝，现在我们听到的是灭绝后的复苏。"

又经过漫长而艰难的过程，海中的游动者又开始进入世界的其他部分。旋律渐渐变得复杂而宏大，人们的理解也不再统一。有人想到一条大河奔流而下，有人想到广阔的平原上一支浩荡队伍在跋涉，有人想到漆黑的太空中向黑洞涡旋而下的滚滚星云……但大家都同意，这是在表现一个宏伟的进程，也许是进化的进程。这一乐章很长，不知不觉一个小时过去了，音乐的主题终于发生了变化。旋律渐渐分化成两个，这两个旋律在对抗和搏斗，时而疯狂地碰撞，时而扭缠在一起……

"典型的贝多芬风格。"克莱德曼评论说。这之前很长时间人们都沉浸在宏伟的音乐中没有说话。

秘书长说："好像是一支在海上与巨浪搏斗的船队。"

美国总统摇了摇头："不，不是的，您应该能听出这两种力量没有本质的不同，我想是在表现一场蔓延到整个世界的战争。"

"我说，"一直沉默的日本首相插话说，"你们真的认为自己能够理解外星文明的艺术？也许你们对这音乐的理解，只是牛对琴的理解。"

克莱德曼说："我相信我们的理解基本上正确。宇宙间通用的语言，除了数学可能就是音乐了。"

秘书长说："要证实这一点也许并不难：我们能否预言下一乐章的主题或风格？"

经过稍稍思考，中国领导人说："我想下面可能将表现某种崇拜，旋律将具有森严的建筑美。"

"您是说像巴赫？"

"是的。"

果然如此，在接下来的乐章中，听众们仿佛走进一座高大庄严的教堂，听着自己的脚步在这宏伟的建筑内部发出空旷的回声，对某种看不见但无所不在的力量的恐惧和敬畏压倒了他们。

再往后，已经演化得相当复杂的旋律突然又变得简单了，背景音乐第一次消失了，在无边的寂静中，一串清脆短促的打击声出现了，一声，两声，三声，四声……然后，一声，四声，九声，十六声……一条条越来越复杂的数列穿梭而过。

有人问："这是在描述数学和抽象思维的出现吗？"

接下来音乐变得更奇怪了，出现了由小提琴奏出的许多独立的小节，每小节由三到四个音符组成，各小节中音符都相同，但其音程的长短出现各种组合；还出现一种连续的滑音，它渐渐升高然后降低，最后回到起始的音高。人们凝神听了很长时间，希腊元首说："这好像是在描述基本的几何形状。"人们立刻找到了感觉，他们仿佛看到在纯净的空间中，一群三角形和四边形匀速地飘过，至于那种滑音，让人们看到了圆，椭圆和完美的正圆……渐渐地，旋律开始出现变化，表现直线的单一音符都变成了滑音，但根据刚才乐曲留下的印象，人们仍能感觉到那些飘浮在抽象空间中的几何形状，但这些形状都扭曲了，仿佛浮在水面上……

"时空的秘密被发现了。"有人说。

下一个乐章是以一个不变的节奏开始的，它的频率与脉冲星打出的由昼与夜构成的节拍相同，好像音乐已经停止了，只剩下节拍在空响。但很快另一个不变的节奏也加入进来，频率比前一个稍快。之后，不同频率的不变的节奏在不断地加入，最后出现了一个气势磅礴的大合奏，但在时间轴上，乐曲是恒定不变的，像一堵平坦的声音高墙。

对这一乐章，人们的理解惊人地一致："一部大机器在运行。"

后来，出现了一个纤细的新旋律，如银铃般晶莹地响着，如梦幻般变幻不定，与背后那堵呆板的声音之墙形成鲜明对比，仿佛是飞翔在那部大机器里的一个银色小精灵。这个旋律仿佛是一滴小小的但强有力的催化剂，在钢铁世界中引发了奇妙的反应：

那些不变的节奏开始波动变幻，大机器的粗轴和巨轮渐渐变得如橡皮泥般柔软，最后，整个合奏变得如那个精灵旋律一样轻盈有灵气。

人们议论纷纷："大机器具有智能了！""我觉得，机器正在与它的创造者相互接近。"……

太阳音乐在继续，已经进行到一个新的乐章了。这是结构最复杂的一个乐章，也是最难理解的一个乐章。它首先用类似钢琴的声音奏出一个悠远空灵的旋律，然后以越来越复杂的合奏不断地重复演绎这个主题，每次重复演绎都使得这个主题在上次的基础上变得更加宏大。

在这种重复进行了几次后，中国领导人说："以我的理解，是不是这样的：一个思想者站在一个海岛上，用他深邃的头脑思索着宇宙；镜头向上升，思想者在镜头的视野中渐渐变小，当镜头从空中把整个海岛都纳入视野后，思想者像一粒灰尘般消失了；镜头继续上升，海岛在渐渐变小，镜头升出了大气层，在太空中把整颗行星纳入视野，海岛像一粒灰尘般消失了；太空中的镜头继续远离这颗行星，把整个行星系纳入视野，这时，只能看到行星系的恒星，它在漆黑的太空中看去只有台球般大小，孤独地发着光，而那颗有海洋的行星，也像一粒灰尘般消失了……"

美国总统聆听着音乐，接着说："……镜头以超光速远离，我们发现在我们的尺度上空旷而广漠的宇宙，在更大的尺度上却是一团由恒星组成的灿烂的尘埃，当整个银河系进入视野后，那颗带着行星的恒星像一粒灰尘般消失了；镜头接着跳过无法想象的距离，把一个星系团纳入视野，眼前仍是一片灿烂的尘埃，但尘埃的颗粒已不再是恒星而是恒星系了……"

秘书长接着说："……这时银河系像一粒灰尘般消失了，但终点在哪儿呢？"

保护罩中的人们重新全身心地沉浸在音乐中，乐曲正在达到它的顶峰：在音乐家强有力的思想推动下，那个拍摄宇宙的镜头被推到了已知的时空之外，整个宇宙都被纳入视野，那个包含着银河系的星系团也像一粒灰尘般消失了。人们凝神等待着终极的到来，宏伟的合奏突然消失了，只有开始那种类似钢琴的声音在孤独地响着，空灵而悠远。

"又是返回到海岛上的思想者了吗？"有人问。

克莱德曼倾听着摇了摇头："不，现在的旋律与那时完全不同。"

这时，全宇宙的合奏再次出现，不久停了下来，又让位于钢琴独奏。这两个旋律就这样交替出现，持续了很长时间。

克莱德曼凝神听着，突然恍然大悟："钢琴是在倒着演奏合奏的旋律！"

美国总统点点头："或者说，它是合奏的镜像，哦，宇宙的镜像，这就是镜子了。"

音乐显然已近尾声，全宇宙合奏与钢琴独奏同时进行，钢琴精确地倒奏着合奏的每一处，它的形象凸现在合奏的背景上，但两者又那么和谐。

中国领导人说："这使我想起了一个现代建筑流派，叫光亮派：为了避免新建筑对周围传统环境的影响，就把建筑的表面全部做成镜面，使它通过反射环境来与周围达到和谐，同时也以这种方式表现了自己。"

"是的，当文明达到了一定的程度，它可能也通过反射宇宙来表现自己的存在。"秘书长若有所思地说。

钢琴突然由反奏变为正奏，这样它立刻与宇宙合奏融为一体，太阳音乐结束了。

欢乐颂

镜子说："一场完美的音乐会，谢谢欣赏它的所有人类，好，我走了。"

"请等一下！"克莱德曼高喊一声，"我们有一个最后的要求：你能否用太阳弹奏一首人类的音乐？"

"可以，哪一首呢？"

元首们互相看了看，"弹贝多芬的《命运》吧。"德国总理说。

"不，不应该是《命运》，"美国总统摇摇头说，"现在已经证明，人类不可能扼住命运的喉咙，人类的价值在于：我们明知命运不可抗拒，死亡必定是最后的胜利者，却仍能在有限的时间里专心致志地创造着美丽的生活。"

"那就唱《欢乐颂》吧。"中国领导人说。

镜子说："你们唱吧，我可以通过太阳把歌声向宇宙传播出去，我保证，音色会很好的。"

这 200 多人唱起了《欢乐颂》，歌声通过镜子传给了太阳，太阳再次振动起来，把歌声用强大的电磁脉冲传向太空的各个方向。

......

欢乐啊，美丽神奇的火花，

来自极乐世界的女儿。

天国之女啊，我们如醉如狂，

踏进了你神圣的殿堂。

被时尚无情分开的一切，

你的魔力又把它们重新连接。

......

5 小时后，歌声将飞出太阳系；4 年后，歌声将到达人马座；10 万年后，歌声将传遍银河系；20 多万年后，歌声将到达最近的恒星系大麦哲伦星云；600 万年后，歌声将传遍本星系团的 40 多个恒星系；1 亿年之后，歌声将传遍本超星系团的 50 多个星系群；150 亿年后，歌声将传遍目前已知的宇宙，并向继续膨胀的宇宙传出去，如果那时宇宙还膨胀的话。

......

在永恒的大自然里，

欢乐是强劲的发条，

在宏大的宇宙之钟里，

是欢乐，在推动着指针旋跳。

它催含苞的鲜花怒放，

它使艳阳普照穹苍。

甚至望远镜都看不到的地方，

它也在使天体转动不息。

......

歌唱结束后，音乐会的草坪上，所有人都陷入长时间的沉默，元首们都在沉思着。

"也许，事情还没到完全失去希望的地步，我们应该尽自己的努力。"中国领导人首先说。

美国点点头："是的，世界需要联合国。"

"与未来所避免的灾难相比，我们各自所要做出的让步和牺牲是微不足道的。"俄罗斯总统说。

"我们所面临的，毕竟只是宇宙中一粒沙子上的事，应该好办。"英国首相仰望着星空说。

各国元首纷纷表示赞同。

"那么，各位是否同意延长本届联大呢？"秘书长满怀希望地问道。

"这当然需要我们同各自的政府进行联系，但我想问题应该不大。"美国总统微笑着说。

"各位，今天真是一个值得纪念的日子！"秘书长无法掩饰自己的喜悦，"现在，让我们继续听音乐吧！"

《欢乐颂》又响了起来。

镜子以光速飞离太阳，它知道自己再也不会回来，在那十几亿年的音乐家生涯中，它从未重复演奏过一个恒星，就像人类的牧羊人从不重掷同一块石子。飞行中，他听着《欢乐颂》的余音，那永恒平静的镜面上出现了一圈难以觉察的涟漪。

"嗯，是首好歌。"

2001.06.28　一稿于娘子关

2005.07.11　二稿于娘子关

带上她的眼睛

WITH HER EYES

连续工作了两个多月，我实在累了，便请求主任给我放两天假，出去旅游一下散散心。主任答应了，条件是我再带一双眼睛去，我也答应了，于是他带我去拿眼睛。眼睛放在控制中心走廊尽头的一个小房间里，现在还剩下十几双。

主任递给我一双眼睛，指指前面的大屏幕，把眼睛的主人介绍给我，好像是一个刚毕业的小姑娘，她呆呆地看着我。在肥大的太空服中，她更显得娇小，一副可怜兮兮的样子，显然刚刚体会到太空不是她在大学图书馆中想象的浪漫天堂，某些方面可能比地狱还稍差些。

"麻烦您了，真不好意思。"她连连向我鞠躬。这是我听到过的最轻柔的声音，我想象着这声音从外太空飘来，像一阵微风吹过轨道上那些庞大粗陋的钢结构，使它们立刻变得像橡皮泥一样软。

"一点儿都不，我很高兴有个伴儿的。你想去哪儿？"我豪爽地说。

"什么？您还没决定去哪儿？"她看上去很高兴。但我立刻感到两个异样的地方：其一，地面与外太空通信都有延时，即使在月球，延时也有两秒钟，小行星带延时更长，但她的回答几乎让人感觉不到延时，这就是说，她现在在近地轨道。那里回地面不用中转，费用和时间都不需多少，没必要托别人带眼睛去度假。其二，是她身上的太空服，作为航天个人装备工程师，我觉得这种太空服很奇怪：在服装上看不到防辐射系统，放在她旁边的头盔的面罩上也没有强光防护系统；我还注意到，这套服装的隔热和冷却系统异常发达。

"她在哪个空间站？"我扭头问主任。

"先别问这个吧。"主任的脸色很阴沉。

"别问好吗？"屏幕上的她也说，还是那副让人心软的小可怜样儿。

"你不会是被关禁闭了吧？"我开玩笑地说。因为她所在的舱室十分窄小，显然是一个航行体的驾驶舱，各种复杂的导航系统此起彼伏地闪烁着，但没有窗子，也没有观察屏幕，只有一支在她头顶打转的失重的铅笔说明她是在太空中。听了我的话，她和主任似乎都愣了一下，我赶紧说："好，我不问自己不该知道的事了，还是你决定我们去哪儿吧。"

这个决定对于她来说似乎很艰难，她把戴着太空服手套的双手握在胸前，双眼半闭着，似乎是在决定生存还是死亡，或者认为地球在我们这次短暂的旅行后就要爆炸了。我不由得笑出声来。

"哦，这对我来说不容易，您要是看过海伦·凯勒的《假如给我三天光明》的话，就能明白这多难了！"

"我们没有三天，只有两天。在时间上，这个时代的人都是穷光蛋。但比那个20世纪的盲人幸运的是，我和你的眼睛在三个小时内可到达地球的任何一个地方。"

"那就去我们起航前去过的地方吧！"她告诉了我那个地方，于是我带着她的眼睛去了。

草原

这是高山与平原、草原与森林的交界处，距我工作的航天中心有2000多千米，我乘电离层飞机用了15分钟就到了这儿。面前的塔克拉玛干，经过几代人的努力，已由沙漠变成了草原，又经过几代人强有力的人口控制，这儿再次变成了人迹罕至的地方。现在大草原从我面前一直延伸到天边，背后的天山覆盖着暗绿色的森林，几座山顶还有银色的雪冠。

我掏出她的眼睛戴上。

所谓眼睛，就是一副传感眼镜，当你戴上它时，你所看到的一切图像由超高频信息波发射出去，可以被远方的另一个戴同样传感眼镜的人接收到，于是他就能看到你所看到的一切，就像你带着他的眼睛一样。

现在，长年在月球和小行星带工作的人已有上百万，他们回地球度假的费用是惊人的，于是齐啬的宇航局就设计了这个玩意儿。每个生活在外太空的宇航员在地球上都有了另一双眼睛，由这里真正能去度假的幸运儿带上这双眼睛，让身处外太空的那个思乡者分享他的快乐。这个小玩意儿在刚开始被当作笑柄，但后来由于用它"度假"的人能得到可观的补助，竟流行开来。由于采用了尖端的技术，这人造眼睛越做越精致。现在，它竟能通过采集戴着它的人的脑电波，把他（她）的触觉和味觉一同发射出去。多带一双眼睛去度假，成了宇航系统地面工作人员从事的一项公益活动，可出于度假中的隐私等原因，也并不是每个人都乐意再带双眼睛，但我这次无所谓。

我对眼前的景色大发感叹，但从她的眼睛中，我听到了一阵轻轻的抽泣声。

"上次离开后，我常梦到这里，现在回到梦里来了！"她细细的声音从她的眼睛中传出来，"我现在就像从很深很深的水底冲出来呼吸到空气，我太怕封闭了。"

我真的从中听到她在做深呼吸。

我说："可你现在并不封闭，同你周围的太空比起来，这草原太小了。"

她沉默了，似乎连呼吸都停止了。

"啊，当然，太空中的人还是封闭的，20世纪的一个叫耶格尔的飞行员曾有一句话，是描述飞船中的宇航员的，说他们像……"

"罐头中的肉。"

我们都笑了起来。她突然惊叫："呀，花儿，有花儿啊！上次我来时还没有的！"

是的，广阔的草原上到处点缀着星星点点的小花儿。"能近些看看那朵儿花吗？"我蹲下来看。"呀，真美！能闻闻它吗？不，别摘下它！"我只好半趴到地上闻，一缕淡淡的清香。"啊，我也闻到了，真像一首隐隐传来的小夜曲呢！"

我笑着摇摇头，这是一个闪电变幻疯狂追逐的时代，女孩子们都浮躁到了极点，像这样的见花落泪的林妹妹真是太少了。

"我们给这朵小花儿起个名字好吗？嗯……叫它梦梦吧。我们再看看那一朵好吗？它该叫什么呢？嗯，叫小雨吧。再到那一朵那儿去，啊，谢谢，看它是淡蓝色的，它的名字应该是月光……"

我们就这样一朵朵地看花儿、闻花儿，然后再给它们起名字。她陶醉于其中，没完没了地进行下去，忘记了一切。我对这套小女孩的游戏实在厌烦了，到我坚持停止时，我们已给上百朵花儿起了名字。

一抬头，我发现已走出了好远，便回去拿丢在后面的背包。当我拾起草地上的背包时，又听到了她的惊叫："天啊，你把小雪踩住了！"我扶起那朵白色的野花儿，觉得很可笑，就用两只手各捂住一朵小花儿，问她："它们都叫什么？什么样子？"

"左边那朵叫水晶，也是白色的，它的茎上有分开的三片叶儿；右边那朵叫火苗，粉红色，茎上有四片叶子，上面两片是单的，下面两片连在一起。"

她说得都对，我有些感动了。

"你看，我和它们都互相认识了，以后漫长的日子里，我会好多次一遍遍地想它们每一个的样子，像背一本美丽的童话书。你那里的世界真好！"

"我这里的世界？要是你再这么孩子气地多愁善感下去，这也是你的世界了，那些挑剔的太空心理医生会让你永远待在地球上的。"

我在草原上漫无目的地漫步，很快来到一条隐没在草丛中的小溪旁。我迈过去继续向前走，她叫住了我，说："我真想把手伸到小河里。"我蹲下来把手伸进溪水，一股清凉流遍全身，她的眼睛用超高频信息波把这感觉传给远在太空中的她，我又听到了她的感叹。

"你那儿很热吧？"我想起了她那窄小的控制舱和隔热系统异常发达的太空服。

"热，热得像……地狱。呀，天啊，这是什么？草原的风？！"这时我刚把手从水中拿出来，微风吹在湿手上凉丝丝的，"不，别动，这真是天国的风呀！"

我把双手举在草原上的微风中，直到手被吹干。然后应她的要求，我又把手在溪水中打湿，再举到风中，把天国的感觉传给她。我们就这样又消磨了很长时间。

再次上路后，沉默地走了一段，她又轻轻地说："你那里的世界真好。"

我说："我不知道，灰色的生活把我这方面的感觉都磨钝了。"

"怎么会呢？！这世界能给人多少感觉啊！谁要能说清这些感觉，就如同说清大雷雨有多少雨点一样。看天边那大团的白云，银白银白的，我这时觉得它们好像是固态的，像发光玉石构成的高山。下面的草原，这时倒像是气态的，好像所有的绿草都飞离了大地，成了一片绿色的云海。看！当那片云遮住太阳又飘开时，草原上光和影的变幻是多么气势磅礴啊！看看这些，您真的感受不到什么吗？"

……

我戴着她的眼睛在草原上转了一天，她渴望看草原上的每一朵野花儿、每一棵小草，看草丛中跃动的每一缕阳光，渴望听草原上的每一种声音。一条突然出现的小溪、小溪中的一条小鱼，都会令她激动不已；一阵不期而至的微风、风中一缕绿草的清香都会让她落泪……我感到，她对这个世界的情感已丰富到病态的程度。

　　日落前，我走到了草原上一间孤零零的白色小屋，那是为旅游者准备的一个小旅店，似乎好久没人光顾了，只有一个迟钝的老式机器人照看着旅店里的一切。我又累又饿，可晚饭只吃到一半，她又提议我们立刻去看日落。

　　"看着晚霞渐渐消失，夜幕慢慢降临森林，就像在听一首宇宙间最美的交响曲。"她陶醉地说。我暗暗叫苦，但还是拖着沉重的双腿去了。

　　草原的落日确实很美，但她对这种美倾泻的情感，使这一切有了一种异样的色彩。

　　"你很珍视这些平凡的东西。"回去的路上我对她说，这时夜色已很重，星星已在夜空中出现。

　　"你为什么不呢，这才像在生活。"她说。

　　"我，还有其他的大部分人，不可能做到这样。在这个时代，得到太容易了。物质的东西自不必说，蓝天绿水的优美环境、乡村和孤岛的宁静等，都可以毫不费力地得到，甚至以前人们认为最难寻觅的爱情，在虚拟现实网上至少也可以暂时体会到。所以人们不再珍视什么了，面对着一大堆伸手可得的水果，他们把拿起的每一个咬一口就扔掉。"

　　"但也有人面前没有这些水果。"她低声说。

我感觉自己刺痛了她，却不知为什么。回去的路上，我们都没再说话。

这天夜里的梦境中，我看到了她，她穿着太空服在那间小控制舱中，眼里含泪，向我伸出手来喊："快带我出去，我怕封闭！"我惊醒了，发现她真的在喊我，我是戴着她的眼睛仰躺着睡的。

"请带我出去好吗？我们去看月亮，月亮该升起来了！"

我脑袋发沉，迷迷糊糊的，很不情愿地起了床。到外面后发现月亮真的刚升起来，草原上的夜雾使它有些发红。月光下的草原也在沉睡，有无数点萤火虫的幽光在朦朦胧胧的草海上浮动，仿佛是草原的梦在显形。

我伸了个懒腰，对着夜空说："喂，你是不是从轨道上看到月光照到这里？"

"告诉我你的飞船的大概方位，说不定我还能看到呢。"我肯定它是在近地轨道上。

她没有回答我的话，而是自己轻轻哼起了一首曲子，一小段旋律过后，她说："这是德彪西的《月光》。"接着又哼下去，陶醉于其中，完全忘记了我的存在。《月光》的旋律同月光一起从太空降落到草原上。我想象着太空中的那个娇弱的女孩，她的上方是银色的月球，下面是蓝色的地球，小小的她从中间飞过，把音乐融入月光……

直到一个小时后我回去躺到床上，她还在哼着音乐，是不是德彪西的我就不知道了，但那轻柔的乐声一直在我的梦中飘荡着。

不知过了多久，音乐变成了呼唤，她又叫醒了我，还要出去。

"你不是看过月亮了吗？！"我生气地说。

"可现在不一样了，记得吗？刚才西边有云的，现在那些云可能飘过来了，月亮正在云中时隐时现呢，想想草原上的光和影，多美啊，那是另一种音乐了，求你带我的眼睛出去吧！"

我十分恼火，但还是出去了。云真的飘过来了，月亮在云中穿行，草原上大块的光斑在缓缓浮动，如同大地深处浮现的远古的记忆。

"你像是来自18世纪的多愁善感的诗人，完全不适合这个时代，更不适合当宇航员。"我对着夜空说，然后摘下她的眼睛，挂到旁边一棵红柳的枝上，"你自己看月亮吧，我真的得睡觉去了，明天还要赶回航天中心，继续我那毫无诗意的生活呢。"

她的眼睛中传出了她细细的声音，我听不清她说什么，径自回去了。

我醒来时天已大亮，阴云已布满了天空，草原笼罩在蒙蒙的小雨中。她的眼睛仍挂在红柳枝上，镜片上蒙上了一层水雾。我小心地擦干镜片，戴上它。原以为她看了一夜月亮，现在还在睡觉，却从眼睛中听到了她低低的抽泣声，我的心一下子软了下来。

"真对不起，我昨天晚上实在太累了。"

"不，不是因为你，呜呜，天从3点半就阴了，5点多又下起雨……"

"你一夜都没睡？！"

"……呜呜，下起雨，我，我看不到日出了，我好想看草原的日出，呜呜，好想看的，呜……"

我的心像是被什么东西融化了，脑海中出现她眼泪汪汪、小鼻子一抽一抽的样儿，眼睛竟有些湿润。不得不承认，在过去的一天一夜里，她教会了我某种东西，一种说不清的东西，像月夜中草原上的光影一样朦胧。由于它，以后我眼中的世界会与以前有些不同。

"草原上总还会有日出的，以后我一定会再带你的眼睛来，或者带你本人来看，好吗？"

她不哭了，突然，她低声说："听……"

我没听见什么，但紧张起来。

"这是今天的第一声鸟叫，雨中也有鸟呢！"她激动地说，那口气如同听到世纪钟声一样庄严。

"落日六号"

我又回到了灰色的生活和忙碌的工作中，以上的经历我很快就淡忘了。很长时间后，当我想起洗那些旅行时穿的衣服时，在裤脚上发现了两三颗草籽。

同时，在我的意识深处，也有一颗小小的种子留了下来。在我孤独寂寞的精神沙漠中，那颗种子已长出了令人难以察觉的绿芽。虽然是无意识的，当一天的劳累结束后，我已能感觉到晚风吹到脸上时那淡淡的诗意，鸟儿的鸣叫已能引起我的注意，黄昏时我甚至站在天桥上，看着夜幕降临城市……世界在我的眼中仍是灰色的，但星星点点的嫩绿在其中出现，并在增多。当这种变化发展到让我觉察出来时，我又想起了她。

也许是无意识的，在我闲暇时，甚至睡梦中，她身处的环境常在我的脑海中出现，那窄小的封闭的控制舱、奇怪的隔热太空服……后来这些东西在我的意识中都隐去了，只有一样东西凸显出来，那就是在她头顶上打转的失重的铅笔。不知为什么，一闭上眼睛，那支铅笔总在我的眼前飘浮。终于有一天，上班时我走进航天中心高大的门厅，一幅见过无数次的巨大壁画把我吸引住了，壁画上是从太空中拍摄的蔚蓝色的地球。那支飘浮的铅笔又在我的眼前出现了，同壁画叠印在一起，我又听到了她的声音："我怕封闭……"一道闪电在我的脑海里出现。

除了太空，还有一个地方会失重！

我发疯似的跑上楼，猛砸主任办公室的门，他不在，我心有灵犀地知道他在哪儿，就飞跑到存放眼睛的那个小房间，他果然在里面，看着大屏幕。她在大屏幕上，还在那个封闭的控制舱中，穿着那件"太空服"，画面凝固着，是以前录下来的。"是为了她来的吧？"主任说，眼睛还看着屏幕。

"她到底在哪儿？！"我大声问。

"你可能已经猜到了，她是'落日六号'的领航员。"

一切都明白了，我无力地跌坐在地毯上。

"落日工程"原计划发射10艘飞船，它们是"落日一号"到"落日十号"，但计划由于"落日六号"的失事而中断了。"落日工程"是一次标准的探险航行，它的航行程序同航天中心的其他航行几乎一样。

唯一不同的是，"落日"飞船不是飞向太空，而是潜入地球深处。

第一次太空飞行一个半世纪后，人类开始了向相反方向的探险，"落日"系列地航飞船就是这种探险的首次尝试。

四年前，我在电视中看到过"落日一号"发射时的情景。那时正是深夜，吐鲁番盆地的中央出现了一个如太阳般耀眼的火球，火球的光芒使新疆夜空中的云层变成了绚丽的朝霞。当火球暗下来时，"落日一号"已潜入地层。大地被烧红了一大片，这片圆形的、发着红光的区域中央，是一个岩浆的湖泊，白热化的岩浆沸腾着，激起一根根雪亮的浪柱……那一夜，远至乌鲁木齐，都能感到飞船穿过地层时传到大地上的微微振动。

　　"落日工程"的前5艘飞船都成功地完成了地层航行，安全地返回地面。其中"落日五号"创造了迄今为止人类在地层中航行深度的纪录：海平面下3100千米。"落日六号"不打算突破这个纪录。因为据地球物理学家的结论，在地层3400～3500千米深处，存在着地幔和地核的交界面，学术上把它叫作"古腾堡不连续面"，一旦通过这个交界面，便进入地球的液态铁镍核心，那里物质密度骤然增大，"落日六号"的设计强度是不允许在如此大的密度中航行的。

　　"落日六号"的航行开始很顺利，飞船只用了两个小时便穿过了地表和地幔的交界面——莫霍不连续面，并在大陆板块漂移的滑动面上停留了五个小时，然后开始了在地幔中3000多千米的漫长航行。宇宙航行是寂寞的，但宇航员们能看到无限的太空和壮丽的星群；而地航飞船上的地航员们，只能凭感觉触摸飞船周围不断向上移去的高密度物质。从飞船上的全息后视电视中能看到这样的情景：炽热的岩浆刺目地闪亮着，翻滚着，随着飞船的下潜，在船尾飞快地合拢起来，瞬间充满了飞船通过的空间。有一名地航员回忆：他们一闭上眼睛，就看到了飞快合拢并压下来的岩浆，这个幻象使航行者意识到那压在他们上方的巨量的并不

118

断增厚的物质，一种地面上的人难以理解的压抑感折磨着地航飞船中的每一个人，他们都受到这种封闭恐惧症的袭击。

"落日六号"出色地完成着航行中的各项研究工作。飞船的速度大约是每小时 15 千米，飞船需要航行 20 小时才能到达预定深度。但在飞船航行了 15 小时 40 分钟时，警报出现了。从地层雷达的探测中得知，航行区的物质密度由每立方厘米 6.3 克猛增到 9.5 克，物质成分由硅酸盐类突然变为以铁镍为主的金属，物质状态也由固态变为液态。尽管"落日六号"当时只到达了 2500 千米的深度，但所有的迹象都冷酷地表明，他们闯入了地核！后来得知，这是地幔中一条通向地核的裂隙，地核中的高压液态铁镍充满了这条裂隙，使得在"落日六号"的航线上，古腾堡不连续面向上延伸了近 1000 千米！飞船立刻紧急转向，企图冲出这条裂隙，不幸就在这时发生了：由中子材料制造的船体顶住了突然增加到每平方厘米 1600 吨的巨大压力。但是，飞船分为前部烧熔发动机、中部主舱和后部推进发动机三大部分，当飞船在远大于设计密度和设计压力的液态铁镍中转向时，烧熔发动机与主舱接合部断裂。从"落日六号"用中微子通信发回的画面中我们看到，已与船体分离的烧熔发动机在一瞬间被发着暗红光的液态铁镍吞没了。地层飞船的烧熔发动机用超高温射流为飞船切开航行方向的物质，没有它，只剩下一台推进发动机的"落日六号"在地层中是寸步难行的。地核的密度很惊人，但构成飞船的中子材料密度更大，液态铁镍对飞船产生的浮力小于它的自重，于是，"落日六号"便向地心沉下去。

人类登月后，用了一个半世纪才有能力航行到土星。在地层探险方面，人类也要用同样的时间才有能力从地幔航行到地核。

现在的地航飞船误入地核，就如同 20 世纪中期的登月飞船偏离月球迷失于外太空一样，获救的希望是丝毫不存在的。

好在"落日六号"主舱的船体是可靠的，船上的中微子通信系统仍和地面控制中心保持着完好的联系。在以后的一年中，"落日六号"航行组坚持工作，把从地核中得到的大量宝贵资料发送到地面。他们被裹在几千千米厚的物质中，这里别说空气和生命，连空间都没有，周围是温度高达 5000 摄氏度、压力可以把碳在一秒钟内变成金刚石的液态铁镍！它们密密地挤在"落日六号"的周围，密得只有中微子才能穿过，"落日六号"是处于一个巨大的炼钢炉中！在这样的世界里，《神曲》中的《地狱篇》像是在描写天堂了；在这样的世界里，生命算什么？能仅仅用脆弱来描写它吗？

沉重的心理压力像毒蛇一样撕裂着"落日六号"地航员们的神经。一天，船上的地质工程师从睡梦中突然跃起，竟打开了他所在的密封舱的绝热门！虽然这只是四道绝热门中的第一道，但瞬间涌入的热浪立刻把他烧成了一段木炭。

指令长在一个密封舱内飞快地关上了绝热门，避免了"落日六号"的彻底毁灭。他自己被严重烧伤，在写完最后一页航行日志后死去了。

从那以后，在这个星球的最深处，在"落日六号"上，就只剩下她一个人了。

现在，"落日六号"内部已完全处于失重状态，飞船已下沉到 6800 千米深处，那里是地球的最深处，她是第一个到达地心的人。

她在地心的世界，是那个活动范围不到 10 平方米的闷热的控制舱。飞船上有一个中微子传感眼镜，这个装置使她同地面世界多少保持着一些感性的联系。但这种如同生命线的联系不能长时间延续下去，飞船里中微子通信设备的能量很快就要耗尽，现有的能量已不能维持传感眼镜的超高速数据传输，这种联系在三个月前就中断了，具体时间是在我从草原返回航天中心的飞机上，当时我已把她的眼睛摘下来放到旅行包中。

那个没有日出的、细雨蒙蒙的草原早晨，竟是她最后看到的地面世界。

后来"落日六号"同地面只能保持着语音和数据通信，而这个联系也在一天深夜中断了，她被永远孤独地封闭于地心中。"落日六号"的中子材料外壳足以抵抗地心的巨大压力，而飞船上的生命循环系统还可以运行 50 至 80 年，她将在这不到 10 平方米的地心世界里度过自己的余生。

我不敢想象她同地面世界最后告别的情形，但主任让我听的录音出乎我的意料。这时来自地心的中微子波束已很弱，她的声音时断时续，但这声音很平静。

"……你们发来的最后一份补充建议已经收到，今后，我会按照整个研究计划努力工作的。将来，可能是几代人以后吧，也许会有地心飞船找到'落日六号'并同它对接，有人会再次进入这里，但愿那时我留下的资料会有用。请你们放心，我会在这里安排好自己的生活。我现在已适应这里，不再觉得狭窄和封闭了，整个世界都围着我呀，我闭上眼睛就能看见上面的大草原，还可以清楚地看见每一朵我起了名字的小花儿呢。再见。"

透明地球

在以后的岁月中，我到过很多地方，每到一个地方，我都喜欢躺在那里的大地上。我曾经躺在海南岛的海滩上、阿拉斯加的冰雪上、俄罗斯的白桦林中、撒哈拉烫人的沙漠上……每到那个时刻，地球在我脑海中就变得透明了，在我下面6000多千米深处，在这个巨大的水晶球中心，我看到了停泊在那里的"落日六号"地航飞船，感受到了从几千千米深的地球中心传出的她的心跳。我想象着金色的阳光和银色的月光透射到这个星球的中心，我听到了那里传出的她吟唱的《月光》，还听到她那轻柔的话音：

"……多美啊，这又是另一种音乐了……"

有一个想法安慰着我：不管走到天涯海角，我离她都不会再远了。

地火

FIRE IN THE EARTH

父亲的生命已走到了尽头，他用尽力气呼吸，比他在井下扛起二百多斤的铁支架时用的力气大得多。他的脸色惨白，双目凸出，嘴唇因窒息而呈深紫色，仿佛一条无形的绞索正在脖子上慢慢绞紧。他那艰辛一生的所有纯朴的希望和梦想都已消失，现在他生命的全部渴望就是多吸进一点点空气。但父亲的肺，就像所有患三期矽肺病的矿工的肺一样，成了一块由网状纤维连在一起的黑色灰块，再也无法把吸进去的氧气输送到血液中。组成那个灰块的煤粉是父亲在二十五年中从井下一点点吸入的，是他这一生采出的煤中极小极小的一部分。

　　刘欣跪在病床边，父亲气管发出的尖啸声一下下地割着他的心。突然，他感觉到这尖啸声中有些杂音，他意识到这是父亲在说话。

　　"什么，爸爸？！你说什么呀，爸爸？！"

父亲凸出的双眼死盯着儿子，那垂死呼吸中的杂音更急促地重复着……

刘欣又声嘶力竭地叫着。

杂音没有了，呼吸也变小了，最后成了一下一下轻轻的抽搐，然后一切都停止了，父亲那双已无生命的眼睛焦急地看着儿子，仿佛急切想知道他是否听懂了自己最后的话。

刘欣进入了一种恍惚状态，他不知道妈妈是怎样晕倒在病床前，也不知道护士是怎样从父亲鼻孔中取走输氧管的，他只听到那段杂音在脑海中回响，每个音节都刻在他的记忆中，像刻在唱片上一样准确。后来的几个月，他一直都处在这种恍惚状态中，那段杂音日日夜夜在脑海中折磨着他，最后他觉得自己也窒息了，不让他呼吸的就是那段杂音，他要想活下去，就必须弄明白它的含义！直到有一天，也是久病的妈妈对他说，他已经长大了，该撑起这个家了，别去念高中了，去矿上接爸爸的班吧。他恍惚着拿起父亲的饭盒，走出家门，在1978年冬天的寒风中向矿上走去，向父亲的二号井走去。他看到了黑黑的井口，好像一只眼睛看着他，通向深处的一串防爆灯是那只眼睛的瞳仁，那是父亲的眼睛。那段杂音急促地在他脑海中响起，最后变成一声惊雷，他猛然听懂了父亲最后的话：

"不要下井……"

二十五年后

刘欣觉得自己的奔驰车在这里很不协调，很扎眼。现在矿上建起了一些高楼，路边的饭店和商店也多了起来，但一切都笼罩在一种灰色的不景气之中。

车到了矿务局，刘欣看到局办公楼前的广场上黑压压地坐了一大片人。刘欣穿过坐着的人群向办公楼走去，在这些身着工作服和便宜背心的人中，西装革履的他再次感到了自己与周围一切的不协调。人们无言地看着他走过，无数的目光像钢针一样穿透了他身上的两千美元一套的名牌西装，令他浑身发麻。

在局办公楼前的大台阶上，他遇到了李民生——他的中学同学，现在是地质处的主任工程师。这人还是二十年前那副瘦猴样，不过现在是一副憔悴的倦容，抱着的那卷图纸似乎是很沉重的负担。

"矿上有半年发不出工资了，工人们在静坐。"寒暄后，李民生指着办公楼前的人群说，同时上下打量着他，那目光像看一个异类。

"有了大秦铁路，前两年国家又煤炭限产，还是没好转？"

"有过一段好转，后来又不行了，这行业就这么个东西，我看谁也没办法。"

李民生长叹了一口气，转身走去，好像刘欣身上有什么东西使他想快些离开，但刘欣拉住了他。

"帮我一个忙。"

李民生苦笑着说："十多年前在市一中，你饭都吃不饱，还不肯要我们偷偷放在你书包里的饭票，可现在，你是最不需要谁帮忙的时候了。"

"不，我需要，能不能找到地下一小块煤层，很小就行，贮量不要超过三万吨，关键是这块煤层要尽量孤立，同其他煤层间的联系越少越好。"

"这个……应该行吧。"

"我需要这煤层和周围详细的地质资料，越详细越好。"

"这个也行。"

"那我们晚上细谈。"刘欣说。李民生转身又要走，刘欣再次拉住了他："你不想知道我打算干什么？"

"我现在只对自己的生存感兴趣，同他们一样。"他朝静坐的人群偏了一下头，转身走了。

沿着被岁月磨蚀的楼梯拾级而上，刘欣看到楼内的高墙上沉积的煤粉像一幅幅巨型的描绘雨云和山脉的水墨画。那幅《毛主席去安源》的巨幅油画还挂在那里，画很干净，没有煤粉，但画框和画面都显示出了岁月的沧桑。画中人那深邃沉静的目光在二十多年后又一次落到刘欣的身上，他终于有了回家的感觉。

来到二楼，局长办公室还在二十年前那个地方，那两扇大门后来包了皮革，后来皮革又破了。推门进去，刘欣看到局长正伏在办公桌上看一张很大的图纸，白了一半的头发对着门口。走近了看到那是一张某个矿的掘进进尺图，局长似乎没有注意窗外楼下静坐的人群。

"你是部里那个项目的负责人吧？"局长问，他只是抬了一下头，然后仍低下头去看图纸。

"是的，这是个很长远的项目。"

"呵，我们尽力配合吧，但眼前的情况你也看到了。"局长抬起头来把手伸向他，刘欣又看到了李民生脸上的那种憔悴的倦容，握住局长的手时，感觉到有两根变形的手指，那是早年一次井下工伤造成的。

"你去找负责科研的张副局长，或去找赵总工程师也行，我没空，真对不起了，等你们有一定结果后我们再谈。"局长说完又把注意力集中到图纸上去了。

"您认识我父亲，您曾是他队里的技术员。"刘欣说出了他父亲的名字。

局长点点头："好工人，好队长。"

"您对现在煤炭工业的形势怎么看？"刘欣突然问，他觉得只有尖锐地切入正题才能引起这人的注意。

"什么怎么看？"局长头也没抬地问。

"煤炭工业是典型的传统工业、落后工业和夕阳工业，它劳动密集，工人的工作条件恶劣，产出效率低，产品运输要占用巨量运力……煤炭工业曾是英国工业的一个重要组成部分，但英国在十年前就关闭了所有的煤矿！"

"我们关不了。"局长说，仍未抬头。

"是的，但我们要改变！彻底改变煤炭工业的生产方式！否则，我们将永远无法走出现在这种困境，"刘欣快步走到窗前，指着窗外的人群，"煤矿工人，千千万万的煤矿工人，他们的命运也难以有根本的改变！我这次来……"

"你下过井吗？"局长打断他。

"没有。"一阵沉默后刘欣又说，"父亲死前不让我下。"

"你做到了。"局长说。他伏在图纸上，看不到他的表情和目光，刘欣刚才那种针刺的感觉又回到身上来了。他觉得很热，这个季节，他的西装和领带只适合有空调的房间，但这里没有空调。

"您听我说，我有一个目标，一个梦，这梦在我父亲死的时候就有了。为了我的那个梦、那个目标，我上了大学，又出国读了博士……我要彻底改变煤炭工业的生产方式，改变煤矿工人的命运。"

"简单些，我没空儿。"局长把手向后指了一下，刘欣不知他是不是指的窗外那静坐的人群。

"只要一小会儿，我尽量简单些说。煤炭工业的生产方式是：在极差的工作环境中，用密集的劳动、很低的效率，把煤从地下挖出来，然后占用大量铁路、公路和船舶的运力，把煤运输到使用地点，然后再把煤送到煤气发生器中，产生煤气；或送入发电厂，经磨煤机研碎后送进锅炉燃烧……"

"简单些，直截了当些。"

"我的想法是：把煤矿变成一个巨大的煤气发生器，使煤层中的煤在地下就变为可燃气体，然后用开采石油或天然气地面钻井的方式开采这些可燃气体，并通过专用管道把这些气体输送到使用点。用煤量最大的火力发电厂的锅炉也可以燃烧煤气。这样，矿井将消失，煤炭工业将变成一个同现在完全两样的崭新的现代化工业！"

"你觉得自己的想法很新鲜？"

刘欣不觉得自己的想法新鲜，同时他也知道，局长是矿业学院 20 世纪 60 年代的高才生，国内最权威的采煤专家之一，也不会觉得这个新鲜。局长当然知道，煤的地下气化在几十年前就是一个世界性的研究课题，这几十年中，数不清的研究所和跨国公司开发出了数不清的煤气催化剂，但至今煤的地下气化仍是一个梦，一个人类做了将近一个世纪的梦，原因很简单：那些催化剂的价格远大于它们产生的煤气。

"您听着：我不用催化剂，也可以做到煤的地下气化！"

"怎么个做法呢？"局长终于推开了眼前的图纸，似乎很专心地听刘欣说下去，这给了他很大的鼓舞。

"把地下的煤点着！"

一阵长时间的沉默，局长直直地看着刘欣，同时点上一支烟，兴奋地示意他说下去。但刘欣的热情一下子冷了下来，他已经看出了局长热情和兴奋的实质——在他这日日夜夜艰难而枯燥的工作中，他终于找到了一个短暂的放松消遣的机会：一个可笑的傻瓜来免费表演了。刘欣只好硬着头皮说下去。

"开采是通过在地面向煤层的一系列钻孔实现的，钻孔用现有的油田钻机就可实现。这些钻孔有以下用途：一、向煤层中布放大量的传感器；二、点燃地下煤层；三、向煤层中注水或水蒸气；四、向煤层中通入助燃空气；五、导出气化煤。

"地下煤层被点燃并同水蒸气接触后，将发生以下反应：碳同水生成一氧化碳和氢气，碳同水生成二氧化碳和氢气，然后碳同二氧化碳生成一氧化碳，一氧化碳同水又生成二氧化碳和氢气。最后的结果将产生一种类似于水煤气的可燃气体，其中的可燃成分是百分之五十的氢气和百分之三十的一氧化碳，这就是我们得到的气化煤。

"传感器将煤层中各点的燃烧情况和一氧化碳等可燃气体的产生情况通过次声波信号传回地面，把这些信号汇总到计算机中，生成一个煤层燃烧场的模型，根据这个模型，我们就可从地面通过钻孔控制燃烧场的范围和深度，并控制其燃烧的程度。具体的方法是通过钻孔注水抑制燃烧，或注入高压空气或水蒸气加剧燃烧，这一切都是在计算机根据燃烧场模型的变化自动进行的，使整个燃烧场处于最佳的水煤混合不完全燃烧状态，保持最高的产气量。您最关心的当然是燃烧范围的控制，我们可以在燃烧蔓延的方向上打一排钻孔，注入高压水，形成地下水墙阻断燃烧；在火势较猛的地方，还可采用大坝施工中的水泥高压灌浆帷幕来阻断燃烧……您在听我说吗？"

窗外传来一阵喧闹声，吸引了局长的注意力。刘欣知道，他的话在局长脑海中产生的画面肯定和自己梦想中的不一样，局长当然清楚点燃地下煤层意味着什么。现在，地球上各大洲都有很多燃烧着的煤矿，中国就有几座。

去年，刘欣在新疆第一次见到了地火。在那里，极目望去，大地和丘陵寸草不生，空气中涌动着充满硫黄味的热浪，这热浪使周围的一切像在水中一样晃动，仿佛整个世界都被放在烤架上。入夜，刘欣看到大地上一道道幽幽的红光，这红光是从地上无数裂缝中透出的。刘欣走近一道裂缝探身向里看去，立刻倒吸了一口冷气，这像是地狱的入口。那红光从很深处透上来，幽暗幽暗的，但能感到它强烈的热力。再抬头看看夜幕下这透出道道红光的大地，刘欣一时觉得地球像一块被薄薄地层包裹着的火炭！

陪他来的是一个叫阿古力的强壮的维吾尔族汉子，他是中国唯一一支专业煤层灭火队的队长。刘欣这次来的目的就是要把他招聘到自己的实验室中。

"离开这里我还有些舍不得，"阿古力用生硬的汉话说，"我从小就看着这些地火长大，它在我眼中成了世界必不可少的一部分，像太阳、星星一样。"

"你是说，从你出生时这火就烧着？！"

"不，刘博士，这火从清朝时就烧着！"

当时刘欣呆立着，在这黑夜中的滚滚热浪里打了个寒战。

阿古力接着说："我答应去帮你，还不如说是去阻止你，听我的话刘博士，这不是闹着玩的，你在干魔鬼的事呢！"

……

这时窗外的喧闹声更大了，局长站起身来向外走去，同时对刘欣说："年轻人，我真希望部里用投在这个项目上的那六千万干些别的，你已看到，需要干的事太多了，回见。"

刘欣跟在局长身后来到办公楼外面，看到静坐的人更多了，一位领导在对群众喊话，刘欣没听清他说什么，他的注意力被人群一角的情景吸引了。他看到了那里有一大片轮椅，这个年代，人们不会在别的地方见到这么多的轮椅集中在一块儿，后面，轮椅还在源源不断地出现，每个轮椅上都坐着一位因工伤截肢的矿工……

刘欣感到透不过气来，他扯下领带，低着头疾步穿过人群，钻进自己的汽车。他漫无目的地开车乱转，脑子一片空白。不知转了多长时间，他刹住车，发现自己来到了一座小山的顶上。他小时候常到这里来，从这儿可以俯瞰整个矿山，他呆呆地站在那儿，又不知过了多长时间。

"都看到些什么？"一个声音响起，刘欣回头一看，李民生不知什么时候站在他身后。

"那是我们的学校。"刘欣向远方指了一下，那是一所很大的中学和小学在一起的矿山学校，校园内的大操场格外醒目，在那儿，他们埋葬了自己的童年和少年。

"你自以为记得过去的每一件事。"李民生在旁边的一块石头上坐下来，有气无力地说。

"我记得。"

"那个初秋的下午，太阳灰蒙蒙的，我们在操场上踢足球，突然大家都停下来，呆呆地盯着教学楼上的大喇叭……记得吗？"

"喇叭里传出哀乐，过了一会儿张建军光着脚跑过来说，毛主席逝世了……"

"我们狠揍了他一顿，他哭叫着说那是真的，向毛主席保证是真的，我们没人相信，扭着他往派出所送……"

"但我们的脚步渐渐慢下来，校门外也响着哀乐，仿佛天地间都充满了这种黑色的声音……"

"以后这二十多年中，这哀乐一直在我脑海里响着。最近，在这哀乐声中，尼采光着脚跑过来说，上帝死了，"李民生惨然一笑，"我信了。"

刘欣猛地转身盯着他童年的朋友，说道："你怎么变成这个样子？我不认识你了！"

李民生猛地站起身，也盯着刘欣，同时用一只手指着山下黑灰色的世界。"那矿山怎么变成这个样子？你还认识它吗？！"他又颓然坐下，"那个时代，我们的父辈是多么骄傲的一群人，伟大的煤矿工人是多么骄傲的一群人！就说我父亲吧，他是八级工，一个月能挣一百二十元！毛泽东时代的一百二十元啊！"

刘欣沉默了一会儿，想转移话题："家里人都好吗？你爱人，她叫……什么珊来着？"

李民生又苦笑了一下："现在连我都几乎忘记她叫什么了。去年，她对我说去出差，对单位说请休年假，扔下我和女儿，不见了踪影。两个多月后她来了一封信，信是从加拿大寄来的，她说再也不愿和一个煤黑子一起葬送人生了。"

"有没有搞错，你是高级工程师啊！"

"都一样，"李民生对着下面的矿山画了一个大圈，"在她们眼里都一样，煤黑子。呵，还记得我们是怎样立志当工程师的吗？"

"那年创高产，我们去给父亲送饭，那是我们第一次下井。在那黑乎乎的地方，我问父亲和叔叔们，你们怎么知道煤层在哪儿？怎么知道巷道向哪个方向挖？特别是，你们在深深的地下从两个方向挖洞，怎么能准准地碰到一块儿？"

"你父亲说，孩子，谁都不知道，只有工程师知道。我们上井后，他指着几个把安全帽拿在手中围着图纸看的人说，看，他们就是工程师。当时在我们的眼中，那些人就是不一样，至少，他们脖子上的毛巾白了许多……

"现在我们实现了儿时的愿望，当然说不上什么辉煌，总得尽责任做些什么，要不岂不是自己背叛自己？"

"闭嘴吧！"李民生愤怒地站了起来，"我一直在尽责任，一直在做着什么，倒是你，成天就生活在梦中！你真的认为你能让煤矿工人从矿井深处走出来？能让这矿山变成气田？就算你的那套理论和试验都成功，又能怎么样？你计算过那玩意儿的成本吗？还有，你用什么来铺设几万公里的输气管道？要知道，我们现在连煤的铁路运费都付不起了！"

"为什么不从长远看？几年、几十年以后……"

"见鬼去吧！我们现在连几天以后的日子都没着落呢！我说过，你是靠做梦过日子的，从小就是！当然，在北京六铺炕那幢安静的旧大楼（注：国家煤炭设计院所在地）中你这梦自可以做。我不行，我在现实中！"

李民生转身要走。"哦，我来是告诉你，局长已安排我们处配合你们的试验，工作是工作，我会尽力的。三天后我给你试验煤层的位置和详细资料。"说完他头也不回地走了。

刘欣呆呆地看着他出生并度过了童年和少年时代的矿山，他看到了竖井高大的井架，井架顶端巨大的卷扬轮正转动着，把看不见的大罐笼送入深深的井下；他看到一排排轨道电车从他父亲工作过的井口出入；他看到选煤楼下，一列火车正从一长排数不清的煤斗下缓缓开出；他看到了电影院和球场，在那里他度过了童年最美好的时光；他看到了矿工澡堂高大的建筑，只有在煤矿才有这样大的澡堂，在那宽大澡池被煤粉染黑的水中，他居然学会了游泳！是的，在这远离大海和大河的地方，他是在那儿学会游泳的！他的目光移向远方，看到了高大的矸石山，那是上百年来从采出的煤中拣出的黑石堆成的山，看上去比周围的山都高大，矸石中的硫黄因雨水而发热，正冒出一阵阵青烟……这里的一切都被岁月罩上了一层煤粉，整个矿山呈黑灰色，这是刘欣童年的颜色，这是他生命的颜色。他闭上双眼，听着下面矿山发出的声音，时光在这里仿佛停止了流动。

啊，爸爸的矿山，我的矿山……

这是离矿山不远的一个山谷，白天可以看到矿山的烟雾和蒸气从山后升起，夜里可以看到矿山灿烂的灯火在天空中映出的光晕，矿山的汽笛声也清晰可闻。现在，刘欣、李民生和阿古力站在山谷的中央，看到这里很荒凉，远处山脚下有一个牧羊人赶着一群瘦山羊慢慢走过。这个山谷下面，就是刘欣要做地下气化煤开采试验的那片孤立的小煤层，这是李民生和地质处的工程师们花了一个月的时间，从地质处资料室那堆积如山的地质资料中找到的。

"这里离主采区较远，所以地质资料不太详细。"李民生说。

"我看过你们的资料，从现有资料上看，试验煤层距大煤层至少有二百米，还是可以的。我们要开始干了！"刘欣兴奋地说。

"你不是搞煤矿地质专业的，对这方面的实际情况了解更少，我劝你还是慎重一些。再考虑考虑吧！"

"不是什么考虑，现在试验根本不能开始！"阿古力说，"我也看过资料，太粗了！勘探钻孔间距太大，还都是 20 世纪 60 年代初搞的。应该重新进行勘探，必须确切证明这片煤层是孤立的，试验才能开始。我和李工搞了一个勘探方案。"

"按这个方案完成勘探需要多长时间？还要追加多少投资？"

李民生说："按地质处现有的力量，时间至少一个月；投资没细算过，估计……怎么也得二百万左右吧。"

"我们既没时间也没钱干这事儿。"

"那就向部里请示！"阿古力说。

"部里？部里早就有一帮浑蛋想搞掉这个项目了！上面急于看到结果，我再回去要求延长时间和追加预算，岂不是自投罗网！直觉告诉我不会有太大问题的，就算我们冒个小险吧。"

"直觉？冒险？！把这两个东西用到这件事上？！刘博士，你知道这是在什么上面动火吗？这还是小险？！"

"我已经决定了！"刘欣断然地把手一挥，独自向前走去。

"李工，你怎么不制止这个疯子？我们可是达成过一致看法的！"阿古力对李民生质问道。

"我只做自己该做的。"李民生冷冷地说。

山谷里有三百多人在工作，他们中除物理学家、化学家、地质学家和采矿工程师外，还有一些意想不到的专业人员：有阿古力率领的一支十多人的煤层灭火队，还有来自仁丘油田的两个完整的石油钻井班，以及几名负责建立地下防火帷幕的水工建筑工程师和工人。这个工地上，除几台高大的钻机和成堆的钻杆外，还可以看到成堆的袋装水泥和搅拌机，高压泥浆泵轰鸣着将水泥浆注入地层中，还有成排的高压水泵和空气泵，以及蛛丝般错综复杂的各色管道……

工程已进行了两个月，他们已在地下建立了一圈总长两千多米的灌浆帷幕，把这片小煤层围了起来。这本是一项水电工程中的技术，用于大坝基础的防渗，刘欣想到用它建立地下的防火墙，高压注入的水泥浆在地层中凝固，形成一道地火难以穿透的严密屏障。在防火帷幕包围的区域中，钻机打出了近百个深孔，每个都直达煤层。每个孔口都连接着一根管道，这根管道又分成三根支管，连接到不同的高压泵上，可分别向煤层中注入水、水蒸气和压缩空气。

最后的一项工作是放"地老鼠"，这是人们对燃烧场传感器的称呼。这种由刘欣设计的神奇玩意儿并不像老鼠，倒很像一枚小炮弹。它有二十厘米长，头部有钻头，尾部有驱动轮，当它被放进钻孔中时，它能凭借钻头和驱动轮在地层中钻进移动上百米，自动移到指定位置。能在高温、高压下工作，在煤层被点燃后，它用可穿透地层的次声波通信把所在位置的各种参数传给主控计算机。现在，他们已在这片煤层中放入了上千个"地老鼠"，其中有一半放置在防火帷幕之外，以监测可能透过帷幕的地火。

在一顶宽大的帐篷中，刘欣站在一面投影屏幕前，屏幕上显示出防火帷幕圈，计算机根据收到的信号用闪烁光点标出了所有"地老鼠"的位置，它们密密地分布着，整个屏幕看上去像一幅天文星图。

一切都已就绪，两根粗大的点火电极被人从帷幕圈中央的一个钻孔中放下去，电极的电线直接通到刘欣所在的大帐篷中，接到一个有红色大按钮的开关上。这时所有的工作人员都各就各位，兴奋地等待着。

"你最好再考虑一下，刘博士，你干的事太可怕了，你不知道地火的厉害！"阿古力对刘欣说。

"好了阿古力，从你到我这儿来的第一天，就到处散布恐慌情绪，还告我的状，一直告到煤炭部。但公平地说，你在这个工程中是做了很大贡献的，没有你这一年的工作，我不敢贸然试验。"

"刘博士，别把地下的魔鬼放出来！"

"你觉得我们现在还能放弃？"刘欣笑着摇摇头，然后转向站在旁边的李民生。

李民生说："根据你的吩咐，我们第六遍检查了所有的地质资料，没有问题。昨天晚上我们还在某些敏感处又加了一层帷幕。"他指了指屏幕上帷幕圈外的几个小线段。

刘欣走到点火电极的开关前，把手指放到红色按钮上时，停了一下，闭上双眼，像在祈祷。他的嘴动了动，只有离他最近的李民生听清了他说的两个字。

"爸爸……"

红色按钮按下了，没有任何声音和闪光，山谷还是原来的山谷，但在地下深处，在上万伏的电压下，点火电极在煤层中迸发出雪亮的高温电弧。投影屏幕上，放置点火电极的位置出现了一个小红点，红点很快扩大，像滴在宣纸上的一滴红墨水。刘欣动了一下鼠标，屏幕上换了一个画面，显示出计算机根据"地老鼠"发回的信息生成的燃烧场模型，那是一个洋葱状的不断扩大的球体，洋葱的每一层代表一个等温层。高压空气泵在轰鸣，助燃空气从多个钻孔汹涌地注入煤层，燃烧场像一个被吹起的气球一样扩大着……一个小时后，控制计算机启动了高压水泵，屏幕上的燃烧场像被针刺破了的气球一样，形状变得扭曲复杂起来，但体积并没有缩小。

刘欣走出了帐篷，外面太阳已落下山，各种机器的轰鸣声在黑下来的山谷中回荡。三百多人都聚集在外面，他们围着一个直立的喷口，那喷口有一个油桶般粗。人们为刘欣让开一条路，他走上了喷口下的小平台。平台上已有两个工人，其中一人看到刘欣到来，便开始旋动喷口的开关轮，另一位则用打火机点燃了一个火把，把它递给刘欣。随着开关轮的旋动，喷口中响起了一阵气流的嘶鸣声，这嘶鸣声急剧增大，像一个喉咙嘶哑的巨人在山谷中怒吼。在四周，三百张紧张期待的脸在火把的光亮中时隐时现。刘欣又闭上双眼，再次默念了那两个字：

"爸爸……"

然后他把火把伸向喷口，点燃了人类第一口燃烧气化煤井。

"轰"的一声，一根巨大的火柱腾空而起，猛蹿至十几米高。那火柱紧接喷口的底部呈透明的纯蓝色，向上则很快变成刺眼的黄色，再向上渐渐变红。它在半空中发出低沉强劲的呼声，连离得最远的人都能感觉到它汹涌的热力。周围的群山被它的光芒照得通亮，远远望去，黄土高原上出现了一盏灿烂的天灯！

人群中走出一个头发花白的人，他是局长，他握住刘欣的手说："接受我这个思想僵化的落伍者的祝贺吧，你搞成了！不过，我还是希望尽快把它灭掉。"

"您到现在还不相信我？！它不能灭掉，我要让它一直燃着，让全国和全世界都看看！"

"全国和全世界已经看到了，"局长指了指身后蜂拥而上的电视记者，"但你要知道，试验煤层和周围大煤层的最近距离不到二百米。"

"可在这些危险的位置，我们连打了三道防火帷幕，还有好几台高速钻机随时处于待命状态，绝对没有问题的！"

"我不知道，只是很担心。你们是部里的工程师，我无权干涉，但任何一项新技术，不管看上去多成功，都有潜在的危险。这几十年中在煤炭行业这种危险我见了不少，这可能是我思想僵化的原因吧，我真的很担心……不过，"局长再次把手伸给了刘欣，"我还是谢谢你，你让我看到了煤炭工业的希望，"他又凝望了火柱一会儿，"你父亲也会很高兴的！"

以后的两天，又点燃了两个喷口，使火柱达到了三根。这时，试验煤层的产气量按标准供气压力计算已达每小时五十万立方米，相当于上百台大型煤气发生炉。

对地下煤层燃烧场的调节全部由计算机完成，燃烧场的面积严格控制在帷幕圈总面积的三分之二，且界限稳定。应矿方的要求，多次做了燃烧场控制试验，刘欣在计算机上用鼠标画一个圈圈住燃烧场，然后按住鼠标把这个圈缩小。随着外面高压泵轰鸣声的改变，在一个小时内，实际燃烧场的面积退到缩小的圈内。

同时，在距离大煤层较近的危险方向上，又增加了两道长二百多米的防火帷幕。

刘欣没有太多的事可做，他把所有的时间都花在接受记者采访和对外联络上。国内外的许多大公司蜂拥而至，对这个项目提出了庞大的投资资金和合作意向，其中包括像杜邦和埃克森这样的巨头。

第三天，一个煤层灭火队队员找到刘欣，说他们队长要累垮了。这两天阿古力带领灭火队发疯似的一遍遍地搞地下灭火演习。他还自作主张，租用国家遥感中心的一颗卫星监视这一地区的地表温度。他自己已连着三夜没睡觉，晚上在帷幕圈外面远远近近地转，一转就是一夜。

刘欣找到阿古力，看到这个强壮的汉子消瘦了许多，双眼红红的。

"我睡不着，"他说，"一合眼就做噩梦，看到大地上到处喷着这样的火柱子，像一个火的森林……"

刘欣说："租用遥感卫星是一笔很大的开销，虽然我觉得没必要，但既然已做了，我尊重你的决定。阿古力，我以后还是很需要你的，虽然我觉得你的煤层灭火队不会有太多的事可做，但再安全的地方也是需要消防队的。你太累了，先回北京去休息几天吧。"

"我现在离开？！你疯了！"

"你在地火上面长大，对它形成了一种根深蒂固的恐惧感。现在，我们还控制不了新疆煤矿地火那么大的燃烧场，但我们很快就能做到的！我打算在新疆建立第一个投入商业化运营的气化煤田，到时候，那里的地火将在我们的控制中，你家乡的土地将布满美丽的葡萄园。"

"刘博士，我很敬重你，这也是我跟你干的原因，但你总是高估自己。对于地火，你还只是孩子呢！"阿古力苦笑着，摇着头走了。

灾难是在第五天降临的。当时天刚亮，刘欣被推醒，看到面前站着阿古力，他气喘吁吁，双眼发直，像得了热病，裤腿都被露水打湿了。他把一张激光打印机打出的照片举到刘欣眼前，举得那么近，快挡住他的双眼了。那是一幅卫星发回的红外假彩色温度遥感照片，像一幅色彩斑斓的抽象画，刘欣看不懂，迷惑地望着他。

"走！"阿古力大吼一声，拉着刘欣的手冲出帐篷。

刘欣跟着他向山谷北面的一座山上攀去，一路上，刘欣越来越迷惑。首先，这是最安全的一个方向，在这个方向上，试验煤层距大煤层有上千米远；其次，阿古力现在领他走得也太远了，他们已接近山顶，帷幕圈远在下面，在这儿能出什么事呢。到达山顶后，刘欣喘息着正要质问，却见阿古力把手指向山另一边更远的地方。刘欣放心地笑了，笑阿古力神经过敏。向阿古力所指的方向望去，矿山尽收眼底，在矿山和这座山之间，有一段平缓的山坡，在山坡的低处有一块绿色的草地，阿古力指的就是那块草地。放眼望去，矿山和草地像平时一样平静，但顺着阿古力手指的方向看了好一会儿后，刘欣终于发现了草地有些异样：在草地上出现了一个圆，圆内的绿色比周围略深一些，不仔细看根本无法察觉。刘欣的心猛然抽紧了，他和阿古力向山下跑去，向草地上那个暗绿色的圆跑去。

跑到那里后，刘欣跪到草地上看圆内的草，并把它们同圆外的相比较，发现这些草已蔫软，并倒伏在地，像被热水泼过一样。刘欣把手按到草地上，明显地感觉到了来自地下的热力，在圆区域的中心，有一股蒸气在刚刚出现的阳光中升起……

经过一上午的紧急钻探，又施放了上千个"地老鼠"，刘欣终于确定了一个噩梦般的事实：大煤层着火了。燃烧的范围一时还无法确定，因为"地老鼠"在地下的行进速度只有每小时十几米，但大煤层比试验煤层深得多，它的燃烧热量已透至地表，说明已燃烧了相当长的时间，火场已很大了。

事情有些奇怪，在燃烧的大煤层和试验煤层之间的 1000 米土壤和岩石带完好无损，地火是在这上千米隔离带的两边烧起来的，以至于有人提出大煤层的火同试验煤层没有什么关系。但这只是个安慰，连提出这个意见的人自己也不太相信这个说法。随着勘探的深入，事情终于在深夜搞清楚了。

从试验煤层中伸出了八条狭窄的煤带，这些煤带最窄处只有半米，很难察觉。其中五条煤带被防火帷幕截断，而有三条煤带呈向下的走向，刚刚爬过了帷幕的底部。这三条"煤蛇"中的两条中途中断了，但有一条一直通向千米外的大煤层。这些煤带实际是被煤填充的地层裂缝，这些裂缝都与地表相通，为燃烧提供了良好的供氧，于是，那条煤带成了连接试验煤层和大煤层的一根导火索。

这三条煤带都没有在李民生提供的地质资料上标明。事实上，这种狭长的煤带在煤矿地质上是罕见的，大自然开了一个残酷的玩笑。

"我没有办法，孩子得了尿毒症，要不停地做透析，这个工种项目的酬金对我太重要了！所以我没有尽全力阻止你……"李民生脸色苍白，回避着刘欣的目光。

现在，他们和阿古力三人站在隔开两片地火的那座山峰上，这又是一个早晨，矿山和山峰之间的草地已全部变成了深绿色，而昨天他们看到的那个圆形区域现在已成了焦黄色！蒸气在山下弥漫，矿山已看不清楚了。

阿古力对刘欣说："我在新疆的煤矿灭火队带着大批设备已乘专机到达太原，很快就到这里了。全国其他地区的力量也在向这儿集中。从现在的情况看，火势很凶，蔓延飞快！"

刘欣默默地看着阿古力，好大一会儿才低声问："还有救吗？"

阿古力轻轻地摇摇头。

"你就告诉我，还有多大的希望？如果封堵供氧通道，或注水灭火……"

阿古力又摇摇头："我有生以来一直在干那事，可地火还是烧毁了我的家乡。我说过，在地火面前，你只是个孩子。你不知道地火是什么，在那深深的地下，它比毒蛇更光滑，比幽灵更莫测，它想去哪儿，凡人是拦不住的。这里地下巨量的优质无烟煤，是这魔鬼渴望了上亿年的东西，现在你把它放出来了，它将拥有无穷的能量和力量，这里的地火将比新疆的大百倍！"

刘欣抓住这个维吾尔族汉子的双肩绝望地摇晃着："告诉我还有多大希望？！求求你说真话！"

"百分之零。"阿古力轻轻地说，"刘博士，你此生很难赎清自己的罪了。"

在局大楼里召开了紧急会议，与会的除矿务局主要领导和五个矿的矿长外，还有包括市长在内的市政府的一群忧心忡忡的官员。会上首先成立了危机指挥中心，中心总指挥由局长担任，刘欣和李民生都是领导小组的成员。

　　"我和李工将尽自己最大的努力做好工作，但还是请大家明白，我们现在都是罪犯。"刘欣说。

　　李民生在一边低头坐着，一言不发。

　　"现在还不是讨论责任的时候，只干，别多想。"局长看着刘欣说，"知道最后这五个字是谁说的吗？你父亲。那时我是他队里的技术员，有一次为了达到当班的产量指标，我不顾他的警告，擅自扩大了采掘范围，结果造成工作面大量进水，队里二十几个人被水困在巷道的一角。当时大家的头灯都灭了，也不敢用打火机，一怕瓦斯，二怕消耗氧气，因为水已把这里全封死了。黑得伸手不见五指，你父亲这时告诉我，他记得上面是另一条巷道，顶板好像不太厚。然后我就听到他用镐挖顶板，我们几个也都摸到镐跟着他在黑暗中挖了起来。氧气越来越少，开始感到胸闷头晕，还有那黑暗，那是地面上的人见不到的绝对黑暗，只有镐头撞击顶板的火星在闪动。当时对我来说，活着真是一种折磨，是你父亲支撑着我，他在黑暗中反复对我说那五个字：'只干，别多想。'不知挖了多长时间，当我就要在窒息中昏迷时，顶板被挖塌了一个洞，上面巷道防爆灯的光亮透射进来……后来你父亲告诉我，他根本不知道顶板有多厚，但那时人只能是：只干，别多想。这么多年，这五个字在我的脑子中越刻越深，现在我替你父亲把它传给你了。"

　　会上，从全国各地紧急赶到的专家们很快制订了灭火方案。

可供选择的方式不多，只有三个：一、隔绝地下火场的氧气；二、用灌浆帷幕切断火路；三、通过向地下火场大量注水灭火。这三个行动同时进行，但第一个方法早就证明难以奏效，因为通向地下的供氧通道极难定位，就是找到了，也很难堵死；第二个方法只对浅煤层火场有效，且速度太慢，赶不上地下火势的迅速蔓延；最有希望的是第三个灭火方法了。

消息仍然被封锁，灭火工作在悄悄进行。从仁丘油田紧急调来的大功率钻机在人们好奇的目光中穿过煤城的公路，军队在进入矿山，天空出现了盘旋的直升机……一种不安的情绪笼罩着矿山，各种谣言开始像野火一样蔓延。

大型钻机在地下火场的火头上一字排开，钻孔完成后，上百台高压水泵开始向冒出青烟和热浪的井孔中注水。注水量是巨大的，以致矿山和城市生活区全部断水，这使得社会的不安和骚动进一步加剧。但注水结果令人鼓舞，在指挥中心的大屏幕上，红色火场的前锋面出现了一个个以钻孔为中心的暗色圆圈，标志着注水在急剧降低火场温度。如果这一排圆圈连接起来，就有希望截断火势的蔓延。

但这使人稍稍安慰的局势并没有持续多长时间。在高大的钻塔旁边，来自油田的钻井队队长找到了刘欣。

"刘博士，有三分之二的井位不能再钻了！"他在钻机和高压泵的轰鸣声中大喊。

"你开什么玩笑？！我们现在必须在火场上大量增加注水孔！"

"不行！那些井位的井压都在急剧增大，再钻下去要井喷的！"

"你胡说！这儿不是油田，地下没有高压油气层，怎么会井喷？！"

"你懂什么？！我要停钻撤人了！"

刘欣愤怒地抓住队长满是油污的衣领。"不行！我命令你钻下去！不会有井喷的！听到了吗？不会！"

话音未落，钻塔方向传来了一声巨响，两人转头望去，只见沉重的钻孔封瓦成两半飞了出来，一股黄黑色的浊流嘶鸣着从井口喷出，浊流中，折断的钻杆七零八落地飞出。在人们的惊叫声中，那股浊流的色调渐渐变浅，这是其中泥沙含量减少的缘故。后来它变成了雪白色，人们明白了这是注入地下的水被地火加热后变成的高压蒸气。刘欣看到了司钻的尸体被挂在钻塔高高的顶端，在白色蒸气的冲击下疯狂地摇晃，时隐时现。而钻台上的另外三个工人已不见踪影！

更恐怖的一幕出现了，那条白色巨龙的头部脱离了地面，渐渐升起，最后白色蒸气全部升到了钻塔以上，仿佛横空出世的一个白发魔鬼，而这魔鬼同地面的井口之间，除了破损的井架竟空无一物！只能听到那可怕的啸声，以至于几个年轻工人以为井喷停了，犹豫地向钻台迈步，但刘欣死死抓住了他们中的两个，高喊："不要命了！过热蒸气！"

在场的工程师们很快明白了眼前这奇景的含义，但让其他人理解并不容易。同人们的常识相反，水蒸气是看不到的，人们看到的白色只是水蒸气在空气中冷凝后结成的微小水珠。而水在高温高压下会形成可怕的过热蒸气，其温度高达400至500摄氏度！它不会很快冷凝，所以现在只能在钻塔上方看到它显形。这样的蒸气平常只在火力发电厂的高压汽轮机中存在，它一旦从高压输汽管中喷出（这样的事故不止一次发生），可以在短时间内穿透一堵砖墙！人们惊恐地看到，刚才潮湿的井架在无形的过热蒸气中很快被烤干了，几根悬在空中的粗橡胶管像蜡做的一样被融化了。这魔鬼蒸气冲击井架，发出让人头皮发麻的巨响……

地下注水已不可能了，即使可能，注入地下火场中的水的助燃作用已大于灭火作用。

危机指挥部的全体成员来到距地火前沿最近的三矿四号井井口前。

"火场已逼近这个矿的采掘区，"阿古力说，"如果火头到达采掘区，矿井巷道将成为地火强有力的供氧通道，那时地火火势将猛增许多倍……情况就是这样。"他打住了话头，不安地望着局长和三矿的矿长，他知道采煤人最忌讳的是什么。

"现在井下情况怎么样？"局长不动声色地问。

"八个井的采煤和掘进工作都在正常进行，这主要是为了安定着想。"矿长回答。

"全部停产，井下人员立即撤出，然后……"局长停了下来，沉默了两三秒钟。

人们觉得这两三秒很长很长。

"封井。"局长终于说出了那两个最让采煤人心碎的字。

"不！不行！！！"李民生失声叫道，然后才发现自己还没想好理由，"封井……封井……社会马上就会乱起来，还有……"

"好了。"局长轻轻挥了一下手，他的目光说出了一切：我知道你的感觉，我也一样，大家都一样。

李民生抱头蹲到地上，他的双肩在颤抖，但哭不出声来。矿山的领导者和工程师们面对井口默默地站着，宽阔的井口像一只巨大的眼睛看着他们，就像二十多年前看着童年的刘欣一样。

他们在为这座百年老矿致哀。

不知过了多长时间，局总工程师低声打破沉默："井下的设备，看看能弄出多少就弄出多少。"

"那么，"矿长说，"组织爆破队吧。"

局长点点头："时间很紧，你们先干，我同时向部里请示。"

局党委书记说："不能用工兵吗？用矿工组成的爆破队……怕要出问题。"

"考虑过，"矿长说，"但现在到达的工兵只有一个排，即使干一个井人力也远远不够，再说他们也不熟悉井下爆破作业。"

……

距火场最近的四号井最先停产，当井下矿工一批批乘电轨车上到井口时，发现上百人的爆破队正围在一堆钻杆旁边等待着什么。人们围上去打听，但爆破队的矿工们也不知道自己要干什么，他们只是接到命令带着钻孔设备集合。突然，人们的注意力都被吸引到一个方向，一个车队正在朝井口开来，第一辆卡车上坐满了持枪的武警士兵，跳下车来为后面的卡车围出了一块停车场。后面有十一辆卡车，它们停下后，篷布很快被掀开，露出了码放整齐的黄色木箱，矿工们惊呆了，他们知道那是什么。

整整十卡车，是每箱二十四公斤装的硝酸铵二号矿井炸药，总重约有五十吨。最后一辆较小的卡车上有几捆用于绑药条的竹条，还堆着一大堆黑色塑料袋，矿工们知道那里面装的是电雷管。

刘欣和李民生刚从一辆车的驾驶室里跳下来，就看到刚任命的爆破队队长，一个长着络腮胡的壮汉，手里拿着一卷图纸迎面走来。

"李工，这是让我们干什么？"队长问，同时展开图纸。

李民生指点着图纸，手微微发抖："三条爆破带，每条长35米，具体位置在下面那张图上。爆孔分150毫米和75毫米两种，装药量分别是每米28公斤和每米14公斤，爆孔密度……"

"我问你要我们干什么？！"

在队长那喷火的双眼逼视下，李民生无声地低下了头。

"弟兄们，他们要炸毁主巷道！"队长转身冲人群高喊。矿工人群中一阵骚动，接着如一堵墙一样围逼上来，武警士兵组成半圆形阻止人群靠近卡车，但在那势不可当的黑色人海的挤压下，警戒线弯曲变形，很快就要被冲破了。这一切都是在阴沉无声中发生的，只听到脚步的摩擦声和拉枪栓的声响。在最后关头，人群停止了涌动，矿工们看到局长和矿长出现在一辆卡车的踏板上。

"我15岁就在这口井干了，你们要毁了它？！"一个老矿工高喊，他脸上那刀刻般的皱纹在厚厚的煤灰下也很清晰。

"炸了井，往后的日子怎么过？！"

"为什么炸井？！"

"现在矿上的日子已经很难了，你们还折腾什么？！"

……

人群炸开了，愤怒的声浪一阵高过一阵，在那落满煤灰的黑脸的海洋中，白色的牙齿十分醒目。局长冷静地等待着，人群在愤怒的声浪中又骚动起来，在即将再次失去控制时，他才开始说话。

"大家往那儿看——"他手向井口旁边的一个小山丘指去。他的声音不高，却使愤怒的人群立刻安静下来，所有的人朝他指的方向看去。

那座小山丘顶上立着一根黑色的煤柱子，有两米多高，粗细不一。有一圈落满煤尘的石栏杆圈着那根煤柱。

"大家都管那东西叫老炭柱，但你们知道吗，它立起来的时候并不是一根柱子，而是一块四四方方的大煤块。那是一百多年前，清朝的张之洞总督在建矿典礼时立起的。它是让这一百多年的风风雨雨蚀成一根柱子了。这一百多年，我们这个矿山经历了多少风风雨雨，多少大灾大难，谁还能记得清呢？这时间不短啊同志们，四五辈人啊！这么长时间，我们总该记下些什么，总该学会些什么。如果实在什么也记不下，什么也学不会，总该记下和学会一样东西，那就是——"局长对着黑色的人海挥起双手，"天，塌不下来！"

人群在空气中凝固了，似乎连呼吸都已停止。

"中国的产业工人，中国的无产阶级，没有比我们的历史更长了，没有比我们经历的风雨和灾难更多了，煤矿工人的天塌了吗？没有！我们这么多人现在能站在这儿看那老煤柱，就是证明。我们的天塌不了！过去塌不了，将来也塌不了！！！

"说到难，有什么稀罕啊同志们，我们煤矿工人什么时候容易过？从老祖宗辈算起，我们什么时候有过容易日子啊！你们再掰着指头算算，中国的，世界的，工业有多少种，工人有多少种，哪种比我们更难？！没有，真的没有。难有什么稀罕？不难才怪，因为我们不但要顶起天，还要撑起地啊！怕难，我们早断子绝孙了！

"但社会和科学都在发展，很多有才能的人在为我们想办法，这办法现在想出来了，我们有希望完全改变自己的生活，我们要走出黑暗的矿井，在太阳底下，在蓝天底下采煤了！煤矿工人，将成为最让人羡慕的工作！这希望刚刚出现，不信，就去看看南山沟那几根冲天的大火柱！但正是这个努力，引发了一场灾难，关于这个，我们会对大家有个详细的交代。现在大家只需明白，这可能是煤矿工人的最后一难了，这是为我们美好明天付出的代价，就让我们抱成一团渡过这个难关吧。我还是那句话，多少辈人都过来了，天塌不下来！"

人群默默地散去后，刘欣对局长说："你和我父亲，认识你们两人，我死而无憾。"

"只干，别多想。"局长拍拍刘欣的肩膀，又在那里攥了一下。

四号井主巷道爆破工程开始一天后，刘欣和李民生并肩走在主巷道里，他们的脚步发出空洞的回响。他们正在走过第一爆破带，昏暗的顶灯下，可以看到高高的巷道顶上密密地布满了爆孔，引爆电线如彩色的瀑布从上面泻下来，在地上堆成一堆。

李民生说："以前我总觉得自己讨厌矿井，恨矿井，恨它吞掉了自己的青春。但现在才知道，我已同它融为一体了，恨也罢，爱也罢，它就是我的青春了。"

"我们不要太折磨自己了，"刘欣说，"我们毕竟干成了一些事，不算烈士，就算阵亡吧。"

他们沉默下来，同时意识到，他们谈到了死。

这时阿古力从后面气喘吁吁地跑过来，"李工，你看！"他指着巷道顶说。他指的是几根粗大的帆布管子，那是井下通风用管，现在它们瘪下来了。

"天啊，什么时候停的通风？！"李民生大惊失色。

"两个小时了。"

李民生用对讲机很快叫来了矿通风科科长和两名通风工程师。

"没法恢复通风了，李工，下面的通风设备：鼓风机、马达、防爆开关，甚至部分管路，都拆了呀！"通风科科长说。

"你浑蛋！谁让你们拆的，你找死啊！"李民生一反常态，破口大骂起来。

"李工，这是怎么讲话嘛！谁让拆的？封井前尽可能多地转移井下设备可是局里的意思，停产安排会你我都是参加了的！我们的人没日没夜干了两天，拆上来的设备有上百万元，就落你这一顿臭骂？！再说井都封了，还通什么风！"

李民生长叹一口气，直到现在事情的真相还没有公布，因而出现了这样的协调问题。

"这有什么？"通风科的人走后刘欣问，"通风不该停吗？这样不是还可以减少向地下输送的氧气流量？"

"刘博士，你真是个理论的巨人、行动的矮子，一接触到实际，你就什么都不懂了，真像李工说的，你只会做梦！"阿古力说。煤层失火以来，他对刘欣一直没有客气过。

李民生解释："这里的煤层是瓦斯高发区，通风一停，瓦斯在井下很快聚集，地火到达时可能引起大爆炸，其威力有可能把封住的井口炸开，至少可能炸出新的供氧通道。不行，必须再增加一条爆破带！"

"可，李工，上面第二条爆破带才只干到一半，第三条还没开工，地火距南面的采区已很近了，把原计划的三条做完都怕来不

154

及啊！"

"我……"刘欣小心地说，"我有个想法不知行不行？"

"哈，这可是……用你们的话怎么说，破天荒了！"阿古力冷笑着说，"刘博士还有拿不准的事儿？刘博士还有需要问别人才能决定的事儿？"

"我是说，现在这最深处的一条爆破带已做好，能不能先引爆这一条，这样一旦井下发生爆炸，至少还有一道屏障。"

"要行早这么做了。"李民生说，"爆破规模很大，引爆后巷道里的有毒气体和粉尘长时间散不去，会让后面的施工无法进行。"

地火的蔓延速度比预想的快，施工领导小组决定只打两条爆破带就引爆，尽快从井下撤出施工人员。天快黑时，大家正在离井口不远的生产楼中，围着一张图纸研究如何利用一条支巷最短距离引出起爆线，李民生突然说："听！"

一声低沉的响声隐隐约约从地下传上来，像大地在打嗝。几秒钟后又一声。

"是瓦斯爆炸，地火已到采区了！"阿古力紧张地说。

"不是说还有一段距离吗？"

没人回答，刘欣的地老鼠探测器已用完，现有落后的探测手段很难准确把握地火的位置和推进速度。

"快撤人！"

李民生拿起对讲机，但任凭他大喊，没有回答。

"我上井前看张队长干活时怕碰坏对讲机，把它和导线放一块儿了，下面几十台钻机同时干，声儿很大！"一个爆破队的矿工说。

李民生跳起来冲出生产楼，安全帽也没戴，叫了一辆电轨车，以最快速度向井下开去。当电轨车在井口消失前的一瞬间，追出来的刘欣看到李民生在向他招手，还向他笑，他很长时间没笑过了。

地下又传来几阵打嗝声，然后平静下来。

"刚才的一阵爆炸，能不能把井下的瓦斯消耗掉？"刘欣问身边的一名工程师，对方惊奇地看了他一眼。

"消耗？笑话，它只会把煤层中更多的瓦斯释放出来！"

一声冲天巨响，仿佛地球在脚下爆炸！井口淹没于一片红色火焰之中。气浪把刘欣高高抛起，世界在他眼中疯狂地旋转，同他一起飞落的是纷乱的石块和枕木，刘欣还看到了电轨车的一节车厢从井口的火焰中飞出来，像一粒被吐出的果核。刘欣被重重地摔到地上，碎石在他身边纷纷掉下，他觉得每一块碎石上都有血……刘欣又听到了几声沉闷的巨响，那是井下炸药被引爆的声音。失去知觉前，他看到井口的火焰消失了，代之以滚滚的浓烟……

一年以后

刘欣仿佛行走在地狱中。整个天空都是黑色的烟云，太阳是一个刚刚能看见的暗红色圆盘。由于尘粒摩擦产生的静电，烟云中不时出现幽幽的闪电，每次闪电出现时，地火之上的矿山就在青光中凸显出来，那图景一次次像用烙铁烙在他的脑海中。烟尘是从矿山的一个个井口中冒出的，每个井口都吐出一根烟柱，那烟柱的底部映着地火狰狞的暗红光，向上渐渐变成黑色，如天地间一条条扭动的怪蛇。

公路是滚烫的，沥青路面融化了，每走一步几乎要撕下刘欣的鞋底。路上挤满了难民和车辆，闷热的空气充满了硫黄味，还不时有雪花状的灰末从空中落下，每个人都戴着呼吸面罩，身上落满了白灰。道路拥挤不堪，全副武装的士兵在维持秩序，一架直升机穿行在烟云中，在空中用高音喇叭劝告人们不要惊慌……疏散迁民在冬天就开始了，本计划在一年时间内完成，但现在地火势头突然变猛，只得紧急加快进程。一切都乱了，法院对刘欣的开庭一再推迟，以至于今天早上他所在的候审间一时没人看管了，他迷迷糊糊地就走了出来。

公路以外的地面干燥开裂，裂纹又被厚厚的灰尘填满，脚踏上去扬起团团尘雾。一个小池塘，冒出滚滚蒸气，黑色的水面上浮满了鱼和青蛙的尸体。现在是盛夏，可见不到一点绿色，地面上的草全部枯黄了，埋在灰尘中。树也都是死的，有些还冒出青烟，已变成木炭的枝丫像怪手一样伸向昏暗的天空。所有的建筑都已人去楼空，有些浓烟从窗子中冒出。刘欣看到了老鼠，它们被地火的热力从穴中赶出，数量惊人，大群大群地涌向路面……随着刘欣向矿山深处走去，越来越感受到地火的热力，这热力从他的脚踝沿身体升腾上来。空气更加闷热污浊，即使戴上面罩也难以呼吸。地火的热量在地面上并不均匀，刘欣本能地避开灼热的地面，能走的路越来越少了。地火热力突出的区域，建筑燃起了大火，一片火海中不时响起建筑物倒塌的声音……刘欣已走到了井区，他走过一个竖井，那竖井已变成了地火的烟道，高大的井架被烧得通红，热流冲击井架发出让人头皮发麻的尖啸声，滚滚热浪让他不得不远远绕行。选煤楼被浓烟吞没了，后面的煤山已燃烧了多日，成了发出红光和火苗的一块巨大的火炭……

这里已看不到一个人了，刘欣的脚已被烫得起了皮，身上的汗已几乎流干，艰难的呼吸使他到了休克的边缘，但他的意识是清楚的，他用生命最后的能量向最后的目标走去。那个井口喷出的地火的红色光芒在召唤着他，他到了，他笑了。

刘欣转身朝井口对面的生产楼走去。还好，虽然从顶层的窗中冒出浓烟，但楼还没有着火。他走进开着的楼门，向旁边拐入一间宽大的班前更衣室。井口有地火从窗外照进来，使这里充满了朦胧的红光，一切都在地火的红光中跃动，包括那一排衣箱。刘欣沿着这排衣箱走去，仔细地辨认着上面的号码，很快他找到了要找的那个。关于这衣箱他想起了儿时的一件事：那时父亲刚调到这个采煤队当队长，这是最野的一个队，出了名地难带。那些野小子根本不把父亲放在眼里，本来嘛，看他在班前会上那可怜样儿，怯生生地让人把一个掉了的衣箱门钉上去，当然没人理他，小伙子们只顾在边上甩扑克、说脏话，父亲只好说那你们给我找几个钉子我自己钉吧，有人扔给他几个钉子。父亲说再找个锤吧，这次真没人理他了。但接着，小伙子们突然鸦雀无声，他们目瞪口呆地看着父亲用大拇指把那些钉子一根根轻松地按进木头中去！事情有了改变，小伙子们很快站成一排，敬畏地听着父亲的班前讲话……现在这箱子没锁，刘欣拉开后发现里面的衣物居然还在！他又笑了，心里想象着这二十多年用过父亲衣箱的那些矿工的模样。他把里面的衣服取出来，首先穿上厚厚的工作裤，再穿上同样厚的工作衣，这套衣服上涂满了厚厚的油腻的煤灰，发出一股浓烈的、刘欣熟悉的汗味和油味，这味道使他真正镇静下来，并处于一种类似于幸福的状态中。他接着穿上胶靴，然后拿起安全帽，把放在衣箱最里面的矿灯拿出来，用袖子擦干灯上的灰，把它卡到帽檐上。他又找电池，但没有，只好另开了一个衣箱，有。他把那块笨重的矿灯电池用皮带系到腰间，突然想到电池还没充电，毕竟矿上完全停产一年了。但他记得灯房的位置，就在更衣室对面，他小时候不止一次在那儿看到灯房的女工们把冒着白烟的硫酸喷到电池上充电。但现在不行了，灯房笼罩在硫酸的黄烟之中。他庄重地戴上有矿灯的安全帽，走到一面布满灰尘的镜子面前，在那红光闪动的镜子中，他看到了父亲。

"爸爸，我替您下井了。"刘欣笑着说，转身走出楼，向喷着地火的井口大步走去。

后来有一名直升机驾驶员回忆说，他当时低空飞过二号井，在那一带做最后的巡视，好像看到井口有一个人影，那人影在井内地火的红光中呈一个黑色的剪影，他好像在向井下走去，一转眼，那井口又只有火光，别的什么都看不见了。

一百二十年后
（一个初中生的日记）

过去的人真笨，过去的人真难。

知道我上面的印象是怎么来的吗？今天我参观了煤炭博物馆，但给我印象最深的是一件事：

居然有固体的煤炭！

我们首先穿上了一身奇怪的衣服，那衣服上有一个头盔，头盔上有一盏灯，那灯通过一根导线同挂在我们腰间的一个很重的长方形物体连着，我原以为那是一台电脑（也太大了些），谁想到那竟是这盏灯的电池！这么大的电池，能驱动一辆高速赛车的，却只用来点亮这盏小小的灯。我们还穿上了高高的雨靴，老师告诉我们，这是早期矿工的井下服装。有人问井下是什么意思，老师说你们很快就会知道的。

我们上了一辆行驶在小铁轨上的铁车，有点像早期的火车，但小得多，上方有一根电线为车供电。车开动起来，很快钻进一个黑黑的洞口中。里面真黑，只有上方不时掠过的一盏暗暗的小灯，我们头上的灯发出的光很弱，只能看清周围人的脸。风很大，在我们耳边呼啸，我们好像在向一个深渊坠下去。艾娜尖叫起来，讨厌，她就会这样叫。

"同学们，我们下井了！"老师说。

不知过了多长时间，车停了，我们由这个较为宽大的隧洞进入了它的一个分支，这个洞又窄又小，要不是戴着头盔，我的脑袋早就碰起好几个包了。我们头灯的光圈来回晃着，但什么都看不清楚，艾娜和几个女孩子又叫着说害怕。

过了一会儿，我们眼前的空间开阔了一些，这个空间有许多根柱子支撑着顶部。在对面，我又看到许多光点，也是我们头盔上的这种灯发出的。走近一看，发现那里有许多人在工作，他们有的在用一种钻杆很长的钻机在洞壁上打孔，那钻机不知是用什么驱动的，响起的声音让人头皮发麻；有的在用铁锹把什么看不清楚的黑色东西铲到轨道车上和传送皮带上，不时有一阵尘埃扬起，把他们隐没其中，许多头灯在尘埃中射出一道道光柱……

"同学们，我们现在所在的地方叫采煤工作面，你们看到的是早期矿工工作的景象。"

有几个矿工向我们这个方向走来，我知道他们都是全息影像，没有让路，几个矿工的身体和我互相穿过，我把他们看得很清楚，对看到的很吃惊。

"老师，那时的中国煤矿全部雇用黑人吗？"

"为了回答这个问题，我们将真实地体验一下当时采煤工作面的空气。注意，只是体验，所以请大家从右衣袋中拿出呼吸面罩戴上。"

我们戴好面罩后，又听到老师的声音："孩子们注意，这是真实的，不是全息影像！"

一片黑尘飘过来，我们的头灯也散射出了道道光柱，我惊奇地看着光柱中密密的尘粒在纷飞闪亮。这时艾娜又惊叫起来，像合唱队的领唱，好几个女孩子也跟着她大叫起来。再后来，竟有男孩的声音加入进来！我扭头想笑他们，但看到他们的脸时自己也叫出声来，所有人也都成了黑人，只有呼吸面罩盖住的一小部分是白的。这时我又听到一声尖叫，立刻汗毛直立——这是老师在叫！

"天啊，斯亚！你没戴面罩！！！"

斯亚真没戴面罩，他同那些全息矿工一样，成了最地道的黑人。"您在历史课上反复强调，学这门课的关键在于对过去时代的感觉，我想真正感觉一下。"他说着，黑脸上白牙一闪一闪的。

警报声不知从什么地方响起，不到一分钟，一辆水滴状微型悬浮车无声地停到我们中间，这种现代东西出现在这里真是煞风景。从车上下来两个医护人员，现在真正的煤尘已被完全吸收，只剩下全息的还飘浮在周围，所以医生在穿过"煤尘"时雪白的服装一尘不染。他们拉住斯亚往车里走。

"孩子,"一个医生盯着他说,"你的肺已受到很严重的损伤,至少要住院一个星期,我们会通知你家长的。"

"等等!"斯亚叫道,手里抖动着那个精致的全隔绝内循环面罩,"一百多年前的矿工也戴这东西吗?"

"不要说废话,快去医院!你这孩子也太不像话了!"老师气急败坏地说。

"我和先辈同样是人,为什么……"

斯亚话没说完就被硬塞进了车里。

"这是博物馆第一次出这样的事故,您要对此事负责的!"一个医生上车前指着老师严肃地说。悬浮车同来时一样无声地开走了。

我们继续参观,老师说:"井下的每一项工作都充满危险,且需消耗巨大的体力。随便举个例子:这些铁支柱,在这个工作面的开采工作完成后,都要回收,这项工作叫放顶。"

我们看到一个矿工用铁锤击打支架中部的一个铁销,使支架折为两段取下,然后把它扛走了。我和一个男孩试着搬已躺在地上的一个支架,才知道它重得要命。"放顶是一项很危险的工作,因为在撤走支架的过程中,工作面顶板随时都会塌落……"

这时我们头顶发出不祥的摩擦声,我抬起头来,在矿灯的光圈中看到头顶刚撤走支架的那部分岩石正在张开一个口子,我没来得及反应它就塌了下来,大块岩石的全息影像穿透了我的身体落到地上,发出一声巨响,尘埃腾起遮住了一切。

"这样的井下事故叫作冒顶。"老师的声音在旁边响起,"大家注意,伤人的岩石不只是来自上部……"

话音未落，我们旁边的一面岩壁竟垂直着向我们扑来，这一大面岩壁冲出相当的距离才化为一堆岩石砸下来，好像有一个巨大的手掌从地层中把它推出来一样。岩石的全息影像把我们埋没了，一声巨响后我们的头灯全灭了，在一片黑暗中，在女孩们的尖叫声中，我又听到老师的声音。

　　"这样的井下事故叫瓦斯突出。瓦斯是一种气体，它被封闭在岩层中，有巨大的气压。刚才我们看到的景象，就是工作面的岩壁抵挡不住这种压力，被它推出的情景。"

　　所有人的头灯又亮了，大家长出一口气。这时我听到了一个奇怪的声音，有时高亢，如万马奔腾；有时低沉，好像几个巨人在耳语。

　　"孩子们注意，洪水来了！"

　　正当我们迷惑之际，不远处的一个巷道口喷出了一道粗大汹涌的洪流，整个工作面很快淹没在水中。我们看着浑浊的水升到膝盖上，然后又没过了腰部，水面反射着头灯的光芒，在顶上的岩石上映出一片模糊的亮纹。水面上漂浮着被煤粉染黑的枕木，还有矿工的安全帽和饭盒……当水到达我的下巴时，我本能地长吸一口气，然后我全身没在水中了，只能看到自己头灯的光柱照出的一片混沌的昏黄和下方不时升上来的一串串水泡。

　　"井下的洪水有多种来源，可能是地下水，也可能是矿井打通了地面的水源，但它比地面洪水对人生命的威胁要大得多。"老师的声音在水下响着。

　　水的全息影像在瞬间消失了，周围的一切又恢复了原样。这时我看到了一个奇怪的东西，像一个肚子鼓鼓的大铁蛤蟆，很大很重，我指给老师看。

"那是防爆开关，因为井下的瓦斯是可燃气体，防爆开关可避免一般开关产生的电火花。这关系到我们就要看到的最可怕的井下危险……"

又一声巨响，但同前两次不一样，似乎是从我们体内发出，冲破我们的耳膜来到外面，来自四方的强大的冲击压缩着我的每一个细胞，在一股灼人的热浪中，我们都被淹没在一片红色的光晕里，这光晕是周围的空气发出的，充满了井下的每一寸空间。红光迅速消失，一切都陷入无边的黑暗中……

"很少有人真正看到瓦斯爆炸，因为这时井下的人很难生还。"老师的声音像幽灵般在黑暗中回荡。

"过去的人来这样可怕的地方，到底为了什么？"艾娜问。

"为了它。"老师举起一块黑石头，在我们头灯的光柱中，它的无数小平面闪闪发光。就这样，我第一次看到了固体的煤炭。

"孩子们，我们刚才看到的是 20 世纪中叶的煤矿，后来，出现了一些新的机械和技术，比如液压支架和切割煤层的大型机器等，这些设备在那个世纪的后二十年进入矿井，使井下的工作条件有了一些改善，但煤矿仍是一个工作环境恶劣、充满危险的地方，直到……"

以后的事情就索然无味了，老师给我们讲气化煤的历史，说这项技术是在八十年前全面投入应用的。那时，世界石油即将告罄，各大国为争夺仅有的油田陈兵中东，世界大战一触即发，是气化煤技术拯救了世界……这我们都知道，没意思。

我们接着参观现代煤矿，有什么稀奇的，不就是我们每天看到的从地下接出并通向远方的许多大管子。不过这次我倒是第一次进入了那座中控大楼，看到了燃烧场的全息图，真大！还看了看监测地下燃烧场的中微子传感器和引力波雷达，还有激光钻机……也没意思。

老师在回顾这座煤矿的历史时，说一百多年前这里被失控的地火烧毁过，那火烧了十八年才被扑灭。那段时期，我们这座美丽的城市草木生烟，日月无光，人民流离失所。失火的原因有多种说法，有人说是一次地下武器试验造成的，也有人说与当时的绿色和平组织有关。

我们不必留恋所谓过去的好时光，那个时候生活充满艰难、危险和迷惘。我们也不必为今天的时代过分沮丧，因为今天也总有一天会被人们称作是过去的好时光。

过去的人真笨，过去的人真难。

思想者 THE THINKER

太阳

他仍记得 34 年前第一次看到思云山天文台时的感觉，当救护车翻过一道山梁后，思云山的主峰在远方出现，观象台的球形屋顶反射着夕阳的金光，像镶在主峰上的几粒珍珠。

那时他刚从医学院毕业，是一名脑外科见习医生，作为主治医生的助手，到天文台来抢救一个不能搬运的重伤员，那是一名到这里做访问研究的英国学者，散步时不慎跌下山崖摔伤了脑部。到达天文台后，他们为伤员做了颅骨穿刺，吸出了部分瘀血，降低了脑压，当病人的情况改善到能搬运的状态后，便用救护车送他到省城医院做进一步的手术。

离开天文台时已是深夜，在其他人向救护车上搬运病人时，他好奇地打量着周围那几座球顶的观象台，它们的位置组合似乎有某种晦涩的含义，如月光下的巨石阵。在一种他在以后的一生中都百思不得其解的神秘力量的驱使下，他走向最近的一座观象台，推门走了进去。

里面没有开灯，但有无数小信号灯在亮着，他感觉是从有月亮的星空走进了没有月亮的星空。只有一缕细细的月光从球顶的一道缝隙中透下来，投在高大的天文望远镜上，用银色的线条不完整地勾画出它的轮廓，使它看上去像深夜的城市广场中央一件抽象的现代艺术品。

他轻步走到望远镜的底部，在微弱的光亮中看到了一大堆装置，其复杂程度超出了他的想象。正在他寻找着可以把眼睛凑上去的镜头时，从门那边传来一个轻柔的女声：

"这是太阳望远镜，没有目镜的。"

一个穿着白色工作服的苗条身影走进门来，很轻盈，仿佛从月光中飘来的一片羽毛。这女孩子走到他面前，他感到了她带来的一股轻风。

"传统的太阳望远镜，是把影像投在一块幕板上，现在大多是在显示器上看了。医生，您好像对这里很感兴趣。"

他点点头："天文台，总是一个超脱和空灵的地方，我挺喜欢这种感觉的。"

"那您干吗要从事医学呢？噢，我这么问很不礼貌的。"

"医学并不仅仅是琐碎的技术，有时它也很空灵，比如我所学的脑医学。"

"哦？您用手术刀打开大脑，能看到思想？"她说。他在微弱的光线中看到了她的笑容，想起了那从未见过的投射到幕板上的太阳，消去了逼人的光焰，只留下温柔的灿烂，不由得心动了一下。他也笑了笑，并希望她能看到自己的笑容。

"我，尽量看吧。不过你想想，那用一只手就能托起的蘑菇状的东西，竟然是一个丰富多彩的宇宙，从某种哲学观点看，这个宇宙比你所观察的宇宙更为宏大，因为你的宇宙虽然有几百亿光年大，但好像已被证明是有限的；而我的宇宙无限，因为思想无限。"

"呵呵，不是每个人的思想都是无限的，但医生，您可真像是有无限想象的人。至于天文学，它真没有您想象的那么空灵，在几千年前的尼罗河畔和几百年前的远航船上，它曾是一门很实用的技术，那时的天文学家，往往长年累月在星图上标注成千上万颗恒星的位置，把一生消耗在星星的'人口普查'中。就是现在，天文学的具体研究工作大多也是枯燥乏味没有诗意的，比如我从事的项目，我研究恒星的闪烁，没完没了地观测记录、再观测再记录，很不超脱，也不空灵。"

他惊奇地扬起眉毛："恒星在闪烁吗？像我们看到的那样？"看到她笑而不语，他自嘲地笑着摇摇头，"噢，我当然知道那是大气折射。"

她点点头："不过呢，作为一个视觉比喻这还真形象，去掉基础恒量，只显示输出能量波动的差值，闪烁中的恒星看起来还真是那个样子。"

"是由黑子、耀斑什么的引起的吗？"

她收起笑容，庄严地摇摇头："不，这是恒星总体能量输出的波动，其动因要深刻得多，如同一盏电灯，它的光度变化不是由于周围的飞蛾，而是由于电压的波动。当然恒星的闪烁波动是很微小的，只有十分精密的观测仪器才能觉察出来，要不我们早被太阳的闪烁烤焦了。研究这种闪烁，是了解恒星深层结构的一种手段。"

"你已经发现了什么？"

"还远不到发现什么的时候，到目前为止我们还只观测了一颗最容易观测的恒星——太阳的闪烁，这种观测可能要持续数年，同时把观测目标由近至远，逐步扩展到其他恒星。您知道吗，我们可能花十几年的时间在宇宙中采集标本，然后才谈得上归纳和发现。这是我博士论文的题目，但我想我会一直把它做下去的，用一生也说不定。"

"如此看来，你并不真觉得天文学枯燥。"

"我觉得自己在从事一项很美的事业，走进恒星世界，就像进入一个无限广阔的花园，这里的每一朵花都不相同。您肯定觉得这个比喻有些奇怪，但我确实有这种感觉。"

她说着，似乎是无意识地向墙上指指，向那个方向看去，他看到墙上挂着一幅画，很抽象，画面只是一条连续起伏的粗线。注意到他在看什么时，她转身走过去从墙上取下那幅画递给他，他发现那条起伏的粗线是用思云山上的雨花石镶嵌而成的。

"很好看，但这表现的是什么呢？一排邻接的山峰吗？"

"最近我们观测到太阳的一次闪烁，其剧烈的程度和波动方式在近年来的观测中都十分罕见，这幅画就是它那次闪烁时辐射能量波动的曲线。呵呵，我散步时喜欢收集山上的雨花石，所以……"

但此时吸引他的是另一条曲线，那是信号灯的弱光在她身躯的一侧勾出的一道光边，而她的其余部分都与周围的暗影融为一体，如同一位卓越的国画大师在一张完全空白的宣纸上信手勾出

172

的一条飘逸的墨线，仅由于这条柔美曲线的灵气，宣纸上所有一尘不染的空白就立刻充满了生机和内涵……在山外他生活的那座大都市里，每时每刻都有上百万个青春靓丽的女孩子在追逐着浮华和虚荣，像一大群做布朗运动的分子，没有给思想留出哪怕一瞬间的宁静。但谁能想到，在这远离尘嚣的思云山上，却有一个文静的女孩子在长久地凝视星空……

"你能从宇宙中感受到这样的美，真是难得，也很幸运。"他觉察到了自己的失态，收回目光，把画递还给她，但她轻轻地推了回来。

"送给您做个纪念吧，医生，威尔逊教授是我的导师，谢谢你们救了他。"

10分钟后，救护车在月光中驶离了天文台。后来，他渐渐意识到自己的什么东西留在了思云山上。

时光之一

直到结婚时，他才彻底放弃了与时光抗衡的努力。这一天，他把自己单身宿舍的东西都搬到了新婚公寓，除了几件不适于两人共享的东西，他把这些东西拿到了医院的办公室，漫不经心地翻看着，其中有那幅雨花石镶嵌画，看着那条多彩的曲线，他突然想到，思云山之行已经是10年前的事了。

人马座 α 星

这是医院里年轻人组织的一次春游，他很珍惜这次机会，因为以后这类事越来越不可能请他参加了。这次旅行的组织者故弄玄虚，在路上一直把所有车窗的帘子紧紧拉上，到达目的地下车后让大家猜这是哪儿，第一个猜中者会有一份不错的奖励。他一下车就立刻知道了答案，但沉默不语。

思云山的主峰就在前面，峰顶上那几个珍珠似的球形屋顶在阳光下闪亮。

当有人猜对这个地方后，他对领队说要到天文台去看望一个熟人，然后径自沿着那条通向山顶的盘山公路徒步走去。

他没有说谎，但心里也清楚那个连姓名都不知道的她并不是天文台的工作人员，10年后她不太可能还在这里。其实他压根儿就没想走进去，只是想远远地看看那个地方，10年前在那里，他那阳光灿烂、燥热异常的心灵泻进了第一缕月光。

一小时后他登上了山顶，在天文台的油漆已斑驳褪色的白色栅栏旁，他默默地看着那些观象台，这里变化不大，他很快便认出了那座曾经进去过的圆顶建筑。他在草地上的一块方石上坐下，点燃一支烟，出神地看着那扇已被岁月留下痕迹的铁门，脑海中一遍遍地重放着那珍藏在他记忆深处的画面：那铁门半开着，一缕如水的月光中，飘进了一片轻盈的羽毛……他完全沉浸在那逝去的梦中，以至于现实的奇迹出现时他并不吃惊：那个观象台的铁门真的开了，那片曾在月光中出现的羽毛飘进阳光里，她那轻盈的身影匆匆而去，进入了相邻的另一座观象台。这过程只有十几秒钟，但他坚信自己没有看错。

5 分钟后，他和她重逢了。

他是第一次在充足的光线下看到她，她与自己想象的完全一样，对此他并不惊奇，但转念一想已经 10 年了，那时在月光和信号灯弱光中隐现的她与现在应该不太一样，这让他很困惑。

她见到他时很惊喜，但除了惊喜似乎没有更多的东西："医生，您知道我是在各个天文台巡回搞观测项目的，一年只能有半个月在这里，又遇上了您，看来我们真有缘分！"她轻易地说出了最后那句话，更证实了他的感觉：她对他并没有更多的东西。不过，想到 10 年后她还能认出自己，他也感到一丝安慰。

他们谈了几句那个脑部受伤的英国学者后来的情况，然后他问："你还在研究恒星闪烁吗？"

"是的。对太阳闪烁的观测进行了两年，然后我们转向其他恒星，您容易理解，这时所需的观测手段与对太阳的观测完全不同，项目没有新的资金，中断了好几年，我们三年前才重新恢复了这个项目，现在正在观测的恒星有 25 颗，数量和范围还在扩大。"

"那你一定又创作了不少雨花石画。"

他这 10 年中从记忆深处无数次浮现的那月光中的笑容，这时在阳光下出现了："啊，您还记得那个！是的，我每次来思云山还是喜欢收集雨花石，您来看吧！"

她带他走进了 10 年前他们相遇的那座观象台，他迎面看到一架高大的望远镜，不知道是不是 10 年前的那架太阳望远镜，但周围的电脑设备都很新，肯定不是那时留下来的。她带他来到一面高大的弧形墙前，他在墙上看到了熟悉的东西：大小不一的雨花石镶嵌画。每幅画都只是一条波动曲线，长短不一，有的平缓如海波，有的陡峭如一排高低错落的塔松。

她挨个儿告诉他这些波形都来自哪些恒星："这些闪烁我们称为恒星的 A 类闪烁，与其他闪烁相比，它们出现的次数较少。A 类闪烁与恒星频繁出现的其他闪烁的区别，除了其能量波动的剧烈程度大几个数量级外，其闪烁的波形在数学上也更具美感。"

他困惑地摇摇头："你们这些基础理论科学家时常在谈论数学上的美感，这种感觉好像是你们的专利，比如你们认为很美的麦克斯韦方程，我曾经看懂了它，但看不出美在哪儿……"

像 10 年前一样，她突然又变得庄严了："这种美像水晶，很硬，很纯，很透明。"

他突然注意到了那些画中的一幅，说："哦，你又重作了一幅？"看到她不解的神态，他又说，"就是你 10 年前送给我的那幅太阳闪烁的波形图呀。"

"可……这是人马座 α 星的一次 A 类闪烁的波形，是在，嗯，去年 10 月观测到的。"

他相信她表现出的迷惑是真诚的，但他更相信自己的判断，这个波形他太熟悉了，不仅如此，他甚至能够按顺序回忆出组成那条曲线的每一粒雨花石的色彩和形状。他不想让她知道，在过去 10 年里，除去他结婚的最后一年，他一直把这幅画挂在单身宿舍的墙上，每个月总有那么几天，熄灯后窗外透进的月光足以使躺在床上的他看清那幅画，这时他就开始默数那组成曲线的雨花石，让自己的目光像一只甲虫沿着曲线爬行，一般来说，当爬完一趟又返回一半路程时他就睡着了，在梦中继续沿着那条来自太阳的曲线漫步，像踏着块块彩石过一条永远见不到彼岸的河……

"你能够查到 10 年前的那条太阳闪烁曲线吗？日期是那年的4 月 23 日。"

"当然能。"她用很特别的目光看了他一眼，显然对他如此清晰地记得那年的日期有些吃惊。她来到电脑前，很快就调出了那列太阳闪烁波形，然后又调出了墙上的那幅画上的人马座 α 星闪烁波形。他立刻在屏幕前呆住了。

两列波形完美地重叠在一起。

当沉默延长到无法忍受时，他试探着说："也许，这两颗恒星的结构相同，所以闪烁的波形也相同，你说过，A 类闪烁是恒星深层结构的反映。"

"它们虽同处主星序，光谱型也同为 G2，但结构并不完全相同。关键在于，就是结构相同的两颗恒星也不会出现这样的情况，都是榕树，您见过长得完全相同的两棵吗？如此复杂的波形竟然完全重叠，这就相当于有两棵连最末端的枝丫都一模一样的大榕树。"

"也许，真有两棵一模一样的大榕树。"他安慰说，但知道自己的话毫无意义。

她轻轻地摇摇头，突然又想到了什么，猛地站起来，目光中除了刚才的震惊又多了恐惧。

"天哪！"她说。

"什么？"他关切地问。

"您……想过时间吗？"

他是个思维敏捷的人，很快便捕捉到了她的想法："据我所知，人马座 α 星是距我们最近的恒星，这距离好像是……4 光年吧。"

"1.3 秒差距，就是 4.25 光年。"她仍处于震惊状态，这话仿佛是别人通过她的嘴说出的。

现在事情清楚了：两个相同的闪烁出现的时间相距 8 年零 6 个月，正好是光在两颗恒星间往返一趟所需的时间。当太阳的闪烁光线在 4.25 光年后传到人马座 α 星时，后者发生了相同的闪烁，又过了同样长的时间，人马座 α 星的闪烁光线传回来，被观测到。

她又伏在计算机上进行了一阵演算，自语道："即使把这些年来两颗恒星的相互退行考虑进去，结果仍能精确地对上。"

"让你如此不安我很抱歉，不过这毕竟是一件无法进一步证实的事，不必太为此烦恼吧。"他又想安慰她。

"无法进一步证实吗？也不一定：太阳那次闪烁的光线仍在太空中传播，也许会再次导致一颗恒星产生相同的闪烁。"

"比人马座 α 星再远些的下一颗恒星是……"

"巴纳德星，1.81 秒差距，但它太暗，无法进行闪烁观测；再下一颗，佛耳夫 359，2.35 秒差距，同样太暗，不能观测；再往远处，莱兰 21185，2.52 秒差距，还是太暗……只有到天狼星了。"

"那好像是我们能看到的最亮的恒星了，有多远？"

"2.65 秒差距，也就是 8.6 光年。"

"现在太阳那次闪烁的光线在太空中已行走了 10 年，已经到了那里，也许天狼星已经闪烁过了。"

"但它闪烁的光线还要再等 7 年多才能到达这里。"

她突然像从梦中醒来一样，摇着头笑了笑："呵，天哪，我这是怎么了？太可笑了！"

"你是说，作为一名天文学家，有这样的想法很可笑？"

她很认真地看着他："难道不是吗？作为脑外科医生，如果您同别人讨论思想是来自大脑还是心脏，有什么感觉？"

他无话可说了，看到她在看表，他便起身告辞，她没有挽留他，但沿下山的公路送了他很远。他克制了向她要电话号码的冲动，因为他知道，自己在她眼中不过是一个10年后又偶然重逢的陌路人而已。

告别后，她转身向天文台走去，山风吹拂着她那白色的工作衣，突然唤起他10年前那次告别的感觉，阳光仿佛变成了月光，那片轻盈的羽毛正离他远去……

像一个落水者极力抓住一根稻草，他决意要维持他们之间那蛛丝般的联系，几乎是本能地，他冲她的背影喊道："如果，7年后你看到天狼星真的那样闪烁了……"

她停下脚步转过身来，微笑着回答他："那我们就还在这里见面！"

时光之二

婚姻使他进入了一种完全不同的生活，但真正彻底改变生活的是孩子。自从孩子出生后，生活的列车突然由慢车变成特快车，越过一个又一个沿途车站，永不停息地向前赶路。旅途的枯燥使他麻木了，他闭上双眼不再看沿途那千篇一律的景色，在疲倦中自顾睡去。但同许多在火车上睡觉的旅客一样，心灵深处的一个小小的时钟仍在走动，使他在到达目的地前的一分钟醒来。

这天深夜，妻儿都已睡熟，他难以入睡，一种神秘的冲动使他披衣来到阳台上。他仰望着在城市的光雾中暗淡了许多的星空，在寻找着，找什么呢？好一会儿他才在心里回答自己：找天狼星。这时他不由得打了一个寒战。

7年已经过去，现在，距他和她相约的那个日子只有两天了。

天狼星

昨天下了今年的第一场雪，路面很滑，最后一段路出租车不能走了，他只好再一次徒步攀登思云山的主峰。

路上，他不止一次地质疑自己的精神是否正常。事实上，她赴约的可能性为零，理由很简单：天狼星不可能像17年前的太阳那样闪烁。在这7年里，他涉猎了大量的天文学和天体物理学知识，7年前的那个发现可笑得让他无地自容，她没有当场嘲笑，已让他感激万分。现在想想，她当时那副认真的样子，不过是一种得体的礼貌而已，7年间他曾无数次回味分别时她的那句诺言，越来越从中体会出一种调侃的意味……

随着天文观测向太空轨道的转移，思云山天文台在4年前就不存在了，那里的建筑变成了度假别墅，在这个季节已空无一人，他到那儿去干什么？想到这里他停下了脚步，这7年的岁月显示出了它的力量，他再也不可能像当年那样轻松地登山了。他犹豫了一会儿，最终还是放弃了返回的念头，继续向前走。

在这人生过半之际，就让自己最后追一次梦吧。

所以，当他看到那个白色的身影时，真以为是幻觉。天文台旧址前的那个穿着白色风衣的身影与积雪的山地背景融为一体，最初很难分辨，但她看到他时就向这边跑过来，这使他远远看到了那片飞过雪地的羽毛。他只是呆立着，一直等她跑到面前。她喘息着，一时说不出话来。他看到，除了长发换成短发，她没变太多，7年不是太长的时间，对于恒星的一生来说连弹指一挥间都算不上，而她是研究恒星的。

她看着他的眼睛说："医生，我本来不抱希望能见到您，我来只是为了履行一个诺言，或者说满足一个心愿。"

"我也是。"他点点头。

"我甚至，甚至差点儿错过了观测时间，但我没有真正忘记这事，只是把它放到记忆中一个很深的地方，在几天前的一个深夜里，我突然想到了它……"

"我也是。"他又点点头。

他们沉默了，只听到阵阵松涛声在山间回荡。"天狼星真的那样闪烁了？"他终于问道，声音微微发颤。

她点点头："闪烁波形与17年前太阳那次和7年前人马座 α 星那次精确重叠，一模一样，闪烁发生的时间也很精确。这是'孔子三号'太空望远镜的观测结果，不会有错的。"

他们又陷入长时间的沉默，松涛声在起伏轰响，他觉得这声音已从群山间盘旋而上，充盈在天地之间，仿佛是宇宙间的某种力量在进行着低沉而神秘的合唱……他不由得打了个寒战。她显然也有同样的感觉，打破沉默，似乎只是为了摆脱这种恐惧。

"但这种事情，这种已超出了所有现有理论的怪异，要想让科学界严肃地面对它，还需要更多的观测和证据。"

他说："我知道，下一个可观测的恒星是……"

"本来小犬座的南河二星可以观测，但 5 年前该星的亮度急剧减弱到可测值以下，可能是因飘浮到它附近的一片星际尘埃所致，这样，下一次只能观测天鹰座的河鼓二星了。"

"它有多远？"

"5.1 秒差距，16.6 光年，17 年前的太阳闪烁信号刚刚到达那颗恒星。"

"这就是说，还要再等将近 17 年？"

她缓缓地点点头："人生苦短啊。"

她最后这句话触动了他心灵深处的什么东西，他那被冬风吹得发干的双眼突然有些湿润："是啊，人生苦短。"

她说："但我们至少还有时间再这样相约一次。"

这话使他猛地抬起头来，呆呆地望着她，难道又要分别17 年？！

"请您原谅，我现在心里很乱，我需要时间思考。"她拂开被风吹到额前的短发说，然后看透了他的心思，动人地笑了起来，"当然，我给您我的电话和邮箱，如果您愿意的话，我们以后常联系。"

他长长地松了一口气，仿佛缥缈大洋上的航船终于看到了岸边的灯塔，心中充满了一种难言的幸福感："那……我送你下山吧。"

她笑着摇摇头，指指后面的圆顶度假别墅："我要在这里住一阵儿，别担心，这里有电，还有一户很好的人家，是常驻山里的护林哨……我真的需要安静，很长时间的安静。"

他们很快分手，他沿着积雪的公路向山下走去，她站在思云山的顶峰上久久地目送着他，他们都准备好了这17 年的等待。

时光之三

在第三次从思云山返回后，他突然看到了生命的尽头，他和她的生命都再也没有多少个 17 年了，宇宙的广漠使光都慢得像蜗牛，生命更是灰尘般微不足道。

在这 17 年的头 5 年里他和她保持着联系，他们互通电子邮件，有时也打电话，但从未见过面，她居住在另一座很远的城市。以后，他们各自都走向了人生的巅峰，他成为著名脑医学专家和这家大医院的院长，她则成为国家科学院院士。他们要操心的事情多了起来，同时他明白，同一个已取得学术界最高地位的天文学家过多地谈论那件把他们联系在一起的神话般的事件是不适宜的。于是他和她相互间的联系渐渐少了，到 17 年过完一半时，联系完全断了。

但他很坦然，他知道他们之间还有一个不可能中断的纽带，那就是在广漠的外太空中正在向地球日夜兼程的河鼓二星的星光，他们都在默默地等待它的到达。

河鼓二星

他和她在思云山主峰见面时正是深夜，双方都想早来些，以免让对方等自己，所以都在凌晨 3 点多攀上山来。他们各自的飞行车都能轻而易举地到达山顶，但两人不约而同地把车停在了山脚下，徒步走上山来，显然都想找回过去的感觉。

自从 10 年前被划为自然保护区后，思云山成了这世界上少有的越来越荒凉的地方，昔日的天文台和度假别墅已成为一片被藤蔓覆盖的废墟，他和她就在这星光下的废墟间相见。他最近还在电视上见过她，所以已熟悉岁月在她身上留下的痕迹，但今夜没有月亮，无论怎样想象，他都觉得面前的她还是 34 年前那个月光中的少女，她的双眸映着星光，让他的心融化在往昔的感觉中。

她说："我们先不要谈河鼓二星好吗？这几年我在主持一个研究项目，就是观测恒星间 A 类闪烁的传递。"

"我一直以为你不敢触及这个发现，或干脆把它忘了呢！"

"怎么会呢？真实的存在就应该去正视，其实就是经典的相对论和量子力学描述的宇宙，其离奇和怪异已经不可思议了。这几年的观测发现，A 类闪烁的传递是恒星间的一种普遍现象，每时每刻都有无数颗恒星在发生初始的 A 类闪烁，周围的恒星再把这个闪烁传递开去，任何一颗恒星都可能成为初始闪烁的产生者或其他恒星闪烁的传递者，所以整个星际看起来很像是雨中泛起无数圈涟漪的池塘……怎么，你并不感到吃惊？"

"我只是感到不解：仅观测了四颗恒星的闪烁传递就用了 30 多年，你们怎么可能……"

"你是个十分聪明的人，应该能想到一个办法。"

"我想……是不是这样：寻找一些相互之间相距很近的恒星来观测，比如两颗恒星 A 和 B，它们距地球都有一万光年，但它们之间相距仅 5 光年，这样你们就能用 5 年的时间观察到它们一万年前的一次闪烁传递。"

"你真的是聪明人！银河系内有上千亿颗恒星，可以找到相当数量的这类恒星对。"

他笑了笑，并像 34 年前一样，希望她能在夜色中看到自己的笑。

"我给你带来了一件礼物。"他说着，打开背上山来的一个旅行包，拿出一个很奇怪的东西，足球大小，初看上去像是一个胡乱团起的渔网，对着天空时，透过它的孔隙可以看到断断续续的星光。他打开手电，她看到那东西是由无数米粒大小的小球组成的，每个小球都伸出数目不等的几根细得几乎看不见的细杆与其他小球相连，构成了一个极其复杂的网架系统。他关上手电，在黑暗中按了一下网架底座上的一个开关，网架中突然充满了快速移动的光点，令人眼花缭乱，她仿佛在看着一个装进了几万只萤火虫的空心玻璃球。再定睛细看，她发现光点最初都是由某一个小球发出的，然后向周围的小球传递，每时每刻都有一定比例的小球在发出原始光点，或传递别的小球发出的光点，她形象地看到了自己的那个比喻：雨中的池塘。

"这是恒星闪烁传递模型吗？！啊，真美，难道……你已经预见到这一切？！"

"我确实猜测恒星闪烁传递是宇宙间的一种普遍现象，当然是仅凭直觉。但这个东西不是恒星闪烁传递模型。我们院里有一个脑科学研究项目，用三维全息分子显微定位技术研究大脑神经元之间的信号传递，这就是一小部分右脑皮层的神经元信号传递模型，当然只是很小很小的一部分。"

她着迷地盯着这个星光窜动的球体："这就是意识吗？"

"是的，正如巨量的 0 和 1 的组合产生了计算机的运算能力一样，意识也只是由巨量的简单连接产生的，这些神经元间的简单连接聚集到一个巨大的数量时，就产生了意识，换句话说，意识，就是超巨量的节点间的信号传递。"

他们默默地注视着这个星光灿烂的大脑模型，在他们周围的宇宙深渊中，飘浮着银河系的千亿颗恒星和银河系外的千亿个恒星系，在这无数的恒星之间，无数的 A 类闪烁正在传递。

她轻声说："天快亮了，我们等着看日出吧。"

于是他们靠着一堵断墙坐下来，看着放在前面的大脑模型，那闪闪的荧光有一种强烈的催眠作用，她渐渐睡着了。

思想者

她逆着一条苍茫的灰色大河飞行，这是时光之河，她在飞向时间的源头，群星像寒冷的冰碛飘浮在太空中。她飞得很快，扑动一下双翅就越过上亿年时光。宇宙在缩小，群星在汇聚，背景辐射在剧增，百亿年过去了，群星的冰碛开始在能量之海中溶化，很快消散为自由的粒子，后来粒子也变为纯能。太空开始发光，最初是暗红色，她仿佛潜行在能量的血海之中；后来光芒急剧增强，由暗红变成橘黄，再变为刺目的纯蓝，她似乎在一个巨大的霓虹灯管中飞行，物质粒子已完全溶解于能量之海中。透过这炫目的空间，她看到宇宙的边界球面如巨掌般收拢，她悬浮在这已收缩到只有一间大厅般大小的宇宙中央，等待着奇点的来临。终于一切陷入漆黑，她知道已在奇点中了。

一阵寒意袭来，她发现自己站立在广阔的白色平原上，上面是无限广阔的黑色虚空。看看脚下，地面是纯白色的，覆盖着一层湿滑的透明胶液。她向前走，来到一条鲜红的河流边，河面覆盖着一层透明的膜，可以看到红色的河水在膜下涌动。她离开大地飞升而上，看到血河在不远处分了岔，还有许多条树枝状的血河，构成了一个复杂的河网。再上升，血河细化为白色大地上的血丝，而大地仍是一望无际。她向前飞去，前面出现了一片黑色的海洋，飞到海洋上空时她才发现这海不是黑的，呈黑色是因为它深而完全透明，广阔海底的山脉历历在目，这些水晶状的山脉呈放射状，由海洋的中心延伸到岸边……她拼命上升，不知过了多长时间才再次向下看，这时整个宇宙已一览无余。

这宇宙是一只静静地看着她的巨大的眼睛。

……

她猛地醒来，额头湿湿的，不知是汗水还是露水。他没睡，一直在身边默默地看着她，在他们前面的草地上，大脑模型已耗完了电池，穿行于其中的星光熄灭了。

在他们上方，星空依旧。

"'他'在想什么？"她突然问。

"现在吗？"

"在这 34 年里。"

"源于太阳的那次闪烁可能只是一次原始的神经元冲动，这种冲动每时每刻都在发生，大部分像蚊子在水塘中点起的微小涟漪，转瞬即逝，只有传遍全宇宙的冲动才能成为一次完整的感受。"

"我们耗尽了一生时光，只看到'他'的一次甚至自己都感觉不到的瞬间冲动？"她迷茫地说，仿佛仍在梦中。

"耗尽整个人类文明的寿命，可能也看不到'他'的一次完整的感觉。"

"人生苦短啊。"

"是啊，人生苦短……"

"一个真正意义上的孤独者。"她突然没头没脑地说。

"什么？"他不解地看着她。

"哦，我是说'他'之外全是虚无，'他'就是一切，还在想，也许还做梦，梦见什么呢……"

"我们还是别试图做哲学家吧！"他一挥手，像赶走什么似的说。

她突然想起了什么，从靠着的断墙上直起身说："按照现代宇宙学的宇宙暴涨理论，在膨胀的宇宙中，从某一点发出的光线永远也不可能传遍宇宙。"

"这就是说，'他'永远也不可能有一次完整的感觉。"

她两眼平视着无限远方，沉默许久，突然问道："我们有吗？"

她的这个问题令他陷入对往昔的追忆中，这时，思云山的丛林中传来了第一声鸟鸣，东方的天际出现了一线晨光。

"我有过。"他很自信地回答。是的，他有过，那是34年前，在这个山峰上的一个宁静的月夜，一个月光中羽毛般轻盈的身影，一双仰望星空的少女的眼睛……他的大脑中发生了一次闪烁，并很快传遍了他的整个心灵宇宙，在以后的岁月中，这闪烁一直没有消失。这个过程更加宏伟壮丽，大脑中所包含的那个宇宙，要比这个星光灿烂的已膨胀了150亿年的外部宇宙更为宏大，外部宇宙虽然广阔，毕竟已被证明是有限的，而思想无限。

东方的天空越来越亮，群星开始隐没，思云山露出了剪影般的轮廓，在它高高的主峰上，在那被藤蔓覆盖的天文台废墟中，这两个年近60岁的人期待地望着东方，等待着那个光辉灿烂的脑细胞升出地平线。

吞食者 DEVOURER

一、波江座晶体

即使距离很近，上校也不可能看到那块透明晶体，它飘浮在漆黑的太空中，就如同一块沉在深潭中的玻璃。他凭借晶体扭曲的星光确定其位置，但很快在一片星星稀疏的背景上把它追丢了。突然，远方的太阳变形扭曲了，那永恒的光芒也变得闪烁不定，这使他吃了一惊，但以"冷静的东方人"著称的他并没有像飘浮在旁边的十几名同事那样惊叫，他很快明白，那块晶体就在他们和太阳之间，距他们有十几米，距太阳有一亿千米。以后的三个多世纪里，这诡异的景象时常出现在他的脑海中，他真怀疑这是不是后来人类命运的一个先兆。

作为联合国地球防护部队在太空中的最高指挥官，他率领的这支小小的太空军队装备着人类有史以来当量最大的热核武器，敌人却是太空中没有生命的大石块，在预警系统发现有威胁地球安全的陨石和小行星时，他的部队负责使其改变轨道或摧毁它们。这支部队在太空中巡逻了 20 多年，从来没有一次使用这些核弹的机会，那些足够大的太空石块似乎都躲着地球走，故意不给他们辉煌的机会。但现在晶体在两个天文单位外被探测到，它沿一条陡峭的绝非自然形成的轨道精确地飞向地球。

上校和同事们谨慎地向晶体靠近，他们太空服上推进器的尾迹像条条蛛丝把晶体缠在正中。就在上校与它的距离缩小到不足 10 米时，晶体的内部突然出现了迷雾般的白光，使它规则的长棱状轮廓清晰地显示了出来。它大约有 3 米长，再近一些，还可以看到内部像是推进系统的错综复杂的透明管道。当上校把戴着太空手套的右手伸向晶体表面，以进行人类与外星文明的首次接触时，晶体再次变得透明，内部浮现出一个色彩亮丽的影像。那是一个卡通小女孩儿，眼睛像台球那么大，长发直到脚跟，同漂亮的长裙一起像在水中那样缓缓漂动着。

"警报！呀！警报！吞食者来了！"她惊慌失措地大叫着，大眼睛盯着上校，一只细而柔软的手臂指向与太阳相反的方向，像在指一条追着她的大狼狗。

"那你是从哪里来的呢？"上校问。

"波江座—e 星，你们好像是这么叫的，按你们的时间，我已经飞行了 6 万年……吞食者来了！吞食者来了！"

"你有生命吗？"

"当然没有，我只是一封信……吞吞食者来了！吞食者来了！"

"你怎么会讲英语？"

“路上学的……吞吞食者来了……吞食者来了！”

“那你这个样子是……？”

“路上看到的……吞食者来了！吞食者来了！呀，你们真不怕吞食者吗？”

“吞食者是什么？”

“样子像个大轮胎，这是你们的比喻。”

“你对我们世界的东西真熟悉。”

“路上熟悉的……吞食者来了！”

波江女孩儿喊叫着，闪向晶体的一端，在她空出的空间里出现了那个“轮胎”的图像。它确实像轮胎，表面发着磷光。

“它有多大？”另一名军官问。

“总的直径为 5 万千米，‘轮胎’宽为 1 万千米，内圆直径为 3 万千米。”

“……你说的千米是我们的长度单位吗？”

“当然是，它大着呢，可以把一颗行星套进去，就像你们的轮胎套一个足球一样。套住那颗行星后，它就掠夺行星的资源，把它吸干榨尽后吐出去，就像你们吃水果吐核儿一样……”

“我们还是不明白吞食者到底是什么。”

“一艘世代飞船，我们不知道它从哪里来要到哪里去。事实上，驾驶吞食者的那些大蜥蜴肯定也不知道，这个世界已在银河系中飘行了几千万年，它的拥有者一定早已忘记了它的本源和目的。但可以肯定：它被创造出来时远没有那么大，它是靠吃行星长大的，我们的行星就被它吃了！”

这时，晶体中显示的吞食者在变大，渐渐占满了整个画面，显然正在向摄像者的世界缓缓降下来。现在在这个世界居民的眼中，大地仿佛处于一口宇宙巨井的井底，太空就是一圈缓缓转动的井壁，可以看清井壁表面的复杂结构。开始让上校想到了在显微镜下看到的微处理器的电路，后来他发现那是连绵不断的城市。再向上，井壁的顶端是一圈蓝色光焰，在天空中形成一个围绕着群星的巨大火圈。波江女孩儿告诉他们，那是吞食者尾部的环形推进发动机。在晶体的一端，女孩儿的手胡乱挥舞，她那飘飘的长发也像许多只挥动的手臂，极力表达着她的惊恐。

"这就是波江座—e星的第三颗行星被吞食时的情形。这时你要是身在我们的世界，第一个感觉是身体在变轻，这是由吞食者巨大质量产生的引力抵消行星引力所致。这引力的扰动产生了毁灭性的灾难：海洋先是涌向行星朝向吞食者的那一极，当行星被套入轮胎后又涌向赤道，产生的巨浪能够吞没云层。接着，引力异常，将大陆像薄纸一样撕成碎片。火山在海底和陆地密密麻麻地出现……当'轮胎'套到行星的赤道时，吞食者便停止了推进，以后，其相对于恒星的轨道运动始终与行星保持同步，一直把这颗行星含在口里。

"这时对行星的掠夺开始了，无数条上万千米长的缆索从筒壁伸到行星表面，使得行星如同一只被蛛网粘住的虫子。巨大的运载舱频繁地往来于行星表面与筒壁之间，运走行星的海水和空气，更有无数大机器深深地钻进行星的地层，狂采吞食者需要的矿藏……由于吞食者的引力与行星引力的相互抵消，行星与'轮胎'之间的一围空间是低重力区，这使得行星的资源向吞食者的运输变得很容易，大掠夺因此有很高的效率。

"按地球时间，吞食者对被吞入的每颗行星大约要'咀嚼'一个世纪左右，在这段时间里，行星包括水和空气在内被掠夺一空，由于'轮胎'长时间的引力作用，行星向赤道方向渐渐变扁，最后变成……还用你们的比喻吧：铁饼状。当吞食者最后移走，'吐出'这颗已被榨干的行星时，行星的形状会恢复成圆形，这又引发了最后一场全球范围的地质灾难。这时，行星的表面呈现其几十亿年前刚刚形成时的熔岩状，早已是一个没有任何生命的地狱了。"

"吞食者距太阳系还有多远？"上校问。

"它紧跟在我后面，按你们的时间，再过一个世纪就到了。警报！吞食者来了！吞食者来了！"

二、使者大牙

正当人们为波江晶体带来的信息是否可信而争论不休时，吞食者的一艘先遣小型飞船进入了太阳系，到达地球。

首先与之接触的仍是上校率领的太空巡逻队，但这次接触的感觉与上次完全不同。通透的波江晶体代表了一种纤细精致的技术文明，而吞食者飞船则相反，其外形极其笨重，如同在旷野中被遗弃了一个世纪的大锅炉，令人想起凡尔纳描述的粗放的大机器时代。吞食帝国的使者也同样粗陋笨重，它那蜥蜴状的粗壮身躯披着大块的石板般的鳞甲，直立起来有近 10 米高。它自我介绍的名字发音为"达雅"，根据他的外形特点和后来的行为方式，人们管它叫"大牙"。

当大牙的小型飞船在联合国大厦前着陆时，发动机把地面冲撞出了一个大坑，飞溅的石块把大厦打得千疮百孔。由于外星使者太高大，无法进入会议大厅，各国首脑就在大厦前的广场上与他见面，他们中的几个人用手帕捂着刚才被玻璃和碎石划破的头。大牙每走一步地面都颤抖一下，说话时声音像十台老式火车头同时鸣笛，让人头皮发麻，而它胸前的一个外形粗笨的翻译器把话译成地球英语（也是路上学的），由一个粗犷的男音读出来，音虽比大牙低了许多，但仍然让听者心惊肉跳。

"呵呵，白嫩的小虫虫，有趣的小虫虫。"大牙乐呵呵地说。人们捂住耳朵等他轰鸣着说完，然后稍微放开耳朵听翻译器里的声音。"我们有一个世纪的时间相处，相信我们会互相喜欢对方的。"

"尊敬的使者，您知道，我们现在最为关心的，是您那伟大的母舰到太阳系的目的。"联合国秘书长仰望着大牙说。尽管他大声喊着，声音听起来仍像蚊子嗡嗡。

大牙做了一个类似于人类立正的姿势，地面为之一颤。"伟大的吞食帝国将吃掉地球，以便继续它壮丽的航程，这是不可改变的！"

"那么人类的命运呢？"

"这正是我今天要决定的事。"

元首们纷纷相互交换目光，秘书长点点头："这确实需要我们之间充分交流。"

大牙摇摇头："这是一件十分简单的事情，我只需要品尝一下——"说着，它伸出强壮的大爪，从人群中抓起一个欧洲国家的首脑，从三四米远处优雅地将他扔进嘴里，细细地嚼了起来。不知是出于尊严还是过度的恐惧，那个牺牲品一直没有叫出声，只听到他的骨骼在大牙嘴里碎裂时清脆的咔嚓声。半分钟后，大牙"噗"的一声吐出了那人的衣服和鞋子，衣服虽然浸透了血，但几乎完好无损，这时不止一个旁观者联想到了人类嗑瓜子的情形。

整个地球世界一时间陷入一片死寂，这寂静似乎无限期地持续着，直到被一个人类的声音打破——

"您怎么拿起来就吃啊？"站在人群后面的上校问。

大牙向他走去，人群散开一条道，这个庞然大物咚咚地走到上校面前，用一双篮球大小的黑眼睛盯着他："不行吗？"

"您怎么这么肯定他能吃呢？一个相距如此遥远的世界上的生物能被食用，从生物化学上讲几乎是不可能的。"

大牙点点头，大嘴一咧做出类似于笑的表情："我一开始就注意到你了，你一直冷眼看着我，若有所思，在想什么？"

上校也笑笑："您呼吸我们的空气，通过声波说话，有两只眼睛一个鼻子一张嘴，还有四个对称的肢体……"

"这不可理解吗？"大牙把巨头凑近上校，喷出一股让人作呕的血腥气。

"是的，因为太好理解所以不可理解，我们不应该这么相似。"

"我也有不理解之处，那就是你的冷静，你是军人？"

"我是一名保卫地球的战士。"

"哼，不过是推开一些小石头而已，那能让你成为真正的战士？"

"我准备着更大的考验。"上校庄严地昂起头。

"有趣的小虫虫。"大牙笑着点点头，直起身来，"我们还是回到正题吧：人类的命运。你们的味道不错，有一种滑爽的清淡，很像我在波江座行星上吃过的一种蓝色的浆果。所以祝贺你们，你们的种族将延续下去，你们将作为一种小家禽在吞食帝国饲养，到 60 岁左右上市。"

"您不觉得那时我们的肉太老了吗？"上校冷笑着说。

大牙大笑起来，声音如火山爆发："哈哈哈哈，吞食人喜欢有嚼头的小吃。"

三、蚂蚁

联合国又同大牙进行了几次接触，虽然再没有人被吃掉，但关于人类命运的谈判结果都一样。

人们把下一次会面精心安排在非洲的一处考古挖掘现场。

大牙的飞行器准时在距挖掘现场几十米处降落。同每次一样，降落就像是一场大爆炸，震耳欲聋，飞沙走石。据波江女孩儿介绍，飞行器是由一台小型核聚变发动机驱动的。对于有关吞食者的信息，她一解释人类的科学家就立刻明白了，但波江人的技术却令地球人迷惑，比如那块晶体，着陆后便在空气中融化，最后把与星际航行有关的推进部分全化掉了，只剩下薄薄的一片，在空气中轻盈地飘行。

大牙来到挖掘现场时，有两个联合国工作人员抬着一本一米见方的大画册递给它，画册是按它的个头精心制作的，有上百页精美的彩页。内容是人类文明的各个方面，很像一本儿童启蒙教材。在挖掘现场的大坑旁，一名考古学家绘声绘色地描述了地球文明的辉煌历程，他竭力想让外星人明白这个蓝色行星上有那么多值得珍惜的东西，说到动情处声泪俱下，好不凄惨。最后，他指着挖掘现场的大坑说："尊敬的使者，您看，这是我们刚刚发现的一处城市遗址，是迄今发现的最早的人类城市，距今已有近5万年，你们真的忍心毁灭一个历经5万年的岁月一点一滴发展到今天的灿烂文明？"

大牙在这个过程中一直在翻看那本画册，好像觉得那是一件很好玩的东西。考古学家的最后一句话让它抬起头来，看了看大坑："考古虫虫，我对这个坑和坑里的旧城市不感兴趣，倒是很想看看从坑里挖出的土。"他指了指大坑旁边的一个几米高的土堆。

听完翻译器中的话，考古学家很迷惑："土？那堆土里什么也没有啊。"

"那是你的看法。"大牙说着走到土堆旁，蹲下高大的身躯伸出两只大爪在土里挖起来。

人们围成一圈看着，很惊叹它那看似粗笨的大爪的灵活。它拨动着松土，不时拾起什么极小的东西放到画册上。就这样专心致志地干了10多分钟，它端着画册直起身来，走到人们面前，让大家看画册上的东西。

上百只蚂蚁，有的活着，有的已经死了，蜷成一团，仔细辨认才能看出是什么。

"我想讲一个故事，"大牙说，"是关于一个王国的故事。这个王国的前身是一个更大的帝国，它们先祖的先祖可以追溯到地球白垩纪末期，在恐龙那高耸入云的骨架下，那些先祖建起帝国宏伟的城市……但那些历史太久太久了，帝国最后一世女王能记起的，就是冬天的降临。在那漫长的冬天中，大地被冰川覆盖，失去已延续了上千万年的生机，生活变得万分艰难。

"在最后一次冬眠醒来时，女王只唤醒了帝国不到百分之一的成员，其他的都已在寒冷中长眠，有的已变成透明的空壳。女王摸摸城市的墙壁，冷得像冰块，硬得像金属，她知道这是冻土，在这严寒时代中，它夏天都不化。女王决定离开这片先祖留下的疆域，去找一块不冻的土地建立新的王国。

"于是女王率领所有的幸存者来到地面，在高大的冰川间开始艰难的跋涉。大部分成员都在漫漫的路途中死于严寒，但女王与不多的幸存者终于找到了一块不冻土，这是一块被溢出的地热温暖的土地。女王当然不明白，为什么在这严寒世界中有这么一小片潮湿柔软的土地，但她对能到达这里并不感到意外：一个延续了 6000 万年的种族是不会灭绝的！

"面对冰川纵横的大地和昏暗的太阳，女王宣布要在这里建立一个新的伟大的王国，它将延续万代！她站在一座高大的白色山峰下，就把这个新王国命名为白山王国，那座白色山峰是一头猛犸象的头骨。这是第四纪冰川末期的一个正午，这时的人类虫虫还是零星地龟缩在岩洞中发抖的愚钝的动物，9 万年之后，你们的文明的第一点烛光才在另一个大陆的美索不达米亚平原上出现。

"以附近冰冻的猛犸遗体为生，白山王国度过了一万年的艰难岁月。之后，地球冰期结束，大地回春。各大陆又重新披上了生命的绿色。在这新一轮的生命大爆炸中，白山王国很快达到了鼎盛，拥有数不清的成员和广大的疆域。在其后的几万年中，王国经历了数不清的朝代，创造了数不清的史诗。"

大牙指指眼前的大坑："这就是那个王国最后的位置，在考古虫虫专心挖掘下面那已死去5万年的城市时，并没有想到在它上面的土层中还有一座活着的城市。它的规模绝不比纽约小，后者只是一座二维的平面城市，而它是一座宏大的立体城市，有很多层。每一层都密布着迷宫般的街道，有宽阔的广场和宏伟的宫殿，整座城市的供排水系统和消防系统的设计也比纽约高明得多。城市有着复杂的社会结构、严格的行业分工。整个社会以一种机器般的精密和协调高效地运转着，不存在吸毒和犯罪问题，也没有沉沦和迷茫。但它们并非没有感情，当有成员死亡时，它们表现出长时间的悲伤。它们甚至还有墓地，位于城市附近的地面上，掩埋深度为3厘米。最值得说明的是：在城市的底层有一个庞大的图书馆，其中有数量巨大的容器，这就是一本书，每个容器中都装有成分极其复杂的化学味剂，这些味剂用其复杂的成分记录着信息。这里有对白山王国漫长历史的史诗般的记载：你能看到在一次森林大火中，王国的所有成员抱成无数个团，顺一条溪流漂下逃出火海的壮举；还能看到王国与白蚁帝国长达百年的战争史；还有王国的远征队第一次看到大海的记载……

"但所有这一切在三个小时之内被毁灭。当时，在惊天动地的轰鸣声中，挖掘机那遮盖了整个天空的钢铁巨掌凌空劈下，把包含着城市的土壤一把把抓起，城市和其中的一切在巨掌中被碾得粉碎，包括城市最下层的所有孩子和将成为孩子的几万只雪白的卵。"地球世界再一次陷入死寂之中，这次寂静比大牙吃人的那一次延续得更长。面对外星使者，人类第一次无话可说。

大牙最后说："我们以后有很长的时间相处，有很多的事要谈，但不要再从道德的角度谈了，在宇宙中，那东西没意义。"

四、加速度

大牙走后，考古现场的人们仍沉浸在迷茫和绝望之中，还是上校首先打破寂静，他对周围的各国政要说："我知道自己是个小人物，只是因为首先接触外星文明而有幸亲临这些场合，我只想说两句话：一、大牙是对的；二、人类的唯一出路是战斗。"

"战斗？唉，上校，战斗……"秘书长苦笑着摇头。

"对，战斗！战斗！战斗！"波江女孩儿大喊，此时她所在的晶体片正飘飞在人们头上几米高处，在阳光下的晶体中，那长发女孩儿兴奋地手舞足蹈。有人说："你们波江人也战斗了，结果怎么样？人类得为自己种族的生存着想，我们并没有义务满足你那变态的复仇欲望。"

"不，先生，"上校对所有人说，"波江人是在对敌人完全陌生的情况下进行自卫战争的，加上他们本来就是一个历史上完全没有战争的社会，所以失败是不足为奇的。但在这场长达一个世纪的惨烈战争中，他们对吞食者有了细致深刻的了解。现在大量的资料通过这艘飞船送到了我们手中，这就是我们的优势。

"冷静地初步研究这些资料，我们发现吞食者并没有最初想象的那么可怕。首先，除了不可思议的庞大外，吞食者并没有太多超出人类已有知识之外的东西。就生命形式而言，吞食者（据说在'轮胎'上居住着上百亿个）与地球人一样是碳基生物，且生命在分子层次的构造十分相似。人类与敌人处于相同的生物学基础上，使我们有可能真正深刻地理解它们的各个方面，这比我们面对一群由力场和中子星物质构成的入侵者要幸运多了。

"更让我们宽慰的是，吞食者并没有太多的'超技术'。吞食

202

者人的技术比人类要先进许多，但这主要表现在技术的规模上而不是理论基础上。吞食者的推进系统的能量来源主要是核聚变，它所掠夺的行星水资源除了用于吞食者人的生活外，主要是被作为聚变燃料。吞食者发动机的推进方式也是基于动量守恒的反冲的方式，并没有时空跃迁之类玄妙的玩意儿……这些信息可能使科学家们深感失落，因为吞食者毕竟是一个延续了几千万年的文明，它们的技术层次也就标明了科学力量的极限；同时也使我们知道，敌人不是不可战胜的神。"

秘书长说："仅凭这些，就能使人类建立起必胜的信心吗？"

"当然还有许多具体的信息，使我们能够制定出一个成功率较高的战略，比如……"

"加速度！加速度！"波江女孩儿在人们头顶大叫。

上校对周围迷惑的人们解释说："从波江人送来的资料看，吞食者航行时的加速度有一个极限，在长达两个世纪的观察中，他们从未发现它突破过这个极限。为证实这一点，我们根据波江座飞船送来的其他资料，如吞食者的结构和构成它的材料的强度等，建立了一个数学模型。模型的演算证实了波江人对吞食者加速度极限的观察，这个极限是由它的结构强度所决定的，一旦超出，这个庞然大物就会被撕裂。"

"那又怎么样？"一位大国元首问道。

"我们应该冷静下来，用自己的脑子好好想想。"上校微笑着说。

五、月球避难所

人类与外星使者的谈判终于有了一点点进展。大牙对人类关于月球避难所的要求做出了让步。

"人是恋家的动物。"在一次谈判中，秘书长眼泪汪汪地说。

"吞食人也是，虽然我们没有家。"大牙同情地点点头。

"那么，能否让我们留下一些人，等伟大的吞食帝国吃完后吐出地球，待它的地质变化稳定下来，再回来重建我们的文明？"

大牙摇摇头："吞食帝国吃东西是吃得很干净的，那时的地球将比现在的火星还荒凉，凭你们虫虫的技术能力，不可能重建文明。"

"总得试试吧，这样我们的灵魂也会安定，特别是在吞食帝国上被饲养的那些小家禽，如果记得在遥远的太阳系还有一个家，会多长些肉的，虽然这个家不一定真的存在。"

大牙点点头："可是当地球被吞下时，这些人去哪儿呢？除了地球，我们还要吃掉金星、木星，海王星太大了，我们吃不下，但要吃它们的卫星，吞食帝国需要上面的碳氢化合物和水；连贫瘠的火星和水星我们也想嚼一嚼，我们想要上面的二氧化碳和金属，这些星球的表面将是一片火海。"

"我们可以去月球避难。据我们所知，吞食帝国在吃地球之前要把月球推开。"

大牙又点点头："是的，由吞食帝国和地球组成的联合星体引力很大，有可能使月球坠落在大环表面，这种撞击足以毁灭帝国。"

"那就对了，让我们住上去一些人吧，这对你们也没有太大损失。"

"你们打算留多少人？"

"从维持一个文明的最低限度着想，10万吧。"

"可以，但你们得干活儿。"

"干活儿？什么活儿？"

"把月球从地球轨道推开，这对我们来说也是一件很麻烦的事。""可是……"秘书长绝望地抓着头发，"您这等于拒绝了人类这点小小的可怜的要求，您知道我们没有这种技术力量的！"

"呵，虫虫，那我不管，再说，不是还有一个世纪吗？"

六、播种核弹

在泛着白光的月球平原上，一群穿着太空服的人站在一个高高的钻塔旁边，吞食帝国高大的使者站在更远一些的地方，仿佛是另一个钻塔。他们注视着一个钢铁圆柱体从钻塔顶端缓缓吊下，沉入钻塔下的深井中，吊索飞快地向井中放下去，38万千米外的整个地球世界都在注视着这一幕。当放置物到达井底的信号传来时，包括大牙在内的所有观察者都鼓起掌来，庆祝这一历史性时刻的到来。

推进月球的最后一颗核弹已经就位，这时，距波江晶体和吞食帝国使者到达地球已有一个世纪。这是一个绝望的世纪，人类在进行着痛苦的奋斗。

上半个世纪，全世界竭尽全力建造月球推进发动机，但这种超级机器始终没能建成，那几台试验用的样机只是给月球表面增加了几座废铁高山，还有几台在试运行时被核聚变的高温熔化成了一片钢水湖泊。人类曾向吞食帝国使者请求技术支援，推进月球需要的发动机还不及吞食者上那无数超级发动机的十分之一大，但大牙不答应，还讥讽道："别以为知道了核聚变就能造出行星发动机，造出爆竹离造出火箭还差得远呢。其实你们完全没有必要费这么大劲儿，在银河系，一个文明成为更强大文明的家禽是很正常的，你们会发现被饲养是一种多么美妙的生活，衣食无忧，快乐终生，有些文明还求之不得呢。你们感到不舒服，完全是陈腐的人类中心论在作怪。"

于是，人类把希望寄托在波江晶体上，但这希望同样落空了。波江文明是沿着一条与地球和吞食者完全不同的技术路线发展的，他们的所有技术力量都来自本星的生物体，比如这块晶体，就是波江行星海洋中的一种浮游生物的共生体。对这个世界中生命的这些奇特能力，波江人只是组合和利用，也不知其深层的秘密，而一旦离开本星的生物，波江人的技术就寸步难行了。

浪费了宝贵的 50 多年后，绝望的人类突然想出了一个极其疯狂的月球推进方案。这个方案首先由上校提出，当时他是月球推进计划的主要领导人之一，已升为元帅。这个方案尽管疯狂，在技术上要求却不高，人类现有的技术完全可以胜任，以至于人们惊奇为什么没有及早想到它。

新的推进方案很简单，就是在月球的一面大量埋设核弹，这些核弹的埋设深度一般为 3000 米左右，其埋设的密度以不被周围核弹的爆炸所摧毁为准，这样，将在月球的推进面埋设 500 万核弹。与这些热核炸弹相比，人类在冷战时期所制造的威力最大的核弹也算常规武器。因此，当这些埋在月球地下的超级核弹爆炸时，与在以前的地下核试验中被窒息在深洞中的核爆炸完全不同，它会将上面的地层完全掀起炸飞。在月球的低重力下，被炸飞的地层岩石会达到逃逸速度，脱离月球冲进太空，进而对月球本身产生巨大的推进力。如果每一时刻都有一定数量的核弹爆炸，这种脉冲式的推进力就会变得连续不断，等于给月球装上了强劲的发动机，而使不同位置的核弹爆炸，可以操纵月球的飞行方向。进一步的设计计划在月面下埋设两层核弹，另一层在第一层之下，深度约6000米。这样，当上层的推进面被剥去3000米厚的一层时，第二层接着被不断引爆，使"发动机"的运行时间延长一倍。

当晶体中的波江女孩儿听到这个计划时，认为人类真的疯了："现在我知道，如果你们有吞食者那样的技术力量，会比他们还野蛮！"

但这个计划使大牙赞叹不已："呵呵，虫虫们竟能有这样美妙的想法，我喜欢，喜欢它的粗野，粗野是最美的！"

"荒唐，粗野怎么会美？"波江女孩儿反驳说。

"粗野当然美，宇宙就是最粗野的！漆黑寒冷的深渊中燃烧着狂躁的恒星，不粗野吗？宇宙是雄性的，明白吗？像你们那种女人气的文明，那种弱不禁风的精致和纤细，只是宇宙小角落中一种微不足道的病态而已。"

100年过去了，大牙仍然生机勃勃，晶体中的波江女孩儿仍然鲜艳动人，但元帅感受到了岁月的力量，135岁，是老年人了。

这时，吞食者已越过冥王星轨道，它从由波江座—e星开始的6万年漫长的航程中苏醒了。太空中那个巨大的轮胎变得灯火辉煌，庞大的社会运转起来，准备好了对太阳系的掠夺。

吞食者掠过外围行星，沿着陡峭的轨道向地球扑来。

七、人类的第一次和最后一次星战

月球脱离地球的加速开始了。

推进面的核弹开始爆炸时，月球正处于地球白昼的一面，每次爆炸的闪光，都把月球在蓝天上短暂地映现一下，这使得天空中仿佛出现了一只不断眨巴的银色的眼睛。入夜，月球一侧的闪光传过近40万千米仍能在地面上映出人影，这时还能在月球的后面看到一条淡淡的银色尾迹，它是由从月面炸入太空的岩石构成的。从安装在推进面的摄像机中可以看到，月面被核爆掀起的地层如滔天洪水般涌向太空，向前很快变细，在远方成为一条极细的蛛丝，弯向地球的另一面，描绘出月球加速的轨道。但人们的注意力都集中在天空中出现的那个恐怖的大环上：吞食者此时已驶近地球，它的引力产生的巨大潮汐已摧毁了所有的沿海城市。吞食者尾部的发动机闪着一圈蓝色的光芒，它正在进行最后的轨道调整，以使其绕太阳运行的轨道与地球保持同步，同时使自己与地球的自转轴线对准在同一直线上，然后它将缓缓向地球移动，将其套入大环中。月球的加速持续了两个月，这期间在它的推进面平均两三秒钟就爆炸一枚核弹，到目前为止已引爆了250多万枚。加速后的月球环绕地球第二圈的软道形状已变得很扁，当月球运行到这条轨道的顶端时，应元帅的邀请，大牙同他一起来到了月球面向前进方向一面，他们站在环形山环绕的平原上，感受着从月球另一面传来的震动，仿佛这颗地球卫星的中心有一颗强劲的心脏。在漆黑的太空背景下，吞食者的巨环光彩夺目，占据了半个天空。

"太棒了，元帅虫虫，真的太棒了！"大牙对元帅由衷地赞叹着，"不过你们要抓紧，只剩下一圈的加速时间了，吞食帝国可没有等待别人的习惯。我还有个疑问：你们下面 10 年前就已建成的地下城还空着，那些移民什么时候来？你们的月地飞船能在一个月时间里从地球迁移 10 万人？"

"不会迁移任何人了，我们将是月球上最后的人类。"

听到这话，大牙吃惊地转过身去，看到了元帅所说的"我们"——这是地球太空部队的 5000 名将士，在环形山平原上站成严整的方阵。方阵前面，一名士兵展开一面蓝色的旗帜。

"看，这是我们行星的旗帜，地球对吞食帝国宣战了！"

大牙呆呆地站着，迷惑多于惊讶，紧接着，他四脚朝天摔倒了。这是由于月面突然增加的重力所致。大牙一动不动地趴在地上。它那庞大的身体激起的月尘在周围缓缓降落，但很快月尘又扬起来，这是从月球另一面传来的剧烈震波所致，这震动使平原蒙上了一层白色的尘被。大牙知道，在月球的另一面，核弹的爆炸密度突然增加了几倍，从重力的激增上它也能推测出月球的加速度也增加了几倍。它翻了个滚，从太空服胸前的口袋里掏出硕大的袖珍电脑，调出了月球目前的轨道。它看到，如果这剧增的加速度持续下去，轨道将不再闭合，月球将脱离地球引力冲向太空，一条闪着红光的虚线标示出预测的方向。

月球将径直撞向吞食者！

大牙缓缓地站了起来，任手中的电脑掉下去。它抬头看去，在突然增加的重力和波浪般的尘雾中，地球军团的方阵仍如磐石般稳立着。

"持续了一个世纪的阴谋。"大牙喃喃地说。

元帅点点头："你明白得晚了。"

大牙长叹道："我应该想到地球人与波江人是完全不同的两个物种，波江世界是一个以共生为进化基础的生态圈，没有自然选择和生存竞争，更不知战争为何物……我们却用这种习惯思维来套地球人，而你们，自从从树上下来后就厮杀不断，怎么可能轻易被征服呢？我……不可饶恕的失职啊！"

元帅说："波江人为我们提供了大量重要的信息，其中关于吞食者的加速度极限值就是人类这个作战方案的基础：如果引爆月球上的转向核弹，月球的轨道机动加速度将是吞食音速度极限值的三倍，这就是说它比吞食还灵活三倍，你们不可能躲开这次撞击的。"

大牙说："其实我们也不是完全没有戒备，当地球开始生产大量核弹时，我们时刻监视着这些核弹的去向，确保它们被放置在月球地层中，可没有想到……"

元帅在面罩后面微微一笑："我们不会傻到用核弹直接攻击吞食者，地球人那些简陋的导弹在半途中就会被身经百战的吞食帝国全部拦截，但你们无法拦截巨大的月球。也许凭借吞食者的力量最终能击碎它或使其转向，但现在距离已经很近，时间来不及了。"

"狡诈的虫虫，阴险的虫虫，恶毒的虫虫……吞食帝国是心肠实在的文明，把什么都说在明处，可是最终被阴险的地球虫虫骗了。"大牙咬牙切齿地说，狂怒中想用大爪子抓元帅，但在士兵们指向它的冲锋枪前停住了，它没有忘记自己也是血肉之躯，一梭子子弹足以让它丧命。元帅对大牙说："我们要走了，劝你也离开月球吧，不然会死在吞食帝国的核弹之下的。"

元帅说得很对，大牙和人类太空部队刚刚飞离月球，吞食者的截击导弹就击中了月面。这时月球的两面都闪烁着强光，朝向前进方向的一面也有大量的岩石被炸飞到太空中，与推进面不同的是，这些岩石是朝着各个方向漫天目标地飞散开。从地球上看去，撞向吞食者的月球如一个披着怒发的斗士，任何力量都无法阻挡它！在能看到月球的大陆上，人山人海中爆发出狂热的欢呼。

吞食者的拦截行动只持续了不长的时间就停止了，因为他们发现这毫无意义，在月球走完短暂的距离之前，既不可能使它转向，更不可能击碎它。

月球上的推进核弹也停止了爆炸，速度已经足够，地球保卫者要留下足够的核弹进行最后的轨道机动。一切都沉静下来，在冷寂的太空中，吞食者和地球的卫星静静地相向飘行着，它们之间的距离在急剧缩短。当两者的距离缩短至 50 万千米时，从地球统帅部所在的指挥舰上看去，月球已与"轮胎"重叠，像是轴承圈上的一粒钢珠。

直到这时，吞食者的航向也没有任何变化，这是容易理解的：过早的轨道机动会使月球也做出相应的反应，真正有意义的躲避动作要在月球最后撞击前进行。这就像两名用长矛决斗的中世纪骑士，他们骑马越过长长的距离逼近对方，但真正决定胜负是在即将相互接触的一小段距离内。

银河系的两大文明都屏住了呼吸，等待着那最后的时刻。

当距离缩短至 35 万千米时，双方的机动航行开始了。吞食者的发动机首先喷出了上万千米的蓝色烈焰，开始躲避；月球上的核弹则以空前的密度和频率疯狂地引爆，进行着相应的攻击方向修正，它那弯曲的尾迹清楚地描绘出航线的变化。吞食者喷出的上万千米长的蓝色光河的头部镶嵌着月球核弹银色的闪光，构成了太阳系有史以来最壮观的景象。

双方的机动航行进行了三个小时，它们的距离已缩短至 5 万千米，计算机显示的结果令指挥舰上的人们不敢相信自己的眼睛：吞食者的变轨加速度四倍于波江晶体提供的极限值！以前人们深信不疑的吞食者的加速度极限，一直是地球人取胜的基础，现在，月球上剩余的核弹已没有能力对攻击方向做出足够的调整。计算表明，即使尽全力变轨，半小时后，月球也将以 400 千米的距离与吞食者擦肩而过。

在一阵令人目眩的剧烈闪光后，月球耗尽了最后的核弹，几乎与此同时，吞食者的发动机也关闭了。在死一般的寂静中，惯性定律完成了这篇宏伟史诗的最后章节：月球紧擦着吞食者的边缘飞过，由于其速度很快，吞食者的引力没能将其捕获，但扭弯了它的飘行轨迹。月球掠过吞食者后，无声地向远离太阳的方向飞去。

指挥舰上，统帅部的人们在死一般的沉默中度过了几分钟。

"波江人骗了我们。"一位将军低声说。

"也许，那块晶体只是吞食帝国的一个圈套！"一位参谋喊道。

统帅部瞬间陷入一片混乱，每个人都声嘶力竭地叫喊着，以掩盖或发泄自己的绝望，几名文职人员或哭泣或抓着自己的头发，精神已到了崩溃的边缘。只有元帅仍静静地站在大显示屏前，他慢慢转过身来，用一句话稳住了局面："我提醒各位注意一个现象：吞食者的发动机为什么要关闭？"

这话引起了所有人的思考，是的，在月球耗尽核弹后，敌人的发动机没有理由关闭，因为他们不可能知道月球上是否还剩有核弹。同时考虑到吞食者的引力捕获月球的危险，也应该继续进行躲避加速，继续拉开与月球攻击线的距离，而不可能仅仅满足于这 400 千米的微小间距。

"给我吞食者外表面的近距离图像。"元帅说。

大屏幕上出现了一幅全息画画，这是一个吞食者的地球小型高速侦察器在其表面 500 千米上空传回的，吞食者灯光灿烂的大陆历历在目，人们敬畏地看着那线条粗放的钢铁山和峡谷缓缓移过。一条黑色的长缝引起了元帅的注意。在过去的一个世纪中，他已记熟了吞食者外表面的每一个细节，肯定这条长缝以前是不存在的。很快别人也注意到了：

"这是什么？一条……裂缝？"

"是的，裂缝，一条长达 5000 千米的裂缝。"元帅点点头说，"波江人没有骗我们，晶体带来的资料是真实的，那个加速度极限确实存在。但当月球逼近时，绝望的吞食者不顾一切地用超限四倍的加速度来躲避，这就是超限加速的后果：它被撕裂了。"

接下来，人们又发现了另外几条裂缝。

"看啊，那又是什么？"又有人惊叫，这时，吞食者的自转正使它表面的另一部分进入视野，金属大陆的边缘出现了一个刺目的光球，如同它那辽阔地平线上的日出一般。

"自转发动机！"一名军官说。

"是的，是吞食者赤道上很少启动的自转发动机，它此时正在以最大功率刹住自转！"

"元帅，这证实了您的看法！"

"尽快用各种观测手段取得详细资料，进行模拟！"元帅说，但在这之前一切已在进行中了。

经过一个世纪建立起来的精确描述吞食者物理结构的数学模型，在从前方取得必需的数据后高速运转，模拟结果很快出来了：需近四十小时的时间，自转发动机才能把吞食者的自转速度减至毁灭值之下，而如果高于这个转速，离心力将使已被撕裂的吞食者在十八个小时内完全解体。

人们欢呼起来。大屏幕上接着映出了吞食者解体时的全息模拟图像：解体的过程很慢，如梦似幻。在漆黑太空的背景上，这个巨大的世界如同一团浮在咖啡上的奶沫一样散开来，边缘的碎块渐渐隐没于黑暗之中，仿佛被太空融化了，只有不时出现的爆炸的闪光才使它们重新现形。

元帅并没有同人们一起观赏这令人心旷神怡的画面，他远离人群，站在另一块大屏幕前注视着现实中的吞食者，脸上没有一点胜利的喜悦。冷静下来的人们注意到了他，也纷纷站到这个屏幕前，他们发现，吞食者尾部的蓝色光环又出现了，它再次启动了推进发动机。

在环体已经被严重损伤的情况下，这似乎是一个不可理解的错误，这时，任何微小的加速度都可能导致大环解体。而吞食者的运行方向更让人迷惑：它正在缓缓回到躲避月球攻击前所在的位置，谨慎地建立与地球同步的太阳轨道，并使自己和地球的自转轴对准在一条直线上。

"怎么？这时它还想吃地球？"

有人吃惊地说，他的话引起了稀疏的笑声，但笑声戛然而止，人们看到了元帅的表情，他已不再看屏幕，而是双眼紧闭，苍白的脸上毫无表情。一个世纪以来，作为抗击吞食者的精神支柱之一，太空将士们已经熟悉了他的音容，他们从来没有见到他像这样。人们慢慢冷静下来，再看屏幕，终于明白了一个严峻的现实——吞食者还有一条活路。

吞食地球的航行开始了，已与地球运行同步自转同轴的吞食者向着这颗行星的南极移动。如果它慢了，会在自转的离心力下解体；如果太快，推进的加速度可能使其提前解体。吞食者正走在一条生存的钢丝绳上，它必须绝对准确地把握住时间和速度的平衡。

在地球的南极被套入大环前的一段时间，太空中的人们看到，南极大陆的海岸线形状在急剧变化，这个大陆像一块热煎锅上的牛油一样缩小着面积，地球的海水在吞食者引力的拉动下涌向南极，地球顶端那块雪白的大陆正在被滔天巨浪吞没。这时吞食者大环上的裂缝越来越多，且都在延长扩宽。最初出现的那几条裂缝已不再是黑色的，里面透出了暗红色的火光，像几千千米长的地狱之门。有几条蛛丝般的白色细线从大环表面升起，接下来这样的细线越来越多，出现在大环的每一部分，仿佛吞食者长出了稀疏的头发。这是从大环上发射的飞船的尾迹，吞食者开始从他们将要毁灭的世界逃命了。

但当地球被大环吞入一半时，情况发生了逆转：地球的引力像无数根无形的辐条拉住了正在解体的大环，吞食者表面不再有新的裂缝出现，已有的裂缝也停止了扩展。14 小时过去后，地球被完全套入大环，它那引力的辐条变得更加强劲有力，吞食者表面的裂缝开始缩小，又过了 5 小时，这些裂缝完全合拢了。

在指挥舰上，统帅部的大聊欢已结束了，甚至连灯都灭了，只有太阳从舷窗中投进惨白的光芒。为了产生人工重力，飞船中部仍在缓缓旋转，使得太阳从不同位置的舷窗中升升降降，光影流转，仿佛在追述着人类那已永远成为过去的日日夜夜。

"谢谢各位在过去一个世纪中尽职尽责地工作，谢谢。"元帅说，并向统帅部的全体人员敬礼。在将士们的注视下，他平静地整理了一下自己的军装，其他的人也这样做了。

人类失败了，但地球保卫者们已经尽到了自己的责任。对于尽责的战士来说，这一时刻仍是辉煌的，他们接受了平静的良心授予自己的无形勋章，他们有权享受这一时光。

尾声：归宿

"真的有水啊！"一名年轻上尉惊喜地叫出来，面前确实是一片广阔的水面，在昏黄的天空下泛着粼粼的波光。

元帅摘下太空服的手套，捧起一点水，推开面罩尝了尝，又赶紧将面罩合上："喂，还不是太咸。"看到上尉也想打开面罩，他制止说，"会得减压病的，大气成分倒没问题，硫黄之类的有毒成分已经很淡了，但气压太低，相当于战前的 10000 米高空。"

又一名将军在脚下的沙子中挖着什么。"也许会有些草种子的。"他抬头对元帅笑笑说。元帅摇摇头："这里战前是海底。""我们可以到离这里不远的 11 号新陆去看看，那里说不定会有。"那名上尉说。

"有也早烤焦了。"有人叹息道。

大家举目四望，地平线处有连绵的山脉，它们是最近一次造山运动的产物。青色的山体由赤裸的岩石构成，从山顶流下的医河发着暗红的光，使山脉像一个巨人淌血的躯体，但大地上的岩浆河已经消失了。

这是战后 230 年的地球。

战争结束后，统帅部幸存的 100 多人在指挥舰上进入冬眠器，等待着地球被吞食者吐出后重返家园。指挥舰则成为一颗卫星，在一条宽大的轨道上围绕着由吞食者和地球组成的联合星体运行。在以后的时间里，吞食帝国并没有打扰他们。

战后第 125 年，指挥舰上的传感系统发现吞食者正在吐出地球，就唤醒了一部分冬眠者。当这些人醒来后，吞食者已飞离地球，向金星方向航行，而这时的地球已变成一颗人们完全陌生的行星，像一块刚从炉子里取出的火炭，海洋早已消失，大地上覆盖着蛛网般的河流。他们只好继续冬眠，重新设定传感器，等待着地球冷却，这一等又是一个世纪。

冬眠者们再次醒来时，发现地球已冷却成一个荒凉的黄色行星，剧烈的地质运动已经平息下来。虽然生命早已消失，但有稀薄的大气，他们甚至还发现了残存的海洋，于是他们就在一个大小如战前内陆湖泊的残海边着陆了。

一阵轰鸣声，就是在这稀薄的空气中也震耳欲聋，那艘熟悉的外形粗笨的吞食帝国飞船在人类的飞船不远处着陆，高大的舱门打开后，大牙挂着一根电线杆长度的拐杖颤巍巍地走下来。

"啊，您还活着！有 500 岁了吧？"元帅同他打招呼。

"我哪能活那么久啊，战后 30 年我也冬眠了，就是为了能再见你们一面。"

"吞食者现在在哪儿？"

大牙指向天空的一个方向："晚上才能看见，只是一个暗淡的小星星，它已航出木星轨道。"

"它在离开太阳系吗？"

大牙点点头："我今天就要启程去追它了。"

"我们都老了。"

"老了……"大牙黯然地点点头，哆嗦着把拐杖换了手，"这个世界，现在……"它指指天空和大地。

"有少量的水和大气留了下来，这算是吞食帝国的仁慈吗？"

大牙摇摇头："与仁慈无关，这是你们的功绩。"

地球战士们不解地看着大牙。

"哦，在那场战争中，吞食帝国遭受了前所未有的创伤，在那次大环撕裂中死了上亿人，生态系统也被严重损坏，战后用了50个地球年的时间才初步修复。这以后才有能力开始对地球的咀嚼。但你知道，我们在太阳系的时间有限，如果不能及时离开，有一片星际尘埃会飘到我们前面的航线上，如果绕道，我们到达下一个恒星系的时间就会晚17000年，那颗恒星将会发生变化，烧毁我们要吞食的那几颗星，所以对太阳几颗行星的咀嚼就很匆忙，吃得不大干净。"

"这让我们感到许多的安慰和荣誉。"元帅看看周围的人们说。

"你们当之无愧，那真是一场伟大的星际战争。在吞食帝国漫长的征战史中，你们是最出色的战士之一！直到现在，帝国的行吟诗人还在到处传唱着地球战士史诗般的战绩。"

"我们更想让人类记住这场战争。对了，现在人类怎样了？"

"战后大约有 20 亿人类移居到吞食帝国，占人类总数的一半。"大牙说着，打开了它的手提电脑宽大的屏幕，上面映出人类在吞食者上生活的画面：蓝天下一片美丽的草原，一群快乐的人在唱歌跳舞。一时难以分辨出这些人的性别，因为他们的皮肤都是那么细腻白嫩，都身着轻纱般的长服，头上装饰着美丽的花环。远处有一座漂亮的城堡，其形状显然来自地球童话，色彩之鲜艳如同用奶油和巧克力建造的。镜头拉近，元帅细看这些漂亮人儿的表情，确信他们真的是处于快乐之中，这是一种真正无忧无虑的快乐，如水晶般单纯，战前的人类只在童年短暂地享受过这种快乐。

"必须保证他们的绝对快乐，这是饲养中起码的技术要求，否则肉质得不到保证。地球人是高档食品，只有吞食帝国的上层社会才有钱享用，这种美味像我都是吃不起的。哦，元帅，我们找到了您的曾孙，录下了他对您说的话，想看吗？"

元帅吃惊地看了大牙一眼，点点头。屏幕上出现了一个皮肤细嫩的漂亮男孩儿，从面容上看他可能只有 10 岁，但身材却有成年人那么高，他一双女人般的小手拿着一个花环，显然是刚被从舞会上叫过来，他眨着一双水灵灵的大眼睛说："听说曾祖父您还活着？我只求您一件事，千万不要来见我啊！我会恶心死的！想到战前人类的生活我们都会恶心死的，那是狼的生活、蟑螂的生活！你和你的那些地球战士还想维持这种生活，差一点儿真的阻止人类进入这个美丽的天堂了！变态！您知道您让我多么羞耻，您知道您让我多么恶心吗？呸！不要来找我！呸！快死吧你！"说完他又蹦跳着加入到草原上的舞会中去了。大牙首先打破了尴尬的沉默："他将活过 60 岁，能活多久就活多久，不会被宰杀。"

"如果是因为我的话，十分感谢。"元帅凄凉地笑了一下说。

"不是，在得知自己的身世后，他很沮丧，也充满了对您的仇恨，这类情绪会使他的肉质不合格。"

大牙感慨地看着面前这最后一批真正的人，他们身上的太空服已破旧不堪，脸上都深深地刻着岁月的沧桑，在昏黄的阳光中如同地球大地上一群锈迹斑斑的铁像。

大牙合上电脑，充满歉意地说："本来不想让大家看这些的，但你们都是真正的战士，能够勇敢地面对现实，要承认……"它犹豫了一下才说，"人类文明完了。"

"是你们毁灭了地球文明，"元帅凝视着远方说，"你们犯下了滔天罪行！"

"我们终于又开始谈道德了。"

大牙咧嘴一笑说。

"在入侵我们的家园并极其野蛮地吞食一切后，我不认为你们还有这个资格。"元帅冷冷地说。其他的人不再关注他们的谈话，吞食者文明冷酷残暴的程度已超出人类的理解力，人们现在真的没有兴趣再同其进行道德方面的交流了。

"不，我们有资格，我现在还真想同人类谈谈道德……'您怎么拿起来就吃啊？'"

大牙最后这句话让所有人浑身一震，这话不是从翻译器中传出，而是大牙亲口说的，虽然嗓门震耳，但他对三个世纪前元帅的声调模仿得惟妙惟肖。

大牙通过翻译器接着说："元帅您在 300 年前的那次感觉是对

的：星际间的不同文明，其相似要比差异更令人震惊，我们确实不应该这么像。"

人们都把目光聚焦在大牙身上，他们都预感到，一个惊天的大秘密将被揭开。

大牙动动拐杖使自己站直，看着远方说："朋友们，我们都是太阳的孩子，地球是我们共同的家园，但我们比你们更有权利拥有它！因为在你们之前的1亿4000万年，我们的祖先就在这个美丽的行星上生活，并创造了灿烂的文明。"

地球战士们呆呆地看着大牙，身边的残海跳跃着昏黄的阳光，远方的新山脉流淌着血红的岩浆。越过6000万年的沧桑时光，曾经覆盖地球的两大物种在这劫后的母亲星球上凄凉地相会了。

"恐——龙——"有人低声惊叫。

大牙点点头："恐龙文明崛起于1亿地球年之前，就是你们地质纪年的中生代白垩纪中期，在白垩纪晚期达到鼎盛。我们是一个体形巨大的物种，对生态的消耗量极大，随着恐龙人口的急剧增加，地球生态圈已难以维持恐龙社会的生存，接着又吃光了刚刚拥有初级生态的火星。地球上恐龙文明的历史长达2000万年。但恐龙社会真正的急剧膨胀也就是几千年的事，其在生态上造成的影响从地质纪年的长度看很像一场突然爆发的大灾难，这就是你们所猜测的白垩纪灾难。

"终于有那么一天，所有的恐龙都登上了十艘巨大的世代飞船，航向茫茫星海。这十艘飞船最后合为一体，每到达一个有行星的恒星就扩建一次，经过6000万年，就成为现在的吞食帝国。"

"为什么要吃掉自己的家园呢？恐龙没有一点怀旧感吗？"有

人问。

大牙陷入了回忆："说来话长，星际空间确实茫茫无际，但与你们的想象不同，真正适合我们高等碳基生物生存的空间并不多。从我们所在的位置向银河系的中心方向，走不出两千光年就会遇到大片的星际尘埃，在其中既无法航行也无法生存，再向前则会遇到强辐射和大群游荡的黑洞……如果向相反的方向走呢，我们已在旋臂的末端，不远处就是无边无际的荒凉虚空。在适合生存的这片空间中，消耗量巨大的吞食帝国已吃光了所有的行星。现在，我们的唯一活路是航行到银河系的另一旋臂去，我们也不知道那里有什么，但在这片空间待下去肯定是死路一条。这次航行要持续 1500 万年，途中一片荒凉，我们必须在启程前储备好所有的消耗品。这时的吞食帝国就像干涸的小水洼中的一条鱼，它必须在水洼完全干掉之前猛跳一下，虽然多半是落到旱地上在烈日下死去，但也有可能落到相邻的另一个水洼中活下去……至于怀旧感，在经历了几千万年的太空跋涉和数不清的星际战争后，恐龙种族早已是铁石心肠了，为了前方千万年的航程，吞食帝国要尽可能多吃一些东西……文明是什么？文明就是吞食，不停地吃啊吃，不停地扩张和膨胀，其他的一切都是次要的。"

元帅深思着说："难道生存竞争是宇宙间生命和文明进化的唯一法则？难道不能建立起一个自给自足的、内省的、多种生命共生的文明吗，就像波江文明那样？"

大牙长出一口气，说："我不是哲学家，也许可能吧。关键是谁先走出第一步呢？自己生存是以征服和消灭别人为基础的，这是这个宇宙中生命和文明生存的铁的法则，谁要首先不遵从它而自省起来，就必死无疑。"

大牙转身走上飞船，再出来时端着一个扁平的方盒子，那个盒子有三四米见方，起码要四个人才能抬起来。大牙把盒子平放到地上，掀起顶盖，人们看到盒子里装满了土，土上长着一片青草，在这已无生命的世界中，这绿色令所有人心动。

"这是一块战前地球的土地，战后我使这片土地上的所有植物和昆虫都进入冬眠，现在过了两个多世纪，又使它们同我一起苏醒。本想把这块土地带走做个纪念的，唉，现在想想还是算了吧，还是把它放回它该在的地方吧，我们从母亲星球拿走的够多了。"

看着这一小片生机盎然的地球土地，人们的眼睛湿润了。他们现在知道，恐龙并非铁石心肠，在那比钢铁和岩石更冷酷的鳞甲后面，也有一颗渴望回家的心。

大牙一挥爪子，似乎想把自己从某种情绪中解脱出来："好了，朋友们，我们一起走吧，到吞食帝国去。"看到人们的表情，它举起一只爪子，"你们到那里当然不是作为家禽饲养，你们是伟大的战士，都将成为帝国的普通公民，你们还会得到一份工作：建立一个人类文明博物馆。"

地球战士们都把目光集中在元帅身上，他想了想，缓缓地点点头。

地球战士们一个接一个地上了大牙的飞船，那为恐龙准备的梯子他们必须一节一节引体向上爬上去。元帅是最后一个上飞船的人，他双手抓住飞船舷梯最下面的一节踏板的边缘，在把自己的身体拉离地面的时候，他最后看了一眼脚下地球的土地，此后他就停在那里看着地面，很长时间一动不动，他看到了——

蚂蚁。

这蚂蚁是从那块盒子中的土地里爬出来的，元帅放开抓着踏板的双手，蹲下身，让它爬到手上，举起那只手，再细细地看看它，它那黑宝石般的小身躯在阳光下闪闪发亮。元帅走到盒子旁，把这只蚂蚁放回到那片小小的草丛中，这时他又在草丛间的土面上发现了其他几只蚂蚁。

他站起身来，对刚来到身边的大牙说："我们走后，这些草和蚂蚁就是地球上仅有的生命了。"

大牙默默无语。

元帅说："地球上的文明生物有越来越小的趋势，恐龙、人，然后可能是蚂蚁。"他又蹲下来深情地看着那些在草丛间穿行的小生命，"该轮到它们了。"

这时，地球战士们又纷纷从飞船上下来，返回到那块有生命的地球土地前，围成一圈深情地看着它。

大牙摇摇头说："草能活下去，这海边也许会下雨的，但蚂蚁不行。"

"因为空气稀薄吗？看样子它们好像没受影响。"

"不，空气没问题。与人不同，在这样的空气中它们能存活，关键是没有食物。"

"不能吃青草吗？"

"那就谁也活不下去了：在稀薄的空气中青草长得很慢，蚂蚁会吃光青草然后饿死，这倒很像吞食文明可能的最后结局。"

"您能给它们留下些吃的吗？"

大牙又摇头："我的飞船上除了生命冬眠系统和饮用水外什么都没有，我们在追上帝国前需要冬眠，你们的飞船上还有食物吗？"

元帅也摇摇头："只剩几支维持生命的注射营养液，没用的。"

大牙指指飞船："我们还是抓紧时间吧，帝国加速很快，晚了我们追不上它的。"

沉默。

"元帅，我们留下来。"一名年轻中尉说。

元帅坚定地点点头。

"留下来？干什么？"大牙挨个儿看他们，惊讶地问，"你们飞船上的冬眠装置已接近报废，又没有食品，留下来等死吗？"

"留下来走出第一步。"元帅平静地说。

"什么？"

"您刚才提过的新文明的第一步。"

"你们……要作为蚂蚁的食物？"

地球战士们都点点头。大牙无言地注视了他们很长时间，然后转身拄着拐杖慢慢走向飞船。

"再见，朋友。"元帅在大牙身后高声说。

老恐龙长长地叹息了一声："在我和我的子孙前面，是无尽的暗夜、不休的征战，茫茫宇宙，哪里是家哟！"人们看到它的脚下湿了一片，不知道是不是一滴眼泪。

恐龙的飞船在轰鸣声中起飞，很快消失在天空。在那个方向，太阳正在落下。

最后的地球战士们围着那块有生命的土地默默地坐了一会儿，然后，从元帅开始，大家纷纷掀起面罩，在沙地上躺了下来。

时间在流逝，太阳落下，晚霞使劫后的大地映在一片美丽的红光中，不久，有稀疏的星星在天空中出现。元帅发现，一直昏黄的天空这时居然现出了蓝色。在稀薄的空气夺去他的知觉前，令他欣慰的是，他的太阳穴上有轻微的骚动感，蚂蚁正在爬上他的额头，这感觉让他回到了遥远的童年，在海边两棵棕榈树上拴着的小吊床上，他仰望着灿烂的星海，妈妈的手抚过他的额头……

夜晚降临了，残海平静如镜，毫不走样地映着横天而过的银河。这是这个行星有史以来最宁静的一个夜晚。

在这宁静中，地球重生了。

MOUNTAIN

一、山在那儿

"我今天一定要搞清楚你这个怪癖：你为什么从不上岸？"船长对冯帆说，"5 年了，我都记不清'蓝水号'停泊过多少个国家的多少个港口，可你从没上过岸；回国后你也不上岸；前年船在青岛大修改造，船上乱哄哄地施工，你也没上岸，就在一间小舱里过了两个月。"

"我是不是让你想到了那部叫《海上钢琴师》的电影？"

"如果'蓝水号'退役了，你是不是也打算像电影的主人公那样随它沉下去？"

"我会换条船，海洋考察船总是欢迎我这种不上岸的地质工程师的。"

"这很自然地让人想到，陆地上有什么东西让你害怕？"

"相反，陆地上有东西让我向往。"

"什么？"

"山。"

他们现在站在"蓝水号"海洋地质考察船的左舷，看着赤道上的太平洋。一年前"蓝水号"第一次过赤道时，船上还娱乐性地举行了那个古老的仪式，但随着这片海底锰结核沉积区的发现，"蓝水号"在一年中反复穿越赤道无数次，人们也就忘记了赤道的存在。

现在，夕阳已沉到了海平线下，太平洋异常平静，冯帆从未见过这么平静的海面，竟让他想起了那些喜马拉雅山上的湖泊，清澈得发黑，像地球的眸子。

一次，他和两个队员偷看湖里的藏族姑娘洗澡，被几个牧羊汉子拎着腰刀追，后来追不上，就用石抛子朝他们抛石头，贼准，他们只好做投降状停下，那几个汉子走近打量了他们一阵儿就走了，冯帆听懂了他们嘀咕的那几句藏语：还没见过外面来的人能在这地方跑这么快。

"喜欢山？那你是山里长大的了。"船长说。

"这你错了，"冯帆说，"山里长大的人一般都不喜欢山，在他们的感觉中山把自己与世界隔绝了。我认识一个尼泊尔夏尔巴族登山向导，他登了 41 次珠峰，但每一次都在距峰顶不远处停下，看着雇用他的登山队登顶，他说只要自己愿意，无论从北坡还是南坡，他都可以在 10 个小时内登上珠峰，但他没有兴趣。山的魅力是从两个方位感受到的：一是从平原上远远地看山；二是站在山顶上。

"我的家在河北大平原上，向西能看到太行山。家和山之间就像这海似的一马平川，没遮没挡。我生下来不久，妈妈第一次把我抱到外面，那时我脖子刚硬得能撑住小脑袋，就冲着西边的山咿咿呀呀地叫。学走路时，总是摇摇晃晃地朝山那边走。大了些后，曾在一天清晨出发，沿着石太铁路向山走，一直走到中午肚子饿了才回头，但那山看上去还是那么远。上学后还骑着自行车向山的方向走，那山似乎随着我前进而向后退，丝毫没有近些的感觉。时间长了，远山对于我已成为一种象征，像我们生活中那些清晰可见但永远无法到达的东西，那是凝固在远方的梦。"

"我去过那一带。"船长摇摇头说，"那里的山很荒，上面只有乱石和野草，所以你以后注定要面临一次失望。"

"不，我和你想的不一样，我只想到山那里，爬上去，并不指望得到山里的什么东西。第一次登上山顶时，看着生我养我的平原在下面伸延，真有一种重新出生的感觉。"

冯帆说到这里，发现船长并没有专注于他们的谈话，他在仰头看天，那里，已出现了稀疏的星星。"那儿，"船长用烟斗指着正上方天顶的一处说，"那儿不应该有星星。"

但那里有一颗星星，很暗淡，丝毫不引人注意。

"你肯定？"冯帆将目光从天顶转向船长，"GPS 早就代替了六分仪，你肯定自己还是那么熟悉星空？"

"那当然，这是航海专业的基础知识……你接着说。"

冯帆点点头："后来在大学里，我组织了一支登山队，登过几座 7000 米以上的高山，最后登的是珠峰。"

船长打量着冯帆："我猜对了，果然是你！我一直觉得你面熟，改名了？"

"是的，我曾叫冯华北。"

"几年前你可引起不小的关注啊，媒体上说的那些都是真的？"

"基本上是吧，反正那四个大学登山队员确实是因我而死的。"

船长划了根火柴，将灭了的烟斗重新点着："我感觉，做登山队长和做远洋船长有一点是相同的：最难的不是学会争取，而是学会放弃。"

"可我当时要是放弃了，以后也很难再有机会。你知道登山运动是一件很花钱的事，我们是一支大学生登山队，好不容易争取到赞助……由于我们雇的登山协同和向导闹罢工，在建一号营地时耽误了时间。然后就预报有风暴，但从云图上看，风暴到那儿至少还有 20 个小时的时间，我们这时已经建好了 7900 米的二号营地，立刻登顶时间上应该够了。你说我这时能放弃吗？我决定登顶。"

"那颗星星在变亮。"船长又抬头看了看。

"是啊，天黑了嘛。"

"好像不是因为天黑……说下去。"

"后面的事你应该都知道：风暴来时，我们正在海拔 8680 米到 8710 米最险的一段上，那是一道接近 90 度的峭壁，登山界管它叫'第二台阶''中国梯'。当时峰顶已经很近了，天还很晴，只在峰顶的一侧雾化出一缕云，我清楚地记得，当时觉得珠峰像一把锋利的刀子，把天划破了，流出那缕白血……很快一切都看不见了，风暴刮起的雪雾那个密啊，密得成了黑色的，一下子把那 4 名队员从悬崖上吹下去了，只有我死死拉着绳索。可我的登山镐当时只是卡在冰缝里，根本不可能支撑 5 个人的重量，也就是出于本能吧，我割断了登山索上的钢扣，任他们掉下去……其中两个人的遗体到现在还没找到。"

"这是 5 个人死还是 4 个人死的问题。"

"是，从登山运动紧急避险的准则来说，我也没错，但就此背上了这辈子的一个十字架……你说得对，那颗星星不正常，还在变亮。"

"别管它，那你现在的这种……状况，与这次经历有关吗？"

"还用说吗？你也知道当时媒体上铺天盖地的谴责和鄙夷，说我不负责任，说我是个自私怕死的小人，为了自己活命竟牺牲了 4 个同伴……我至少可以部分澄清后一项指责，于是那天我穿上那件登山服，戴上太阳镜，顺着排水管登上了学院图书馆的顶层。就在我跳下去前，导师也上来了，他在我后面说：'你这么做是不是太轻饶自己了？你这是在逃避更重的惩罚。'我问他有那种惩罚吗，他说：'当然有，你找一个离山最远的地方过一辈子，让自己永远看不见山，这不就行了？'于是我就没有跳下去。这当然招来了更多的耻笑，但只有我自己知道导师说得对，那对我真的是一个比死更重的惩罚。我视登山为生命，学地质也是为的这个，让我一辈子永远离开自己痴迷的高山，再加上良心的折磨，很合适。于是我毕业后就找到了这个工作，成为'蓝水号'考察船的海洋地质工程师，来到海上——离山最远的地方。"

船长盯着冯帆看了好半天，不知该说什么好，终于认定最好的选择是摆脱这人，好在现在头顶上的天空中就有一个转移话题的目标："再看看那颗星星。"

"天哪，它好像在显出形状来！"冯帆抬头看后惊叫道，那颗星已不是一个点，而是一个小小的圆形，那圆形在迅速扩大，转眼间成了天空中一个醒目的发着蓝光的小球。

一阵急促的脚步声把他们的目光从空中拉回了甲板，头上戴着耳机的大副急匆匆地跑来对船长说："收到消息，有一艘外星飞船正在向地球飞来，我们所处的赤道位置看得最清楚，看，就是那个！"

三人仰望，天空中的小球仍在急剧膨胀，像吹了气似的，很快胀到满月大小。

"所有的电台都中断了正常播音，在说这事儿呢！那个东西早被观测到了，现在才证实它是什么，它不回答任何询问，但从运行轨道看它肯定是有巨大动力的，正在高速向地球扑过来！他们说那东西有月球大小呢！"

现在看来，太空中的那个球体已远不止月亮大小了，它的内部现在可以装下 10 个月亮，占据了天空相当大的一部分，这说明它比月球距地球要近得多。大副捂着耳机接着说："……他们说它停下了，正好停在 3.6 万千米高的同步轨道上，成了地球的一颗同步卫星！"

"同步卫星？就是说它悬在那里不动了？！"

"是的，在赤道上，正在我们上方！"

冯帆凝视着太空中的球体，它似乎是透明的，内部充盈着蓝幽幽的光。真奇怪，他竟有盯着海面看的感觉，每当海底取样器升上来之前，海呈现出来的那种深邃都让他着迷，现在，那个蓝色巨球的内部就是这样深不可测，像是地球海洋在远古丢失的一部分正在回归。

"看啊，海！海怎么了？！"船长首先将目光从具有催眠般魔力的巨球上挣脱出来，用早已熄灭的烟斗指着海面惊叫。

前方的海天连线处开始弯曲，变成了一条向上拱起的正弦曲线。海面隆起了一个巨大的水包，这水包急剧升高，像是被来自太空的一只无形的巨手提了起来。

"是飞船质量的引力！它在拉起海水！"冯帆说，他很惊奇自己这时还能进行有效的思考。飞船的质量相当于月球，而它与地球的距离仅是月球的十分之一！幸亏它静止在同步轨道上，引力拉起的海水也是静止的，否则滔天的潮汐将毁灭世界。

现在，水包已升到了顶天立地的高度，呈巨大的秃锥形，它的表面反射着空中巨球的蓝光，而落日暗红的光芒又用艳丽的血红勾勒出它的边缘。水包的顶端在寒冷的高空雾化出了一缕云雾，那云飘出不远就消失了，仿佛是傍晚的天空被划破了似的，这景象令冯帆心里一动，他想起了……

"测测它的高度！"船长喊道。

过了一分钟有人喊道："大约 9100 米！"

在这地球上有史以来最恐怖也最壮美的奇观面前，所有人都像被咒语定住了。

"这是命运啊……"冯帆梦呓般地说。

"你说什么？！"船长大声问，目光仍被固定在水包上。

"我说这是命运。"

是的，是命运。为逃避山，冯帆来到太平洋中，而就在这距山最远的地方，出现了一座比珠穆朗玛峰还高 200 多米的水山，现在，它是地球上最高的山。

"左舵五，前进四！我们还是快逃命吧！"船长对大副说。

"逃命？有危险吗？"冯帆不解地问。

"外星飞船的引力已经造成了一个巨大的低气压区，大气旋正在形成，我告诉你吧，这可能是有史以来最大的风暴，说不定能把'蓝水号'像树叶似的刮上天！但愿我们能在气旋形成前逃出去。"

大副示意大家安静，他戴着耳机听了一会儿，说："船长，事情比你想的更糟！电台上说，外星人是来毁灭地球的，他们仅凭着飞船巨大的质量就能做到这一点！飞船的引力产生的不是普通的大风暴，而是地球大气的大泄漏！"

"泄漏？向什么地方泄漏？"

"飞船的引力会在地球的大气层上拉出一个洞，就像扎破气球一样，空气会从那个洞中逃逸到太空中去，地球大气会跑光的！"

"这需要多长时间？"船长问。

"专家们说，只需一个星期左右，全球的大气压就会降到致命的低限……他们还说，当气压降到一定程度时，海洋会沸腾起来，天哪，那是什么样子啊……现在各国的大城市都陷入混乱，人们一片疯狂，都涌进医院和工厂抢劫氧气……呵，还说，美国卡纳维拉尔角的航天发射基地都有疯狂的人群涌入，他们想抢作为火箭发射燃料的液氧……唉，一切都完了！"

"一个星期？就是说我们连回家的时间都不够了。"船长说，他这时反倒显得镇静了，摸出火柴来点烟斗。

"是啊，回家的时间都不够了……"大副茫然地说。

"要是这样，我们还不如分头去做自己最想做的事。"冯帆说，他突然兴奋起来，感到热血沸腾。

"你想做什么？"船长问。

"登山。"

"登山？登……这座山？！"大副指着海水高山吃惊地问。

"是的，现在它是世界最高峰了，山在那儿了，当然得有人去登。"

"怎么登？"

"登山当然是徒步的——游泳。"

"你疯了？！"大副喊道，"你能游上9000米高的水坡？那坡看上去有45度！那和登山不一样，你必须不停地游动，一松劲就滑下来了！"

"我想试试。"

"让他去吧。"船长说，"如果我们在这个时候还不能照自己的愿望生活，那什么时候能行呢？这里离水山的山脚有多远？"

"20千米左右吧。"

"你开一艘救生艇去吧，"船长对冯帆说，"记住多带些食品和水。"

"谢谢！"

"其实你挺幸运的。"船长拍拍冯帆的肩说。

"我也这么想。"冯帆说，"船长，还有一件事我没告诉你，在珠峰遇难的那4名大学登山队员中，有我的恋人。当我割断登山索时，脑子里闪过的念头是这样的：我不能死，还有别的山呢。"

船长点点头："去吧。"

"那……我们怎么办呢？"大副问。

"全速冲出正在形成的风暴，多活一天算一天吧。"

冯帆站在救生艇上，目送着"蓝水号"远去，他原准备在其上度过一生的。

另一边，在太空中的巨球下，海水高山静静地耸立着，仿佛亿万年来它一直就在那儿。

海面仍然很平静，波澜不惊，但冯帆感觉到了风在缓缓增强，空气已经开始向海山的低气压区聚集了。救生艇上有一面小帆，冯帆升起了它，风虽然不大，但方向正对着海山，小艇平稳地向山脚驶去。随着风力的加强，帆渐渐鼓满，小艇的速度很快增加，艇首像一把利刃划开海水，到山脚的 20 千米路程只走了 40 分钟左右。当感觉到救生艇的甲板在水坡上倾斜时，冯帆纵身一跃，跳入被外星飞船的光芒照得蓝幽幽的海中。

他成为第一个游着泳登山的人。

现在，已经看不到海山的山顶，冯帆在水中抬头望去，展现在他面前的，是一面一望无际的海水大坡，坡度有 45 度，仿佛是一个巨人把海洋的另一半在他面前掀起来一样。

冯帆用最省力的蛙式游着，想起了大副的话。他大概心算了一下，从这里到顶峰有 13 千米左右，如果是在海平面，以他的体力游出这么远是不成问题的，但现在是在爬坡，不进则退，登上顶峰几乎是不可能的，但冯帆不后悔这次努力，能攀登海水珠峰，本身已是自己登山梦想的一个超值满足了。

这时，冯帆有某种异样的感觉。他已明显地感到了海山的坡度的增加，身体越来越随着水面向上倾斜，游起来却没有感到更费力。回头一看，看到了被自己丢弃在山脚的救生艇，他离艇之前已经落下了帆，却见小艇仍然稳稳地停在水坡上，没有滑下去。他试着停止了游动，仔细观察着周围，发现自己也没有下滑，而是稳稳地浮在倾斜的水坡上！冯帆一砸脑袋，骂自己和大副都是白痴：既然水坡上呈流体状态的海水都不会下滑，上面的人和船怎么会滑下去呢？

空中巨球的引力与地球引力相互抵消，使得沿坡面方向的重力逐渐减小，这种重力的渐减抵消了坡度，使得重力对水坡上的物体并不产生使其下滑的重力分量，对于重力而言，水坡或海水高山其实是不存在的，物体在坡上的受力状态，与海平面上是一样的。

现在冯帆知道，海水高山是他的了。

冯帆继续向上游，渐渐感到游动变得更轻松了，主要是头部出水换气的动作能够轻易完成，这是因为他的身体变轻了。重力减小的其他迹象也开始显现出来，冯帆游泳时溅起的水花下落的速度变慢了，水坡上海浪起伏和行进的速度也在变慢，这时大海阳刚的一面消失了，呈现出了正常重力下不可能有的轻柔。

随着风力的增大，水坡上开始出现排浪，在低重力下，海浪的高度增加了许多，形状也发生了变化，变得薄如蝉翼，在缓慢的下落中自身翻卷起来，像一把无形的巨刨在海面上推出的一卷卷玲珑剔透的刨花。海浪并没有增加冯帆游泳的难度，浪的行进方向是向着峰顶的，推送着他向上攀游。随着重力的进一步减小，更美妙的事情发生了：薄薄的海浪不再是推送冯帆，而是将他轻轻地抛起来，有一瞬间他的身体完全离开了水面，旋即被前面的海浪接住，再抛出，他就这样被一只只轻柔而有力的海之手传递着，快速向峰顶进发。他发现，这时用蝶泳的姿势效率最高。

风继续增强，重力继续减小，水坡上的浪已超过了 10 米，但起伏的速度更慢了。由于低重力下水之间的摩擦并不剧烈，这样的巨浪居然不发出声音，只能听到风声。身体越来越轻盈的冯帆从一个浪峰跃向另一个浪峰，他突然发现，现在自己腾空的时间已大于在水中的时间，不知道自己是在游泳还是在飞翔。有几次，薄薄的巨浪把他盖住了，他发现自己进入了一个由翻滚卷曲的水膜卷成的隧道中，在他的上方，薄薄的浪膜缓缓卷动，浸透了巨球的蓝光。透过浪膜，可以看到太空中的外星飞船，巨球在浪膜后变形抖动，像是用泪眼看去一般。

冯帆看看左腕上的防水表，他已经"攀登"了一个小时，照这样出人意料的速度，最多再有这么长时间就能登顶了。

冯帆突然想到了"蓝水号"，照目前风力增长的速度看，大气旋很快就要形成，"蓝水号"无论如何也逃不出超级风暴了。他突然意识到船长犯了一个致命的错误：应该将船径直驶向海水高山，既然水坡上的重力分量不存在，"蓝水号"登上顶峰将如同在平海上行驶一样轻而易举，而峰顶就是风暴眼，是平静的！想到这里，冯帆急忙掏出救生衣上的步话机，但没人回答他的呼叫。

冯帆已经掌握了在浪尖飞跃的技术，他从一个浪峰跃向另一个浪峰，又"攀登"了20分钟左右，已经走过了三分之二的路程，浑圆的峰顶看上去不远了，它在外星飞船洒下的光芒中柔和地闪亮，像是等待着他的一个新的星球。这时，呼呼的风声突然变成了恐怖的尖啸，这声音来自所有方向。风力骤然增大，二三十米高的薄浪还没来得及落下，就在半空中被飓风撕碎，冯帆举目望去，水坡上布满了被撕碎的浪峰，像一片在风中狂舞的乱发，在巨球的照耀下发出一片炫目的白光。

冯帆进行了最后的一次飞跃，他被一道近30米高的薄浪送上半空，那道浪在他脱离的瞬间就被疾风粉碎了。他向着前方的一排巨浪缓缓下落，那排浪像透明的巨翅缓缓向上张开，似乎也在迎接他，就在冯帆的手与升上来的浪头接触的瞬间，这面晶莹的水晶巨膜在强劲的风中粉碎了，化作一片雪白的水雾，浪膜在粉碎时发出一阵很像是大笑的怪声。与此同时，冯帆已经变得很轻的身体不再下落，而是离癫狂的海面越来越远，像一片羽毛般被狂风吹向空中。

冯帆在低重力下的气流中翻滚着，晕眩中，只感到太空中发光的巨球在围绕着他旋转。当他终于能够初步稳住自己的身体时，竟然发现自己在海水高山的顶峰上空盘旋！水山表面的排排巨浪从这个高度看去像一条条长长的曲线，这些曲线标示出了旋风的形状，呈螺旋状汇聚在山顶。冯帆在空中盘旋的圈子越来越小，速度越来越快，他正在被吹向气旋的中心。

当冯帆飘进风暴眼时，风力突然减小，托着他的无形的气流之手松开了，冯帆向着海水高山的峰顶坠下去，在峰顶的正中扎入了蓝幽幽的海水中。

冯帆在水中下沉着，过了好一会儿才开始上浮，这时周围已经很暗了。当窒息的恐慌出现时，冯帆突然意识到了他所面临的危险：入水前的最后一口气是在海拔近万米的高空吸入的，含氧量很少，而在低重力下，他在水中的上浮速度很慢，即使是自己努力加速游动，肺中的空气怕也支持不到自己浮上水面。一种熟悉的感觉向他袭来，他仿佛又回到了珠峰的风暴卷起的黑色雪尘中，死的恐惧压倒了一切。就在这时，他发现身边有几个银色的圆球正在与自己一同上浮，最大的一个直径有一米左右，冯帆突然明白这些东西是气泡！低重力下的海水中有可能产生很大的气

241

泡。他奋力游向最大的气泡，将头伸过银色的泡壁，立刻能够顺畅地呼吸了！当缺氧的晕眩缓过去后，他发现自己置身于一个球形的空间中，这是他再一次进入由水围成的空间。透过气泡圆形的顶部，可以看到变形的海面波光粼粼。在上浮中，随着水压的减小，气泡在迅速增大，冯帆头顶的圆形空间开阔起来，他感觉自己是在乘着一个水晶气球升上天空。上方的蓝色波光越来越亮，最后到了刺眼的程度，随着"啪"的一声轻响，大气泡破裂，冯帆升上了海面。在低重力下他冲上了水面近一米高，再缓缓落下来。

冯帆首先看到的是周围无数缓缓飘落的美丽水球，水球大小不一，最大的有足球大小，这些水球映射着空中巨球的蓝光，细看内部还分着许多球层，显得晶莹剔透。这都是冯帆落到水面时溅起的水，在低重力下，由于表面张力而形成球状，他伸手接住一个，水球破碎时发出一种根本不可能是水所发出的清脆的金属声。

海山的峰顶十分平静，来自各个方向的浪在这里互相抵消，只留下一片碎波。这里显然是旋风的中心，是这狂躁的世界中唯一平静的地方。这平静以另一种宏大的轰鸣声为背景，那就是旋风的呼啸声。冯帆抬头望去，发现自己和海山都处于一口巨井中，巨井的井壁是由被气旋卷起的水雾构成的，这浓密的水雾在海山周围缓缓旋转着，一直延伸到高空。巨井的井口就是外星飞船，它像太空中的一盏大灯，将蓝色的光芒投到"井"内。冯帆发现那个巨球周围有一片奇怪的云，那云呈丝状，像一张松散的丝网，它们看上去很亮，像自己会发光似的。冯帆猜测，那可能是泄漏到太空中的大气所产生的冰晶云，它们看上去围绕在外星飞船周围，实际与之相距 3 万多千米。要真是这样，地球大气层的泄漏已经开始了，这口由大旋风构成的巨井，就是那个致命的漏洞。

不管怎么样，冯帆想，我登顶成功了。

二、顶峰对话

周围的光线突然发生了变化，暗了下来，闪烁着，冯帆抬头望去，看到外星飞船发出的蓝光消失了。他这时才明白那蓝光的意义：那只是一个显示屏空屏时的亮光，巨球表面就是一个显示屏。现在，巨球表面出现了一幅图像，图像是从空中俯拍的，是浮在海面上的一个人在仰望，那人就是冯帆。半分钟左右，图像消失了，冯帆明白它的含意，外星人只是表示他们看到了自己。这时，冯帆真正感到自己是站在了世界的顶峰上。

屏幕上出现了两排单词，各国文字的都有，冯帆只认出了英文的"ENGLISH"、中文的"汉语"和日文的"日语"，其他的，也显然是用地球上各种文字所标明的相应语种。有一个深色框在各个单词间快速移动，冯帆觉得这景象很熟悉。他的猜测很快得到了证实，他发现深色框的移动竟然是受自己的目光控制的！他将目光固定到"汉语"上，深色框就停在那里，他眨了一下眼，没有任何反应；应该双击，他想着，连眨了两下眼，深色框闪了一下，巨球上的语言选择菜单消失了，出现了一行很大的中文：

"你好！"

"你好！"冯帆向天空大喊，"你能听到我的声音吗？！"

"能听到，你用不着那么大声，我们连地球上的一只蚊子的声音都能听到。我们从你们行星外泄的电波中学会了这些语言，想同你随便聊聊。"

"你们从哪里来？"

巨球的表面出现了一幅静止的图像，由密密麻麻的黑点构成，复杂的细线把这些黑点连接起来，构成了一张令人目眩的大网，这分明是一幅星图。果然，其中的一个黑点发出了银光，越来越亮。冯帆什么也没看懂，但他相信这幅图像肯定已被记录下来，地球上的天文学家们应该能看懂的。巨球上又出现了文字，星图并没有消失，而是成为文字的背景，或说桌面。

"我们造了一座山，你就登上来了。"

"我喜欢登山。"冯帆说。

"这不是喜欢不喜欢的问题，我们必须登山。"

"为什么？你们的世界有很多山吗？"冯帆问，他知道这显然不是人类目前迫切要谈的话题，但他想谈，既然周围人都认为登山者是傻瓜，他只好与声称必须登山的外星人交流了，他为自己争取到了这一切。

"山无处不在，只是登法不同。"

冯帆不知道这句话是哲学比喻还是现实描述，他只能傻傻地回答："那么你们那里还是有很多山了。"

"对于我们来说，周围都是山，这山把我们封闭了，我们要挖洞才能登山。"

这话令冯帆迷惑，他想了半天也没想出是怎么回事，外星人继续说……

三、泡世界

"我们的世界十分简单，是一个球形空间，按照你们的长度单位计量，半径约为 3000 千米。这个空间被岩层所围绕，向任何一个方向走，都会遇到一堵致密的岩壁。

"我们的第一宇宙模型自然而然地建立起来了。宇宙由两部分构成：其一就是我们生存的半径为 3000 千米的球形空间；其二就是围绕着这个空间的岩层，这岩层向各个方向无限延伸。所以，我们的世界就是这固体宇宙中的一个空泡，我们称它为'泡世界'。这个宇宙理论被称为'密实宇宙论'。当然，这个理论不排除这样的可能：在无限的岩层中还有其他的空泡，离我们或近或远，这就成了以后探索的动力。"

"可是，无限厚的岩层是不可能存在的，会在引力下塌缩的。"

"我们那时不知道万有引力这回事，泡世界中没有重力，我们生活在失重状态中。真正意识到引力的存在是几万年以后的事了。"

"那这些空泡就相当于固体宇宙中的星球了？真有趣，你们的宇宙在密度分布上与真实的正好相反，像是真实宇宙的底片啊。"

"真实的宇宙？这话很浅薄，只能说是现在已知的宇宙。你们并不知道真实的宇宙是什么样子，我们也不知道。"

"那里有阳光、空气和水吗？"

"都没有，我们也都不需要。我们的世界中只有固体，没有气体和液体。"

"没有气体和液体，怎么会有生命呢？"

"我们是机械生命，肌肉和骨骼由金属构成，大脑是超高集成度的芯片，电流和磁场就是我们的血液，我们以地核中的放射性岩块为食物，靠它提供的能量生存。没有谁制造我们，这一切都是自然进化而来，由最简单的单细胞机械和放射性作用下的岩石上偶然形成的 PN 结进化而来。我们的原始祖先首先发现和使用的是电磁能，至于你们意义上的火，从来就没有发现过。"

"那里一定很黑吧？"

"亮光倒是有一些，是放射性物质在地核的内壁上产生的，那内壁就是我们的天空了。光很弱，在岩壁上游移不定，但我们也由此进化出了眼睛。地核中是失重的，我们的城市就悬浮在那昏暗的空间中，它们的大小与你们的城市差不多，远看去，像一团团发光的云。机械生命的进化时间比你们碳基生命要长得多，但我们殊途同归，都走到了对宇宙进行思考的那一天。"

"不过，这个宇宙可真够憋屈的。"

"'憋'……这是个新词语，所以，我们对广阔空间的向往比你们要强烈，早在泡世界的上古时代，向岩层深处的探险就开始了，探险者们在岩层中挖隧道前进，试图发现固体宇宙中的其他空泡。关于这些想象中的空泡，有着很多奇丽的神话，对远方其他空泡的幻想构成了泡世界文学的主体。但这种探索最初是被禁止的，违者将被短路处死。"

"是被教会禁止的吗？"

"不，没什么教会，一个看不到太阳和星空的文明是产生不了宗教的。元老院禁止隧洞探险是出于很现实的理由：我们没有你们近乎无限的空间，我们的生存空间半径只有 3000 千米。隧洞挖出的碎岩会在地核中堆积起来，由于相信有无限厚的岩层，那么隧洞就可能挖得很长，最终挖出的碎岩会把地核空间填满的！换句话说，是把地核的球形空间转换成长长的隧洞空间了。"

"好像有一个解决办法：把挖出的碎岩就放到后面已经挖好的隧洞中，只留下供探险者们容身的空间就行了。"

"后来的探险确实就是这么进行的，探险者们容身的空间其实就是一个移动的小空泡，我们把它叫作'泡船'。但即使这样，仍然有相当于泡船空间的一堆碎石进入地核空间，只有等待泡船返回时这堆碎石才能重新填回岩壁，如果泡船有去无回，那么这小堆碎石占据的地核空间就无法恢复了，就相当于这一小块空间被泡船偷走了，所以探险者们又被称为'空间窃贼'。对于那个狭小的世界，这么一点点空间也是宝贵的，天长日久，随着一艘艘泡船的离去，被占据的空间也很巨大。所以泡船探险在远古时代也是被禁止的。同时，泡船探险是一项十分艰难的活动，一般的泡船中都有若干名挖掘手和一名领航员，那时还没有掘进机，只能靠挖掘手（相当于你们船上的桨手）使用简单的工具不停挖掘，泡船才能在岩层中以极其缓慢的速度前进。在一个刚能容身的小小空洞里机器般劳作，在幽闭中追寻着渺茫的希望，无疑需要巨大的精神力量。由于泡船的返回一般是沿着已经挖松的来路，所以相对容易些，但赌徒般的发现欲望往往驱使探险者越过安全的折返点，继续向前，这时，返回的体力和给养都不够了，泡船就会搁浅在返途中，成为探险者的坟墓。尽管如此，泡世界向外界的探险虽然规模很小，但从未停止过。"

四、哈勃红移

　　"在泡纪元 33281 年的一天（这是按地球纪年法，泡世界的纪年十分古怪，你理解不了），泡世界的岩层天空上突然出现了一个小小的洞，从洞中飞出的一堆碎岩在空中飘浮着，在放射性物质产生的微光中像一群闪烁的星星。中心城市的一队士兵立刻向小破洞飞去（记住泡世界是没有重力的），发现这是一艘返回的探险泡船，它在 8 年前就出发了，谁也没有想到竟能回来。这艘泡船叫'针尖号'，它在岩层中前进了 200 千米，创造了返回泡船航行距离的纪录。'针尖号'出发时有 20 名船员，但返回时只剩随船科学家一人了，我们就叫他哥白尼吧。船上其余的人，包括船长，都被哥白尼当食物吃掉了。事实上，这种把船员当给养的方式，是地层探险早期效率最高的航行方式。

　　"按照严禁泡船探险的法律，以及哥白尼吃人的行为，他将在世界首都被处死。这天，几十万人聚集在行刑的中心广场上，等着观赏哥白尼被短路时美妙的电火花。但就在这时，世界科学院的一群科学家飘过来，公布了他们的一个重大发现：'针尖号'带回了沿途各段的岩石标本，科学家们发现，地层岩石的密度，竟是随着航行距离减小的！"

　　"你们的世界没有重力，怎么测定密度呢？"

　　"通过惯性，比你们要复杂一些。科学家们最初认为，这只是由于'针尖号'偶然进入了一个不均匀的地层区域。但在以后的一个世纪中，在不同方向上，有多艘泡船以超过'针尖号'的航行距离深入地层并返回，带回了岩石标本。人们震惊地发现，所有方向上的地层密度都是沿向外的方向渐减的，而且减幅基本一致！这个发现，动摇了统治泡世界两万多年的密实宇宙论。如果宇宙密度以泡世界为核心呈这样的递减分布，那总有密度减到零的距离，科学家们依照已测得的递减率，很容易计算出，这个距离是 3 万千米左右。"

"嘿，这很像我们的哈勃红移啊！"

"是很像，你们想象不出红移速度能够大于光速，所以把那个距离定为宇宙边缘。而我们的先祖却很容易知道密度为零的状态就是空间，于是新的宇宙模型诞生了，在这个模型中，沿泡世界向外，宇宙的密度逐渐减小，直至淡化为空间，这空间延续至无限。这个理论被称为'太空宇宙论'。

"密实宇宙论是很顽固的，它的占优势地位的拥护者推出了一个打了补丁的密实宇宙论，认为密度的递减只是由于泡世界周围包裹着一层较疏松的球层，穿过这个球层，密度的递减就会停止。他们甚至计算出了这个疏松球层的厚度是 300 千米。其实对这个理论进行证实或证伪并不难，只要有一艘泡船穿过 300 千米的岩层就行了。事实上，这个航行距离很快就达到了，但地层密度的递减趋势仍在继续。于是，密实宇宙论的拥护者又说前面的计算有误，疏松球层的厚度应是 500 千米，10 年后，这个距离也被突破了，密度的递减仍在继续，而且单位距离的递减率有增加的趋势。密实派们接着把疏松球层的厚度增加到 1500 千米……

"后来，一个划时代的伟大发现将密实宇宙论永远送进了坟墓。"

五、万有引力

"那艘深入岩层 300 千米的泡船叫'圆刀号',它是有史以来最大的探险泡船,配备有大功率挖掘机和完善的生存保障系统,因而它向地层深处的航行距离创造了纪录。

"在到达 300 千米的深度(或说高度)时,船上的首席科学家(我们叫他牛顿吧)向船长反映了一件不可思议的事:当船员们悬浮在泡船中央睡觉时,醒来后总是躺在靠向泡世界方向的洞壁上。

"船长不以为意地说:'思乡梦游症而已。他们想回家,所以睡梦中总是向着家的方向移动。'

"但泡船中与泡世界一样是没有空气的,要移动身体有两种方式:一种是蹬踏船壁,这在悬空睡觉时是不可能的;另一种是喷出自己体内的排泄物作为驱动,但牛顿没有发现这类迹象。

"船长仍对牛顿的话不以为然,但这个疏忽使他自己差点儿被活埋了。这天,向前的挖掘告一段落,由于船员十分疲劳,挖出的一堆碎岩没有立刻运到船底,大家就休息了,想等睡醒后再运。船长也与大家一样在船的正中央悬空睡觉,醒来后发现自己与其他船员一起被埋在碎岩中!原来,在他们睡觉时,船首的碎岩与他们一起移到了靠向泡世界方向的船底!牛顿很快发现,船舱中的所有物体都有向泡世界方向移动的趋势,只是它们移动得太慢,平时觉察不出来而已。"

"于是牛顿没有借助苹果就发现了万有引力!"

"哪有那么容易?!在我们的科学史上,万有引力理论的诞生比你们要艰难得多,这是我们所处的环境决定的。当牛顿发现船中的物体定向移动现象时，想当然地认为引力来自泡世界那半径3000千米的空间。于是，早期的引力理论出现了让人哭笑不得的谬误：认为产生引力的不是质量，而是空间。"

"能想象，在那样复杂的物理环境中，你们牛顿的思维任务比我们的牛顿可要复杂多了。"

"是的，直到半个世纪后，科学家们才拨开迷雾，真正认清了引力的本质，并用与你们相似的仪器测定了万有引力常数。引力理论获得承认也经历了一个漫长的过程。但一旦意识到引力的存在，密实宇宙论就完了，引力是不允许无限固体宇宙存在的。

"太空宇宙论得到最终承认后，它所描述的宇宙对泡世界产生了巨大的诱惑力。在泡世界，守恒的物理量除了能量和质量外，还有一个：空间。泡世界的空间半径只有3000千米，在岩层中挖洞增大不了空间，只是改变空间的位置和形状而已。同时，由于失重，地核文明是悬浮在空间中，而不是附着在洞壁（相当于你们的土地）上的，所以在泡世界，空间是最宝贵的东西，整个泡世界文明史，就是一部血腥的空间争夺史。而现在惊闻空间可能是无限的，怎能不令人激动？于是出现了前所未有的探险浪潮，数量众多的泡船穿过地层向外挺进，企图穿过太空宇宙论预言的3.2万千米的岩层，到达密度为0的天堂。"

六、地核世界

"说到这里，如果你足够聪明，应该能够推测出泡世界的真相了。"

"你们的世界，是不是位于一个星球的地心？"

"正确，我们的行星大小与地球差不多，半径约 8000 千米。但这颗行星的地核是空的，空核的半径约为 3000 千米，我们就是地核中的生物。

"不过，发现万有引力后，我们还要过许多个世纪才能最后明白自己世界的真相。"

七、地层战争

"太空宇宙论建立后，追寻外部无限空间的第一个代价却是消耗了泡世界的有限空间，众多的泡船把大量的碎岩排入地核空间，这些碎岩悬浮在城市周围，密密麻麻，无边无际，以至于原来可以自由飘移的城市动弹不得，因为城市一旦移动，就将遭遇毁灭性的密集石雨。这些被碎岩占掉的空间，至少有一半永远无法恢复。

"这时的元老院已由世界政府代替，作为地核空间的管理者和保卫者，疯狂的泡船探险受到了政府严厉的镇压。但最初这种镇压效率并不高，因为当得知探险行为发生时，泡船早已深入地层了。所以政府很快意识到，制止泡船的最好工具就是泡船。于是，政府开始建立庞大的泡船舰队，深入岩层拦截探险泡船，追回被它们盗走的空间。这种拦截行动自然遭到了探险泡船的抵抗，于是，地层中爆发了一场旷日持久的战争。"

"这种战争真的很有意思！"

"也很残酷。首先，地层战争的节奏十分缓慢，因为以那个时代的掘进技术，泡船在地层中的航行速度一般只有每小时 3000 米左右。地层战争推崇巨舰主义，因为泡船越大，续航能力越强，攻击力也更强大。但不管多大的地层战舰，其横截面都应尽可能地小，这样可以将挖掘截面减到最小，以提高航行速度。所以所有泡船的横截面都是一样的，大小只在于其长短。大型战舰的形状就是一条长长的隧道。由于地层战场是三维的，所以其作战方式类似于你们的空战，但要复杂得多。当战舰接触敌舰发起攻击时，首先要快速扩大舰首截面，以增大攻击面积，这时的攻击舰就变成了一根钉子的形状。必要时，泡舰的舰首还可以形成多个分支，像一只张开的利爪那样，从多个方向攻击敌舰。地层作战的复杂性还表现在：每一艘战舰都可以随意分解成许多小舰，多艘战舰又可以快速组合成一艘巨舰。所以当两支敌对的舰队相遇时，是分解还是组合，是一门很深的战术学问。

"地层战争对于未来的探险并非只有负面作用，事实上，在战争的刺激下，泡世界发生了技术革命。除了高效率的掘进机器外，泡世界还发明了地震波仪，它既可用于地层中的通信，又可用作雷达探测，强力的震波还可作为武器。最精致的震波通信设备甚至可以传送图像。

"地层中曾出现过的最大战舰是'线世界号'，它是由世界政府建造的。当处于常规航行截面时，'线世界号'的长度达 150 千米，正如舰名称所示，相当于一个长长的小世界了。身处其中，有置身于你们的英伦海底隧道的感觉，每隔几分钟，隧道中就有一列高速列车驶过，这是向舰尾运送掘进碎石的专列。'线世界号'当然可以分解成一支庞大的舰队，但它大部分时间还是以整体航行的。'线世界号'并非总是呈直线形状，在进行机动航行时，它那长长的舰体隧道可能形成一团自相贯通或交叉的十分复杂的曲线。'线世界号'拥有最先进的掘进机，巡航速度是普通泡舰的一倍，达到每小时 6 千米，作战速度可以超过每小时 10 千米！它还拥有超高功率的震波雷达，能够准确定位 500 千米外的泡船；它的震波武器可以在 1000 米的距离上粉碎目标泡船内的一切。这艘超级巨舰在广阔的地层中纵横驰骋，所向披靡，消灭了大量的探险泡船，并每隔一段时间将吞并的探险泡船空间送还泡世界。

"在'线世界号'的毁灭性打击下，泡世界向外部的探险一度濒于停顿。在地层战争中，探险者们始终处于劣势，他们不能建造或组合长于 10 千米的战舰，因为在地层中这样的目标极易被'线世界号'上或泡世界基地中的雷达探测定位，进而被迅速消灭。但要使探险事业继续下去，就必须消灭'线世界号'。经过长时间的筹划，探险联盟集结了 100 多艘地层战舰围歼'线世界号'，这些战舰中最长的也只有 5 千米。战斗在泡世界向外 1500 千米处展开，史称'1500 千米战役'。

"探险联盟首先调集 20 艘战舰，在 1500 千米处组合成一艘长达 30 千米的巨舰，引诱'线世界号'前往攻击。当'线世界号'接近诱饵，呈一条直线高速冲向目标时，探险联盟埋伏在周围的上百艘战舰沿与'线世界号'垂直的方向同时出击，将这艘 150 千米长的巨舰截为 50 段。'线世界号'被截断后分裂出来的 50 艘战舰仍具有很强的战斗力，双方的 200 多艘战舰缠斗在一起，在地层中展开了惨烈的大混战。战舰空间在不断地组合分化，渐渐已分不清彼此。在战役的最后阶段，半径为 200 千米的战场已成了蜂窝状，就在这个处于星球地下 3500 千米深处的错综复杂的三维迷宫中，到处都是短兵相接的激战。在这个位置，星球的重力已经很明显，而与政府军相比，探险者对重力环境更为熟悉。在迷宫内宏大的巷战中，这微弱的优势渐渐起了决定性的作用，探险联盟取得了最后胜利。"

八、海

"战役结束后，探险者联盟将战场的所有空间合为一体，形成了一个半径为 50 千米的球形空间。就在这个空间中，探险联盟宣布脱离泡世界独立。独立后的探险联盟与泡世界的探险运动遥相呼应，不断地有探险泡船从地核来到联盟，它们带来的空间使联盟领土的体积不断增大，使探险者们在 1500 千米的高度获得了一个前进基地。被漫长的战争拖得筋疲力尽的世界政府再也无力阻止这一切，只得承认探险运动的合法性。

"随着高度的增加，地层的密度也逐渐降低，使得掘进变得容易了；另外重力的增加也使碎岩的处理更加方便。以后的探险变得顺利了许多。在战后第 8 年，就有一艘名叫'螺旋号'的探险泡船走完了剩下的 3500 千米航程，到达了距泡世界边缘——也就是距星球中心 8000 千米，距泡世界边缘 5000 千米的高度。"

"哇，那就是到达星球的表面了！你们看到了大平原和真正的山脉，这太激动人心了！"

"没什么可激动的，'螺旋号'到达的是海底。"

"……"

"当时，震波通信仪的图像摇了几下就消失了，通信完全中断。在更低高度的其他泡船监听到了一个声音，转换成你们的空气声音就是'啵'的一声，这是高压海水在瞬间涌入'螺旋号'空间时发出的。泡世界的机械生命和船上的仪器设备是绝对不能与水接触的，短路产生的强大电流迅速汽化了渗入人体和机器内部的海水，'螺旋号'的乘员和设备在海水涌入的瞬间都像炸弹一样爆裂了。

"接着，联盟又向不同的方向发出了10多艘探险泡船，但都在同样的高度遇到了同样的事情。除了那神秘的'啵'的一声，再没有传回更多的信息。有两次，人们在监视屏幕上看到了怪异的晶状波动，但不知道那是什么。跟随的泡船向上方发出的雷达震波也传回了完全不可理解的回波，那回波的性质既不是空间也不是岩层。

"一时间，太空宇宙论动摇了，学术界又开始谈论新的宇宙模型，新的理论将宇宙半径确定为8000千米，认为那些消失的探险船接触了宇宙的边缘，没入了虚无。

"探险运动面临着严峻的考验，以往无法返回的探险泡船所占用的空间，从理论上说还是有希望回收的。但现在，泡船一旦接触宇宙边缘，其空间可能就永远损失了。到这一步，连最坚定的探险者都动摇了，因为在这个地层中的世界，空间是不可再生的。联盟决定，再派出最后5艘探险泡船，在接近5千米的高度时以极慢速上升。如果发生同样的不测，就暂停探险运动。

"又损失了两艘泡船后，第三艘'岩脑号'取得了突破性的进展。在5千米的高度上，'岩脑号'以极慢的速度小心翼翼地向上掘进，接近海底时，海水并没有像以前那样压塌船顶的岩层瞬间涌入，而是通过岩层上的一道窄裂缝呈一条高压射流喷射进来。'岩脑号'在航行截面上长 250 米，在高地层探险船中算是体积较大的，喷射进来的海水用了近一小时才充满船的空间。在触水爆裂前，船上的震波仪记录了海水的形态，并将数据和图像完整地发回联盟。就这样，地核人第一次见到了液体。

"泡世界的远古时代可能存在过液体，那是炽热的岩浆，后来星球的地质情况稳定了，岩浆凝固，地核中就只有固体了。有科学家曾从理论上预言过液体的存在，但没人相信宇宙中真有那种神话般的物质。现在，从传回的图像中人们亲眼看到了液体。他们震惊地看着那道白色的射流，看着水面在船内空间缓缓上升，看着这种似乎违反所有物理法则的魔鬼物质适应着它的附着物的任何形状，渗入每一道最细微的缝隙；岩石表面接触它后似乎改变了性质，颜色变深了，反光性增强了。最让他们感兴趣的是：大部分物体都会沉入这种物质中，但有部分爆裂的人体和机器碎片却能浮在其液面上！而这些碎片的性质与那些沉下去的没有任何区别。地核人给这种液体物质起了一个名字，叫'无形岩'。

"以后的探索就比较顺利了。探险联盟的工程师们设计了一种叫'引管'的东西，这是一根长达 200 米的空心钻杆，当钻透岩层后，钻头可以像盖子那样打开，以将海水引入管内，管子的底部有一个阀门。携带引管和钻机的泡船上升至 5 千米高度后，引管很顺利地钻透岩层伸入海底。钻探毕竟是地核人最熟悉的技术，但对另一项技术他们却一无所知，那就是密封。由于泡世界中没有液体和气体，所以也没有密封技术。引管底部的阀门很不严实，没有打开海水就已经漏了出来。

"事后证明这是一种幸运，因为如果将阀门完全打开，冲入的高压海水的动能将远大于上次从细小的裂缝中渗入的，那道高压射流会像一道激光那样切断所遇到的一切。现在从关闭的阀门渗入的水流却是可以控制的。你可以想象，泡船中的探险者们看着那一道道细细的海水在他们眼前喷出，是何等震撼啊。他们这时对于液体，就像你们的原始人对于电流那样无知。在用一个金属容器小心翼翼地接满一桶水后，泡船下降，将那根引管埋在岩层中。

"在下降的过程中，探险者们万分谨慎地守护着那桶作为研究标本的海水，很快又有了一个新的发现：无形岩居然是透明的！上次裂缝中渗入的海水由于混入了沙土，使他们没有发现这一点。随着泡船下降深度的增加，温度也在增加，探险者们恐怖地看到，无形岩竟是一种生命体！它在活过来，表面愤怒地翻滚着，呈现由无数涌泡构成的可怕形态。但这怪物在展现生命力的同时也在消耗着自己，化作一种幽灵般的白色影子消失在空中。当桶中的无形岩都化作白色魔影消失后，船舱中的探险者们相继感到了身体的异常，短路的电火花在他们体内闪烁，最后他们都变成了一团团焰火，痛苦地死去。联盟基地中的人们通过监视器传回的震波图像看到了这可怕的情景，但监视器也很快短路停机了。前去接应的泡船也遭遇了同样的命运，在与下降的泡船对接后，接应泡船中的乘员也同样短路而死，仿佛无形岩化作了一种充满所有空间的死神。

"但科学家们也发现，这一次的短路没有上一次那么剧烈，他们得出结论：随着空间体积的增加，无形死神的密度也在降低。接下来，在付出了更多的生命代价后，地核人终于又发现了一种他们从未接触过的物质形态：气体。"

九、星空

"这一系列的重大发现终于打动了泡世界的政府，使其与昔日的敌人联合起来，也投身于探险事业之中，一时间对探险的投入急剧增加，最后的突破就在眼前。

"虽然对水蒸气的性质有了越来越多的了解，但缺乏密封技术的地核科学家一时还无法避免它对地核人生命和仪器设备的伤害。不过他们已经知道，在4500米以上的高度，无形岩是死的，不会沸腾。于是，地核政府和探险联盟一起在4800米高度上建造了一所实验室，装配了更长、性能更好的引管，专门进行无形岩的研究。"

"直到这时，你们才开始做阿基米德的工作。"

"是的，可你不要忘记，我们在原始时代，就做了法拉第的工作。

"在无形岩实验室中，科学家们相继发现了水压和浮力定律，同时与液体有关的密封技术也得以发展和完善。人们终于发现，在无形岩中航行，其实是一件十分简单的事，比在地层中航行要容易得多。只要船体的密封和耐压性达到要求，不需任何挖掘，船就可以在无形岩中以令人难以想象的高速度上升。"

"这就是泡世界的火箭了。"

"应该称作水箭。水箭是一个耐高压的蛋形金属容器，没有任何动力设施，内部仅可乘坐一名探险者，我们就叫他泡世界的'加加林'吧。水箭的发射平台位于5千米的高度，是在地层中挖出的一个宽敞的大厅。在发射前的一小时，加加林进入水箭，关上了密封舱门。确定所有仪器和生命维持系统正常后，自动掘进机破坏了大厅顶部厚度不到 10 米的薄岩层，轰隆一声，岩层在上方无形岩的巨大压力下坍塌了，水箭浸没于深海的无形岩之中。周围的尘埃落定后，加加林透过由金刚石制造的透明舷窗，惊奇地发现发射平台上的两盏探照灯在无形岩中打出了两道光柱，由于泡世界中没有空气，光线不会散射，这时地核人第一次看到了光的形状。震波仪传来了发射命令，加加林扳动手柄，松开了将水箭锚固在底部岩层上的铰链，水箭缓缓升离了海底，在无形岩中很快加速，向上浮去。

"科学家们按照海底压力，很容易就计算出了上方无形岩的厚度，约 10000 米，如无意外，上浮的水箭能够在 15 分钟内走完这段航程，但以后会遇到什么，谁都不知道。

"水箭在一片寂静中上升着，透过舷窗看出去，只有深不见底的黑暗。偶尔有几粒悬浮在无形岩中的尘埃在舷窗透出的光亮中飞速掠过，标示着水箭上升的速度。

"加加林很快感到一阵恐慌，他是生活在固体世界中的生命，现在第一次进入了无形岩的空间，一种无依无靠的虚无感攫住了他的全部身心。15 分钟的航程是那么漫长，它浓缩了地核文明 10 万年的探索历程，仿佛永无止境……就在加加林的精神即将崩溃之际，水箭浮上了这颗行星的海面。

"上浮惯性使水箭冲上了距海面十几米的空中，在下落的过程中，加加林从舷窗中看到了下方无形岩一望无际的广阔表面，这巨大的平面上波光粼粼，加加林并没有时间去想这表面反射的光来自哪里。水箭重重地落在海面上，飞溅的无形岩白花花的一片洒落在周围，水箭像船一样平稳地浮在海面上，随波浪轻轻起伏着。

"加加林小心翼翼地打开舱门，慢慢探出身去，立刻感到了海风的吹拂，过了好一阵儿，他才悟出这是气体。恐惧使他战栗了一下，他曾在实验室中的金刚石管道中看到过水汽的流动，但宇宙中竟然有如此巨量的气体存在，是任何人都始料未及的。加加林很快发现，这种气体与无形岩沸腾后转化的那种不同，不会导致肌体的短路。他在以后的回忆录中有过一段这样的描述：

'我感到这是一只无形的巨手温柔的抚摩，这巨手来自一个我们不知道的无限巨大的存在，在这个存在面前，我变成了另一个全新的我。'

"加加林抬头望去，这时，地核文明 10 万年的探索得到了最后的报偿。

"他看到了灿烂的星空。"

十、山无处不在

"真是不容易，你们经历了那么长时间的探索，才站到我们的起点上。"冯帆赞叹道。

"所以，你们是一个很幸运的文明。"

这时，逃逸到太空中的大气形成的冰晶云面积扩大了很多，天空一片晶亮，外星飞船的光芒在冰晶云中散射出一圈绚丽的彩虹。下面，大气旋形成的巨井仍在轰隆隆地旋转着，像是一台超级机器在一点点碾碎着这个星球。而周围的山顶却更加平静，连碎波都没有了，海面如镜，又让冯帆想起了藏北的高山湖泊……冯帆强迫自己使思想回到了现实。

"你们到这里来干什么？"他问。

"我们只是路过，看到这里有智慧文明，就想找人聊聊，谁先登上这座山顶我们就和谁聊。"

"山在那儿，总会有人去登的。"

"是，登山是智慧生物的一个本性，他们都想站得更高些，看得更远些，这并不是生存的需要。比如你，如果为了生存就会远远逃离这山，可你却登上来了。进化赋予智慧文明登高的欲望是有更深的原因的，这原因是什么我们还不知道。山无处不在，我们都还在山脚下。"

"我在山顶上。"冯帆说，他不容别人挑战自己登上世界最高峰的荣誉，即使是外星人。

"你在山脚下，我们都在山脚。光速是一个山脚，空间的三维是一个山脚，被禁锢在光速和三维这狭窄的时空深谷中，你不觉得……憋屈吗？"

"生来就这样，习惯了。"

"那么，我下面要说的事你会很不习惯的。看看这个宇宙，你感觉到什么？"

"广阔啊，无限啊，这类的。"

"你不觉得憋屈吗？"

"怎么会呢？宇宙在我眼里是无限的，在科学家们眼里，好像也有 200 亿光年呢。"

"那我告诉你，这是一个半径为 200 亿光年的泡世界。"

"……"

"我们的宇宙是一个空泡，一块更大固体中的空泡。"

"怎么可能呢？这块大固体不会因引力而坍缩吗？"

"至少目前还没有，我们这个气泡还在超固体块中膨胀着。引力引起坍缩是对有限的固体块而言的，如果包裹我们宇宙的这个固体块是无限的，就不存在坍缩问题。当然，这只是一种猜测，谁也不知道那个固体超宇宙是不是有限的。有许多种猜测，比如，认为引力在更大的尺度上被另一种力抵消，就像电磁力在微观尺度上被核力抵消一样，我们意识不到这种力，就像处于泡世界中意识不到万有引力一样。从我们收集到的资料上看，对于宇宙的气泡形状，你们的科学家也有所猜测，只是你不知道罢了。"

"那块大固体是什么样子的？也是……岩层吗？"

"不知道，5万年后我们到达目的地时才能知道。"

"你们要去哪里？"

"宇宙边缘，我们是一艘泡船，叫'针尖号'，记得这名字吗？"

"记得，它是泡世界中首先发现地层密度递减规律的泡船。"

"对，不知我们能发现什么。"

"超固体宇宙中还有其他的空泡吗？"

"你已经想得很远了。"

"这让人不能不想。"

"想想一块巨岩中的几个小泡泡，就是有，找到它们也很难，但我们这就去找。"

"你们真的很伟大。"

"好了，聊得很愉快，但我们还要赶路，5万年太久，只争朝夕。认识你很高兴，记往，山无处不在。"

由于冰晶云的遮挡，最后这行字已经很模糊。接着，太空中的巨型屏幕渐渐暗了下来，巨球本身也在变小，很快缩成一点，重新变成星海中一颗不起眼的星星，这变化比它出现时要快许多。这颗星星在夜空中疾驶而去，转眼消失在西方天际。

海天之间黑了下来，冰晶云和风暴巨井都看不见了，天空中只有一片黑暗的混沌。冯帆听到周围风暴的轰鸣声在迅速减小，很快变成了低声的呜咽，再往后完全消失了，只能听到海浪的声音。

冯帆有了下坠的感觉，他看到周围的海面正在缓缓地改变着形状，海山浑圆的山顶在变平，像一把在撑开的巨伞一样。他知道，海水高山正在消失，他正在由9000米高空向海平面坠落。在他的感觉中只有两三分钟，他漂浮的海面就停止了下降，他知道这点，是由于自己身体下降的惯性使他没入了已停降的海面之下，好在这次沉得并不深，他很快就游了上来。

周围已是正常的海面，海水高山消失得无影无踪，仿佛从来就没有存在过一样。风暴也完全停止了，风暴强度虽大但持续时间很短，只是刮起了表层浪，所以海面也很快平静下来。

天空中的冰晶云已经散去很多，灿烂的星空再次出现了。

冯帆仰望着星空，想象着那个遥远的世界，真的太远了，连光都会走得疲惫，那又是很早以前，在那个海面上，泡世界的加加林也像他现在这样仰望着星空。穿越广漠的时空荒漠，他们的灵魂相通了。

冯帆一阵恶心吐出了些什么，凭嘴里的味道他知道是血，他在9000米高的海山顶峰得了高山病，肺水肿出血了，这很危险。在突然增加的重力下，他虚弱得动弹不得，只是靠救生衣把自己托在水面上。不知道"蓝水号"现在的命运，但基本上可以肯定，方圆1000千米内没有船了。

在登上海山顶峰的时候，冯帆感觉此生足矣，那时他可以从容地去死。但现在，他突然变成了世界上最怕死的人。他攀登过岩石的世界屋脊，这次又登上了由海水构成的世界最高峰，下次会登什么样的山呢？这无论如何得活下去才能知道。几年前在珠峰雪暴中的感觉又回来了，那感觉曾使他割断了连接同伴和恋人的登山索，将他们送进了死亡世界，现在他知道自己做对了。如果现在真有什么可背叛的东西来拯救自己的生命，他会背叛的。

　　他必须活下去，因为山无处不在。

WITH HER EYES
CIXIN LIU

TRANSLATED BY JOEL MARTINSEN ET AL.

北京联合出版公司
Beijing United Publishing Co.,Ltd.

CONTENTS

Sea of Dreams _1

Cloud of Poems _35

Ode to Joy _69

With Her Eyes _95

Fire in the Earth _113

The Thinker _151

Devourer _171

Mountain _215

梦之海

SEA OF DREAMS

TRANSLATED BY JOHN CHU

朱中宜 — 译

First Half

The Low-Temperature Artist

It was the Ice and Snow Arts Festival that lured the low-temperature artist here. The idea was absurd, but once the oceans had dried, this was how Yan Dong always thought of it. No matter how many years passed by, the scene when the low-temperature artist arrived remained clear in his[1] mind.

At the time, Yan Dong was standing in front of his own ice sculpture, which he'd just completed. Exquisitely carved ice sculptures surrounded him. In the distance, lofty ice structures towered over a snowfield. These sparkling and translucent skyscrapers and castles were steeped in the winter sun. They were short-lived works of art. Soon, this glittering world would become a pool of clear water in the spring breeze. People were sad to see them melt but the process embodied many of life's ineffable mysteries. This, perhaps, was the real reason why Yan Dong clung dearly to the ice and snow arts.

Yan Dong tore his gaze away from his own work, determined not to look at it again before the judges named the winners. He sighed, then glanced at the sky. It was at this moment that he saw the low-temperature artist for the first time.

Initially, he thought it was a plane dragging a white vapor trail behind it, but the flying object was much faster than a plane. It swept a great arc through the air. The vapor trail, like a giant piece of chalk, drew a hook in

---

1　英文版对主人公性别进行了转换，本版遵循原文进行了修订。

the blue sky. The flying object suddenly stopped high in the air right above Yan Dong. The vapor trail gradually disappeared from its tail to its head, as though the flying object were inhaling it back in.

Yan Dong studied the bit of the vapor trail that was the last to disappear. It was flickering oddly, and he decided it had to be from something reflecting the sunlight. He then saw what *it* was—a small, ash-gray spheroid. Then quickly realized that the spheroid wasn't small—it looked small in the distance, but was now expanding rapidly. The spheroid was falling right toward him, it seemed, and from an incredibly high altitude. When the people around him realized this, they fled in all directions. Yan Dong also ducked his head and ran, darting in and around the ice sculptures.

An enormous shadow hung over the area, and for a moment, Yan Dong's blood seemed to freeze. The expected impact never came, though. The artists and judges and festival spectators stopped running. They gazed upward, dumbstruck. He looked up, too. The massive gray spheroid floated a hundred meters over their heads. It wasn't wholly spheroid, as if the vapor expelled during its high-speed flight had warped its shape. The half in the direction of its flight was smooth, glossy, and round. The other half sprouted a large sheaf of hair, making it look like a comet whose tail had been trimmed. It was massive, well over one hundred meters in diameter, a mountain suspended in midair. Its presence felt oppressive to everyone beneath it.

After the spheroid halted, the air that had driven it charged the ground, sending up a rapidly expanding ring of dirt and snow. It's said that when people touched something they didn't expect to be as cold as an ice cube, it'd feel so hot that they'd shout as their hand recoiled. In the instant that the mass of air fell on him, that's how Yan Dong felt. Even someone from the bitterly cold Northeast would have felt the same way. Fortunately, the air diffused quickly, or else everyone on the ground would have frozen stiff. Even so, practically everyone with exposed skin suffered some frostbite.

Yan Dong's face was numb from the sudden cold. He looked up, transfixed by the spheroid's surface. It was made of a translucent ash-gray substance he recognized intimately: ice. This object suspended in the air was a giant ball of ice.

Once the air settled, large snowflakes were fluttering around the floating mountain of ice. An oddly pure white against the blue sky, they glittered in the sunlight. However, these snowflakes were only visible within a certain distance around the spheroid. When they floated farther away, they dissolved. They formed a snow ring with the spheroid as its center, as though the spheroid were a streetlamp lighting the snowflakes around it on a cold night.

'I am a low-temperature artist!' a clear, sharp voice emitted from the ball of ice. 'I am a low-temperature artist!'

'This ball of ice is you?' Yan Dong shouted back.

'You can't see my true form. The ball of ice you see is formed by my freeze field from the moisture in the air,' the low-temperature artist replied.

'What about those snowflakes?'

'They are crystals of the oxygen and nitrogen in the air. In addition, there's dry ice formed from the carbon dioxide.'

'Wow. Your freeze field is so powerful!'

'Of course. It's like countless tiny hands holding countless tiny hearts tight. It forces all the molecules and atoms within its range to stop moving.'

'It can also lift this gigantic ball of ice into the air?'

'That's a different kind of field, the antigravity field. The ice-sculpting tools you all use are so fascinating. You have small shovels and small chisels of every shape. Not to mention watering cans and blowtorches. Fascinating! To make low-temperature works of art, I also have a set of tiny tools. They are various types of force fields. Not as many tools as you have, but they work extremely well.'

'You create ice sculptures, too?'

'Of course. I'm a low-temperature artist. Your world is extremely suitable for the ice-and-snow-molding arts. I was shocked to discover they've long existed in this world. I'm thrilled to say that we're colleagues.'

'Where do you come from?' the ice sculptor next to Yan Dong asked.

'I come from a faraway place, a world you have no way to understand. That world is not nearly as interesting as yours. Originally, I focused solely on the art. I didn't interact with other worlds. However, seeing exhibitions like this one, seeing so many colleagues, I found the desire to interact. But, frankly, very few of the low-temperature works below me deserve to be called works of art.'

'Why?' someone asked.

'Excessively realistic, too reliant on form and detail. Besides space, there's nothing in the universe. The actual world is just a big pile of curved spaces. Once you understand this, you'll see how risible these works are. However, hm, this piece moves me a little.'

Just as the voice faded away, a delicate thread extended from the snowflakes around the ball of ice, as if it flowed down following an invisible funnel. The snowflake thread stretched from midair to the top of Yan Dong's ice sculpture before dissolving. Yan Dong stood on his tiptoes, and tentatively stretched a gloved hand toward the snowflake thread. As he neared it, his fingers felt that burning sensation again. He jerked his hand back, but it was already painfully cold inside the glove.

'Are you pointing to my work?' Yan Dong rubbed his frozen hand with the other. 'I, I didn't use traditional methods. That is, carve it from ready-made blocks of ice. Instead, I built a structure composed of several large membranes. For a long time, steam produced from boiling water rose from the bottom of the structure. The steam froze to the membrane, forming a complex crystal. Once the crystal grew thick enough, I got rid of the membrane and the result is what you see here.'

'Very good. So interesting. It so expresses the beauty of the cold. The inspiration for this work comes from . . .'

'Windowpanes! I don't know whether you will be able to understand my description: When you wake during a hard winter's night just before sunrise, your bleary gaze falls on the windowpane filled with crystals. They reflect the dark blue first light of early dawn, as though they were something you dreamed up overnight. . . .'

'Yes, yes, I understand!' The snowflakes around the low-temperature artist danced in a lively pattern. 'I have been inspired. I want to create! I must create!'

'The Songhua River is that way. You can select a block of ice, or . . .'

'What? Your form of art is as pitiable as bacteria. Do you think my form of low-temperature art is anything like that? This place doesn't have the sort of ice I need.'

The ice sculptors on the ground looked bewildered at the interstellar low-temperature artist. Yan Dong said, blankly, 'Then, you want to go . . .'

'I want to go to the ocean!'

Collecting Ice

An immense fleet of airplanes flew at an altitude of five kilometers along the coastline. This was the most motley collection of airplanes in history. It was composed of all types, ranging from Boeing jumbo jets to mosquito-like light aircraft. Every major press service in the world had dispatched news planes. In addition, research organizations and governments had dispatched observation planes. This chaotic air armada trailed closely behind a short wake of thick white vapor, like a flock of sheep chasing after its shepherd. The wake was left by the low-temperature artist. It constantly urged the planes behind it to fly faster. To wait for them, it had to endure a rate of flight slower than crawling. (For someone who jumped through space-time at will, light speed was already crawling.) The whole way, it grumbled that this pace would kill its inspiration.

In the airplanes behind it, reporters rattled away, asking endless questions over the radio. The low-temperature artist had no desire to answer any of them. It was only interested in talking to Yan Dong, sitting in the Harbin Y-12 that China Central Television had rented. As a result, the reporters grew quiet. They listened carefully to the conversation between the two artists.

'Is your home within the Milky Way?' Yan Dong asked. The Harbin Y-12 was the plane closest to the low-temperature artist. He could see the flying ball of ice intermittently through the white vapor. This wake trailing it was formed from oxygen, nitrogen, and carbon dioxide in the atmosphere condensing in the ultralow temperatures around the ice ball. Sometimes, the plane would accidentally brush the wake's billows of white mist. A thick coat of frost would immediately coat the plane's windows.

'My home isn't part of any galaxy. It sits in the vast and empty void between galaxies.'

'Your planet must be extremely cold.'

'We don't have a planet. The low-temperature civilization developed in a cloud of dark matter. That realm is indeed extremely cold. With difficulty, life snatched a little heat from the near-absolute-zero environment. It sucked in every thread of radiation that came from distant stars. Once the low-temperature civilization learned how to leave, we couldn't wait to go to the closest warm planet in the Milky Way. On this world, we had to maintain a low-temperature environment to live, so we became that warm planet's low-temperature artists.'

'The low-temperature art you're talking about is sculpting ice and snow?'

'Oh, no. No. Using a temperature far lower than a world's mean temperature to affect the world so as to produce artistic effects, this is all part of the low-temperature art. Sculpting ice and snow is just the low-temperature art that suits this world. The temperature of ice and snow is what this world considers a low temperature. For a dark-matter world, that would be a high temperature. For a stellar world, lava would be considered low-temperature material.'

'We seem to overlap in what art we consider beautiful.'

'That's not unusual. So-called warmth is just a brief effect of an equally brief spasm produced after the universe was born. It's gone in an instant like light after sunset. Energy dissipates. Only the cold is eternal. The beauty of the cold is the only enduring beauty.'

'So you're saying the final fate of the universe is heat death?!' Yan Dong heard someone ask over his earpiece. Later, he learned the speaker was a theoretical physicist sitting in one of the planes following behind.

'No digressions. We will discuss only art,' the low-temperature artist scolded.

'The ocean is below us!' Yan Dong happened to glance out the porthole. The crooked coastline passed below.

'Further ahead, we'll reach the deepest part of the ocean. That will be the most convenient place to collect ice.'

'Where will there be ice?' Yan Dong asked, uncomprehending, as he looked at the vast, blue ocean.

'Wherever a low-temperature artist goes, there will be ice.'

The low-temperature artist flew for another hour. Yan Dong stared out the window as they traveled. The view had long become a boundless surface of water. At that moment, the plane suddenly pulled up. He nearly blacked out from acceleration.

'We almost hit it!' the pilot shouted.

The low-temperature artist had stopped suddenly. Taken by surprise, the planes behind it scrambled to change direction.

'Damn it! The law of inertia doesn't apply to the bastard. Its speed seemed to drop to zero in an instant. By all rights, this sort of deceleration should have cracked the ball of ice into pieces,' the pilot said to Yan Dong.

As he spoke, he steered the plane around. The other pilots did the same, rotating majestically around the ball of ice, which just lingered in midair. It produced oxygen and nitrogen snowflakes, but due to strong wind at the altitude, the snowflakes were all blown away. They seemed like white hair whirling in the wind around the ball of ice.

'I am about to create!' the low-temperature artist said. Without waiting for Yan Dong to respond, it suddenly dropped straight down as if the giant invisible hand that had held it suddenly let it go. It free-fell faster and faster until it disappeared into the blue backdrop that was the ocean, leaving only a faint thread of atoms stretching down from midair. A ring of white spray shot up from the sea surface. When it fell, a wave spread out in a circle on the water.

'This alien threw itself into the ocean and committed suicide,' the pilot said to Yan Dong.

'Don't be ridiculous!' Yan Dong stretched out his Northeastern accent and glared at the pilot. 'Fly a little lower. The ball of ice will float back up any moment now.'

But the ball of ice didn't float back up. In its place, a white dot appeared on the ocean. It quickly expanded into a disk. The plane descended and Yan Dong could observe in detail.

The white disk was actually a white fog that covered the ocean. Soon, between its quick expansion and the airplane's continued descent, the only ocean he could see oozed a white fog from its surface. A noise from the sea covered the roaring of the plane's engine. It sounded both like rolling thunder and the cracking of the plains and mountains.

The airplane hovered close to sea level. Yan Dong peered at the surface of the ocean below the fog. The light the ocean reflected was mild, not like moments ago when glints of gold had slashed Yan Dong's eyes. The ocean grew deeper in color. Its rough waves grew level and smooth. What shocked him, though, was the next discovery: The waves became solid and motionless.

'Good heavens. The ocean froze!'

'Are you crazy?' The pilot turned his head to look at Yan Dong.

'See for yourself. . . . Hey! Why are you still descending? Do you want to land on the ice?!'

The pilot yanked the control stick. Once again, the world in front of Yan Dong grew black. He heard the pilot say, 'Ah, no, how strange . . .' The pilot looked as though he were sleepwalking. 'I wasn't descending. The ocean, no, the ice is rising by itself!'

At that moment, Yan Dong heard the low-temperature artist's voice: 'Get your flying machine out of the way. Don't block the path of the rising ice. If there weren't a colleague in the flying machine, I would simply crash into you. I can't stand disruptions to my inspiration while I'm creating. Fly west, fly west, fly west. That direction is closer to the edge.'

'Edge? The edge of what?' Yan Dong asked.

'The cube of ice I'm taking!'

Planes took off like a flock of startled birds, climbing into the sky and heading in the direction the low-temperature artist indicated. Below, because the white fog created by the temperature drop had dissipated, the dark blue ice field stretched to the horizon. Even though the plane was climbing, the ice field climbed even faster. As a result, the distance between the planes and the ice field continued to shrink.

'The Earth is chasing us!' the pilot screamed.

The plane now flew pressed against the ice field. Frozen dark blue waves roiled past the plane's wings.

The pilot yelled, 'We have no choice but to land on the ice field. My god, climbing and landing at the same time. That's just too strange.'

Just at that moment, the Harbin Y-12 reached the end of the ice. A straight edge swept past the fuselage. Below them, liquid sea reemerged, rippling and shimmering. It was like what a fighter jet saw the instant it leapt off the deck of an aircraft carrier, except the 'aircraft carrier' was several kilometers tall.

Yan Dong snapped his head around. Behind them, an immense, dark blue cliff was receding, whose surface was extremely smooth and stretched all the way to the horizon. Its bottom was still connected to the sea, flapped by white waves. But a few seconds later, those waves disappeared, revealing an accurately straight edge. The bottom of the massive block of ice had cleared the ocean.

As the chunk of ice continued to rise, Yan Dong finally understood what the low-temperature artist had meant: This was literally a giant block of ice. The dark blue cube occupied two-thirds of the sky. Afterward, radar observation indicated that the block of ice was sixty kilometers long, twenty kilometers wide, and five kilometers tall, a thin and flat cuboid. Its flat surface reflected the sunlight, like streaks of eye-piercing lightning high in the sky. Several planes crawling slowly against the enormous block looked like tiny birds hovering around a skyscraper, and one would need to try hard to distinguish them.

The giant block of ice kept rising, casting an unimaginably large shadow onto the sea. And when it shifted, it revealed the most terrifying sight since the dawn of history.

The planes were flying over a long, narrow basin, the empty space in the ocean that was left once the giant block of ice was removed. On each side was a mountain of seawater five kilometers high. Hundred-meter-high waves surged at the bottom of these liquid cliffs. At the top, the cliffs were collapsing, advancing as they did. Their surface rippled, but they remained perpendicular to the seafloor. As the seawater cliffs advanced, the basin shrank.

This was the reverse of Moses parting the Red Sea.

What startled Yan Dong the most was how slow the entire process seemed. This was, he assumed, due to the scale. He'd seen the Huangguoshu waterfalls. The water had seemed to fall slowly there, too. And these cliffs of seawater before him were magnitudes larger than those waterfalls. Watching them felt like an endless moment of unparalleled wonder.

The shadow cast by the block of ice had completely disappeared. Yan Dong looked up. The block of ice was now just the size of two full moons.

As the two seawater cliffs advanced, the basin shrank into a canyon. Then the two seawater cliffs, tens of kilometers long, five thousand meters high, crashed into each other. An incredible roar echoed between the sea and sky. The space in the ocean the ice block left was gone.

'We aren't dreaming, are we?' Yan Dong said to himself.

'If this were a dream, everything would be fine. Look!'

The pilot pointed below. Where the two cliffs had crashed into each other, the sea hadn't yet settled. Two waves as long as those cliffs rose, as if they were the reincarnation of those two seawater cliffs on the sea's surface. They parted, heading in opposite directions. From high above, the waves weren't that impressive, but careful measurements showed they were over two hundred meters tall. Viewed from up close, they'd seem like two moving mountain ranges.

'Tidal waves?' Yan Dong asked.

'Yes. Could be the largest ever. The coast is in for a disaster.'

Yan Dong looked up. He could no longer see the frozen block in the blue sky. According to radar, it had become an ice satellite of Earth.

For the rest of the day, the low-temperature artist removed, in the same way, hundreds of blocks of ice of the same size from the Pacific Ocean. It sent them into orbit around the Earth.

By nightfall, a cluster of twinkling points could be seen flying across the sky every couple of hours. You could distinguish them from the usual stars because, on careful inspection, someone could make out the shape of each point. They were each a small cuboid. They all, in their own orientations, spun on their own axes. As a result, they reflected the sunlight and twinkled at different rates.

People thought for a long time, but were never quite able to adequately describe these small objects in space. Finally, a reporter came up with an analogy that got some traction.

'They're like a handful of crystalline dominoes scattered by a space giant.'

A Dialogue Between Two Artists

'We ought to have a chat,' Yan Dong said.

'I asked you to come just to do that, but only about art,' the low-temperature artist said.

Yan Dong stood on a giant block of ice suspended five thousand meters in the air. The low-temperature artist had invited him here. The helicopter that had brought him had landed and now waited to the side. Its rotors were still spinning, ready to take off at any moment.

Ice fields stretched to the horizon on all sides. The ice surface reflected the dazzling sunlight. The layer of blue ice below him seemed bottomless. At this altitude, the sky was clear and boundless. The wind blew stiffly.

This was one of the five thousand giant blocks of ice the low-temperature artist had taken from the oceans. Over the past five days, it had taken, on average, one thousand blocks a day from the oceans and sent them into orbit. All across the Pacific and Atlantic oceans, giant blocks of ice were being frozen and then carried into the air to become one of an increasing number of glittering 'space dominoes.' Tidal waves assaulted every major city along the world's coasts. Over time, though, these disasters became less frequent. The reason was simple: The sea level had dropped.

Earth's oceans had become blocks of ice revolving around it.

Yan Dong stamped his feet on the hard ice surface. 'Such a large block of ice, how did you freeze it in an instant? How did you do it in one piece without it cracking? What force are you using to send it into orbit? All of this is beyond our understanding and imagination.'

The low-temperature artist said, 'This is nothing. In the course of creation, we've often destroyed stars! Didn't we agree to discuss only art? I, creating art in this way, you, using small knives and shovels to carve ice sculptures, from the perspective of art, aren't all that different.'

'When those ice blocks orbiting in space are exposed to intense sunlight, why don't they melt?'

'I covered every ice block with a layer of extremely thin, transparent, light-filtering membrane. It only allows cold light, whose frequencies don't generate heat, to get into the block of ice. The frequencies that do generate heat are all reflected. As a result, the block of ice doesn't melt. This is the last time I'll answer this sort of question. I didn't stop work to discuss these trivial things. From now on, we'll discuss only art, or else you might as well leave. We'll no longer be colleagues and friends.'

'In that case, how much ice do you ultimately plan to take from the oceans? This is surely relevant to the creation of art!'

'Of course, I'll only take as much as there is. I've talked to you before about my design. I'd like to realize it perfectly. Initially, I planned to take ice from Jupiter's satellites because it had turned out that Earth's oceans aren't enough, but it would take too much trouble, so I just make do.'

The wind mussed Yan Dong's hair. He smoothed it back into place. The cold at this altitude made him shiver. 'Is art important to you?'

'It's everything.'

'But . . . there are other things in life. For example, we still need to work to survive. I'm an engineer at the Changchun Institute of Optics. I can only make art in my spare time.'

The low-temperature artist's voice rumbled from the depths of the ice. The vibrating ice surface tickled Yan Dong's feet. 'Survival. Ha! It's just the diaper of a civilization's infancy that needs to be changed. Later, that's as easy as breathing. You'll forget there ever was a time when it took effort to survive.'

'What about societal and political matters?'

'The existence of individuals is also a troublesome part of infant civilizations. Later, individuals melt into the whole. There's no society or politics as such.'

'What about science? There must be science, right? Doesn't a civilization need to understand the universe?'

'That is also a course of study infant civilizations take. Once exploration has been carried out to the proper extent, everything down to the slightest will be revealed. You will discover that the universe is so simple, even science is unnecessary.'

'So that just leaves art?'

'Yes. Art is the only reason for a civilization to exist.'

'But we have other reasons. We want to survive. The several billion people on this planet below us and even more of other species want to survive. You want to dry our oceans, to make this living planet a doomed desert, to make us all die of thirst.'

A wave of laughter propagated from the depths of the ice. Again, it tickled Yan Dong's feet.

'Colleague, look, in the midst of my violent surge of creative inspiration, I stopped to talk to you about art. But, every time, you gossip with me about trivialities. It disappoints me greatly. You ought to be ashamed. Go. I'm going to work.'

Yan Dong finally lost his patience. 'screw your ancestors!' He shouted, then continued to swear in a Northeastern dialect of Chinese.

'Are those obscenities?' the low-temperature artist asked placidly. 'Our species is one where the same body matures as it evolves. No ancestors. As for treating your colleague like this . . .' It laughed. 'I understand. You're jealous of me. You don't have my ability. You can only make art at the level of bacteria.'

'But, you just said that our art requires different tools but there's no essential difference.'

'I've just now changed my perspective. At first, I thought I'd run into a real artist, but, as it turns out, you're a mediocre, pitiful creature who chatters on about the oceans drying, ecological collapse, and other inconsequential things that have nothing to do with art. Too trivial, too trivial, I tell you. Artists cannot be like this.'

'screw your ancestors anyway.'

'Yes, well. I'm working. Go.'

For a moment, Yan Dong felt heavy. He fell ass-first onto the slick ice as a gust of wind swept down from above. The ice block was rising again. He scrambled into the helicopter, which, with difficulty, took off from the nearest edge of the block of ice, nearly crashing in the tornado produced as the block of ice rose.

Communication between humanity and the low-temperature artist had failed.

Sea of Dreams

Yan Dong stood in a white world. The ground below his feet and the surrounding mountains were covered in a silvery white cloak. The mountains were steep and treacherous. He felt as though he were in the snow-covered Himalayas. But in fact, it was the opposite; he was at the lowest place on Earth. The Marianas Trench. Once the deepest part of the Pacific Ocean. The white material that covered everything was not snow but the minerals that had once made the water salty. After the seawater froze, these minerals separated out and were deposited on the seafloor. At the thickest, these deposits were as much as one hundred meters deep.

In the past two hundred days, the oceans of the Earth were exhausted by the low-temperature artist. Even the glaciers of Greenland and Antarctica were completely pillaged.

Now, the low-temperature artist invited Yan Dong to participate in its work's final rite of completion.

In the ravine ahead lay a surface of blue water. The blue was pure and deep. It seemed all the more touching among so many snow-white mountain peaks. This was the last ocean on Earth. It was about the area of Dianchi Lake in Yunnan. Its great waves had long ceased. Only gentle ripples swayed on the water, as though it were a secluded lake deep in the mountains. Three rivers converged into this final ocean. These were great rivers that had survived by luck, trudging through the vast, dehydrated seafloor. They were the longest rivers on Earth ever. By the time they'd arrived here, they'd become slender rivulets.

Yan Dong walked to the oceanfront. Standing on the white beach, he dipped his hand into the lightly rippling sea. Because the water was so saturated with salt, its waves seemed sluggish. A gentle breeze blew Yan Dong's hand dry, leaving a layer of white salt.

The sharp sound that Yan Dong knew so well pierced the air. It tore through the air whenever the low-temperature artist slid toward the ground. Yan Dong spotted it in the sky as it approached. It still appeared as a ball of ice, except much smaller compared to its initial appearance. This was due to its relatively short journey through the atmosphere this time. Since the blocks of ice were sent into the orbit, humanity had tried every method to observe the low-temperature artist when it left the blocks, but had seen nothing. The ball of ice which grew larger and larger after it entered the atmosphere was the only indication to its location.

The low-temperature artist didn't greet Yan Dong. The ball of ice fell into the middle of this last ocean, causing a tall column of water to spout.

Afterward, once again, a familiar scene emerged: A disk of white fog oozed out from the point where the low-temperature artist hit the water. Rapidly, the white fog covered the entire ocean. The water quickly froze with a loud cracking sound. Once again, the fog dissipating revealed a frozen ocean surface. Unlike before, this time, the entire body of water was frozen. There wasn't a drop of liquid water left. The ocean surface also didn't have frozen waves. It was as smooth as a mirror. Throughout the freezing process, Yan Dong felt a cold draft on his face.

The now-frozen final ocean was lifted off the ground. At first, it was lifted only several careful centimeters off the ground. A long black fissure emerged from the edge of the ice field between the ice and white salt beach. Air, forming a strong wind low to the ground, rushed into the long fissure, filling the newly created space. It blew the salt around, so that it now buried Yan Dong's feet. The rate the lake was rising at increased. In the blink of an eye, the final ocean was in midair. So much volume rising so quickly produced violent, chaotic winds. A gust swirled up the salt into a white column in the ravine. Yan Dong spit out the salt that flew into his mouth. It wasn't salty like he'd imagined. It tasted bitter in a way that was hard to express, like the reality that humanity was up against.

The final ocean wasn't a cuboid. Its bottom was an exact impression of the contours of the seafloor. Yan Dong watched it rise until it became a small point of light that dissolved into the mighty ring of ice.

The ring of ice was about as wide as the Milky Way in the sky. Unlike the rings of Uranus and Neptune, the surface of the ring of ice was parallel, instead of perpendicular, to the surface of the Earth. So it was like a broad belt of light in space. A broad belt composed of two hundred thousand blocks of ice completely surrounding the Earth. From the ground, one could clearly make out every block of ice. Some of them rotated while others seemed static. Throughout the day, the ring of ice varied with dramatic changes in brightness and color. The two hundred thousand points of light, some twinkling, some not, formed a majestic, heavenly river that flowed solemnly across the Earth's sky.

Its colors were the most dramatic at dawn and dusk. The ring of ice changed gradually from the orange-red of the horizon to a dark red and then to dark green and dark blue, like a rainbow in space.

During the daytime, the ring of ice assumed a dazzling silver color against the blue sky, like a great river of diamonds flowing across a blue plain. The daytime ring of ice looked most spectacular during an eclipse, when it blocked the sun. Massive blocks of ice refracted the sunlight. Like a strange and magnificent fireworks show in the sky.

How long the sun was blocked by the ice ring depended on whether it was an intersecting eclipse or a parallel eclipse. What was known as a parallel eclipse was when the sun followed the ring of ice for some distance. Every year, there was one total parallel eclipse. For a day, the sun, from sunrise to sunset, followed the path of the ice ring for its entire journey. On this day, the ring of ice seemed like a belt of silver gunpowder set loose on the sky. Ignited at sunrise, the dazzling fireball burned wildly across the sky. When it set in the west, the sight was magnificent, too difficult to put into words. Some people proclaimed, 'Today, God strolled across the sky.'

Even so, the ring of ice's most enchanting moment was at night. It was twice as bright as a full moon. Its silver light filled the Earth. It was as though every star in the universe had lined up to march solemnly across the night sky. Unlike the Milky Way, in this mighty river of stars, one could clearly make out every cuboid star. Of these thickly clustered stars, half of them glittered. Those hundred thousand twinkling stars formed a ripple that surged, as though driven by a gale. It transformed the river of stars into an intelligent whole. . . .

With a sharp squeal, the low-temperature artist returned from space for the last time. The ball of ice was suspended over Yan Dong. A ring of snowflakes appeared and wrapped itself tightly around it.

'I've completed it. What you do think?' it asked.

Yan Dong stayed silent for a long time, then said only one short phrase: 'I give up.'

He had truly given up. Once, he'd stared up at the ring of ice for three consecutive days and three nights, without food or drink, until he collapsed. Once he could get out of bed again, he went back outside to stare at the ice ring again. He felt as if he could gaze at it forever and it wouldn't be enough. Beneath the ring of ice, he was sometimes dazed, sometimes steeped in an indescribable happiness. This was the happiness of when an artist found ultimate beauty. He was completely conquered by this immense beauty. His entire soul was dissolved in it.

'As an artist, now that you're able to see such work, are you still striving for it?' the low-temperature artist asked.

'Truly, I'm not,' Yan Dong answered sincerely.

'However, you're merely looking. Certainly, you can't create such beauty. You're too trivial.'

'Yes. I'm too trivial. We're too trivial. How can we? We have to support ourselves and our children.'

Yan Dong sat on the saline soil. Steeped in sorrow, he buried his head in his hands. This was the deep sorrow that arose when an artist saw beauty he could never produce, when he realized he would never be able to transcend his limitations.

'So, how about we name this work together? Call it—*Ring of Dreams,* perhaps?'

Yan Dong considered this. Slowly, he shook his head. 'No, it came from the sea or, rather, was sublimated from the sea. Not even in our dreams could we conceive that the sea possessed this form of beauty. It should be called—*Sea of Dreams.*'

'*Sea of Dreams* . . . very good, very good. We'll call it that, *Sea of Dreams.*'

Then, Yan Dong remembered his mission. 'I'd like to ask, before you leave, can you return *Sea of Dreams* to become our actual seas?'

'Have me personally destroy my own work? Ridiculous!'

'Then, after you leave, can we restore the seas ourselves?'

'Of course you can. Just return these blocks of ice and everything should be fine, right?'

'How do we do that?' Yan Dong asked, his head raised. All of humanity strained to hear the answer.

'How should I know?' the low-temperature artist said indifferently.

'One final question: As colleagues, we all know that works of art made from ice and snow are short-lived. So *Sea of Dreams* . . .'

'*Sea of Dreams* is also short-lived. A block of ice's light-filtering membrane will age. It'll no longer be able to block heat. But they will dissolve differently than your ice sculptures. The process will be more violent and magnificent. Blocks of ice will vaporize. The pressure will cause the membrane to burst. Every block of ice will turn into a small comet. The entire ring of ice will blur into a silver fog. Then *Sea of Dreams* will disappear into that silver fog. Then the silver fog will scatter and disappear into space. The universe can only look forward to my next work on some other distant world.'

'How long until this happens?' Yan Dong's voice quavered.

'The light-filtering membrane will become ineffective, as you reckon time, hm, in about twenty years. Oh, why are we talking about things other than art again? Trivial, trivial! Okay, colleague. Goodbye. Enjoy the beauty I have left you!'

The ball of ice shot into the air, disappearing into the sky. According to the measurements of every major astronomical organization in the world, the ball of ice flew rapidly in the direction perpendicular to the ecliptic plane. Once it had accelerated to half the speed of light, it abruptly disappeared thirteen astronomical units away from the sun, as if it'd squeezed into an invisible hole. It never returned.

Second Half

Monument and Waveguide

The drought had already lasted for five years.

Withered ground swept past the car window. It was midsummer and there was not a bit of green anywhere on the ground. The trees were all withered. Cracks like black spiderwebs covered the ground. Frequent dry, hot winds kicked up sand that concealed everything. Quite a few times, Yan Dong thought he saw the corpses of people who had died of thirst along the railroad tracks, but they might have just been fallen, dry tree branches, nothing to be afraid of. This harsh, arid world contrasted sharply with the silver *Sea of Dreams* in the sky.

Yan Dong licked his parched lips. He couldn't bring himself to drink from his water flask. That was four days' rations for his entire family. His wife had forced it on him at the train station. Yesterday, his workmates had protested, demanding to be paid in water. In the market, nonrationed water grew scarcer and scarcer. Even the rich weren't able to buy any. . . . Someone touched his shoulder. It was the person in the seat beside him.

'You're that alien's colleague, aren't you?'

Since he'd become the low-temperature artist's messenger, Yan Dong had also become a celebrity. At first, he was considered a role model and a hero. However, after the low-temperature artist left, the situation changed. One way of looking at things is, it was his work that had inspired the low-temperature artist at the Ice and Snow Arts Festival. Without that, none of this would have happened. Most people understood that this was utter nonsense, but having a scapegoat was a good thing. So, in people's eyes he was eventually seen as the low-temperature artist's conspirator. But fortunately, after the artist had left, there were bigger issues to worry about. People gradually forgot about Yan Dong. However, this time, even though he was wearing sunglasses, he had been recognized.

'Give me some water!' the man beside him said, his voice rasping. Two flakes of dry skin fell from his lips.

'What are you doing? Are you robbing me?'

'Be smart, or else I'll scream!'

Yan Dong felt obliged to hand over his water flask. The man drained the flask in one swallow. The people around them watched this with shock on their faces. Even the train attendant who had been passing by stopped in the aisle and stared at him, stupefied. That anyone could be so wasteful was nearly beyond belief. It was like back in the Oceaned Days (what people called the age before the arrival of the low-temperature artist), watching a rich person eat a sumptuous dinner that cost one hundred thousand yuan.

The man returned the empty flask to Yan Dong. Patting Yan Dong's shoulder again, the man said in a low voice, 'It doesn't matter. Soon, it'll all be over.'

Yan Dong understood what the man meant.

The capital seldom had cars on its streets anymore. The rare few had all been retrofitted to be air-cooled. Using a conventional liquid-cooled car was strictly prohibited. Fortunately, the Chinese branch of the World Crisis Organization had sent a car to pick him up. Otherwise, he'd absolutely have had no way to reach their offices. On the way, he saw that sandstorms had covered all the roads with yellow sand. He didn't see many pedestrians. For anyone dehydrated, walking around in the hot, dry wind was too dangerous.

The world was like a fish out of water, already begging for a breath.

When he arrived at the World Crisis Organization, Yan Dong reported to the bureau chief. The bureau chief brought him to a large office and introduced him to the group he would be working with. Yan Dong looked at the office door. Unlike the other ones, this one had no nameplate. The bureau chief said:

'This is a secret group. Everything done here is strictly confidential. In order to avoid social unrest, we call this group the Monument Division.'

Entering the office, Yan Dong realized the people here were all somewhat eccentric: Some had hair that was too long. Some had no hair at all. Some were immaculately dressed, as if the world weren't falling apart around them. Some wore only shorts. Some seemed dejected, others abnormally excited. Many oddly shaped models sat on a long table in the middle of the office. Yan Dong couldn't guess what they might be for.

'Welcome, Ice Sculptor.' The head of the Monument Division enthusiastically shook Yan Dong's hand after the bureau chief's introduction,

'You'll finally have the opportunity to elaborate on the inspiration you received from the alien. Of course, this time, you can't use ice. What we want to build is a work that must last forever.'

'What for?'

The division head looked at the bureau chief, then back at Yan Dong. 'You still don't know? We want to establish a monument to humanity!'

Yan Dong felt even more at a loss with this explanation.

'It's humanity's tombstone,' an artist to his side said. This person had long hair and tattered clothes, and gave the impression of decadence. One hand held a bottle of sorghum liquor that he'd drunk until he was somewhat tipsy. The liquor was left over from the Oceaned Days and now much cheaper than water.

Yan Dong looked all around, then said, 'But . . . we're not dead yet.'

'If we wait until we're dead, it'll be too late.' the bureau chief said. 'We ought to plan for the worst case. The time to think about this is now.'

The division head nodded. 'This is humanity's final work of art, and also its greatest work of art. For an artist, what can be more profound than to join in its creation?'

'It's actually. . . . meaningless,' the long-haired artist said, waving the bottle. 'Tombstones are for your descendants to pay homage to. We'll have no descendants, but we'll still erect a tomb?'

'Pay attention to the name. It's a monument,' the division head corrected solemnly. Laughing, he said to Yan Dong, 'However, the idea he put forth is very good. He proposed that everyone in the world donate a tooth. Those teeth can be used to create a gigantic tablet. Carving a word on each tooth is sufficient to engrave the most detailed history of human civilization on the tablet.' He pointed at a model that looked like a white pyramid.

'This is blasphemy against humanity,' a bald-headed artist shouted. 'The worth of humanity lies in its brains, but he wants to commemorate us with our teeth!'

The long-haired artist took another swig from his bottle. 'Teeth. . . . Teeth are easy to preserve.'

'The vast majority of people are still alive!' Yan Dong repeated solemnly.

'But for how long?' the long-haired artist said. As he asked this question, his enunciation suddenly became precise. 'Water no longer falls from the sky. The rivers have dried. Our crops have utterly failed for three years now. Ninety percent of the factories have stopped production. The remaining food and water, how long can that sustain us?'

'You heap of waste.' The bald-headed artist pointed at the bureau chief. 'Bustling around for five years and you still can't bring even one block of ice back from space.'

The bureau chief laughed off the bald-headed artist's criticism. 'It's not that simple. Given current technology, forcing down one block of ice from orbit isn't hard. Forcing down one hundred, up to one thousand blocks of ice is doable. But forcing back all two hundred thousand blocks of ice orbiting the Earth, that's another matter completely. If we use conventional techniques, a rocket engine could slow a block of ice enough that it would fall back into the atmosphere. That would mean building a large number of reusable high-power engines, then sending them into space. That's a massive-scale engineering project. Given our current technology level and what resources we've stockpiled, there are many insurmountable obstacles. For example, in order to save the Earth's ecosystem, if we start now, we'd need to force down half the blocks of ice within four years, an average of twenty-five thousand per year. The weight of rocket fuel required would be greater than the amount of gasoline humanity used in one year during the Oceaned Days! Except it isn't gasoline. It's liquid hydrogen, liquid oxygen, dinitrogen tetroxide, unsymmetrical dimethylhydrazine, and so on. They need over a hundred times more energy and natural resources to produce than gasoline. Just this one thing makes the entire plan impossible.'

The long-haired artist nodded. 'In other words, doomsday is not far away.'

The bureau chief said, 'No, not necessarily. We can still adopt some nonconventional techniques. There is still hope. While we're working on this, though, we must still plan for the worst.'

'This is exactly why I came,' Yan Dong said.

'To plan for worst?' the long-haired artist asked.

'No, because there's still hope.' He turned to the bureau chief. 'It doesn't matter why you brought me here. I came for my own purpose.' He pointed to his bulky travel bag. 'Please take me to the Ocean Recovery Division.'

'What can you do in the Ocean Recovery Division? They're all scientists and engineers there,' the bald-headed artist wondered.

'I'm a research fellow in applied optics.' Yan Dong's gaze swept past the artists. 'Besides daydreaming along with you, I can also do some practical things.'

After Yan Dong insisted, the bureau chief brought him to the Ocean Recovery Division. The mood here was completely different from the Monument Division. Everyone was tense, working on their computers. A drinking fountain stood in the middle of the office. They could take a drink whenever they wanted. This was treatment worthy of kings. But considering that the hope of the world rested on the people in this room, it wasn't so surprising.

When Yan Dong saw the Ocean Recovery Division's lead engineer, he told him, 'I've brought a plan for reclaiming the ice blocks.'

As he spoke, he opened his travel bag. He took out a white tube about as thick as an arm, followed by a cylinder about a meter long. Yan Dong walked to a window that faced the sun. He stuck the cylinder out of the window, then shook it back and forth. The cylinder opened like an umbrella. Its concave side was plated with a mirror coating. That turned it into something like a parabolic reflector for a solar stove. Next, Yan Dong pushed the tube through a small hole at the bottom of the paraboloid, then adjusted the reflector so that it focused sunlight at the end of the tube. Immediately, the other end of the tube cast an eye-stabbing point of light on the floor. Because the tube lay flat on the floor, the point was an exaggerated oval.

Yan Dong said, 'This uses the latest optical fiber to create a waveguide. There's very little attenuation. Naturally, an actual system would be much larger than this. In space, a parabolic reflector only about twenty meters in diameter can create a point of light at the other end of the waveguide with a temperature of over three thousand degrees.'

Yan Dong looked around. His demonstration hadn't produced the reaction he'd expected. The engineers took a look, then returned to their computer screens, paying him no mind. It wasn't until a stream of dark smoke rose from the point of light on the antistatic floor that the nearest person came over and said, 'What did you do? It's already so hot here.'

At the same time, the person nudged back the waveguide, moving the light coming through the window away from the focal length of the parabolic reflector. Although the point was still on the floor, it immediately darkened and lost heat. Yan Dong was surprised at how adept the person was at adjusting the thing.

The lead engineer pointed at the waveguide. 'Pack up your gear and drink some water. I heard you took the train. The one to here from Changchun is still running? You must be extremely thirsty.'

Yan Dong desperately wanted to explain his invention, but he truly was thirsty. His throat burned and it was painful to speak.

'Very good. This is a really practical plan.' The lead engineer handed Yan Dong a glass of water.

Yan Dong drained the glass of water in one gulp. He looked blankly at the lead engineer. 'Are you saying that someone has already thought of this?'

The lead engineer laughed. 'Spending time with aliens has made you underestimate human intellect. In fact, from the moment the low-temperature artist sent the first block of ice into space, many people have come up with this plan. Afterward, there were lots of variants. For example, some used solar panels instead of reflectors. Some used wires and electric heating elements instead of waveguides. The advantage is that the equipment is easy to manufacture and transport. The disadvantage is the efficiency is not as high as waveguides. We've been researching this for five years now. The technology is already mature. The equipment we need has mostly been manufactured.'

'Then why haven't you carried the plan out?'

An engineer next to them said, 'With this plan, the Earth will lose twenty-one percent of its water. Either during propulsion as vaporized steam or during reentry from high-temperature dissociation.'

The lead engineer turned to that engineer. 'You may have not heard of this yet; the latest American simulations show, below the ionosphere, the hydrogen produced by high-temperature dissociation during reentry will immediately recombine with the surrounding oxygen into water. We overestimated the high-temperature-dissociation loss. The total loss estimate is around eighteen percent.' He turned back to Yan Dong. 'But this percentage is high enough.'

'Then do you have a plan to bring back all of the water from space?'

The lead engineer shook his head. 'The only possibility is to use a nuclear fusion engine. But, right now, on Earth, controlled nuclear fusion isn't within our capabilities.'

'Then why aren't you acting more quickly? You know, if you dither around, the Earth will lose one hundred percent of its water.'

The lead engineer nodded. 'So, after a long time of hesitation, we've decided to act. Soon, the Earth will be in for the fight of its life.'

Reclaiming the Oceans

Yan Dong joined the Ocean Recovery Division, in charge of receiving and checking the waveguides that had been produced. Although this wasn't a core posting, he found it fulfilling.

One month after Yan Dong arrived at the capital, humanity's project to reclaim the oceans started.

Within one short week, eight hundred large-scale carrier rockets shot into the sky from every launch site in the world, sending fifty thousand tons of freight into Earth orbit. Then, from the North American launch site, twenty space shuttles ferried three hundred astronauts into space. Because launches generally followed the same route, the skies above the launch sites all had a single rocket contrail that never dispersed. Viewed from the orbit, it seemed like threads of spider silk stretching up from every continent into space.

These launches increased human space activity by an order of magnitude, but the technology used was still twentieth-century technology. People realized, under existing conditions, if the entire world worked together and risked everything on one attempt, it could do anything.

On live television, Yan Dong and everyone else witnessed the first time a deceleration propulsion system was installed on a block of ice.

To make things less difficult, the first blocks of ice they forced back weren't the ones that rotated about their own axes. Three astronauts landed on a block of ice. They brought with them the following equipment: an artillery-shell-shaped vehicle that could drill a hole into the block of ice, three waveguides, one expeller tube, and three folded-up parabolic reflectors. It was only now that anyone could get the sense of the immense size of a block of ice. The three people seemed to land on a tiny crystalline world. Under intense sunlight in space, the giant field of ice under their feet seemed unfathomable.

Near and far, innumerable similar crystalline worlds hung in the black sky. Some of them still rotated about their own axes. The surrounding rotating and nonrotating blocks of ice reflected and refracted the sunlight. On the ice the three astronauts stood on, they cast a dazzling pattern of ever-changing light and shadow. In the distance, the blocks of ice in the ring looked smaller and smaller, but gathered closer and closer together, gradually shrinking into a delicate, silver belt twisting toward the other side of the Earth. The closest block of ice was only three thousand meters away from this one. Because it rotated about its minor axis, in their eyes, such a rotation had a breathtaking momentum, as though they were three tiny ants watching a crystalline skyscraper collapsing over and over again. Due to gravity, these two ice blocks would eventually crash into each other. The light-filtering membranes would rupture and the blocks of ice would disintegrate. The smashed blocks of ice would quickly evaporate in the sunlight and disappear. Such collisions had already happened twice in the ring of ice. This was also why this block was the first block of ice to be forced back.

First, an astronaut started the driller vehicle. As the drill head spun, crumbs of ice flew out in a cone-shaped spray, twinkling in the sunlight. The driller vehicle broke through the invisible light-filtering membrane. Like a twisting screw, it dug into the ice, leaving a round hole in its wake. Along with the hole that stretched into the depths of the ice, a faint white line could be seen in the ice itself. Once the hole reached the prescribed depth, the vehicle headed out toward another part of the ice. It then bored another hole. At last, it drilled four holes in total. They all intersected at one point deep in the ice.

The astronauts inserted the three waveguides into three of the holes, then inserted the expeller into the wider fourth hole. The expeller tube's mouth was pointed in the direction of the motion of the block of ice. After that, the astronauts used a thin tube to caulk the gap the three waveguides and the expeller tube left against their holes' walls with a fast-sealing liquid to create a good seal. Finally, they opened the parabolic reflectors. If the initial phase of ocean reclamation employed the latest technology, it was these parabolic reflectors. They were a miracle created by nanotechnology. Folded up, each was only a cubic meter. Unfolded, each formed a giant reflector five hundred meters in diameter. These three reflectors were like three silver lotus leaves that grew on the block of ice. The astronauts adjusted each waveguide so that its receiver coincided with the focal point of its reflector.

A bright point of light appeared where the three holes intersected deep in the ice. It seemed like a tiny sun, illuminating within the block of ice spectacular sights of mythic proportions: a school of silver fish, dancing seaweed drifting with the waves . . . Everything retained its lifelike appearance at the instant it was frozen. Even the strings of bubbles spat from fishes' mouths were clear and distinct. Over one hundred kilometers away, inside another ice block being reclaimed, the sunlight that the waveguides led into the ice revealed a giant black shadow. It was a blue whale over twenty meters long! This had to be the Earth's seas of old.

Deep in the ice, steam soon blurred the point of light. As the steam dispersed, the point changed into a bright white ball. It swelled in size as the ice melted. Once the pressure had built up to a predetermined level, the expeller mouth cover was broken open. A violent gush of turbulent steam exploded out. Because there were no obstructions, it formed a sharp cone that scattered in the distance. Finally, it disappeared in the sunlight. Some portion of the steam entered another ice block's shadow and condensed into ice crystals that seemed like a swarm of flickering fireflies.

The deceleration propulsion system in the first batch of one hundred blocks of ice activated. Because the blocks of ice were so massive, the thrust the system produced was, relatively speaking, very small. As a result, they needed to orbit fifteen days to a month before they could slow the blocks of ice down enough for them to fall into the atmosphere. Later, reclaiming ice blocks that rotated was much more complicated. The propulsion system had to stop the rotation first, then slow down the block of ice.

Before the blocks of ice entered the atmosphere, astronauts would land on them again to recover the waveguides and reflectors. If they wanted to force all two hundred thousand blocks down, this equipment had to be reused as much as possible.

Ice Meteors

Yan Dong and members of the Crisis Committee arrived together at the flatlands in the middle of the Pacific Ocean to watch the first batch of ice meteors fall.

The ocean bed of former days looked like a snowy white plain, reflecting the intense sunlight—no one could open their eyes unless they were wearing sunglasses. But the white plain before them didn't make Yan Dong think of the snowfields of his native Northeast because, here, it was as hot as hell. The temperature was near fifty degrees Celsius. Hot winds kicked up salty dirt, which hurt when it hit his face. A hundred-thousand-ton oil tanker was in the distance. The gigantic hull lay tilted on the ground. Its propeller, several stories tall, and rudder were completely covered by salt. An unbroken chain of white mountains stood even farther in the distance. That was a mountain range on the seafloor humanity had never seen until now. A two-sentence poem came to Yan Dong's mind:

The open sea is a boat's land. Night is love's day.

He laughed bitterly then. He'd experienced this tragedy, yet he still couldn't shake off thinking like an artist.

Cheers erupted. Yan Dong raised his head and looked to where everyone was pointing. In the distance, a bright red point had appeared in the silver ring of ice that traversed the sky. The point of light drifted out of the ring. It swelled into a fireball. A white contrail dragged behind the fireball. This contrail of steam grew ever longer and thicker. Its color became even denser, even whiter. Soon, the fireball split into ten pieces. Each piece continued to split. A long white contrail dragged behind every small piece. This field of white contrails filled half the sky, as though it were a white Christmas tree and a small, bright lamp hung on the tip of every branch. . . .

Even more ice meteors appeared. Their sonic booms shook the earth like rumbles of spring thunder. As old contrails gradually dissipated, new contrails appeared to replace them. They covered the sky in a complex white net. Several trillion tons of water now belonged to the Earth again.

Most of the ice meteors broke apart and vaporized in the air, but one large fragment of ice fell to the ground about forty kilometers from Yan Dong. The loud crash shook the flatlands. A colossal mushroom cloud rose from somewhere in the distant mountain range. The water vapor shone a dazzling white in the sunlight. Gradually, it dispersed in the wind and became the sky's first cloud layer. The clouds multiplied and, for the first time, blocked the sun that had been scorching the earth for five years. They covered the entire sky. For a while, Yan Dong felt a pleasant coolness that oozed into his heart and lungs.

The cloud layer grew thick and dark. Red light flickered within it. Maybe it was lightning or the light from the continuous waves of ice meteors falling toward the earth.

It rained! This was a downpour so heavy it would have been rare even in the Oceaned Days. Yan Dong and everyone else there ran around screaming wildly in the storm. They felt their souls dissolve in the rain. Then they retreated into their cars and helicopters because, right now, people would suffocate in the rain.

The rain fell nonstop until dusk. Waterlogged depressions appeared on the seafloor flatlands. A crack in the clouds revealed the golden, flickering rays of the setting sun, as though the Earth had just opened its eyes.

Yan Dong followed the crowd, stepping through the thick salty mud. They ran to the nearest depression. He cupped some water in his hands, then splashed that thick brine on his face. As it fell, mixed with his tears, he said, choking with sobs:

'The ocean, our ocean . . .'

Epilogue

Ten years later

Yan Dong walked onto the frozen-over Songhua River. He was wrapped in a tattered overcoat. His travel bag held the tools that he'd kept for fifteen years: several knives and shovels of various shapes, a hammer, and a watering can. He stamped his feet to make sure that the river had truly frozen. The Songhua River had water as early as five years ago, but this was the first time it had frozen, and during the summer, no less.

Due to the arid conditions and, at the same time, the potential energy of the many ice meteors converting into thermal energy in the atmosphere, the global climate had stayed hotter than ever. But in the final stage of ocean reclamation, the largest blocks of ice were forced down. These blocks of ice broke into larger fragments. Most of them crashed onto the ground. This not only destroyed a few cities but also kicked up dust that blocked the sun's heat. Temperatures fell rapidly all over the world. Earth entered a new ice age.

Yan Dong looked at the night sky. This was the starscape of his childhood. The ring of ice had disappeared. He could only make out the vestiges of the remaining small blocks of ice from their rapid motion against the background of stars. *Sea of Dreams* had turned back into actual seas again. This magnificent work of art, its cruel beauty as well as nightmare, would forever be inscribed in the collective memory of humanity.

Although the ocean-reclamation effort had been a success, Earth's climate would be a harsh one from now on. The ecosystem would take a long time to recover. For the foreseeable future, humanity's existence would be extremely difficult. Nevertheless, at least existence was possible. Most people felt content with that. Indeed, the Ring of Ice Era made humanity learn contentment, and also something even more important.

The World Crisis Organization would change its name to the Space Water Retrieval Organization. They were considering another great engineering project: Humanity intended to fly to distant Jupiter, then take water from Jupiter's moons and the rings of Saturn back to Earth in order to make up for the 18 percent lost in the course of the Ocean Reclamation Project.

At first, people intended to use the technology for propelling blocks of ice that they'd already mastered to drive blocks of ice from the rings of Saturn to Earth. Of course, that far away, the sunlight was too weak. Only using nuclear fusion to vaporize the cores of the blocks of ice could provide the necessary thrust. As for the water from Jupiter's moons, that required even larger and more complex technology to acquire. Some people had already proposed pulling the whole of Europa out of Jupiter's deep gravity well, pushing it to Earth, and making it Earth's second moon. This way, Earth would receive much more water than 18 percent. It could turn Earth's ecosystem into a glorious paradise. Naturally, this was a matter for the far future. No one alive hoped to see it during their lifetime. However, this hope made people in their hard lives feel a happiness they'd never felt before. This was the most valuable thing humanity received from the Ring of Ice Era: Reclaiming *Sea of Dreams* made humanity see its own strength, taught it to dream what it had never before dared to dream.

Yan Dong saw in the distance a group of people gathered on the ice. He walked to them, gliding with each step. When they spotted him, they began to run toward him. Some slipped and fell, then picked themselves up and raced to catch up with the others.

'Our old friend! Hello!' The first one to reach Yan Dong wrapped him in a warm hug. Yan Dong recognized him. He was one of the ice sculpture judges from so many ice and snow festivals before the Ring of Ice Era. Yan Dong had sworn never to speak with those judges again, because during the last festival, they gave the top prize to a young woman for her pretty face instead of her work of art.

As they neared, he recognized the others, most of them ice sculptors from before the Ring of Ice Era. Like everyone else of this era, they wore tattered clothes. Suffering and time had dyed the hair on their temples white. Yan Dong felt as though he'd come home after years of wandering.

'I heard that the Ice and Snow Arts Festival has started back up again?' he asked.

'Of course. Otherwise, what are we all doing here?'

'I've been thinking. Times are so hard . . .'

Yan Dong wrapped his large overcoat tighter around himself. He shivered in the cold wind, constantly stamping his numb feet against the ice. Everyone else did the same, shivering, stamping their feet, like a group of begging refugees.

'So what if times are hard? Even in hard times, you can't not make art, right?' an old ice sculptor said through chattering teeth.

'Art is the only reason for a civilization to exist!' someone else said.

'screw that, I have plenty of reasons to go on,' Yan Dong said loudly.

Everyone laughed, then fell silent as they thought back on ten years of hard times. One by one, they counted their reasons to go on. Finally, they changed themselves from survivors of a disaster back to artists again.

Yan Dong took a bottle of sorghum liquor from his bag. They warmed up as each one took a swig then passed it on to the next. They built a fire on the vast riverbank and heated up a chainsaw until it would start in the bitter cold. They all stepped onto the river, and the chainsaw growled as it cut into the ice. White crumbs of ice fell around them. Soon, they pulled their first block of glittering, translucent ice from the Songhua River.

诗云

CLOUD OF POEMS

TRANSLATED BY CARMEN YILING YAN

刘慈欣 一 著

二〇一〇 一 译

A yacht bore Yi Yi and his two companions across the South Pacific on a voyage dedicated to poetry. Their destination was the South Pole. Upon a successful arrival in a few days, they would climb through the Earth's crust to view the Cloud of Poems.

Today, the sky and seas were clear. For the purposes of poem making, the workings of the world seemed to be laid out in glass. Looking up, one could see the North American continent in rare clarity in the sky. On the vast world-encompassing dome as seen from the eastern hemisphere, the continent looked like a patch of missing plaster on a wall.

Oh, yes, humanity lived inside the Earth nowadays. To be more accurate, humanity lived inside the Air, for the Earth had become a gas balloon. The Earth had been hollowed out, leaving only a thin shell about a hundred kilometers thick. The continents and oceans remained in their old places, only they had all migrated to the inside of the shell. The atmosphere also remained, moved inside as well. So now the Earth was a balloon, with the oceans and continents clinging to its inner surface. The hollow Earth still rotated, but the significance of the rotation was much different than before: It now produced gravity. The attractional force generated by the bit of mass forming Earth's crust was so weak as to be insignificant, so now the Earth's 'gravity' had to come from the centrifugal force of rotation. But this kind of 'gravity' was unevenly distributed across the regions of the world.

It was strongest at the equator, being about 1.5 times Earth's original gravity. With increase of latitude came a gradual decrease in gravity—the two poles experienced weightlessness. The yacht was currently at the exact latitude that experienced 1.0 gees as per the old scale, but Yi Yi nonetheless found it difficult to recall the sensation of standing on the old, solid Earth.

At the heart of the hollow Earth hovered a tiny sun, which currently illuminated the world with the light of noon. The sun's luminosity changed continuously in a twenty-four-hour cycle, from its maximum to total darkness, providing the hollow Earth with alternating day and night. On suitable nights, it even gave off cold moonlight. But the light came from a single point; there was no round, full moon to be seen.

Of the three people on the yacht, two of them were not, in fact, people. One was a dinosaur named Bigtooth[1]. The yacht swayed and tilted with every shift of his ten-meter-tall body, to the annoyance of the one reciting poetry at the boat's prow. This was a thin, wiry old man, garbed in the loose, archaic robes of the Tang Dynasty, whose snow-white hair and snow-white whiskers flowed in the wind as one. He resembled a bold calligraphy character splashed in the space between sea and sky.

This was the creator of the new world, the great poet Li Bai.

The Gift

The matter began ten years ago, when the Devouring Empire completed its two-century-long pillage of the solar system. The dinosaurs from Earth's ancient past departed for Cygnus in their ring-shaped world fifty thousand kilometers in diameter, leaving the sun behind them. The Devouring Empire took 1.2 billion humans with them as well, to be raised as livestock. But as the ring world approached the orbit of Saturn, it suddenly began to decelerate, before, incredibly, returning along its earlier route to the inner reaches of the solar system.

One ring-world week after the Devouring Empire began its return, the emissary Bigtooth piloted away from the ring in his spaceship shaped like an old boiler, a human named Yi Yi in his pocket.

'You're going to be a present!' Bigtooth told Yi Yi, eyes on the black void

---

1 大牙，《吞食者》中表述为'Fangs'，本版无意取舍，保留原始译法。

outside the window port. His booming voice rattled Yi Yi's bones.

'For whom?' Yi Yi threw his head back and shouted from the pocket. From the opening, he could see the dinosaur's lower jaw, like a boulder jutting out from the top of a giant cliff.

'You'll be given to a god! A god came to the solar system. That's why the Empire is returning.'

'A real god?'

'Their kind controls unimaginable technology. They've transformed into beings of pure energy, and can instantaneously jump from one side of the Milky Way to the other. They're gods, all right. If we can get just a hundredth of their ultra-advanced technology, the Devouring Empire will have a bright future ahead. We're entering the final step of this important mission. You need to get the god to like you!'

'Why did you pick me? My meat is very low-grade,' said Yi Yi. He was in his thirties. Next to the tender, pale-fleshed humans cultivated with so much care by the Devouring Empire, he appeared rather old and world-worn.

'The god doesn't eat bug-bugs, just collects them. I heard from the breeder that you're really special. Apparently you have many students?'

'I'm a poet. I currently teach Classic literature to the livestock humans on the feedlot.' Yi Yi struggled to pronounce 'poet' and 'literature,' rarely used words in the Devourer language.

'Boring, useless knowledge. Your breeder turns a blind eye to your classes because their spiritual effects improve the bug-bugs' meat quality. . . . From what I've observed, you think highly of yourself and give little notice to others. They must be very interesting traits for a head of livestock to have.'

'All poets are like this!' Yi Yi stood tall in the pocket. Even though he knew that Bigtooth couldn't see, he raised his head proudly.

'Did your ancestors participate in the Earth Defense War?'

Yi Yi shook his head. 'My ancestors from that era were also poets.'

'The most useless kind of bug-bug. Your kind was already rare on Earth back then.'

'They lived in the world of their innermost selves, untouched by changes to the outside world.'

'Shameless . . . ha, we're almost there.'

Hearing this, Yi Yi stuck his head out of the pocket. Through the huge window port, he could see the two white, glowing objects ahead of the ship: a square and a sphere, floating in space. When the spaceship reached the level of the square, the latter briefly disappeared against the backdrop of the stars, revealing that it had virtually zero thickness. The perfect sphere hovered directly above the plane. Both shone with soft, white light, so evenly distributed that no features could be distinguished on their surfaces. They looked like objects taken from a computer database, two concise yet abstract concepts in a disorderly universe.

'Where's the god?' Yi Yi asked.

'He's the two geometric objects, of course. Gods like to keep it nice and simple.'

As they approached, Yi Yi saw that the plane was the size of a soccer field. The spaceship descended upon the plane thruster side down, but the flames left no marks on the surface, as if the plane were nothing but an illusion. Yet Yi Yi felt gravity, and the jarring sensation when the spaceship touched down proved that the plane was real.

Bigtooth must have come here before; he opened the hatch without hesitation and walked out. Yi Yi's heart seized up when he saw that Bigtooth had simultaneously opened the hatches on both side of the airlock, but the air inside the chamber didn't howl outward. As Bigtooth walked out of the ship, Yi Yi smelled fresh air from inside his pocket. When he poked his head out, a soft, cool breeze caressed his face. This was ultra-advanced technology beyond the comprehension of either humans or dinosaurs. Its comfortable, casual application astounded Yi Yi, in a way that pierced the soul more deeply than what humanity must have felt in its first encounter with Devourers. He looked up. The sphere floated overhead against the backdrop of the radiant Milky Way.

'What little gift have you brought me this time, Emissary?' asked the god in the language of the Devourers. His voice was not loud, seeming to come from a boundless distance away, from the deep void of outer space. It was the first time Yi Yi had found the crude language of the dinosaurs pleasing to the ear.

Bigtooth extended a claw into his pocket, caught Yi Yi, and set him down on the plane. Yi Yi could feel the elasticity of the plane through the soles of his feet.

'Esteemed god,' Bigtooth said. 'I heard you like to collect small organisms from different star systems, so I brought you this very entertaining little thing: a human from Earth.'

'I only like *perfect* organisms. Why did you bring me such a filthy insect?' said the god. The sphere and the plane flickered twice, perhaps to express disgust.

'You know about this species?' Bigtooth raised his head in astonishment.

'Not intimately, but I've heard about them from certain visitors to this arm of the galaxy. They made frequent visits to Earth in the brief course of these organisms' evolution, and were revolted at the vulgarness of their thoughts, the lowliness of their actions, the disorder and filth of their history. Not a single visitor would deign to establish contact with them up to the destruction of Earth. Hurry and throw it away.'

Bigtooth seized Yi Yi, rotating his massive head to look for a place to throw him. 'The trash incinerator is behind you,' said the god. Bigtooth turned and saw that a small, round opening had appeared in the plane behind him. Inside shimmered a faint blue light. . . .

'Don't dismiss us like that! Humanity created a magnificent civilization!' Yi Yi shouted with all his might in the language of the Devourers.

The sphere and the plane again flickered twice. The god gave two cold laughs. 'Civilization? Emissary, tell this insect what civilization is.'

Bigtooth lifted Yi Yi to his eye level; Yi Yi could even hear the *gululu* of the dinosaur's giant eyeballs turning in their sockets. 'Bug-bug, in this universe, the standard measure of any race's level of civilization is the number of dimensions it can access. The basic requirement for joining civilization at large is six or more. Our esteemed god's race can already access the eleventh dimension. The Devouring Empire can access the fourth dimension in small-scale laboratory environments, and only qualifies as a primitive, uncivilized tribe in the Milky Way. You, in the eyes of a god, are in the same category as weeds and lichen.'

'Throw it away already, it's disgusting,' the god urged impatiently.

Having finished speaking, Bigtooth headed for the incinerator's aperture. Yi Yi struggled frantically. Numerous pieces of white paper fluttered loose from his clothing. The sphere shot out a needle-thin beam of light, hitting one of the sheets, which froze unmoving in midair. The beam scanned rapidly over its surface.

'Oh my, wait, what's this?'

Bigtooth allowed Yi Yi to dangle over the incinerator's aperture as he turned to look at the sphere.

'That's . . . my students' homework!' Yi Yi managed laboriously, struggling in the dinosaur's giant claw.

'These squarish symbols are very interesting, and the little arrays they form are quite amusing too,' said the god. The sphere's beam of light rapidly scanned over the other sheets of paper, which had since landed on the plane.

'They're Ch-Chinese characters. These are poems in Classical Chinese!'

'Poems?' the god exclaimed, retracting its beam of light. 'I trust you understand the language of these insects, Emissary?'

'Of course, esteemed god. Before the Devouring Empire ate Earth, we spent a long time living on their world.' Bigtooth set Yi Yi down on the plane next to the incinerator, bent over, and picked up a sheet of paper. He held it just in front of his eyes, trying with effort to distinguish the small characters on it. 'More or less, it says—'

'Forget it, you'll distort the meaning!' Yi Yi waved a hand to interrupt Bigtooth.

'How so?' asked the god interestedly.

'Because this is a form of art that can only be expressed in Classical Chinese. Even translating these poems into other human languages alters them until they lose much of their meaning and beauty.'

'Emissary, do you have this language in your computer database? Send me the relevant data, as well as all the information you have on Earth history. Just use the communications channel we established during our last meeting.'

Bigtooth hurried back to the spaceship and banged around on the computer inside for a while, muttering, 'We don't have the Classical Chinese portion here, so we'll have to upload it from the Empire's network. There might be some delay.' Through the open hatchway, Yi Yi saw the morphing colors of the computer screen reflected off the dinosaur's huge eyeballs.

By the time Bigtooth got off the ship, the god could already read the poem on one sheet of paper with perfect modern Chinese pronunciation.

Bai ri yi shan jin,
Huang he ru hai liu,
Yu qiong qian li mu,
Geng shang yi ceng lou.

'You're a fast learner!' Yi Yi exclaimed.

The god ignored him, silent.

Bigtooth explained, 'It means, the star has set behind the orbiting planet's mountains. A liquid river called the Yellow River is flowing in the direction of the ocean. Oh, the river and the ocean are both made of the chemical compound consisting of one oxygen atom and two hydrogen atoms. If you want to see further, you must climb further up the edifice.'

The god remained silent.

'Esteemed god, you visited the Devouring Empire not long ago. The scenery there is almost identical to that of the world known to this poem's author bug-bug, with mountains, rivers, and seas, so . . .'

'So I understand the meaning of the poem,' said the god. The sphere suddenly moved so it was right above Bigtooth's head. Yi Yi thought it looked like a giant pupilless eye staring at Bigtooth. 'But, didn't you feel something?'

Bigtooth shook his head, confused.

'That is to say, something hidden behind the outward meaning of that simple, elegant array of square symbols?'

Bigtooth looked even more confused, so the god recited another Classical poem:

> *Qian bu jian gu ren,*
> *Hou bu jian lai zhe,*
> *Nian tian di zhi you you,*
> *Du chuang ran er ti xia.*

Bigtooth hurried eagerly to explain. 'This poem means, looking in front of you, you can't see all the bug-bugs who lived on the planet in the distant past. Looking behind you, you can't see all the bug-bugs who will live on the planet in the future. So you feel how time and space are just too big and end up crying.'

The god brooded.

'Ha, crying is one way for Earth bug-bugs to express their grief. So at that point their visual organs—'

'Do you still feel nothing?' the god interrupted Bigtooth. The sphere descended further, nearly touching Bigtooth's snout.

Bigtooth shook his head firmly this time. 'Esteemed god, I don't think there's anything inside. It's just a simple little poem.'

Next, the god recited several more poems, one after the other. They were all short and simple, yet imbued with a spirit that transcended their topics. They included Li Bai's 'Downriver to Jiangling' ,'Still Night Thoughts' and 'Bidding Meng Haoran Farewell at Yellow Crane Tower'; Liu Zongyuan's 'River Snow'; Cui Hao's 'Yellow Crane Tower'; Meng Haoran's 'Spring Dawn'; and so forth.

Bigtooth said, 'The Devouring Empire has many historical epic poems with millions of lines. We would happily present them all to you, esteemed god! In comparison, the poems of human bug-bugs[1] are so puny and simple,

---

1　虫虫，《吞食者》中表述为 'worm' ，本版无意取舍，保留原始译法。

like their technology—'

The sphere suddenly departed its position above Bigtooth's head, drifting in unthinking arcs in midair. 'Emissary, I know your people's greatest hope is that I'll answer the question "The Devouring Empire has existed for eight million years, so why is its technology still stalled in the Atomic Age?" Now I know the answer.'

Bigtooth gazed at the sphere passionately. 'Esteemed god, the answer is crucial to us! Please—'

'Esteemed god,' Yi Yi called out, raising a hand. 'I have a question too. May I speak?'

Bigtooth glared resentfully at Yi Yi, as if he wanted to swallow him in one bite. But the god said, 'Though I continue to despise Earth insects, those little arrays have won you the right.'

'Is art common throughout the universe?'

The sphere vibrated faintly in midair, as if nodding. 'Yes—I'm an intergalactic art collector and researcher myself, in fact. In my travels, I've encountered the various arts of numerous civilizations. Most are ponderous, unintelligible setups. But using so few symbols, in so small and clever an array, to encompass such rich sensory layers and subtle meaning, all the while operating under such sadistically exacting formal rules and rhyme schemes? I have to say, I've never seen anything like it. . . . Emissary, you may now throw away this insect.'

Once again, Bigtooth seized Yi Yi with his claw. 'That's right, we ought to throw it away. Esteemed god, we have fairly abundant resources on human civilization stored in the Devouring Empire's central networks. All those resources are now in your memory, while this bug-bug probably doesn't know any more than a couple of the little poems.' He carried Yi Yi toward the incinerator as he spoke.

'Throw away those pieces of paper too,' the god said. Bigtooth hurriedly returned and used his other claw to collect the papers. At this point, Yi Yi hollered from between the massive claws.

'O god, save these papers with the ancient poems of humanity, as a memento! You've discovered an unsurpassable art. You can spread it throughout the universe!'

'Wait.' The god once again stopped Bigtooth. Yi Yi was already hanging above the incinerator aperture, feeling the heat of the blue flames below him. The sphere floated over, coming to a stop a few centimeters from Yi Yi's forehead. Yi Yi, like Bigtooth earlier, felt the force of the enormous pupilless eye's gaze.

'Unsurpassable?'

Bigtooth laughed, holding up Yi Yi. 'Can you believe the pitiable bug-bug, saying these things in front of a magnificent god? Hilarious! What remains to humanity? You've lost everything on Earth. Even the scientific knowledge you've managed to bring with you has been largely forgotten. One time at dinner, I asked the human I was about to eat, what were the atomic bombs used by the humans in the Earth Defense War made of? He told me they were made of atoms!'

'Hahahaha . . .' The god joined Bigtooth in laughter, the sphere vibrating so hard it became an ellipsoid. 'It's certainly the most accurate answer of them all, hahaha . . .'

'Esteemed god, all these dirty bug-bugs have left are a couple of those little poems! Hahaha—'

'But they cannot be surpassed!' Yi Yi said solemnly in the middle of the claw, puffing out his chest.

The sphere stopped vibrating. It said, in an almost intimate whisper, 'Technology can surpass anything.'

'It has nothing to do with technology. They are the quintessence of the human spiritual realm. They cannot be surpassed!'

'Only because you haven't witnessed the power of technology in its ultimate stage, little insect. Little, little insect. You haven't seen.' The god's tone of voice became as gentle as a father's, but Yi Yi shivered at the icy killing edge hidden deep within. The god said, 'Look at the sun.'

Yi Yi obeyed. They were in the vacuum between the orbits of Earth and Mars. The sun's radiance made him squint.

'What's your favorite color?' asked the god.

'Green.'

The word had barely left his lips before the sun turned green. It was a bewitching shade; the sun resembled a cat's eye floating in the void of space. Under its gaze, the whole universe looked strange and sinister.

Bigtooth's claw trembled, dropping Yi Yi onto the plane. When their reason returned, they realized a fact even more unnerving than the sun turning green: the light should have taken more than ten minutes to travel here from the sun, but the change had occurred instantaneously!

Half a minute later, the sun returned to its previous condition, emitting brilliant white light once more.

'See? This is technology. This is the force that allowed my race to ascend from slugs in ocean mud to gods. Technology itself is the true God, in fact. We all worship it devotedly.'

Yi Yi blinked his dazzled eyes. 'But that god can't surpass this art. We have gods too, in our minds. We worship them, but we don't believe they can write poems like Li Bai and Du Fu.'

The god laughed coldly. 'What an extraordinarily stubborn insect,' it said to Yi Yi. 'It makes you even more loathsome. But, for the sake of killing time, let me surpass your array-art.'

Yi Yi laughed back. 'It's impossible. First of all, you aren't human, so you can't feel with a human's soul. Human art to you is only a flower on a stone slab. Technology can't help you surmount this obstacle.'

'Technology can surmount this obstacle as easily as snapping your fingers. Give me your DNA!'

Yi Yi was confused. 'Give the god one of your hairs!' Bigtooth prompted him. Yi Yi reached up and plucked out a hair; an invisible suction force drew the hair into the sphere. A while later, the hair fell from the sphere, drifting to the plane. The god had only extracted a bit of skin from its root.

The sphere roiled with white light, then gradually became clear. It was now filled with transparent liquid in which strings of bubbles rose. Next, Yi Yi spotted a ball the size of an egg yolk inside the liquid, made pale red by the sunlight shining through, as if it were luminous in and of itself. The ball soon grew. Yi Yi realized that it was a curled-up embryo, its bulging eyes squeezed shut, its oversized head crisscrossed with red blood vessels. The embryo continued to mature. The tiny body finally uncurled and swam frog-like in the sphere of liquid. The liquid gradually became cloudy, so that the sunlight coming through the sphere revealed only a blurry silhouette that continued to rapidly mature until it became that of a swimming grown man. At this point, the sphere reverted to its original opaque, glowing state, and a naked human fell out of it and onto the plane.

Yi Yi's clone stood up unsteadily, the sunlight glistening off his wet form. He was long-haired and long-bearded, but one could tell that he was only in his thirties or forties. Aside from the wiry thinness, he didn't look at all like the original Yi Yi.

The clone stood stiffly, gazing dully into the infinite distance, as if completely oblivious to the universe he'd just joined. Above him, the sphere's white light dimmed, before extinguishing altogether. The sphere itself disappeared as if evaporating. But just then, Yi Yi thought he saw something else light up, and realized that it was the clone's eyes. The dullness had been replaced with the divine gleam of wisdom. In this moment, Yi Yi would learn, the god had transferred all his memories to the clone body.

'Cold . . . so this is cold?' A breeze had blown past. The clone had wrapped his arms around his slick shoulders, shivering, but his voice was full of delighted surprise. 'This is cold! This is pain, immaculate, impeccable pain, the sensation I scoured the stars for, as piercing as the ten-dimensional string through time and space, as crystalline as a diamond of pure energy at the heart of a star, ah . . .' He spread his emaciated arms and beheld the Milky Way. '*Qian bu jian gu ren, hou bu jian lai zhe, nian tian di zhi*—' A spate of shivers left the clone's teeth chattering. He hurriedly stopped commemorating his birth and ran over to warm himself over the incinerator.

The clone extended his hands over the blue flames inside the aperture, shivering as he said to Yi Yi, 'Really, this is something I do all the time. When researching and collecting a civilization's art, I always lodge my consciousness inside a member organism of that civilization, to ensure my complete understanding of the art.'

The flames inside the incinerator's aperture suddenly flared. The plane surrounding it roiled with multicolored light as well, so that Yi Yi felt as if the entire plane were a sheet of frosted glass floating on a sea of fire.

'The incinerator has turned into a fabricator,' Bigtooth whispered to Yi Yi. 'The god is performing energy-matter exchange.' Seeing Yi Yi's continued puzzlement, he explained again, 'Idiot, he's making objects out of pure energy, the handicraft of a god!'

Suddenly, a white mass burst from the fabricator, unfurling in midair as it fell—clothing, which the clone caught and put on. Yi Yi saw that it was a loose, flowing Tang Dynasty robe, made of snow-white silk and trimmed with a wide band of black. The clone, who had appeared so pitiable earlier, looked like an ethereal sage with it on. Yi Yi couldn't imagine how it had been made from the blue flames.

The fabricator completed another object. Something black flew from the aperture and thudded onto the plane like a rock. Yi Yi ran over and picked it up. He might not trust his eyes, but his hand clearly registered a heavy inkstone, icy cold at that. Something else smacked onto the plane; Yi Yi picked up a black rod. No doubt about it—it was an inkstick! Next came several brush pens, a brush holder, a sheet of snow-white mulberry paper (paper, out of the flames!), and several little decorative antiques. The last object out was also the largest: an old-fashioned writing desk! Yi Yi and Bigtooth hurriedly righted the desk and arranged the other objects on top of it.

'The amount of energy he converted into these objects could have pulverized a planet,' Bigtooth whispered to Yi Yi, his voice shaking slightly.

The clone walked over to the desk, nodding in satisfaction when he saw the arrangement on it. One hand stroked his newly dry beard, he said, 'I, Li Bai.'

Yi Yi examined the clone. 'Do you mean you want to become Li Bai, or do you really think you're Li Bai?'

'I'm Li Bai, pure and simple. A Li Bai to surpass Li Bai!'

Yi Yi laughed and shook his head.

'What, do you question me even now?'

Yi Yi nodded. 'I concede that your technology far exceeds my understanding. It's indistinguishable from human ideas of magic and acts of God. Even in the fields of art and poetry, you've astonished me. Despite such an enormous cultural, spatial, and temporal gap, you've managed to sense the hidden nuances of Classical Chinese poetry. . . . But understanding Li Bai is one matter, and exceeding him is another. I continue to believe that you face an unsurpassable body of art.'

A mysterious amusement appeared on the clone's—Li Bai's—face, only to quickly vanish. He pointed at the desk. 'Grind ink!' he bellowed to Yi Yi, before striding away. He was nearly at the edge of the plane before he stopped, stroking his whiskers, gazing toward the distant Milky Way, descending into thought.

Yi Yi took the Yixing clay pot on the desk and poured a trickle of clear water into the depression in the inkstone. Then he began to grind the inkstick against the stone. It was the first time he'd done this; he clumsily angled the stick to scrape at its corners. As he watched the liquid thicken and darken, Yi Yi thought of himself, 1.5 astronomical units away from the sun, perched on this infinitely thin plane in the vastness of outer space. (Even while it was making things out of pure energy, a distant viewer would have perceived zero thickness.) It was a stage floating in the void of the universe, on which a dinosaur, a human raised as dinosaur livestock, and a technological god in period dress planning to surpass Li Bai were performing bizarre live theater. With that thought, Yi Yi shook his head and laughed wanly.

Once he thought the ink was ready, Yi Yi stood and waited next to Bigtooth. The breeze on the plane had ceased by this time; the sun and Milky Way shone calmly, as if the whole universe were waiting in anticipation.

Li Bai stood steadily at the edge of the plane. The layer of air above the plane created almost no scattering effect, so that the sunlight cast him in crispest light and shadow. Aside from the movements of his hand when he smoothed his beard now and then, he was practically a statue hewn from stone.

Yi Yi and Bigtooth waited and waited. Time flowed past silently. The brush on the desk, plump with ink, began to dry. The position of the sun changed unnoticed in the sky; they, the desk, and the spaceship cast long shadows, while the white paper that was spread out on the desk appeared as if it had become part of the plane.

Finally, Li Bai turned and slowly stepped over to the desk. Yi Yi hurriedly re-dipped the brush in ink and offered it with both hands, but Li Bai held up a hand in refusal. He only stared at the blank paper on the desk in continued deep thought, something new in his gaze.

Yi Yi, with glee, saw that it was perplexity and unease.

'I need to make some more things. They're all . . . fragile goods. Be sure to catch them.' Li Bai pointed at the fabricator; the flames within, which had dimmed, grew bright once more. Just as Yi Yi and Bigtooth ran over, a tongue of blue flame pushed out a round object. Bigtooth caught it agilely. Upon closer inspection, it was a large earthen jar. Next, three large bowls sprang out of the blue flames. Yi Yi caught two of them, but the third fell and shattered. Bigtooth carried the jar to the desk and carefully unsealed it. The powerful fragrance of wine emerged. Bigtooth and Yi Yi exchanged astonished looks.

'There wasn't much documentation on human winemaking in the Earth-related data I received from the Devouring Empire, so I'm not sure I fabricated this correctly,' said Li Bai, pointing to the jar of wine to indicate that Yi Yi should taste it.

Yi Yi took a bowl, scooped a little from the jar, and took a sip. Fiery heat ran past his throat down into his belly. He nodded. 'It's wine, albeit much too strong compared to the kind we drink to improve our meat quality.'

Li Bai pointed to the other bowl on the desk. 'Fill it up.' He waited for Bigtooth to pour a bowlful of the strong wine, then picked it up and glugged the whole thing down. Then he turned and once again walked off into the distance, weaving a stagger here and there along the way. Once he reached the edge of the plane, he stood there and resumed his pondering in the direction of the stars, only this time his body swayed rhythmically left and right, as if to some unheard melody. Li Bai didn't ponder for long before returning to the desk once more, and on the walk back he staggered every step. He grabbed the brush being proffered by Yi Yi and threw it into the distance.

'Fill it up,' Li Bai said, eyes fixed on the empty bowl. . . .

An hour later, Bigtooth's two immense claws carefully lowered a passed-out Li Bai onto the cleared desk, only for him to roll over and fall right off, muttering something in a language incomprehensible to dinosaur and human alike. He'd already vomited a particolored pile (although no one knew when he'd had the occasion to eat in the first place), some of it staining his flowing robes. With the white light of the plane passing through, the vomit formed some sort of abstract image. Li Bai's mouth was black with ink: after finishing his fourth bowl, he'd tried to write something on the paper, but had ended up merely stabbing his ink-plump brush heavily upon the table. After that, he'd tried to smooth the brush with his mouth, like a child at his first calligraphy lesson. . . .

'Esteemed god?' Bigtooth bent down and asked carefully.

'Wayakaaaaa . . . kaaaayiaiwa,' said Li Bai, tongue lolling.

Bigtooth straightened, shook his head, and sighed. He said to Yi Yi, 'Let's go.'

The Second Path

Yi Yi's feedlot was located on the Devourers' equator. While the planet had lain within the inner reaches of the solar system, this had been a beautiful prairie between two rivers. When the Devourers left the orbit of Jupiter, a harsh winter had descended, the prairie disappearing and the rivers freezing. The humans raised there had all been relocated to an underground city. After the Devourers received the summons from the god and returned, spring had come back to the land with the approach of the sun. The two rivers quickly defrosted, and the prairie began to turn green as well.

In times of good weather, Yi Yi lived alone in the crude grass hut he'd built himself by the riverside, tilling the land and amusing himself. A normal human wouldn't have been allowed, but as Yi Yi's feedlot lectures on ancient literature had edifying properties, imparting a unique flavor to the flesh of his students, the dinosaur breeder didn't stop him.

It was dusk, two months after Yi Yi had first met Li Bai, the sun just tipping over the perfectly straight horizon line of the Devouring Empire. The two rivers reflected the sunset, meeting at the edge of the sky. In the riverside hut, a breeze carried faint, distant sounds of song and celebration over the prairie. Yi Yi was alone, playing weiqi with himself.

He looked up and saw Li Bai and Bigtooth walking along the riverbank toward him. Li Bai was much changed from before: his hair was unkempt, his beard even longer, his face sun-browned. He had a rough cloth pack slung over his left shoulder and a large bottle-gourd in his right hand. His robes had been reduced to rags; his woven-straw shoes were mangled with wear. But Yi Yi thought that he now seemed more like a human being.

Li Bai walked over to the weiqi table. Like the last few times, he slammed the gourd down without looking at Yi Yi and said, 'Bowl!' When Yi Yi had brought over the two wooden bowls, Li Bai uncorked the gourd and filled them with wine, then took a paper package from his pack. Yi Yi opened it to discover cooked meat, already sliced, its aroma greeting his nose enthusiastically. He couldn't help but grab a piece and start chewing.

Bigtooth only stood, a few meters away, watching them silently. He knew from before that the two of them were going to discuss poetry again, a topic in which he had no interest and no ability.

'Delicious,' Yi Yi said, nodding approvingly. 'Is the beef made directly from energy too?'

'No, I've gone natural for a long while now. You might not know, but there's a pasture a long distance away from here where they raise Earth cows. I cooked the beef myself in the Shanxi Pingyao style. There's a trick to it. When you stew the meat, you have to add . . .' Li Bai whispered mysteriously into Yi Yi's ear, 'Urea.'

Yi Yi looked at him uncomprehendingly.

'Oh, that's what you get when you take human urine, let it evaporate, and extract the white stuff. It makes the cooked meat red and juicy with a tender texture, while keeping the fatty parts from being cloying and the lean parts from being leathery.'

'The urea . . . it's made from pure energy, right?' Yi Yi asked, horrified.

'I told you, I've gone natural! It took me a lot of work to collect the urea from several human feedlots. This is a very traditional folk cuisine technique, faded from use long before the destruction of Earth.'

Yi Yi had already swallowed his bite of beef. He picked up the wine bowl to prevent himself from vomiting.

Li Bai pointed at the gourd. 'Under my direction, the Devouring Empire has built a number of distilleries, already capable of producing many of the wines famous on Earth. This is bona-fide zhuyeqing, made by steeping bamboo leaves in sorghum liquor.'

Yi Yi only now discovered that the wine in his bowl was different from what Li Bai had brought previously. It was emerald green, with a sweet aftertaste of herbs.

'Looks like you've really mastered human culture,' Yi Yi said feelingly to Li Bai.

'That's not all. I've also spent a lot of time on personal enrichment. As you know, the scenery of many parts of the Devouring Empire is near identical to what Li Bai saw on Earth. In these two months, I've wandered the mountains and waters, feasting my eyes on picturesque landscapes, drinking wine under moonlight, declaiming poetry on mountain summits, even having a few romantic encounters in the human feedlots everywhere . . .'

'Then, you should be ready to show me your works of poetry.'

Li Bai set down his wine bowl suddenly. He stood and paced uneasily. 'I've composed some poems, yes, and I'm certain you'd be astonished at them. You'd find that I'm already a remarkable poet, even more remarkable than you and your great-grandfather. But I don't want you to see the poems, because I'm equally certain you'd think they fail to surpass Li Bai's. And I . . .' He looked up and far away, at the residual radiance of the setting sun, his gaze dazed and pained. 'I think so too.'

On the distant prairie, the dances had ended. People were happily turning to their abundant dinner. A group of girls ran to the riverbank to splash in the shallows near shore. Circlets of flowers adorned their heads, and light gauze like mist draped over their bodies, forming an intoxicating scene in the lighting of dusk. Yi Yi pointed at one girl near the hut. 'Is she beautiful?'

'Of course,' Li Bai said, looking uncomprehendingly at Yi Yi.

'Imagine cutting her open with a sharp knife, removing her every organ, plucking out her eyes, scooping out her brain, picking out all her bones, slicing apart her muscles and fat according to position and function, gathering her blood vessels and nerves into two bundles. Finally, imagine laying out a big white cloth and arranging all those pieces, classified according to anatomical principles. Would you still think her beautiful?'

'How do you think of such a thing while drinking? Disgusting,' Li Bai said, wrinkling his brow.

'How is it disgusting? Is this not the technology you worship?'

'What are you trying to say?'

'Li Bai saw nature like you see the girls down by the riverside. But in technology's eyes, nature is its components, perfectly arrayed and dripping blood on a white cloth. Therefore, technology is antithetical to poetry.'

'Then you have a suggestion for me?' Li Bai said thoughtfully, stroking his beard.

'I still don't think you stand a chance at surpassing Li Bai, but I can point your energies in the correct direction. Technology has clouded your eyes, blinding you to the beauty of nature. Therefore, you must first forget all your ultra-advanced technological knowledge. If you can transplant all your memories into your current brain, you can certainly delete some of them.'

Li Bai exchanged looks with Bigtooth. Both burst into laughter. 'Esteemed god, I told you from the start, these are tricky bug-bugs,' said Bigtooth. 'A moment of carelessness and you'll fall into one of their traps.'

'Hahahaha, tricky indeed, but entertaining as well,' Li Bai said to Bigtooth, before turning toward Yi Yi with cold amusement. 'Did you really think I came here to admit defeat?'

'You could not surpass the pinnacle of human poetry. That's a fact.'

Abruptly, Li Bai raised a finger and pointed to the river. 'How many ways are there to walk to the riverbank?'

Yi Yi looked uncomprehendingly at Li Bai for a few seconds. 'It seems . . . there's only one.'

'No, there's two. I can also walk in this direction,' Li Bai indicated the direction opposite from the river, 'and keep going, all the way around the Devouring Empire, crossing the river from the other side to reach this bank. I can even make a full circuit around the Milky Way and return here. With our technology, it's just as easy. Technology can surpass anything! I am now forced to take the second path!'

Yi Yi pondered this for a long time before shaking his head in bewilderment. 'Even if you have the technology of a god, I can't think of a second path to surpassing Li Bai.'

Li Bai stood. 'It's simple. There are two ways to surpass Li Bai. The first is to write poems that surpass his. The other is to write every poem!'

Yi Yi looked even more confused, but Bigtooth beside him seemed to have had an epiphany.

'I will write every five-character-line and seven-character-line poem possible. They were Li Bai's specialty. In addition, I'm going to write down every possible lyrical poem for the common line formats! How do you not understand? I'm going to try every possible permutation of Chinese characters that fits the format rules!'

'Ah, magnificent! What a magnificent undertaking!' Bigtooth crowed, forgetting all dignity.

'Is this hard?' Yi Yi asked ignorantly.

'Of course, incredibly so! The largest computer in the Devouring Empire might not be able to finish the calculations before the death of the universe!'

'Surely not,' Yi Yi said, skeptical.

'Of course yes!' Li Bai nodded with satisfaction. 'But by using quantum computing, which you're still a long way from mastering, we can complete the calculations in an acceptable length of time. Then I'll have written every single poem, including everything that's been written in the past, and, much more importantly, everything that may be written someday in the future! This will naturally include poems that surpass Li Bai's best works. In fact, I've ended the art of poetry. Every poet from now on to the destruction of the universe, no matter how great, will be no more than a plagiarist. Their works will turn up in a search of my enormous storage device.'

Bigtooth suddenly gave a guttural cry, his gaze on Li Bai changing from excitement to shock. 'An enormous . . . storage device? Esteemed god, do you mean to say, you're going to . . . *save* all the poems the quantum computer writes?'

'What's the fun in deleting everything right after I write it? Of course I'm going to save them! It will be a monument to the artistic contributions my race has made to this universe!'

Bigtooth's expression changed from shock to horror. He extended his bulky claws and bent his legs, as if trying to kneel to Li Bai. 'You mustn't, esteemed god,' he cried. 'You mustn't!'

'What's got you so scared?' Yi Yi regarded Bigtooth with astonishment.

'You idiot! Don't you know that atomic bombs are made of atoms? The storage device will be made of atoms too, and its storage precision can't possibly exceed the atomic level! Do you know what atomic-level storage is? It means that all of humanity's books can be stored in an area the size of the point of a needle! Not the couple of books you have left, but all the books that existed before we ate Earth!'

'Ah, that sounds plausible. I've heard that a glass of water contains more atoms than the Earth's oceans contained cups of water. Then, he can just write down those poems and take the needle with him,' Yi Yi said, pointing at Li Bai.

Bigtooth nearly burst with outrage. He had to rapidly pace a few steps to summon a little more patience. 'Okay, okay, tell me, if the god writes all those five-character-and seven-character-line poems, and the common lyrical poetry formats, one time each, how many characters would that be?'

'Not many, no more than two or three thousand, right? Classical poetry is the most concise art form there is.'

'Fine, you idiot bug-bug, let me show you how concise it really is!' Bigtooth strode to the table and pointed at the game board with one claw. 'What is it you call this stupid game . . . ah yes, weiqi. How many grid intersections are on the board?'

'There are nineteen lines in both the vertical and horizontal directions, for a total of three hundred and sixty-one points.'

'Very good, each intersection can be occupied by a black piece, a white piece, or no piece, a total of three states in all. So you can think of each game state as using three characters to write a poem of nineteen lines and three hundred and sixty-one characters.'

'That's a clever comparison.'

'Now, if we exhaust all the possible permutations of these three characters in this poem format, how many poems can we write? Let me tell you: 3^{361}, or, let me think, 10^{172}!'

'Is . . . is that a lot?'

'Idiot!' Bigtooth spat the word at him for the third time. 'In all the universe, there are only . . . grargh!' He was too infuriated to speak.

'How many?' Yi Yi still wore a befuddled expression.

'10^{80} atoms! You idiot bug-bug—'

Only now did Yi Yi show any sign of astonishment. 'You mean to say, if we could save one poem in every atom, we might use up every atom in the universe and still not be able to fit all of his quantum computer's poems?'

'Far from it! Off by a factor of 10^{92}! Besides, how can one atom store a whole poem? The memory devices of human bug-bugs would have needed more atoms to store one poem than your population. As for us, *ai,* technology to store one bit per atom is still in the laboratory stage. . . .'

'Here you display your shortsightedness and lack of imagination, Emissary, one of the reasons behind the laggardly advancement of Devouring Empire technology,' Li Bai said, laughing. 'Using quantum storage devices based on the quantum superposition principle, the poems can be stored in very little matter. Of course, quantum storage is none too stable. To preserve the poems forever, it needs to be used in tandem with more traditional storage techniques. Nonetheless, the amount of matter required is minuscule.'

'How much?' Bigtooth asked, looking as if his heart were in his throat.

'Approximately 10^{57} atoms, a pittance really.'

'That's . . . that's exactly the amount of matter in the solar system!'

'Correct, including all the planets orbiting the sun, and of course including the Devouring Empire.'

Li Bai said this last sentence easily and naturally, but it struck Yi Yi like a bolt out of the blue. Bigtooth, on the other hand, seemed to have calmed down. After the long torment of sensing disaster on the horizon, the actual onslaught only left a sense of relief.

'Can't you convert pure energy into matter?' asked Bigtooth.

'You should know how much energy it would take to create such an enormous amount of matter. The prospect is unimaginable even to us. We'll go with ready-made.'

'His Majesty's concerns weren't unjustified,' Bigtooth murmured to himself.

'Yes, yes,' Li Bai said happily. 'I informed the Emperor of the Devourers the day before yesterday. This great ring-world empire shall be used for an even greater goal. The dinosaurs should feel honored.'

'Esteemed god, you'll see how the Devouring Empire feels,' Bigtooth said darkly. 'I also have one more concern. Compared to the sun, the amount of matter in the Devouring Empire is insignificantly minuscule. Is it really necessary to destroy a civilization millions of years of evolution in the making, just to obtain a few scraps?'

'I fully understand your reservations. But you must know, extinguishing, cooling, and disassembling the sun will take a long time. The quantum calculations should begin before then, and we need to save the resulting poems elsewhere so that the computer can clear its internal storage and continue work. Therefore the planets and the Devouring Empire, which can immediately provide matter for manufacturing storage devices, are crucial.'

'I understand, esteemed god. I have one last question: Is it necessary to store all the results? Why can't you add an analytical program at the end, to delete all the poems that don't warrant saving? From what I know, Classical Chinese poetry has to follow a strict structure. If we delete all the poems that violate the formal rules, we'll greatly decrease the volume of the results.'

'Formal rules? Ha.' Li Bai shook his head contemptuously. 'Shackles upon inspiration, and nothing more. Classical Chinese poetry wasn't bound by these rules before the Northern and Southern Dynasties. Even after the Tang Dynasty, which popularized the strict jintishi form, many master poets ignored the rules to write some extraordinary biantishi works. That's why, for this ultimate poetry composition, I won't take formal rules into consideration.'

'But, you should still consider the poem's content, right? Ninety-nine percent of the results are obviously going to be rubbish. What's the point of storing a bunch of randomly generated character arrays?'

'Rubbish?' Li Bai shrugged. 'Emissary, you are not the one who decides whether a poem is meaningful. Neither am I, nor any other person. Time decides. Many poems once considered worthless at the time of their writing were later lauded as masterpieces. Many of the masterpieces of today and tomorrow would have been considered worthless in the distant past. I'm going to write all the poems there are. Trillions of years from now, who knows which of them mighty Time will choose as the finest?'

'That's absurd!' Bigtooth bellowed, startling several birds hidden in the distant grass into flight. 'If we go by the human bug-bugs' preexisting Chinese character database, the first poem your quantum computer writes should be:

a a a a a

a a a a a

a a a a a

a a a a ai

'Might I ask, would mighty Time choose *this* as a masterpiece?!'

Yi Yi broke his silence to cheer. 'Wow! Who needs mighty Time to choose? It's a masterpiece right now! The first three lines and the first four characters of the fourth are the exclamations—*ah!*—of living beings witnessing the majestic grandeur of the universe. The last character is the clincher, where the poet, having witnessed the vastness of the universe, expresses the insignificance of life in the infinity of time and space with a single sigh of inevitability.'

'Hahahaha . . .' Li Bai stroked his whiskers, unable to stop smiling. 'A fine poem, my bug-bug Yi Yi, a fine poem indeed, hahaha . . .' He took up the gourd and poured Yi Yi wine.

Bigtooth raised his massive claws and flung Yi Yi into the distance with one swat. 'Nasty bug-bug, I know you're happy now. But don't forget, once the Devouring Empire is destroyed, your kind won't survive either!'

Yi Yi rolled all the way to the riverbank. It took a long time before he could crawl back up. A grin cracked across his dirt-covered face; he was laughing despite his pain, truly happy. 'This is great! This universe is motherfucking incredible!' he yelled with no thought to dignity.

'Any other questions, Emissary?' asked Li Bai. Bigtooth shook his head. 'Then I'll leave tomorrow. The day after the next, the quantum computer will execute its poetry-writing software, commencing the ultimate poetry composition. At the same time, the work to extinguish the sun and dismantle the planets and the Devouring Empire shall commence.'

Bigtooth straightened. 'Esteemed god, the Devouring Empire will complete preparations for battle tonight!' he said solemnly.

'Good, very good, the coming days will be interesting. But before all else, let us finish this gourd.' Li Bai nodded happily as he took up the gourd and poured the remaining wine. He looked at the river, now shrouded in night, and continued to savor those words: 'A fine poem indeed, the first, haha, the first and already so fine.'

The Ultimate Poetry Composition

The poetry-composition software was in fact very simple. Represented in humanity's C language, it would be no more than two thousand lines of code, with an additional database of modest size appended storing the Chinese characters. Once the software was uploaded onto the quantum computer in the orbit of Neptune, an enormous transparent cone floating in the vacuum, the ultimate poetry composition began.

Only now did the Devouring Empire learn that the god version of Li Bai was merely one individual member of his ultra-advanced civilization. The dinosaurs had previously assumed that any society that had advanced to this level of technology would have melded their consciousness into one being long ago; all five of the ultra-advanced civilizations they'd met in the past ten million years had done so. That Li Bai's race had preserved their individual existences also somewhat explained their extraordinary ability to grasp art. When the poetry composition began, more individuals from Li Bai's race jumped into the solar system from various places in distant space and began construction on the storage device.

The humans living in the Devouring Empire couldn't see the quantum computer in space, or the new arrivals from the race of gods. To them, the process of the ultimate poetry composition was simply the increase and decrease of the number of suns in space.

One week after the poetry software began execution, the gods successfully extinguished the sun, reducing the sun count to zero. But the cessation of nuclear fission inside the sun caused the star's outer layer to lose support, and it quickly collapsed into a new star that illuminated the darkness once more. However, this sun's luminosity was a hundred times greater than before; smoke rose from the grass and trees on the surface of the Devouring Empire. The new star was once again extinguished, but a while later it burst alight again. So it went on, lighting only to be extinguished, extinguishing only to light once more, as if the sun were a cat with nine lives, struggling stubbornly. But the gods were highly practiced at killing stars. They patiently extinguished the new star again and again, until its matter had, as much as possible, fused into the heavier elements needed in the construction of the storage device. Only after the eleventh star dimmed was the sun snuffed out for good.

At this point, the ultimate poetry composition had run for three Earth months. Long before then, during the appearance of the third new star, other suns had appeared in space. These suns rose and fell in succession throughout space, brightening and dimming. At one point, there were nine new suns in the sky. They were releases of energy as the gods dismantled the planets. With the star-sized sun diminishing in brightness later on, people could no longer tell the suns apart.

The dismantlement of the Devouring Empire commenced the fifth week after the start of the poetry composition. Before it, Li Bai had made a suggestion to the Empire: The gods could jump all the dinosaurs to a world on the other side of the Milky Way. The civilization there was much less advanced than the gods', its members being unable to convert themselves into pure energy, but still much more advanced than the Devourers' civilization. There, the dinosaurs would be raised as a form of livestock and live happy lives with all their needs taken care of. But the dinosaurs would rather break than bend, and angrily refused this suggestion.

Next, Li Bai made another request: that humanity be allowed to return to their mother planet. To be sure, Earth had been dismantled, and most of it went toward the storage device. But the gods saved a small amount of matter to construct a hollow Earth, about the same size as the original, but with only a hundredth of its mass. To say that the hollow Earth was Earth hollowed-out would be incorrect, because the layer of brittle rock that originally covered the Earth could hardly be used to make the spherical shell. The shell material was perhaps taken from the Earth's core. In addition, razor-thin but extremely strong reinforcing hoops crisscrossed the shell, like lines of latitude and longitude, made from the neutronium produced in the collapse of the sun.

Movingly, the Devouring Empire not only immediately agreed to Li Bai's request, allowing all humans to leave the great ring world, but also returned the seawater and air they'd taken from Earth in their entirety. The gods used them to restore all of Earth's original continents, oceans, and atmosphere inside the hollow Earth.

Next, the terrible battle to defend the great ring began. The Devouring Empire launched barrages of nuclear missiles and gamma rays at the gods in space, but these were useless against their foe. The gods launched a powerful, invisible force that pushed at the Devourers' ring, spinning it faster and faster, until it finally fell apart under the centrifugal forces of such rapid rotation. At this time, Yi Yi was en route to the hollow Earth. From twelve million kilometers away, he witnessed the complete course of the Devouring Empire's destruction:

EXTRACT-A

The ring came apart very slowly, dreamlike. Against the pitch-black backdrop of space, this immense world dispersed like a piece of milk foam on coffee, the fragments at its edges slowly sinking into darkness, as if being dissolved by space. Only by the flashes of sporadic explosions would they reappear.

Excerpt from Devourer

END EXTRACT-A

The great, fierce civilization from ancient Earth was thus destroyed, to Yi Yi's deepest lament. Only a few dinosaurs survived, returning to Earth with humanity, including the emissary Bigtooth.

On the return journey to Earth, the humans were largely in low spirits, but for different reasons than Yi Yi: Once they were back on Earth, they'd have to farm and plow if they wanted to eat. To humans accustomed to having every need provided for in their long captivity, grown indolent and ignorant of labor, it really did seem like a nightmare.

But Yi Yi believed in Earth's future. No matter how many challenges lay ahead, humans were going to become people once more.

The Cloud of Poems

The poetry voyage arrived on the shores of Antarctica.

The gravity here was already weak; the waves cycled slowly in a dreamlike dance. Under the low gravity, the impact of waves upon shore sent spray dozens of meters into the air, where the seawater contracted under surface tension into countless spheres, some as large as soccer balls, some as small as raindrops, which fell so slowly that one could draw rings around them with one's hand. They refracted the rays of the little sun, so that when Yi Yi, Li Bai, and Bigtooth disembarked, they were surrounded by crystalline brilliance.

Due to the forces of rotation, the Earth was slightly stretched at the North and South Poles, causing the hollow Earth's pole regions to maintain their old chilly state. Low-gravity snow was a wonder, loose and foamy, waist-high in the shallow parts and deep enough at others that even Bigtooth disappeared beneath it. But having disappeared, they could still breathe normally inside the snow! The entire Antarctic continent was buried underneath this snow-foam, creating an undulating landscape of white.

Yi Yi and company rode a snowmobile toward the South Pole. The snowmobile skimmed across the snow-foam like a speedboat, throwing waves of white to either side.

The next day, they arrived at the South Pole, marked by a towering pyramid of crystal, a memorial dedicated to the Earth Defense War of two centuries ago. Neither writing nor images marked its surface. There was just the crystal form in the snow-foam at the apex of the Earth, silently refracting the sunlight.

From here, one could gaze upon the entire world. Continents and oceans surrounded the radiant little sun, so that it looked as if it had floated up from the waters of the Arctic Sea.

'Will that little sun really be able to shine forever?' Yi Yi asked Li Bai.

'At the very least, it will last until the new Earth civilization is advanced enough to create a new sun. It is a miniature white hole.'

'White hole? Is that the inverse of a black hole?' asked Bigtooth.

'Yes, it's connected through a wormhole to a black hole orbiting a star, two million light-years away. The black hole sucks in the star's light, which is released here. Think of the sun as one end of a fiber-optic cable running through hyperspace.'

The apex of the monument was the southern starting point of the Lagrangian axis, the thirteen-thousand-kilometer line of zero gravity between the North and South Poles of the hollow Earth, named after the zero-gravity Lagrangian point that had existed between the Earth and moon before the war. In the future, people were certain to launch various satellites onto the Lagrangian axis. Compared to the process on Earth before the war, this would be easy: one would only have to ship the satellite to the North or South Pole, by donkey if one wanted to, and give it a good kick up with one's foot.

As the party viewed the memorial, another larger snowmobile ferried over a crowd of young human tourists. After disembarking, the tourists bent their legs and jumped straight into the air, flying high along the Lagrangian axis, turning themselves into satellites. From here, one could see many small, black specks in the air, marking out the position of the axis: tourists and vehicles drifting in zero gravity. They would have been able to fly directly to the North Pole if it weren't for the sun, placed at the midpoint of the Lagrangian axis. In the past, some tourists flying along the axis had discovered their handheld miniature air-jet thrusters broken, been unable to decelerate, and flown straight into the sun. Well, in truth, they vaporized a considerable distance from it.

In the hollow Earth, entering space was also easy. One only needed to jump into one of the five deep wells on the equator (called Earthgates) and fall (fly?) a hundred kilometers through the shell, then be flung by the centrifugal forces of the hollow Earth's rotation into space.

Yi Yi and company also needed to pass through the shell to see the Cloud of Poems, but they were heading through the Antarctic Earthgate. Here, there were no centrifugal forces, so instead of being flung into space, they would only reach the outer surface of the hollow Earth. Once they'd put on lightweight space suits at the Antarctic control station, they entered the one-hundred-kilometer well—although, without gravity, it was better termed a tunnel. Being weightless here, they used the thrusters on their space suits to move forward. This was much slower than the free fall on the equator; it took them half an hour to arrive on the outside.

The outer surface of the hollow Earth was completely barren. There were only the crisscrossing reinforcing hoops of neutronium, which divided the outside by latitude and longitude into a grid. The South Pole was indeed where all the longitudinal hoops met. When Yi Yi and company walked out of the Earthgate, they saw that they were located on a modestly sized plateau. The hoops that reinforced Earth resembled many long mountain ranges, radiating in every direction from the plateau.

Looking up, they saw the Cloud of Poems.

In place of the solar system was the Cloud of Poems, a spiral galaxy a hundred astronomical units across, shaped much like the Milky Way. The hollow Earth was situated at the edge of the Cloud, much as the sun had been in the actual Milky Way. The difference was that Earth's position was not coplanar with the Cloud of Poems, which allowed one to see one face of the Cloud head-on, instead of only edge-on as with the Milky Way. But Earth wasn't nearly far enough from the plane to allow people here to observe the full form of the Cloud of Poems. Instead, the Cloud blanketed the entire sky of the southern hemisphere.

The Cloud of Poems emitted a silvery radiance bright enough to cast shadows on the ground. It wasn't that the Cloud itself was made to glow, apparently, but rather that cosmic rays would excite it into silver luminescence. Due to the uneven spatial distribution of the cosmic rays, glowing masses frequently rippled through the Cloud of Poems, their varicolored light rolling across the sky like luminescent whales diving through the Cloud. Rarely, with spikes in the cosmic radiation, the Cloud of Poems emitted dapples of light that made the Cloud look utterly unlike a cloud. Instead, the entire sky seemed to be the surface of a moonlit sea seen from below.

Earth and the Cloud did not move in sync, so sometimes Earth lay in the gaps between the spiral arms. Through the gap, one could see the night sky and the stars, and most thrillingly, a cross-sectional view of the Cloud of Poems. Immense structures resembling Earthly cumulonimbuses rose from the spiraling plane, shimmering with silvery light, morphing through magnificent forms that inspired the human imagination, as if they belonged to the dreamscape of some super-advanced consciousness.

Yi Yi tore his gaze from the Cloud of Poems and picked up a crystal chip off the ground. These chips were scattered around them, sparkling like shards of ice in winter. Yi Yi raised the chip against a sky thick with the Cloud of Poems. The chip was very thin, and half the size of his palm. It appeared transparent from the front, but if he tilted it slightly, he could see the bright light of the Cloud of Poems reflect off its surface in rainbow halos. This was a quantum memory chip. All the written information created in human history would take up less than a millionth of a percent of one chip. The Cloud of Poems was composed of 10^{40} of these storage devices, and contained all the results of the ultimate poem composition. It was manufactured using all the matter in the sun and its nine major planets, of course including the Devouring Empire.

'What a magnificent work of art!' Bigtooth sighed sincerely.

'Yes, it's beautiful in its significance: a nebula ten billion kilometers across, encompassing every poem possible. It's too spectacular!' Yi Yi said, gazing at the nebula. 'Even I'm starting to worship technology.'

Li Bai gave a long sigh. He had been in a low mood all this time. '*Ai*, it seems like we've both come around to the other person's viewpoint. I witnessed the limits of technology in art. I—' He began to sob. 'I've failed. . . .'

'How can you say that?' Yi Yi pointed at the Cloud of Poems overhead. 'This holds all the possible poems, so of course it holds the poems that surpass Li Bai's!'

'But I can't get to them!' Li Bai stomped his foot, which shot him meters into the air. He curled into a ball in midair, miserably burying his face between his knees in a fetal position; he slowly descended under the weak gravitational pull of the Earth's shell. 'At the start of the poetry composition, I immediately set out to program software that could analyze poetry. At that point, technology once again met that unsurpassable obstacle in the pursuit of art. Even now, I'm still unable to write software that can judge and appreciate poetry.' He pointed up at the Cloud of Poems. 'Yes, with the help of mighty technology, I've written the ultimate works of poetry. But I can't find them amid the Cloud of Poems, *ai . . .*'

'Is the soul and essence of intelligent life truly untouchable by technology?' Bigtooth loudly asked the Cloud of Poems above. He'd become increasingly philosophical after all he'd endured.

'Since the Cloud of Poems encompasses all possible poems, then naturally some portion of those poems describes all of our pasts and all of our futures, possible and impossible. The bug-bug Yi Yi would certainly find a poem that describes how he felt one night thirty years ago while clipping his fingernails, or a menu from a lunch twelve years in his future. Emissary Bigtooth, too, might find a poem that describes the color of a particular scale on his leg five years from now. . . .'

Li Bai had touched down once more on the ground; as he spoke, he took out two chips, shimmering under the light of the Cloud of Poems. 'These are my parting gifts for you two. The quantum computer used your names as keywords to search through the Cloud of Poems, and found several quadrillion poems that describe your various possible future lives. Of course, these are only a tiny portion of the poems with you as subject in the Cloud of Poems. I've only read a couple dozen of these. My favorite is a seven-character-line poem about Yi Yi describing a romantic riverbank scene between him and a beautiful woman from a faraway village. . . .

'After I leave, I hope humanity and the remaining dinosaurs can get along with each other, and that humanity can get along with itself even better. If someone nukes a hole into the shell of the hollow Earth, it's going to be a real problem. . . . The good poems in the Cloud of Poems don't belong to anyone yet. Hopefully humans will be able to write some of them.'

'What happened to me and the woman, afterward?' Yi Yi asked.

Under the silver light of the Cloud of Poems, Li Bai chuckled. 'Together, you lived happily ever after.'

欢乐颂

ODE TO JOY

AN ALTERNATE HISTORY OF THE SOPHON

TRANSLATED BY JOEL MARTINSEN

周华 译

The Concert

The concert held to close the final session of the United Nations was a depressing one.

A utilitarian attitude toward the body, dating back to bad precedents set at the start of the century, had been on the rise; countries assumed the UN was a tool to achieve their interests, and interpreted its charter to their own benefit. Smaller nations challenged the authority of the permanent members, while each permanent member believed it deserved more authority within the organization, which lost all authority of its own as a result. A decade on, all efforts at a rescue had failed, and everyone agreed that the UN and the idealism it represented no longer applied to the real world. It was time to be rid of it.

All heads of state assembled for the final session, to observe a solemn funeral for the UN. The concert, held on the lawn outside the General Assembly building, was the final item on the program.

It was well after sunset. This was the most bewitching time of day, the handover from day to night when the cares of reality were masked by the growing dusk. The world was still visible under the last light from the setting sun, and on the lawn, the air was thick with the scent of budding flowers.

The secretary general was the last to arrive. On the lawn, he[1] ran across Richard Clayderman,[2] one of the evening's featured performers, and struck

---

1　英文版对人物性别进行了转换，本版遵循原文进行了修订。

2　The French musician's 1992 performance in China was the first by a major foreign pianist, and he has remained the most recognized classical musician in the decades since.

up a cheerful conversation.

'Your playing fascinates me,' he told the prince of pianists with a smile.

Clayderman, dressed in his favorite snow-white suit, looked uncomfortable. 'If that's genuine, then I'm overjoyed. But I've heard there have been complaints about my appearance at a concert like this.'

Not merely complaints. The head of UNESCO, a noted art theorist, had publicly criticized Clayderman's playing as 'busker-level,' and his performances as 'blasphemy against piano artistry.'

The secretary general lifted a hand to stop him. 'The UN can have none of classical music's arrogance. You've erected a bridge from classical music to the masses, and so must we bring humanity's highest ideals directly to the common people. That's why you were invited here tonight. Believe me, when I first heard your music under the sweltering sun in Africa, I had the feeling of standing in a ditch looking up at the stars. It was intoxicating.'

Clayderman gestured toward the leaders on the lawn. 'It feels more like a family gathering than a UN event.'

The secretary general looked over the crowd. 'On this lawn, for tonight at least, we have realized a utopia.'

He crossed the lawn and reached the front row. It was a glorious evening. He had planned on switching off his political sixth sense and just relaxing for once, taking his place as an ordinary member of the audience, but this proved impossible. That sense had picked up a situation: The president of China, engaged in conversation with the president of the United States, looked up at the sky for a moment. The act itself was utterly unremarkable, but the secretary general noticed that it was a little on the long side, perhaps just an extra second or two, but he'd noticed it. When the secretary general sat down after shaking hands with the other world leaders in the front row, the Chinese president looked up at the sky again, confirming his perception. Where national leaders are concerned, apparently random actions are in fact highly precise, and under normal circumstances, this act would not have been repeated. The US president also noticed it.

'The lights of New York wash out the stars. The sky's far brighter than this over DC,' he said.

The Chinese president nodded but said nothing.

The US president went on, 'I like looking at the stars, too. In the ever-changing course of history, our profession needs an immovable reference object.'

'That object is an illusion,' the Chinese president said.

'Why do you say that?'

Instead of responding directly, the Chinese president pointed at a cluster of stars that had just come out. 'Look, that's the Southern Cross, and that's Canis Major.'

The US president smiled. 'You've proven they're immovable enough. Ten thousand years ago, primitive man would have seen the same Southern Cross and Canis Major as we do today. They may have even come up with those names.'

'No, Mr. President. In fact, the sky might even have been different just yesterday.' The Chinese president looked up for a third time. He remained calm, but the steel in his eyes made the other two nervous. They looked at the same placid sky they had seen so many times before; nothing seemed wrong. They looked questioningly at the Chinese president.

'The two constellations I just noted should only be visible from the southern hemisphere,' he said without pointing them out or looking upward. He turned thoughtfully toward the horizon.

The secretary general and US president looked questioningly at him.

'We're looking at the sky from the other side of the Earth,' he said.

The US president yelped, but then restrained himself and said in a voice even lower than before, 'You've got to be kidding.'

'Look, what's that?' the secretary general said, pointing at the sky with a hand raised only to eye level so as not to alarm the others.

'The moon, of course,' the US president said after a brief glance overhead. But when the Chinese president slowly shook his head, he looked up a second time and was less certain. At first, the semicircular shape in the sky looked like the moon in first quarter, but it was bluish, as if a scrap of daytime sky had gotten stuck. The US president looked more closely at the blue semicircle. He became a keen observer once he was focused. He held out a finger and measured the blue moon against it. 'It's growing.'

The three politicians stared up at the sky, not caring anymore if they'd startle the others. The heads of state in the surrounding seats noticed their movements, and more people looked upward. The orchestra on the outdoor stage abruptly stopped its warm-up.

By now, it was clear that the blue semicircle was not the moon, because its diameter had grown to twice that, and its darkness-shrouded other half was now visible in dim blue. In its brighter half, details could be made out; its surface was not a uniform blue but had patches of brown.

'God! Isn't that North America?' someone shouted. They were right. You could distinguish the familiar shape of the continent, which lay smack on the border between the light and dark halves. (It may have occurred to someone that was the very same position they occupied.) Then they found Asia, and the Arctic Ocean and Bering Strait. . . .

'It's . . . Earth!'

The US president drew back his finger. The blue sphere in the sky was now growing at a rate visible without a reference object, and was now at least three times the diameter of the moon. At first, it looked like a balloon rapidly inflating in the sky, but then a shout from the crowd abruptly changed that impression:

'It's falling!'

The shout provided a reasonable interpretation of the scene before them. Regardless of its accuracy, they immediately had a new sense of what was happening: another Earth was crashing toward them in space! The approaching blue planet now occupied a third of the sky, and surface details could be made out: brown continents covered in mountain wrinkles, cloud coverage looking like unmelted snow, outlined in black from the shadows cast on the ground. There was white at the North Pole, parts of which glittered— ice, rather than clouds. On a blue ocean, a snow-white object spiraled lazily with the delicate beauty of a velvet flower in a blue crystal vase—a newborn hurricane. . . . But when the huge blue sphere grew to cover half the sky, their perception experienced an almost simultaneous transformation.

'God! We're falling!'

The feeling of inversion came in an instant. The sphere filling half the sky gave them a feeling of height, or that the ground beneath their feet had vanished and they were now falling toward the other Earth. Its surface was clearer now, and on the dark side, not far from the shadow line, those with keen eyes could see a faint glowing band: the lights of America's East Coast cities, their own location in New York a somewhat brighter spot within it. The other planet now filled two-thirds of the sky, and it seemed as if the two Earths would collide. There were screams from the crowd, and many of them shut their eyes.

Then all was still. The Earth overhead was no longer falling (or the ground they stood on was no longer falling toward it). The sphere hung motionless covering two-thirds of the sky, bathing the land in its blue glow.

Now sounds of chaos could be heard from the city, but the occupants of the lawn had the strongest nerves on the planet in unstable situations, so they held back their panic at the nightmarish scene and approached it more quietly.

'It's a hallucination,' the secretary general said.

'Yes,' the Chinese president said. 'If it were real, we'd feel the gravity. And this close to the sea, we'd be drowned by the tide.'

'It's more than just the tides,' the Russian president said. 'The two Earths would be torn to pieces by their mutual attraction.'

'The laws of physics don't permit two Earths to remain motionless,' the Japanese prime minister said, and, turning to the Chinese president, added, 'When that Earth first appeared, you were saying that the stars of the southern hemisphere were in the sky above us. Could the two phenomena be connected?' It was a tacit admission of eavesdropping, but they were past caring at this point.

'Perhaps we're about to find out,' the US president said. He spoke into a mobile phone; the secretary of state, at his elbow, informed the others that he was speaking with the International Space Station. And so they focused their anticipation on the president, who listened attentively to the phone but said only a few words. Silence reigned on the lawn, where in the blue light of that other Earth they looked like a throng of ghosts. After about two minutes, the president set down the phone, climbed onto a chair, and shouted to the expectant crowd:

'It's simple. A huge mirror has appeared next to the Earth!'

The Mirror

There was no way to describe it other than a huge mirror. Its surface perfectly reflected visual light as well as radar with no energy or image loss. Viewed from the right distance, the Earth would look like a stone on a go board ten billion square kilometers in area.

It shouldn't have been difficult for *Endeavor*'s astronauts to obtain preliminary data, since an astronomer and a space physicist were on board and had all the necessary equipment available and at their disposal, including the ISS, to conduct observations; however, their momentary panic had nearly sent the orbiter to its doom. The ISS was a fully-equipped observation platform, but its orbit was not conducive to observing an object situated 450 kilometers above the North Pole nearly perpendicular to the Earth's axis. *Endeavor*'s orbit sent it over the poles so it could carry out observations of the ozone holes; at a height of 280 kilometers, it was flying right between the Earth and the mirror.

Flying with an Earth on either side was nightmarish, like speeding along a canyon with blue cliffs towering above them. The pilot insisted it was a mirage, like the spatial disorientation he had experienced twice during his three thousand hours in a fighter jet, but the commander was convinced there really were two Earths. He ordered their orbit adjusted to compensate for the gravitational pull of the second one, but the astronomer stopped him in time. Once they got over their initial shock and learned from observations of the shuttle's orbit that one of the two Earths had no mass, they let out a sigh of relief: if they had made the compensational adjustments, *Endeavor* would be nothing more than a shooting star over the North Pole.

The astronauts carefully observed the massless Earth. Visual inspection indicated the orbiter was much farther away from it, but its North Pole seemed little different from that of the nearer Earth, if not entirely identical. They saw beams of polar lights emitting from both North Poles, two long, dark red snakes twisting slowly in identical shapes at identical positions. Eventually they discovered one thing that the nearer Earth did not have: an object in flight above the massless Earth. Visually they judged it to be in an orbit roughly three hundred kilometers above its surface, but when they attempted to probe its orbit more precisely using shipboard radar, the radar seemed to bounce back from a solid wall a hundred-odd kilometers away. The massless Earth and the flying object were on the opposite side of that wall. Observing the object through the cockpit window using high-powered binoculars, the commander saw another space shuttle flying in low orbit over the frozen Arctic ice pack like a moth crawling along a blue striped wall. There was a figure behind that shuttle's cockpit window, looking through binoculars. The commander waved, and the figure waved at the same time.

And so they discovered the mirror.

They altered course to draw closer to the mirror. At a distance of three kilometers, the astronauts could see clearly *Endeavor*'s reflection six kilometers away, the glow of its aft engines lending it the form of a creeping firefly.

One astronaut took a spacewalk for humanity's first close encounter with the mirror. Thrusters on the suit spurted streams of white, speeding him across the distance. Carefully, he adjusted the jets to bring himself into position ten meters from the mirror. His reflection was remarkably clear, without any distortion. Since he was in orbit but the mirror was stationary with respect to the Earth, he had a relative speed of ten kilometers per second. He was racing past it, but no motion at all was visible. It was the smoothest, shiniest surface in the universe.

When the astronaut decelerated, his thruster jets had been aimed at the mirror for an extended period, and a white fog of benzene propellant had drifted toward it. During previous space walks, whenever the fog had come into contact with the shuttle or the outside wall of the ISS, it would leave a conspicuous smudge; he imagined it would be the same with the mirror, except that with the high relative velocity, the smudge would be a long stripe, like he used to draw with soap on the bathroom mirror as a child. But he saw nothing. The fog vanished upon contact with the mirror, whose surface remained bright as ever.

The shuttle's orbital trajectory gave them only a limited amount of time near the mirror, prompting the astronaut to act quickly. In an almost unconscious act the moment the fog disappeared, he took a wrench out of his tool bag and tossed it at the mirror, but once it left his hand, he and the astronauts aboard the shuttle were paralyzed with the realization that the relative velocity between it and the mirror gave it the force of a bomb. In terror they watched the wrench tumble toward the mirror and had a vision of the spiderweb fractures that in just moments would spread like lightning across the surface from the point of impact, and then the enormous mirror shattering into billions of glittering fragments, a sea of silver in the blackness of space. . . . But when the wrench touched the surface it vanished without a trace, and the mirror remained as smooth as before.

It actually wasn't hard to see that the mirror was massless, not a physical body, since floating motionless over Earth's North Pole would be impossible otherwise. (It might be more accurate to state, given their relative sizes, that the Earth was floating in the middle of the mirror.) Rather than a physical entity, the mirror was a field of some sort. Contact with the fog and the wrench proved that.

Delicately manipulating his thrusters and making continual microadjustments of the jets, the astronaut drew within half a meter of the mirror. He stared straight into his reflection, amazed once again at its fidelity: a perfect copy, one perhaps even more finely wrought than the original. He extended a hand toward it until he and his reflected hand were practically touching, separated by less than a centimeter. His earpiece was silent—the commander did not order him to stop—so he pushed forward, and his hand disappeared into the mirror. He and his image were joined at the wrist. There had been no sensation of contact. He retracted his hand and looked at it carefully. The suit glove was perfectly unharmed. No marks whatsoever.

Below the astronaut, the shuttle was gradually drawing away from the mirror and had to constantly run its engines and thrusters to maintain proximity. However, due to its trajectory its drift was accelerating, and before long such adjustments would be impossible. A second encounter would require waiting an entire orbit, but would the mirror still be there? With this in mind, the astronaut made a decision. He switched on his thrusters and headed straight into the mirror.

His reflection loomed large, filling his field of vision with the quicksilver bubble of his helmet's one-way reflective faceplate. He fought to keep from closing his eyes as his head touched the mirror. At contact he felt nothing, but in that very moment everything vanished before his eyes, replaced by the darkness of space and the familiar Milky Way. He jerked around, and below him was the same view of the galaxy, with one addition: his own reflection receding into the distance, the maneuvering units he and his reflection wore linked by streams of thruster jet fog.

He had crossed the mirror, and the other side of it was a mirror, too.

His earpiece had been chirping with the commander's voice when he was approaching the mirror, but it had cut out. The mirror blocked radio waves. Worse, the Earth wasn't visible from this side. Surrounded entirely by stars gave the astronaut the feeling of being isolated in a different world, and he began to panic. He adjusted the jets and arrested his outward motion. He had passed through the first time with his body parallel to the mirror, but now he oriented himself perpendicular, as if diving headfirst into it. Just before contact, he cut his speed. Then the top of his head touched the top of his reflection, and then he passed through and saw with relief the blue Earth below him, and heard the commander's voice in his ear.

Once his upper torso was through he dropped his drift speed, leaving the remainder of his body on the other side. Then he reversed the direction of his jets and began to back up; fog from the jets on the opposite side of the mirror issued from the surface around him like steam rising from a lake in which he was partially submerged. When the surface reached his nose, he made another startling discovery: The mirror passed through his faceplate and filled the crescent space between it and his face. He looked downward and saw his frightened pupils reflected in the crescent. No doubt the mirror was passing through his entire head, but he felt nothing. He reduced his speed to the absolute minimum, no faster than the tick of a second hand, and advanced millimeter by millimeter until the mirror bisected his pupils and vanished.

Everything was back to normal: Earth's blue sphere on one side, the glittering Milky Way on the other. But that familiar world persisted only for a second or two. He couldn't reduce his speed to zero, so before long the mirror was above his eyes, and the Earth vanished, leaving only the Milky Way. Above him, the mirror blocking his view of Earth extended hundreds of thousands of kilometers into the distance. The angle of reflection distorted his view of the stars into a silver halo on the mirror's surface. He reversed thrusters and drifted back, and the mirror dropped down across his eyes, vanishing momentarily as it passed to reveal both Earth and Milky Way before the galaxy vanished and the halo turned blue on the mirror's surface. He moved slowly back and forth several times, and as his pupils oscillated on either side, he felt like he was passing across a membrane between two worlds. At last he managed a fairly lengthy pause with the mirror invisible at the center of his pupils. He opened his eyes wide for a glimpse of a line at its position, but he saw nothing.

'The thing's got no width!' he exclaimed.

'Maybe it's only a few atoms thick, so you just can't see it. Maybe it approached Earth edgewise and that's why it arrived undetected.' That was the assessment of the shuttle crew, who were watching the images sent back.

The astonishing thing was that the mirror, perhaps just atoms thick but over a hundred Pacific Oceans in area, was so flat as to be invisible from a parallel vantage point; in classical geometry, it was an ideal plane.

Its absolute flatness explained its absolute smoothness. It was an ideal mirror.

A sense of isolation replaced the astronauts' shock and fear. The mirror made the universe strange and rendered them a group of newborn babes abandoned in a new, unfathomable world.

Then the mirror spoke.

The Musician

'I am a musician,' it said. 'I am a musician.'

The pleasing voice resounding through space was audible to all. In an instant, all sleepers on Earth awoke, and all those already awake froze like statues.

The mirror continued, 'Below I see a concert whose audience members are capable of representing the planet's civilization. Do you wish to speak with me?'

The national leaders looked to the secretary general, who was momentarily at a loss for words.

'I have something to say,' the mirror said.

'Can you hear us?' the secretary general ventured.

The mirror answered immediately, 'Of course I can. I could distinguish the voice of every bacterium on the world below me, if I wanted to. I perceive things differently from you. I can observe the rotation of every atom simultaneously. My perception encompasses temporal dimensions: I can witness the entire history of a thing all at once. You only see cross sections, but I see all.'

'How are we hearing your voice?' the US president asked.

'I am emitting superstring waves into your atmosphere.'

'Superstring waves?'

'A strong interactive force released from an atomic nucleus. It excites your atmosphere like a giant hand beating a drum. That's how you hear me.'

'Where do you come from?' the secretary general asked.

'I am a mirror drifting through the universe. I originate so far away in both time and space it is meaningless to speak of it.'

'How did you learn English?'

'I said that I see all. I should note that I'm speaking English because most of the audience at this concert was conversing in that language, not because I believe any ethnic group on the world below is superior to any other. It's all I can do when there's no global common tongue.'

'We do have a world language, but it is little used.'

'Your world language? Less an effort toward world unity than a classic expression of chauvinism. Why should a world language be Latinate rather than based on some other language family?'

This caused a commotion among the world leaders, who whispered nervously to each other.

'We're surprised at your understanding of Earth culture,' the secretary general said earnestly.

'I see all. Besides, a thorough understanding of a speck of dust isn't hard.'

The US president looked up at the sky and said, 'Are you referring to the Earth? You may be bigger, but on a cosmic scale you're on the same order as the Earth. You're a speck of dust, too.'

'I'm less than dust,' the mirror said. 'A long, long time ago I used to be dust, but now I'm just a mirror.'

'Are you an individual or a collective?' the Chinese president asked.

'That question is meaningless. When a civilization travels far enough on the road of time, individual and collective both disappear.'

'Is a mirror your intrinsic form, or one of your many expressions?' the UK prime minister asked.

The secretary general added, 'In other words, are you deliberately exhibiting this form for our benefit?'

'This question is also meaningless. When a civilization travels far enough on the road of time, form and content both disappear.'

'We don't understand your answers to the last two questions,' the US president said.

The mirror said nothing.

Then the secretary general asked the key question: 'Why have you come to the solar system?'

'I am a musician. A concert is being held here.'

'Excellent,' the secretary general said with a nod. 'And humanity is the audience?'

'My audience is the entire universe, even if it will be a century before the nearest civilized world hears my playing.'

'Playing? Where's your instrument?' Richard Clayderman asked from the stage.

They realized the reflected Earth covering most of the sky had begun to slip swiftly toward the east. The change was frightening, like the sky falling, and a few people on the lawn involuntarily buried their head in their hands. Soon the reflection's edge dipped below the horizon, but at practically the same time, everything turned hazy in a sudden bright light. When sight returned, they saw the sun sitting smack in the middle of the sky right where the reflected Earth had been. Brilliant sunlight illuminated their surroundings under a brilliant blue sky that had replaced the black night. The oceans of the reflected Earth, which still covered the eastern sky, blended with the blue of the sky so the land seemed like a patch of clouds. They stared in shock at the change, but then a word from the secretary general explained the change that had taken place.

'The mirror tilted.'

Indeed, the huge mirror had tilted in space, drawing the sun into the reflection and casting its light onto the Earth's nighttime side.

'It rotates fast!' the Chinese president said.

The secretary general nodded. 'Yes, and at that size, the edges must be nearing the speed of light!'

'No physical object can tolerate the stresses from that rotation. It's a field, like our astronaut demonstrated. Near-light-speed motion is entirely normal for a field,' the US president said.

Then the mirror spoke: 'This is my instrument. I am a star player. My instrument is the sun!'

These grand words silenced them all, and they stared mutely at the reflected sun for a long while before someone asked, their voice trembling with awe, how it was played.

'You're all aware that many of the instruments you play have a sound chamber whose thin walls reflect and confine sound waves, allowing them to resonate and produce pleasing sounds. In the case of EM waves, the chamber is a star—it may lack visible walls, but it has a transmission speed gradient that reflects and refracts the waves, confining them to produce EM resonance and play beautiful music.'

'What does this instrument sound like?' Clayderman asked the sky.

'Nine minutes ago, I played tuning notes on the sun. The instrument's sound is now being transmitted at the speed of light. Of course, it's in EM form, but I can convert it to sound in your atmosphere through superstring waves. Listen. . . .'

They heard a few delicate, sustained notes, similar to those of a piano, but with a magic that held everyone momentarily under its spell.

'How does the sound make you feel?' the secretary general asked the Chinese president.

'Like the whole universe is a huge palace, one that's twenty billion light-years tall. And the sound fills it completely.' The Chinese president answered with great emotion.

'Can you still deny the existence of God after hearing that?' the US president asked.

The Chinese president eyed him, and said, 'The sound comes from the real world. If it can produce such a sound, then God is even less essential.'

The Beat

'Is the performance about to start?' the secretary general asked.

'Yes. I'm waiting for the beat,' the mirror replied.

'The beat?'

'The beat began four years ago and is being transmitted here at the speed of light.'

Then there was a fearsome change in the sky. The reflected Earth and sun disappeared, replaced by dancing bright silver ripples that filled the sky, making them feel like Earth had been plunged into an enormous ocean and they were looking up at the blazing sun beyond the water's surface.

The mirror explained: 'I'm blocking intense radiation from outer space. I can't totally reflect it, so what you're seeing is the small portion that gets through. The radiation comes from a star that went supernova four years ago.'

'Four years ago? That's Centauri,' someone said.

'That's right. Proxima Centauri.'

'But that star has none of the necessary conditions for supernova,' the Chinese president said.

'I created the conditions,' the mirror said.

They realized that when the mirror had said it made preparations for this concert four years ago, it was referring to that event; after selecting the sun as its instrument, it had detonated Proxima Centauri. Judging from the audio test of the sun, it was evidently capable of acting through hyperspace and pulsing the sun 1 AU away. But whether it possessed the same ability for a star four light-years away remained unknown. The detonation of Proxima Centauri could have been accomplished in one of two ways: from the solar system via hyperspace, or by teleporting to its vicinity, detonating it, and then teleporting back. Both were godlike power, so far as humanity was concerned, and in any case the light from the supernova would still take four years to reach the sun. The mirror said that music it played would be transmitted to the cosmos by EM, so was the speed of light for that hypercivilization akin to the speed of sound for humans? And if light waves were their sound waves, what was light for them? Humanity would never know.

'Your ability to manipulate the physical world is alarming,' the US president said in awe.

'Stars are stones in the cosmic desert, the most commonplace of objects in my world. Sometimes I use stars as tools, other times as weapons, and other times as musical instruments. . . . I've turned Proxima Centauri into a metronome, basically the same as the stones used by your ancestors. We both take advantage of ordinary objects in our world to enlarge and extend our abilities.'

But the occupants of the lawn could see no similarity between the two, and abandoned the attempt to discuss technology with the mirror. Humanity could no more comprehend it than an ant could understand the ISS.

Little by little the light in the sky began to dim, giving them the impression that it was moonlight shining on the ocean, not sunlight, and that the supernova was going out.

The secretary general said, 'If the mirror hadn't blocked the energy from the supernova, the Earth would be a dead planet.'

By this point the ripples in the sky were gone, and the Earth's enormous reflection again occupied most of the sky.

'Where's the beat?' Clayderman asked. He had left the stage and was standing among the world leaders.

'Look to the east!' someone shouted, and they saw in the eastern sky a dividing line, ramrod straight, bisecting the heavens into two distinct images. The reflected Earth, partially cut off, remained on the western side, but in the east was a dazzling starfield that many of them knew was the correct one for the northern hemisphere rather than the reflected southern sky. The division line marched west, enlarging the starry sky and wiping out the reflected Earth.

'It's flying away!' shouted the secretary general. And they realized he was right: the mirror was leaving the space over Earth. Its edge soon vanished beneath the western horizon, leaving them standing beneath the stars of an ordinary sky. It did not reappear—perhaps it had flown off to the vicinity of its sun instrument.

It comforted them somewhat to see the familiar world, the stars and city lights as they had been, and to smell the blossoms wafting over the lawn.

Then came the beat.

Day arrived without warning with a sudden blue sky and blazing sunlight that flooded the land and lit up their surroundings with brilliant light. But daytime lasted just a second before extinguishing into renewed night as stars and city lights returned. And the night lasted only a second before day returned, only for a second, and then it was night again. Day, and then night, then day, then night . . . like a pulse, or as if the world were a projector switching back and forth between two slides.

A beat formed out of night and day.

They looked up and saw the flashing star, now just a blinding, dimensionless point of light in space. 'A pulsar,' said the Chinese president.

The remains of a supernova, a whirling neutron star, the naked hot spot on its dense surface turning it into a cosmic lighthouse, its revolution sweeping the beam emitted by its hot spot through space, and giving Earth a brief moment of daytime as it swept past the solar system.

'I seem to recall,' the secretary general said, 'that a pulsar's frequency is far faster than this. And it doesn't emit visible light.'

Shielding his eyes with a hand and struggling to adjust to the crazy rhythm of the world, the US president said, 'The high frequency is because the neutron star retains the former star's angular momentum. The mirror may be able to somehow drain that momentum. As for visible light . . . do you really think that's something the mirror can't do?'

'There's another thing,' the Chinese president said. 'There's no reason to believe that the pace of life for all beings in the universe is like that of humanity. The beat for their music might be on a completely different frequency. The mirror's normal beat, for example, may be faster than even our fastest computers.'

'Yes,' the US president said, nodding. 'And there's no reason to believe that what they perceive as visible light is the same EM spectrum.'

'So you're saying that the mirror's music is benchmarked to human senses?' the secretary general asked in surprise.

The Chinese president shook his head. 'I don't know. But it's got to be based on something.'

The pulsar's powerful beam swept across the empty sky like a four-trillion-kilometer-long baton, still growing at the speed of light. At this end, played on the sun by the mirror's invisible fingers and transmitted to the cosmos at the speed of light, the sun concert began.

Sun Music

A rustle like radio jamming or the endless pounding of waves on sand occasionally offered up hints of a vast desolation within its more abundant chaos and disorder. The sound went on for more than ten minutes without changing.

The Russian president broke the silence: 'Like I said, we can't understand their music.'

'Listen!' Clayderman said, pointing at the sky, but it was a long moment before the rest of them heard the melody his trained ears had picked out at once. A simple structure of just two notes, reminiscent of a clock's tick-tock. The notes repeated, separated by lengthy gaps. Then another two-note section, and a third, and a fourth . . . paired tones emerging ceaselessly from the chaos like fireflies in the night.

Then a new melody emerged, four notes. Everyone turned toward Clayderman, who was listening attentively and seemed to have sensed something. The four-note phrases multiplied.

'Here,' he said to the heads of state. 'Let each of us remember a two-note measure.' And so they all listened carefully, and each found a two-note measure and then focused their energy on committing it to memory. After a while, Clayderman said, 'Very well. Now concentrate on a four-note phrase. Quickly, though, or else the music will grow too complex for us to pick them out. . . . Yes, that one. Does anyone hear that?'

'The first half is the pair of notes I memorized!' called the head of Brazil.

'The second half is my pair!' said the head of Canada.

They realized that every four-note phrase was made up of two of the previous note pairs, and as the four-note phrases multiplied they seemed to be depleting the isolated pairs. Then came eight-note phrases, similarly formed out of sets of four-note phrases.

'What do you hear?' the secretary general asked the people around him.

'A primeval ocean lit by flashes of lightning and volcanoes, and small molecules combining into larger ones ...of course, that's purely my own imagination,' the Chinese president said.

'Don't constrain your imagination to the Earth,' the US president said. 'The clustering of these molecules may be taking place in a nebula glowing with starlight. Or maybe they're not molecules, but the nuclear vortices inside a star . . .'

Then came a high-pitched, multi-note phrase that repeated like a bright spark in the dim chaos. 'It's like it's describing a fundamental transformation,' the Chinese president said.

Then they heard a new instrument, a sustained violin-like string sound that repeated a gentle shadow of the standout melody.

'It's expressing a kind of duplication,' the Russian president said.

Now came an uninterrupted melody from the violin voice, changing smoothly as if it were light in curvilinear motion. The UK prime minister said to the Chinese president, 'To borrow your idea, that ocean has something swimming in it now.'

At some point the background music, which they'd nearly forgotten about, had begun to change. From the sound of waves it had turned into an oscillating rush, like a storm assaulting the bare rock. Then it changed again, into wind-like bleakness. The US president said, 'The swimmer has entered a new environment. The land, or perhaps the air.'

Then all the instruments played in unison for a brief moment, a fearsomely loud sound like an enormous physical collapse, then they abruptly dropped out, leaving just the lonely sound of the surf. Then the simple note pairs started up again and turned gradually complex, and everything repeated. . . .

'I can say with certainty that a great extinction was just described, and now we're listening to the revival afterward.'

After another long and arduous process, the ocean swimmer ventured again into other parts of the world. Slowly, the melody grew grander and more complicated, and interpretations diversified. Some people thought it was a river rushing downhill, others imagined the advance of a great army across a vast plain, others saw billowing nebulae in the darkness of space caught in the vortex of a black hole, but they all agreed that it was expressing some grand process, an evolutionary process. The movement was long, and an hour had passed before the theme at last began to change. The melody gradually split into two vying parts that smashed wildly into each other or tangled together. . . .

'The classic style of Beethoven,' Clayderman declared, after a long stretch immersed in the grand music.

The secretary general said, 'It's like a fleet smacking across huge waves on the sea.'

'No,' said the US president, shaking his head. 'Not that. You can tell that the two forces are not essentially different. I think it's a battle that spans a world.'

'Wait a moment,' interrupted the Japanese prime minister, breaking a long silence. 'Do you really imagine you can comprehend alien art? Your understanding of the music may be no better than a cow's appreciation for a lyre.'

Clayderman said, 'I think our understanding is basically correct. The common languages of the cosmos are mathematics and music.'

The secretary general said, 'Proving it won't be difficult. Can we predict the theme or style of the next movement?'

After a moment's thought, the Chinese president said, 'I'd say next will be an expression of worship, and the melody will possess a strict architectural beauty.'

'You mean like Bach?'

'Yes.'

And so it was. The listeners seemed to hear a great imposing church and the echoes of their footsteps inside that magnificent space, and they were overcome by fear and awe of an all-encompassing power.

Then the complicated melody turned simple again. The background music vanished, and a series of short, clear beats appeared in the infinite stillness: one, then two, then three, then four . . . and then one, four, nine, and sixteen . . . and then increasingly complex series.

Someone asked, 'Is this describing the emergence of mathematics and abstract thinking?'

Then it turned even stranger. Isolated three-note and four-note phrases from the violin, each of identically pitched notes held for different durations; then glissandos, rising, falling, and then rising again. They listened intently, and when the president of Greece said, 'It's . . . like a description of basic geometric shapes,' they immediately had the sense they were watching triangles and rectangles shoot by through empty space. The glides conjured up images of round objects, ovals and perfect circles. . . . The melody changed slowly as single-note lines turned into glides, but the previous impression of floating geometric shapes remained, only now they were floating on water and distorted. . . .

'The discovery of the secrets of time,' someone said.

The next movement began with a constant rhythm that repeated along a period resembling a pulsar's day-night beat. The music seemed to have stopped altogether but for the beat echoing in the silence, but it was soon joined by another constant rhythm, this one slightly faster. Then more rhythms at various frequencies were added, until finally a magnificent chorus emerged. But on the time axis the music was constant as a huge flat wall of sound.

Astonishingly, their interpretation of this movement was unanimous: 'A giant machine at work.'

Then came a delicate new melody, a tinkle of crystal, volatile and dreamlike, that contrasted with the thick wall beneath it like a silver fairy flitting over the enormous machine. This tiny drop of a powerful catalyst touched off a wondrous reaction in the iron world: the constant rhythm began to waver, and the machine's shafts and cogs turned soft and rubbery until the whole chorus turned as light and ethereal as the fairy melody.

They debated it: 'The machine has intelligence!' 'I think the machine is drawing closer to its creator.'

The sun music progressed into a new movement, the most structurally complicated yet, and the hardest to understand. First the piano voice played a lonely tune, distant and empty, which was then taken up and extended by an increasingly complex group that turned it grander and more magnificent with every repetition.

After it had repeated several times, the Chinese president said, 'Here's my interpretation: A thinker stands on an island in the sea contemplating the cosmos. As the camera pulls back, the thinker shrinks in the field of view, and when the frame encompasses the entire island, the thinker is no more visible than a grain of sand. The island shrinks as the camera pulls back beyond the atmosphere, and now the entire planet is in frame, with the island just a speck within it. As the camera pulls back into space, the entire planetary system is drawn into frame, but now only the star is visible, a lonely, shining billiard ball against the pitch-black sky, and the ocean planet has vanished like a speck. . . .'

Listening intently, the US president picked up the thought: '. . .The camera pulls back at light speed, and we discover that what from our scale is a vast and boundless cosmos is but glittering star dust, and when the entire galaxy comes into frame, the star and its planetary system vanish like specks. As the camera continues to cross unimaginable distances, a galaxy cluster is pulled into frame. We still see glittering dust, but the dust is formed not of stars but of galaxies . . .'

The secretary general said, '. . .And our galaxy has vanished. But where does it end?'

The audience once again immersed themselves in the music as it approached a climax. The musician's mind had propelled the cosmic camera outside the bounds of known space so its frame captured the entire universe, reducing the Milky Way's galaxy cluster to a speck of dust. They waited intently for the finale, but the grand chorus suddenly dropped out, leaving behind only a lonely piano-like sound, distant and empty.

'A return to the thinker on the island?' someone asked.

Clayderman shook his head. 'No, it's a completely different melody.'

Then the cosmic chorus struck up again, but after a brief moment gave way to the piano solo. The two melodies alternated like this for a long while.

Clayderman listened intently, and suddenly realized something: 'The piano is playing an inversion of the chorus!'

The US president nodded: 'Or maybe it's the mirror of the chorus. A cosmic mirror. That's what it is.'

The music had clearly reached a denouement, and now the piano's inverted melody proceeded alongside the chorus, riding conspicuously on its back but gloriously harmonious.

The Chinese president said, 'It reminds me of the Silvers style of mid-twentieth-century architecture, in which, in order to avoid impact on the surrounding environment, buildings were clad entirely in mirrors. Reflections were a way of putting them in harmony with their surroundings as well as self-expression.'

'Yes,' the secretary general answered thoughtfully. 'When civilization reaches a certain level, it can express itself through its reflection of the cosmos.'

The piano abruptly shifted to the uninverted theme, bringing it into unison with the chorus. The sun music had finished.

Ode to Joy

'A perfect concert,' the mirror said. 'Thank you to all who enjoyed it. And now I will be going.'

'Wait a moment!' shouted Clayderman. 'We have one last request. Could you play a human song on the sun?'

'Yes. Which one?'

The heads of state glanced around at each other. 'Beethoven's Fate

Symphony?'[1] asked the German premier.

'No, not Fate,' said the US president. 'It's been proven that humanity is powerless to strangle fate. Our worth lies in that even knowing that fate can't be resisted and death will have the final victory, we still devote our limited life span to creating beautiful lives.'

'Then 'Ode to Joy,'' said the Chinese president.

The mirror said, 'You all sing. I'll use the sun to transmit the song out into the universe. It will be beautiful, I assure you.'

More than two hundred voices joined in 'Ode to Joy,' their song passed by the mirror to the sun, which again began vibrating to send powerful EM waves into all reaches of space.

> *Joy, thou beauteous godly lightning,*
> *Daughter of Elysium,*
> *Fire drunken we are ent'ring*
> *Heavenly, thy holy home!*
> *Thy enchantments bind together,*
> *What did custom stern divide,*
> *Every man becomes a brother,*
> *Where thy gentle wings abide.*[2]

Five hours later, the song would exit the solar system. In four years, it would reach Proxima Centauri; in ten thousand, it would exit the galaxy; in two hundred thousand, it would reach the galaxy's nearest neighbor, the Large Magellanic Cloud. In six million years, their song would have reached the forty-odd galaxies in the cluster, and in a hundred million years, the fifty-odd clusters in the supercluster. In fifteen billion years, the song would have spread throughout the known universe and would continue onward, should the universe still be expanding.

---

1 Beethoven's Fifth Symphony is known as the Fate Symphony in Chinese.
2 'Ode to Joy' by Friedrich Schiller. Translation by William F. Wertz.

Joy commands the hardy mainspring
Of the universe eterne.
Joy, oh joy the wheel is driving
Which the worlds' great clock doth turn.
Flowers from the buds she coaxes,
Suns from out the hyaline,
Spheres she rotates through expanses,
Which the seer can't divine.

The song concluded, everyone fell silent on the concert lawn. World leaders were lost in thought.

'Maybe things aren't so hopeless just yet, and we ought to renew our efforts,' the Chinese president said.

The US president nodded. 'Yes. The world needs the UN.'

'Concessions and sacrifices are insignificant compared to the future disasters they prevent,' the Russian president said.

'What we're dealing with amounts to a grain of sand in the cosmos. It ought to be easy,' the UK prime minister said, looking up at the stars.

The other leaders voiced their assent.

'So then, do we all agree to extend the present session of the UN?' the secretary general asked hopefully.

'This will of course require contacting our respective governments, but I believe that won't be a problem,' the US president said with a smile.

'Then, my friends, today is a day to remember,' the secretary general said, unable to hide his delight. 'So let's join once more in song.'

'Ode to Joy' started up again.

Speeding away from the sun at the speed of light, the mirror knew it would never return. In more than a billion years as a musician it had never held a repeat performance, just as a human shepherd will never toss the same stone twice. As it flew, it listened to the echoes of 'Ode to Joy,' and a barely perceptible ripple appeared on its smooth mirror surface.

'Oh, that's a good song.'

带上她的眼睛

WITH HER EYES

TRANSLATED BY ZAC HALUZA

何夳子轩 - 译

Prologue

Two months of nonstop work had left me exhausted. I asked my director for a two-day leave of absence so that I could go on a short trip and clear my mind. He agreed, but only on the condition that I take a pair of eyes along with me. I accepted, and he took me to pick them up from the Control Center.

The eyes were stored in a small room at the end of a corridor. I counted about a dozen pairs. The director gestured to the large screen in front of us as he handed me a pair and introduced me to the eyes' owner, a young woman who appeared to be fresh out of university. She was staring blankly at me. The woman's puffy spacesuit made her appear even more petite than she probably was. She looked miserable, to be honest. No doubt she had dreamt of the romance of space from the safety of her university library; now she faced the hellish reality of the infinite void.

'I'm really sorry for the inconvenience,' she said, bowing apologetically. Never in my life had I heard such a gentle voice. Her soft words seemed to float down from space like a gentle breeze, turning those crude and massive orbiting steel structures into rubber.

'Not at all. I'm happy to have some company.' I replied sincerely. 'Where do you want to go?'

'Really? You still haven't decided where you're going?' She looked pleased. But as she spoke, my attention was drawn to two peculiarities.

First off, any transmission from space reaches its destination with some degree of delay. Even transmissions from the moon have a lag of two seconds. The lag time is even longer with communications from the asteroid belt.

Yet somehow her answers seemed to arrive without any perceptible delay. This meant that she had to be in LEO: low Earth orbit. With no need for a transfer mid-journey, returning to the surface from there would be cheap and quick. So why would she want me to carry her eyes on a vacation?

Her spacesuit was the other thing that felt off. I work as an astro-engineer specializing in personal equipment, and her suit struck me as odd for a couple of reasons. For one thing, it lacked any visible anti-radiation system, and the helmet hanging by her side apparently lacked an anti-glare shield on its visor. Her suit's thermal and cooling insulation also looked incredibly advanced.

'What station is she on?' I asked, looking over at my director.

'Don't ask.' His expression was glum.

'Leave it, please,' echoed the young woman on the screen, abjectly enough to tug at my heartstrings.

'You aren't in lockup, are you?' I joked.

The room displayed on the monitor looked exceedingly cramped. It was clearly some sort of cockpit. An array of complex navigation systems pulsed and blinked around her, yet I could see no windows, not even an observation monitor. The pencil spinning near her head was the only visible evidence that she was currently in space.

Both she and the director seemed to stiffen at my words. 'OK,' I continued hurriedly. 'I won't ask about things that aren't my concern. So where are we going? It's your choice.'

Coming to a decision appeared to be a genuine struggle for her. Gloved hands gripped in front of her chest, she shut her eyes. It was as though she were deciding between life and death, or as if she thought the planet would explode after our brief vacation. I couldn't help but chuckle.

'Oh, this isn't easy for me. Have you read the book by Helen Keller? If you have, you'll understand what I'm talking about!'

'We don't have three days, though. Just two. When it comes to time, modern-day folk are dirt-poor. Then again, we're lucky compared to Helen Keller: in three hours, I can take your eyes anywhere on Earth.'

'Then let's go to the last place I visited before leaving!'

She told me the name of the place. I set off, her eyes in hand.

Grassland

Tall mountains, plains, meadows, and forests all converged at this one spot. I was more than 2,000 kilometers from the space center where I worked; the journey by ionospheric jet had taken all of fifteen minutes. The Taklamakan lay before me. Generations of hard graft had transformed the former desert into grassland. Now, after decades of vigorous population control, it was once again devoid of human habitation.

The grassland stretched all the way to the horizon. Behind me, dark green forests covered the Tian Shan mountain range. The highest peaks were capped with silvery snow. I took out her eyes and put them on.

These 'eyes' were, in reality, a pair of multi-sensory glasses. When worn, every image seen by the wearer is transmitted via an ultra-high-frequency radio signal. This transmission can be received by another person wearing an identical set of multi-sensory glasses, letting them view everything that the first individual sees. It's essentially as if the first person is wearing the other person's eyes.

Millions of people worked year-round on the moon and the Asteroid Belt. The cost of a vacation back on Earth was astronomical – pardon the pun – which is why the space bureau, in all their stinginess, designed this little gadget. Every astronaut living in space had a corresponding pair of glasses planet-side. Those on Earth lucky enough to go on a real-life vacation would wear these glasses, allowing a homesick space-worker to share the joy of their trip.

People had originally scoffed at these devices. But as those willing to wear them received significant subsidies for their travels they actually became quite popular. These artificial eyes grew increasingly refined through the constant use of the most cutting-edge technology. The current models even transmitted their wearers' senses of touch and smell by monitoring their brainwaves.

Taking a pair of eyes on vacation became an act of public service among terrestrial workers in the space industry. Not everyone was willing to take an extra pair of eyes with them on vacation, citing reasons such as invasion of privacy. As for me, I had no problem with them.

I sighed deeply at the vista before my eyes. From her eyes, however, came the gentle sound of sobs.

'I have dreamed of this place ever since my last trip. Now I'm back in my dreams!' came her soft voice, drifting out from her eyes. 'I feel like I am rising from the depths of the ocean, like I'm taking my first breath of air. I can't stand being closed in.'

I could actually hear her taking deep, long breaths.

'But you aren't closed in at all. Compared to the vastness of space around you, this grassland might as well be a closet.'

She fell silent. Even her breathing seemed to have stopped.

I continued, if only to break the silence.[1]

'Of course, people in space are still closed in. It's like when Chuck Yeager described the *Mercury* astronauts as being–'

'–Spam in a can.' She finished the thought for me.

We both laughed. Suddenly she called out in surprise.

'Oh! Flowers! I see flowers! They weren't here last time!' Indeed, the broad grassland was adorned with countless small blooms. 'Can you look at the flowers next to you?'

I crouched and looked down.

'Oh, how beautiful! Can you smell her? No, don't pick her!'

Left with little choice, I had to lie almost flat on my belly to pick up the flower's light fragrance.

'Ah, I can smell it too! It's like she's sending us a delicate sonata!'

I shook my head, laughing. In this age of ever-changing fads and wild pursuits, most young women were restless and impulsive. Girls as dainty as this particular specimen, who was practically moved to tears at the sight of a

---

1　此句为译者润色添加，中文版选择保留。后文不再标注。

flower, were few and far between.

'Let's give this little flower a name, shall we? Hmm… We'll call her Dreamy. How about that one? What should we call him? Umm, Raindrop sounds good. Now go to that one over there. Thanks. Her petals are light blue – her name should be Moonbeam.'

We went from flower to flower in exactly this way, first looking, then smelling, and finally naming them. Utterly entranced, she kept at it with no end in sight, all else forgotten. I, however, soon grew bored to death of this girlish game, but by the time I insisted that we stop, we had already named over a hundred flowers.

Looking up, I realized we had wandered a good distance, so I went back to retrieve my backpack. As I bent down to pick it up, I heard a startled shout in my ear.

'Oh no! You crushed Snowflake!'

I gingerly propped the pale little wildflower back up. The whole scene suddenly felt comical. Covering a flower with both hands, I asked her, 'What are their names? What do they look like?'

'That one on the left is Crystal. She's white too, and has three leaves on her stem. To the right we have Flame. He's pink, with four leaves. The top two leaves are separate, and the bottom two are joined.'

She got them all right. Actually, I felt somewhat moved.

'See? We all know each other. I'll think of them over and over again during the long days to come. It'll be like retelling a beautiful fairy tale. This world of yours is absolutely wonderful!'

'This world of mine? It's your world too! And if you keep acting like a temperamental child, those anal-retentive space psychologists will make sure you're grounded on it for the rest of your life.'

I began to roam aimlessly about the plains. It wasn't long before I came across a small brook concealed in the thick grass. I decided to forge ahead, but her voice called me back.

'I want to reach into that stream so much.'

Crouching, I reached my hands into the water. A cool wave of refreshment flowed through my body. I knew she would feel it too, as the ultra-high frequency waves carried the sensation into the far distance of space. Again I heard her sigh.

'Is it hot where you are?' I was thinking of that cramped cockpit, and her spacesuit's oddly advanced insulation system.

'Hot,' she replied. 'As hot as hell.' Her tone changed. 'Hey, what's that? The prairie wind?' I had taken my hands from the water, and the gentle wind was cool against my damp skin. 'No, don't move. This wind is heavenly!' I raised both hands into the breeze, and held them there until they were dry. At her request, I dipped my hands back into the brook and lifted them into the wind. Again it felt divine, and again we shared the experience. We idled away a good while like this.

I set out again, silently wandering for a while. I heard her murmur, 'This world of yours is truly magnificent.'

'I really wouldn't know. The grayness of my life has dulled it all.'

'How could you say that? This world has so many experiences and feelings to offer! Trying to describe them all would be like trying to count the drops of rain in a thunderstorm. Look at those clouds on the horizon, all silvery-white. Right now they look solid to me, like towering mountains of gleaming jade. The meadow below, on the other hand, looks wispy, as if all the grass decided to fly away from the earth and become a green sea of clouds. Look! Look at the clouds floating past the sun! Watch how majestically the light and shadows shift and warp over the grass! Do you honestly feel nothing when you see this?'

Wearing her eyes, I roamed the grassland for an entire day. I could hear the yearning in her voice as she looked at each and every flower, at every blade of grass, at every beam of sunlight leaping through the prairie, and as she listened to all the different voices of the grassy plains. The sudden appearance of a stream, and of the tiny fish swimming within it, would send her into fits of excitement. An unexpected breeze, carrying with it the sweet fragrance of fresh grass, would bring her to tears... Her feelings for this world were so rich that I wondered if something was wrong with her state of mind.

Before sunset, I made my way to a lonely white cabin, standing forlornly on the grassland. It had been set up as an inn for travelers, although I seemed to be its first guest in quite some time. Besides myself, the cabin's only other resident was the glitchy, obsolete android that looked after the entire inn. I was as hungry as I was tired, but before I had a chance to finish my dinner, she suggested that we go outside right away to watch the sun set.

'Watching the evening sky gradually lose its glow, as night falls over the forest – it's like listening to the most beautiful symphony in the universe.'

Her voice swelled with rapture. I dragged my leaden feet outside, silently cursing my misfortune.

*

'You really do cherish these common things,' I told her on our way back to the cabin. Night had already fallen, and stars shone in the sky.

'Why don't you?' she asked. 'That's what it means to truly be alive.'

'I can't really find any satisfaction in those things. Nor can most other people. It's too easy to get what you want these days. I'm not just talking about material things. You can surround yourself with blue skies and crystal-clear waters just like that. If you want the peace and tranquility of the countryside or a remote island, you barely even need to snap your fingers. Even love. Think how elusive that was for previous generations and how desperately they chased it, and now it can be experienced through virtual reality, at least for a few moments at a time.

'People don't cherish anything now. They see a platter of fruit an arm's length away, only to take a bite out of each piece before throwing the rest away.'

'But not everyone has such fruits within reach,' she said quietly.

I felt my words had caused her pain, but I wasn't sure why. The rest of the way back, we said nothing more.

I saw her in my dreams that night. She was in her spacesuit, confined to that tiny cockpit. There were tears in her eyes. She reached out to me, calling out, 'Take me outside! I don't want to be closed in!' I awoke with a start and realized that she really was calling me. I was looking up at the ceiling, still wearing her eyes.

'Please, will you take me outside? Let's go see the moon. It should be up by now!'

My head seemed to be filled with sand as I reluctantly pulled myself out of bed. Once outside I discovered the moon had indeed just risen; the night mist lent it a reddish tinge. The vast wilderness below was sound asleep. Pinprick glows from countless fireflies floated through the hazy ocean of grass, as though Taklamakan's dreams were bleeding into reality.

Stretching, I spoke to the night sky. 'Hey, can you see where the moon is shining from your position in orbit? What's your ship's position? Tell me, and I might even be able to see you. ' I was positive her ship's in LEO.

Instead of answering me, she began humming a song. She stopped after a few bars and said, 'That was Debussy's "Clair de Lune." '

She continued humming, seemingly forgetting that I was still listening on the other end – or that I even existed. From orbit, melody and moonlight descended upon the prairie in unison. I pictured that delicate girl in outer space: the silvery moon shining from above, the blue Earth below. She flew between the two, smaller than a pinpoint, her song dissolving into moonlight...

When I returned to bed an hour later, she was still humming. I had no idea if it was Debussy, but it made no difference. That delicate music fluttered through my dreams.

Some time later – I'm not sure how long – her humming turned into shouting. Her cries stirred me from sleep. She wanted to go outside again.

'Weren't you just looking at the moon?' I was angry.

'But it's different now. Remember the clouds in the west? They might have floated over by now. The moon will be darting in and out of the clouds; I want to see the light and shadows dance on the plains outside. How beautiful that must look. It's a different kind of music. Please, take my eyes outside!'

My head buzzed with anger, but I went out. The clouds had floated on, and the moon was shining through them. Its light filtered hazily over the grassland. It was as though the earth were pondering deep and ancient memories.

'You're like a sentimental eighteenth-century poet. Tragically unfit for these times. Even more so for an astronaut,' I said, peering into the night sky. I took off her eyes and hung them from a branch of a nearby salt cedar. 'If you want to look at the moon, you can do it yourself. I really need to sleep. Tomorrow I have to get back to the space center and continue my woefully prosaic life.'

That soft voice whispered from her eyes, but I could no longer hear what she was saying. I went back to the cabin without another word.

It was daytime when I awoke. Dark clouds covered the sky, shrouding the Taklamakan in a light drizzle. Her eyes were still hanging from the tree, mist covering the lenses. I carefully wiped them clean, and put them on. I assumed that after watching the moon for an entire night, she would be fast asleep by now. However, I heard her sobbing quietly. A wave of pity overwhelmed me.

'I'm really sorry. I was just too tired last night.'

'No, it isn't you,' she said between sobs. 'The sky grew overcast at half past three. And after five o'clock, it started to rain…'

'You didn't sleep at all?' I nearly shouted.

'It started raining, and I – I couldn't see the sun when it rose,' she choked out. 'I really wanted to see the sun rise over the plains. I wanted to see it more than anything…'

Something had melted my heart. Her tears washed through my thoughts, and I pictured her small nose twitching as she sniveled. My eyes actually felt moist. I had to admit – she had taught me something over the past twenty-four hours, though I couldn't put my finger on exactly what. It was hazy, like the light and shadows moving over the grasslands. My eyes now saw a different world because of it.

'There'll always be another sunrise. I'll definitely take your eyes out again to see it. Or maybe I'll see it with you in person. How does that sound?'

Her sobbing stopped. Suddenly she whispered to me.

'Listen...'

I didn't hear anything, but I tensed.

'It's the first bird of the morning! There are birds out, even in the rain!' Her voice was solemn, as though she were listening to the peal of bells marking the end of an era.

Sunset 6

My memories of this experience quickly faded once I had returned to my drab existence and busy job. When I finally remembered to wash the clothes I had worn during my trip – which was some time afterwards – I discovered a few grass seeds in the cuffs of my trousers. At the same time, a tiny seed also remained buried within the depths of my subconscious. In the lonely desert of my soul, that seed had already sprouted, though its shoots were so tiny they were barely perceptible. This may have happened unconsciously, but at the end of each grueling work day, I could feel the natural poetry of the evening breeze stir against my face. Birdsong could catch my attention. I would even stand on the overpass at twilight and watch as night enveloped the city... The world was still dreary to my eyes, but it was now sprinkled with specks of verdant green – specks that grew steadily in number. Once I began to perceive this change, I thought of her again.

She began to drift into my idle mind and even into my dreams. Over and again, I would see that cramped cockpit, that strangely insulated spacesuit... Later on, these things retreated from my consciousness. Only one thing protruded from the void: that pencil, drifting in zero gravity around her head. For some reason, I would see that pencil floating in front of me whenever I shut my eyes.

One day I was walking into the vast lobby of the space center when a giant mural, one that I had passed countless times before, suddenly caught my eye. The mural depicted Earth, viewed from space: a gem of deepest blue.

That pencil again floated before my mind's eye, but now it was superimposed over the mural. I heard her voice again.

I don't want to be closed in.

Realization flashed through my brain like lightning. Space wasn't the only place with zero gravity!

I ran upstairs like a madman and banged on the Director's door. He wasn't in. Guided by what felt like a premonition, I flew down to the small room where the eyes were stored. The director was there, gazing at the girl on the large monitor. She was still inside that sealed-off cockpit, still wearing that 'spacesuit'. The image was frozen; almost certainly a recording.

'You're here for her, I suppose,' he said, still looking at the monitor.

'Where is she?' My voice boomed inside the small room.

'You may have already guessed the truth. She's the navigator of Sunset 6.'

The strength drained from my muscles and I collapsed onto the carpet. It all made sense now.

The Sunset Project had originally planned to launch ten ships, from Sunset 1 to Sunset 10. After the Sunset 6 disaster, however, the project had been abandoned.

The project was an exploratory flight mission like many before it. It followed essentially the same procedures as each of the space center's other flight missions. There was just one difference – the Sunset vessels were not headed to outer space. These ships were to dive into the depths of the Earth.

One-and-a-half centuries after the first space flight, humanity began to probe in the opposite direction. The Sunset-series terracraft were its first attempt at this form of exploration.

Four years ago, I had watched the Sunset 1 launch on television. It was late at night. A blinding fireball lit up the heart of the Turpan Depression, so bright it caused the clouds in Xinjiang's night sky to glow with the gorgeous colors of dawn. By the time the fireball faded, Sunset 1 was already underground. At the center of this circle of red-hot, scorched earth now churned a lake of molten magma. White-hot lava seethed and boiled, hurling bright molten columns into the air... The tremors could be felt as far away as Urumqi, as the terracraft burrowed through the planet's inner layers.

Each of the Sunset Project's first five missions successfully completed their subterranean voyages and returned safely to the Earth's surface. Sunset 5 set a record for the furthest any human had traveled beneath the planet's surface: 3,100 kilometers. It was a record that Sunset 6 did not intend to break, and with good reason. Modern geophysics had concluded that the boundary between the Earth's mantle and core lay between 3,400 and 3,500 kilometers underground; this convergence is referred to academically as the 'Gutenberg Discontinuity.' Breaching this boundary meant entering the planet's iron-nickel core. On entering the core, the density of the surrounding matter would abruptly and exponentially increase to levels that went beyond the Sunset 6's design specifications to navigate.

Sunset 6's voyage began smoothly. It took the terracraft all of two hours to pass through the boundary between the Earth's surface and mantle, also known as the 'Moho.' After resting upon the sliding surface of the Eurasian plate for five hours, the ship began its slow 3,000-plus kilometer journey through the mantle.

Space travel may be lonely, but at least astronauts can gaze at the infinity of the universe and the majesty of the stars. The terranauts voyaging through the planet however, had nothing but the sensation of endlessly increasing density to guide them. All they could glean from peering into the terracraft's holographic rearview monitors, was the blinding glare of the seething magma following in their ship's wake. As the craft plunged deeper, the magma would merge behind the aft section, instantly sealing the path that the ship had just forged.

A terranaut once described the experience. Whenever she and her fellow crew members shut their eyes, they would see the onrushing magma gather behind them, pressing down and sealing them in all over again. The image followed them like a phantom, and it made the voyagers aware of the massive and ever-increasing immensity of matter pressing against their ship. This sense of claustrophobia was difficult for those on the surface to comprehend, but it tortured each and every terranaut.

Sunset 6 completed each of its research tasks with flying colors. The craft traveled at approximately fifteen kilometers per hour; at this rate, it would require twenty hours to reach its target depth. Fifteen hours and forty minutes into their voyage, however, the crew received an alert. Subsurface radar had picked up a sudden increase of density in their vicinity, leaping from 6.3 grams per cubic centimeter to 9.5 grams. The surrounding matter was no longer silicate-based, but primarily an iron-nickel alloy; it was also no longer solid, but liquid. Despite having only achieved a depth of 2,500 kilometers, all signs currently indicated that Sunset 6 and its crew had entered the planet's core!

Later the crew would learn that they had chanced upon a fissure in the Earth's mantle. One that led directly to its core. The fissure was filled with a high-pressure liquid alloy of iron and nickel from the Earth's core. Thanks to this crack, the Gutenberg discontinuity had reached up 1,000 kilometers closer to the Sunset 6's flight path! The ship immediately took emergency measures to change course. It was during this attempt to escape that disaster truly struck.

The ship's neutron-laced hull was strong enough to withstand the massive and sudden pressure increase to 1,600 tons per cubic centimeter, but the terracraft itself was comprised of three parts: a fusion engine at the bow, a central cabin, and a rear mounted drive engine. When it attempted to change direction, the section linking the fusion engine to the main cabin fractured, snapped off by the density and pressure of liquid iron-nickel alloy that far exceeded the ship's operating parameters. The images broadcast from Sunset 6's neutrino communicator showed the forward engine splitting from the hull, only to be instantly engulfed by the crimson glow of the liquid metal. A Sunset ship's fusion engine fired a super-heated jet that cut through the material in front of the vessel. Without it, the drive engine could barely push the Sunset 6 an inch through the planet's solid inner layers.

The density of the Earth's core is startling, but the neutrons in the ship's hull were even denser. As the buoyancy created by the liquid iron-nickel alloy did not exceed the ship's deadweight, Sunset 6 began to sink towards the Earth's core.

One-and-a-half centuries after landing on the moon, humanity was finally capable of venturing to Saturn. It had been anticipated that we would travel from the mantle to the core in a similar time frame. Now, a terracraft had accidentally entered the core, and just like an Apollo-era vessel spinning off course and into the depths of space, the chance of a successful rescue was simply nonexistent.

Fortunately, the hull of the ship's main cabin was sturdy, and Sunset 6's neutrino communications system maintained a solid connection with the control center on the surface. In the year that followed, the crew of the Sunset 6 persisted in their work, sending streams of valuable data gleaned from the core to the surface.

Encased as they were in thousands of kilometers of rock, air and survival were the least of their worries – what they lacked more than anything else was space. They were pummeled by temperatures over 5,000 degrees Celsius and surrounded by pressures that could crush carbon into diamonds within seconds! Only neutrinos could escape the incredible density of the material in which the Sunset 6 was entombed. The ship was completely trapped in a giant furnace of molten metal. To the ship's crew, Dante's would depict a paradise. What could life mean in a world like this? Is there any word beyond 'fragile' that can describe it?

Immense psychological pressure shredded the nerves of the Sunset 6's crew. One day, the ship's geological engineer woke, leapt from his cot and threw open the heat-insulation door protecting his cabin. Even though this was only the first of four such doors, the wave of incandescent heat that washed in through the remaining three layers instantly reduced him to charcoal. To prevent the ship's imminent destruction, the commander rushed to seal the open door. Although he was successful, he suffered severe burns in the process. The man died after making one last entry into the ship's log.

With one crew member remaining, Sunset 6 continued its voyage through the planet's darkest depths.

By now, the interior of the vessel was entirely weightless. The ship had sunk to a depth of 6,800 kilometers – the planet's deepest point. The last remaining terranaut aboard the Sunset 6 had become the first person to reach the Earth's core.

Her entire world had shrunk to the size of a cramped, stuffy cockpit. She had less than ten square meters to move around in. The ship's onboard pair of neutrino glasses allowed her a small measure of sensory contact with the planet's surface. However, this lifeline was doomed to be short-lived, as the craft's neutrino communications system was nearly out of power. By now, the power levels were already too low to support the super-high-speed data relay that these sensory glasses relied on. In fact, the system had lost contact three months ago, just as I was taking the plane back from my vacation in the plains. By that time, her eyes were already stored inside my travel bag.

That misty, sunless morning on the plains had been her final glimpse of the surface world.

From then on, Sunset 6 could only maintain audio and data links with the surface. But late one night this connection had also ceased, sealing her permanently into the planet's lonely core.

Sunset 6's neutron shell was strong enough to resist the core's massive pressure, and the craft's cyclical life support systems were fully capable of an additional fifty to eighty years of operation. So she would remain alive, at the center of the Earth, in a room so small she could traverse its area in less than a minute.

I hardly dared imagine her final farewell to the surface world. However, when the Director played the recording, I was shocked.

The neutrino beam to the surface was already weak when the message was sent, and her voice occasionally cut out, but she sounded calm.

'…have received your final advisement. I'll do all I can to follow the entire research plan in the days to come. Someday, maybe generations from now, another ship might find the 'Sunset 6' and dock with it. If someone does enter here, I can only hope that the data I leave behind will be of use.

Please rest assured; I have made a life for myself down here and adapted to these surroundings; I don't feel constrained or closed-in anymore. The entire world surrounds me. When I close my eyes, I see the great plains up there on the surface. I can still see every one of the flowers that I named.

'Goodbye.'

A Transparent World

Many years have passed, and I have visited many places. Everywhere I go, I stretch out upon the Earth.

I have lain on the beaches of Hainan Island, on Alaskan snow, among Russia's white birches, on the scalding sands of the Sahara. And every time, the world became transparent to my mind's eye. I saw the terracraft anchored more than 6,000 kilometers below me at the center of that translucent sphere, whose hull once bore the name 'Sunset 6'; I felt her heartbeat echo up to me through thousands of kilometers. As I imagined the golden light of the sun and the silvery glow of the moon shining down to the planet's core, I could hear her humming 'Clair de Lune,' and her soft voice:

'... How beautiful that must look. It's a different kind of music...'

One thought comforted me. Even if I traveled to the most distant corner of the Earth, I would never be any farther from her.

地火

FIRE IN THE EARTH

TRANSLATED BY JOEL MARTINSEN

周华 - 译

Father had reached the end of his life. He breathed with difficulty, using far more effort than when he used to hoist hundred-kilo iron struts in the mine. His face was pale, his eyes bulged, and his lips were purple from lack of oxygen. An invisible rope seemed to be slowly tightening around his neck, drowning all of the simple hopes and dreams of his hard life in the all-consuming desire for air. But father's lungs, like those of all miners with stage-three silicosis, were a tangle of dusty black chunks; reticular fibers that could no longer pull oxygen from the air he inhaled into his bloodstream. Bit by bit, through twenty-five years in the mine, his father had inhaled the coal dust that made up those chunks, a tiny part of a lifetime's worth of coal.

Liu Xin knelt by the bed, his heart torn by his father's labored breaths. Suddenly, he sensed another sound in the rasping, and realized his father was trying to speak.

'What is it, Dad? Are you trying to say something?'

His father's eyes locked on him. The noise came again, indecipherable through his father's scratchy gasps, but even more urgent-sounding this time.

Liu Xin repeated his question again, desperate to understand what his father was trying to say.

The noise stopped, and his father's breathing became a light wheeze, then halted altogether. Lifeless eyes stared back at Liu Xin, as if pleading with him to heed his father's last words.

Liu Xin felt frozen; he couldn't look away from his father's eyes. He didn't see his mother fainting at the bedside or the nurse removing the oxygen tube from his father's nose. All he heard, echoing in his brain, was that noise, every syllable engraved on his memory as if etched on a record. He remained in that trance for months, the noise tormenting him day after day, until at last it began to strangle him, too. If he wanted to breathe, to keep on living, he had to figure out what it meant. Then one day, his mother, in the midst of her own long illness, said to him, 'You're grown up. You need to support the family. Drop out of high school and take over your father's job at the mine.' Liu Xin absently picked up his father's lunch box and headed out through the winter of 1978 toward the mine—Shaft No. 2, where his father had been. The black opening of the pit gazed at him like an eye, its pupil the row of explosion-proof lights that stretched off into the depths. It was his father's eye. The noise replayed in his head, urgently, and in a flash he understood his father's dying words:

'Don't go into the pit . . .'

Twenty-five years later

The Mercedes was a little out of place, Liu Xin felt. Too conspicuous. A handful of tall buildings had been erected, and hotels and shops had multiplied along the road, but everything at the mine was still shrouded in dismal gray.

When he reached the Mine Bureau, he saw a throng of people in the square outside the main office. He felt even more out of place in his suit and dress shoes as he made his way through the work-issued coveralls and cheap T-shirts. The crowd watched him silently as he passed. He felt himself blushing, and looked at the ground to avoid the gaze of so many eyes on his two-thousand-dollar suit.

Inside, on the stairs, he ran into Li Minsheng, a high school classmate of his who now worked as chief engineer in the geology department. Li Minsheng was still as wiry as he had been two decades before, though he now had worry lines on his face, and the rolls of paper he carried seemed like a huge weight in his hands.

After greeting him, Li Minsheng said, 'The mine hasn't paid salaries in ages. The workers are demonstrating.' As he spoke, he gestured at the crowd, and also looked Liu Xin over curiously.

'There hasn't been any improvement? Even with the Daqin Railway Company and two years of state coal restrictions?'

'There was for a time, but then things went bad again. I don't think anyone can do anything about this industry.' Li Minsheng gave a long sigh, looking anxious to move past Liu Xin. He seemed uncomfortable talking to him. But as the engineer turned to go, Liu Xin stopped him.

'Can you do me a favor?'

Li Minsheng forced a smile. 'In high school, you were always hungry,' he said, 'but you never accepted the ration tickets we snuck into your book bag. You're the last person who needs help from anyone these days.'

'No, I really do. Can you find me a small coal seam? Just a tiny one. No more than thirty thousand tons. It has to be independent though, that's key. The fewer connections to other seams, the better.'

'That . . . should be doable.'

'I need information on the seam and its surrounding geology. The more detailed the better.'

'That's fine, too.'

'Shall we talk over dinner?' Liu Xin asked. Li Minsheng shook his head and turned to leave, but Liu Xin caught him again. 'Don't you want to know what I'm planning?'

'I'm only interested in surviving, just like the rest,' he said, inclining his head toward the crowd. Then he left.

Taking the weathered stairs, Liu Xin looked at the high walls, the coal dust coated on them appearing for a moment like massive ink wash paintings of dark clouds over dark mountains. A huge painting, *Chairman Mao En Route to Anyuan,* still hung there, the painting itself free of dust but the frame and surface showing their age. When the solemn gaze of the figure in the painting fell upon him after an absence of more than twenty years, Liu Xin finally felt at home.

On the second floor, the director's office was still where it had been two decades earlier. A leather covering had been applied to the doors, but it had since split. He pushed through and saw the director, graying head facing the door, bent over a large blueprint on the desk, which he realized was a mine-tunneling chart as he drew closer. The director seemed not to have noticed the crowd outside.

'You're in charge of that project from the ministry?'[1] the director asked, looking up only briefly before returning to the chart.

'Yes. It's a very long-term project.'

'I see. We'll do our best to cooperate. But you've noticed our current situation.' The director looked up and extended a hand. Liu Xin saw the same weariness he'd seen on Li Minsheng's face, and when he shook the director's hand, he felt two misshapen fingers, the result of an old mining injury.

'Go look up Deputy Director Zhang, who's in charge of scientific research, or Chief Engineer Zhao. I have no time. I'm very sorry. We can talk once you've got results.' The director returned his attention to the blueprint.

'You knew my father. You were a technician on his team,' Liu Xin said, then gave his father's name.

The director nodded. 'A fine worker. A good team leader.'

'What's your opinion of the mining industry now?' Liu Xin asked.

'Opinion about what?' the director asked without looking up. *The only way to get this man's attention is to be blunt,* Liu Xin thought, then said, 'Coal is a traditional, backward, and declining industry. It's labor-intensive, it has wretched work conditions and low production efficiency, and requires enormous transport capacity. . . . Coal used to be a backbone industry in the UK, but that country closed all of its mines a decade ago!'

'We can't shut down,' the director said, head still down.

'That's right. But we can change! A complete transformation of the industry's production methods! Otherwise, we'll never be free of those difficulties,' Liu Xin said, taking quick steps over to the window. He pointed outside. 'Mine workers, millions upon millions of them, with no chance of a

---

1 The Ministry of Coal Industries was abolished in 1998, some of its functions replaced by the State Administration for Coal Industries.

fundamental change to their way of life. I've come today—'

The director cut him off. 'Have you been down below?'

'No.' After a moment, he added, 'Before he died, my father forbade me.'

'And you achieved that,' the director said. Bent over the chart as he was, his expression was unreadable, but Liu Xin felt color flooding his cheeks again. He felt hot. In this season, his suit and tie were appropriate only in air-conditioned rooms, but here there was no air-conditioning.

'Look. I've got a goal, a dream, one my father had before he died. I went to college to realize it, and I did a doctorate overseas. . . . I want to transform coal mining. Transform the lives of the mine workers.'

'Get to the point. I don't have time for childhood dreams and flights of fancy.' The director pointed behind him, but Liu Xin wasn't certain whether he was pointing at the crowd outside or not.

'I'll be as brief as I can. As it stands, the present state of coal production is: Under extremely poor conditions, coal is transported to its point of use, and then put into coal gas generators to produce coal gas, or into electric plants where it's pulverized and burnt . . .'

'I'm well aware of the coal production process.'

'Yes, of course,' Liu Xin faltered momentarily before continuing. 'Well, here's my idea: Turn the mine itself into a massive gas generator. Turn the coal into coal gas underground, in the seam, and then use petroleum or natural gas extraction techniques to extract the combustible gas, and then transport it to its points of use in dedicated pipes. Furnaces in power stations, the largest consumers of coal, can burn coal gas. Mines could disappear, and the coal industry could become a brand-new, totally modern industry, completely different from what it is today!'

'You think your idea is a new one?'

Liu Xin did not think his idea was new. He also knew that the director, who had been a talented student at the Mining Institute in the 1960s and was now one of the country's leading authorities on coal extraction, did not think it was new either. The director was certainly aware that subterranean gasification of coal had been studied throughout the world for decades, during which time no small number of gasification catalysts had been developed by countless labs and multinational companies. But it had remained a pipe dream for the better part of a century for one simple reason: The cost of the catalysts far outstripped the value of the coal gas they produced.

'Listen to this: I can achieve subterranean gasification of coal without using a catalyst!'

'And how would you do that?' the director said, pushing aside his blueprint and giving Liu Xin his full attention. An encouraging sign, Liu Xin thought, and revealed his plan:

'Ignite the coal.'

The director was silent for a moment, then lit a cigarette and motioned for Liu Xin to continue. But Liu Xin felt his enthusiasm drain as he realized the nature of the director's excitement: Here, after days of constant drudgery, he had at last found a brief opportunity to relax. A free performance by an idiot. But Liu Xin pressed stubbornly onward.

'Extraction is accomplished through a series of holes drilled from the surface to the seam, using existing oil drills. These holes have the following effects: First, they distribute a large number of sensors into the seam. Second, they ignite the subterranean coal. Third, they inject water or steam into the seam. Fourth, they introduce combustion air into the seam. Fifth, they remove the gasified coal.

'Once the coal is ignited and comes into contact with the steam, the following reactions occur: Carbon reacts with water to produce carbon monoxide and gaseous hydrogen, and carbon dioxide and hydrogen; then carbon and carbon dioxide react to form carbon monoxide; and carbon monoxide and water react to form more carbon dioxide and hydrogen. The ultimate result is a combustible gas akin to water gas, with a combustible portion consisting of fifty percent hydrogen and thirty percent carbon monoxide. This is the coal gas we will obtain.

'Sensors transmit burn and production conditions of all combustible gases at every point in the seam to the surface by ultrasound. These signals are aggregated by a computer to build a model of the coal-seam furnace, enabling us to control, through the holes, the scale and depth of the subterranean fire as well as the burn rate. Specifically, we can inject water into the holes to arrest the burn, or pressurized air or steam to intensify it. All of this proceeds automatically in response to changes in the computer's burn model so that the fire is kept at an optimum state of incompletely combusted water and coal, to ensure maximum production. You'd be most concerned, of course, with controlling the fire's range. We can drill a series of holes ahead of its advance and inject pressurized water to form a fire barrier. Where the burning is fierce, we can also employ a pressurized cement curtain, the kind used in dam building, to block the fire.' He trailed off. 'Are you listening to me?'

A noise outside had attracted the director's attention. Liu Xin knew that the image his plan evoked in the director's mind was different from his own vision. The director surely knew what igniting subterranean coal meant: right now, coal mines were burning all over the world, including several in China.

The previous year, Liu Xin had seen ground fire for the first time in Xinjiang. Not a stitch of grass on the ground or hillsides as far as the eye could see, and the air churned in hot waves of sulfur, shimmering his vision as if he were underwater or as if the entire world were roasting on a spit. At night, Liu Xin saw ribbons of ghostly red where light seeped through countless cracks in the earth. He had approached one to peer inside, and immediately gulped a nervous breath. It was like the entrance to hell. The light shone dimly from deep within, but he could still sense its ferocious heat. Looking out at the glowing lines beneath the night sky, he'd felt as if the Earth were a burning ember wrapped in a thin layer of crust.

Aygul, the brawny Uighur man who had accompanied him, was the leader of China's sole coal-seam fire brigade, and Liu Xin's aim in making the trip there had been to recruit him for his lab.

'It'll be hard to pull myself away,' Aygul had said in accented Chinese. 'I grew up watching these ground fires, so to me they're an integral part of the world, like the sun or the stars.'

'You mean the fire started burning when you were born?'

'No, Dr. Liu. This fire has been burning since the Qing Dynasty.'

Liu Xin stood rooted in place and shivered as the heat waves rolled over him in the night.

Aygul had continued, 'I'd do better to stand in your way than agree to help you. Listen to me, Dr. Liu. This isn't a game. You're working with devilry!'

Now, in the director's office, the noise outside the window had grown louder. As the director stood up and went over to it, he said to Liu Xin, 'Young man, I really hope that the sixty million the bureau is investing in this project could be put to better use. You can see there's much that needs to be done. Until next time.'

Liu Xin followed the director out of the building, where the workers' sit-in protest had grown larger, and a leader was shouting something he couldn't make out to the crowd. His attention was drawn to a corner of the crowd, where he saw a group of people in wheelchairs. In these days, one rarely saw so many people in wheelchairs gathering. More were filing in, each one a miner who had lost a limb in a work accident.

Liu Xin felt like he couldn't breathe. He loosened his tie, lowered his head, and passed quickly through the crowd before ducking into his car. He drove aimlessly, his mind blank, and after a while slammed on the brakes at the top of a hill. He used to come here as a kid. From here, there was a bird's-eye view of the whole mine. He got out and stood motionless for a long time.

'What are you looking at?' a voice said. Liu Xin looked back and saw Li Minsheng, who had come up at some point to stand behind him.

'That's our school,' Liu Xin said, pointing off at a large mining school that housed both primary and secondary classes. The athletic field on the campus was conspicuously large. It was there they had lain to rest their childhood and youth.

'Do you think you remember everything?' Li Minsheng said tiredly as he sat down on a nearby rock.

'I do.'

'That afternoon in late autumn, when the sun was hazy. We were playing football on the field, when the building's loudspeaker came on . . . do you remember?'

'It was playing a dirge, and then Zhang Jianjun came running over barefoot to say that Chairman Mao had died . . .'

'We walloped him, even as he was crying out that it was true, honest to Chairman Mao it was true. We didn't believe him, though, and dragged him off to the police . . .'

'But we slowed down at the school gate, since the dirge was playing outside too, as if that dark music was filling the whole world . . .'

'That dirge has been playing in my mind for more than two decades. These days, when the music plays it's Nietzsche who runs over barefoot and says, "God is dead." ' Li Minsheng barked out a laugh. 'I believe it.'

Liu Xin stared at his childhood friend. 'When did you turn into this? I hardly even recognize you.'

Li Minsheng jumped up and glared back at him, jabbing a finger at the gray world at the foot of the hill. 'When did the mine turn into that? Do you still recognize it?' Then he sat down heavily again. 'Our fathers were such a proud group. Such a proud, grand group of miners. Take my dad. He was a level-eight worker[1] and earned a hundred and twenty yuan a month. A hundred and twenty yuan in the Chairman Mao era, no less.'

Liu Xin was silent for a moment, then tried to change the subject. 'How's your family? Your wife . . . uh, something Shan, is it?'

Li Minsheng smiled thinly. 'Last year she told me she was taking a work trip, told her work unit she was taking annual leave, and took our daughter and left me and vanished. Two months later she sent a letter, posted from Canada, in which she said she had no wish to waste her life with a dirty coalman.'

'You've got to be kidding. You're a senior engineer!'

'Same difference.' Li Minsheng swept his hand about them. 'To those

---

1 The highest of eight working–class wage levels adopted nationwide in the 1950s.

who've never been below, it's all the same. We're all dirty coalmen. Do you remember how badly we wanted to become engineers?'

'Those were the days of record-chasing production,' Liu Xin said. 'We brought our fathers lunch. It was the first time we'd been down the shaft, and it was so dark down there. I asked my father and those standing near him, 'How do you know where the coal seam is? How do you know where to dig the tunnels? And how are you able to get two tunnels dug from different directions to meet so precisely so far down?' And your father answered, 'Child, no one knows except for the engineers.' And when we got to the surface, he pointed out a few men carrying hard hats and clipboards, and said, 'Look, those are engineers.' Do you remember that, Minsheng? Even we could see that they were different. The towels around their necks, at least, were a bit whiter. We've achieved that childhood dream now. Of course, it's not all that glorious, but we have to at least fulfill our duty and accomplish something. Otherwise, won't we be betraying ourselves?'

'That's enough,' Li Minsheng said, standing up with a sudden anger. 'I've been doing my duty this whole time. I've been accomplishing things. But you? You're living in a dream! Do you really believe you can bring miners up from the mines? Turn this mine into a gas field? Say all that theory is correct and your test succeeds. So what? Have you calculated the cost of the thing? Also, how are you going to lay tens of thousands of kilometers of pipe? You realize that we can't even pay rail shipping fees these days?'

'Can't you take the long view? In a few years, or a few decades . . .'

'The hell with the long view! The people here aren't certain about the next few days, much less the next few decades. I've said before that you live on dreams. You've always been that way. Sure, back in your quiet old institute headquarters in Beijing you can have that dream, but I can't. I live in the real world.'

Li Minsheng turned to leave, then added, 'Oh, I came to tell you that the director has arranged for us to cooperate with your experiment. Work is work, and I'll do it.' Then he set off down the hill without looking back.

Liu Xin silently surveyed the mine where he had been born and spent his childhood. Its towering headframes and their enormous top wheels spinning, lowering large cages down the shaft out of sight; rows of electric trams going in and out of the entrance to the shaft where his father had worked; a train outside the coal-separator building easing past more piles of coal than he could count; the cinema and soccer field where he had spent the best moments of his youth; the huge bathhouse—only miners had ones so large—where he had learned how to swim in water stained black from coal dust. Yes, he had learned to swim in a place so far from rivers and oceans.

Turning his gaze toward the distance, he saw the spoil tip, the accumulation of more than a century's worth of shale dug out of the mine. It seemed taller than the surrounding hills, with smoke rising where the sulfur heated the rain. . . . All of it black, blanketed over time in a layer of coal dust. It was the color of Liu Xin's childhood, the color of his life. He closed his eyes, and as he listened to the sounds of the mine below, time seemed to stop.

Dad's mine. My mine . . .

The valley was not far from the mine, whose smoke and steam were visible beyond the ridge during the day, whose glow projected into the sky at night, and whose steam whistles were always audible. Liu Xin, Li Minsheng, and Aygul stood in the center of the desolate valley. In the distance, a herder was driving a flock of scrawny goats slowly along the foot of the mountain. Beneath the valley lay the small isolated coal seam that Liu Xin wanted to use for his subterranean gasified coal extraction experiment, found by Li Minsheng and the engineers in the geology department after a month of combing through mountains of materials in the archives.

'We're pretty far from the main mining area, so we've got fewer geological details on it,' Li Minsheng said.

'I've read the materials, and from what we have now, the experimental seam is at least two hundred meters from the main seam. That's acceptable. We should get to work,' Liu Xin said excitedly.

'You're not an expert in mining geology, and you're even less familiar with the actual conditions here. I advise you to be more cautious. Think about it some more.'

'There's nothing to think about. The experiment can't proceed,' Aygul said. 'I've read the materials too. They're too sketchy. The separation between exploratory boreholes is too large, and they were made in the sixties. They need to be redone, to prove conclusively that the seam is independent, before the experiment can begin. Li and I have drawn up an exploratory plan.'

'How long until exploration is complete, according to your plan? And how much more investment is needed?'

Li Minsheng said, 'At the geology department's current capacity, at least a month. We didn't run the investment numbers. To estimate . . . at least two million or so.'

'We have neither the time nor the money for that!'

'Then put in a request to the ministry.'

'The ministry? A bunch of bastards in the ministry want to kill this project! The higher-ups are anxious for results, so I'm dooming the entire project if I go back and ask for more time and a bigger budget. Instinct tells me there won't be major problems, so why not take a little risk?'

'Instinct? Risk? Not on a project like this! Dr. Liu, do you realize where we're starting this fire? You call that a small risk?'

'I've made my decision!' Liu Xin cut him off with a wave of his hand and walked off alone.

'Engineer Li, why aren't you stopping that madman? The two of us are on the same side,' Aygul said.

'I'm going to do what I'm required to,' Li Minsheng said.

Three hundred men were at work in the valley. Besides physicists, chemists, geologists, and mining engineers, there were a few unexpected experts. Aygul led a coal-seam fire brigade of more than ten members, and there were two entire drilling squads from Renqiu Oil Field in Hebei Province, as well as a number of hydraulic-construction engineers and workers who would erect subterranean firebreaks. On the work site, in addition to tall rigs and piles of drilling poles, there were piles of cement bags and a mixer, a high-pressure slurry pump whining as it injected liquid cement into the ground, rows of high-pressure water and air pumps, and a spiderweb of crisscrossing multicolored pipes.

Work had been progressing for two months, and an underground cement curtain more than two thousand meters long had been constructed surrounding the seam. Liu Xin had thought of adapting hydraulic engineering technology used in waterproofing the foundation of dams to the subterranean firewall: high-pressure cement was injected underground, where it hardened into a tight fireproof barrier. Within the curtain, the drills had sunk nearly a hundred boreholes, each directly into the seam. The holes were connected by pipes that split into three prongs attached to different high-pressure pumps that could inject water, steam, or compressed air.

The final bit of work was the release of the 'ground rats,' as they called the fire sensors. The curious gizmos, Liu Xin's own design, resembled not rats but bombs. Each was twenty centimeters long with a bit at one end and a drive wheel at the other, and once released into the borehole, it could drill nearly a hundred meters farther into the seam and reach its designated location autonomously. Operable even under high temperatures and pressures, it would transmit the parameters at its location back to the master computer once the seam was ignited via seam-penetrating infrasound. More than a thousand of these ground rats had been released into the seam, half of which were positioned outside of the fire curtain to detect potential breaches.

Liu Xin stood in a large tent in front of a projection screen showing the fire curtain, with flashing lights that indicated the position of each ground rat according to the signals. They were densely distributed, giving the screen the look of an astronomical chart.

Everything was ready. Two bulky ignition electrodes had been lowered down a borehole at the center of the enclosure and were directly wired to a red button switch in the tent where Liu Xin was standing. All of the workers were in place and waiting.

'There's still time to change your mind, Dr. Liu,' Aygul said quietly. 'Or to take more time to think on it.'

'Aygul, that's enough. You've been spreading fear and uncertainty from day one, and you've complained about me all the way to the ministry. To be fair, you've contributed immensely to this project, and without your work this past year, I wouldn't be so quick to conduct the experiment.'

'Dr. Liu . . .' Aygul was pleading now. Liu Xin had never seen him like this. 'We don't have to do this. Don't release the demon from the depths!'

'You think we can quit now?' Liu Xin smiled and shook his head, then turned toward Li Minsheng.

Li Minsheng said, 'As you instructed, we reviewed all of the geological materials a sixth time. We found no problems. Last night we added an additional curtain layer to a few sensitive spots.' He pointed out several short lines on the screen, outside the enclosure.

Liu Xin went up to the ignition switch, and when his hand made contact with the red button he paused and closed his eyes as if in prayer. His lips moved, but only Li Minsheng, standing closest to him, heard the word he said—

'Dad . . .'

The button made no sound or flash. The valley remained the same as ever. But somewhere deep underground, a glittering high-temperature electric arc was created by more than ten thousand volts of electricity in the seam. On the screen, at the location of the electrodes, a small red dot appeared and quickly expanded like a blot of red ink on rice paper. Liu Xin moved the mouse, and the screen switched to a burn model produced from the data returned by the ground rats, a continuously growing, onion-like sphere, where each layer was an isotherm. High-pressure pumps roared, pouring combustion air into the seam through the boreholes, and the fire expanded like a blown-up balloon. . . . An hour later, when the control computer switched on the high-pressure water pumps, the fire onscreen twisted and distorted like a punctured balloon, although its volume remained the same.

Liu Xin exited the tent. The sun had set behind the hill, and the thunder of machines echoed in the darkening valley. More than three hundred people were assembled outside, surrounding a vertical jet the diameter of an oil barrel. They made way for him, and he approached the small platform at the foot of the jet. Two people were standing on the platform, one of whom twisted the knob when he saw Liu Xin coming; the other struck a lighter to light a torch, which he passed to Liu Xin. The turning of the knob produced a hiss of gas from the jet that rose dramatically in volume until it roared throughout the valley like a hoarse giant. On all sides, three hundred nervous faces watched in the faint torchlight. Liu Xin closed his eyes and spoke silently to himself again. 'Dad. . .' Then he brought the torch to the mouth of the jet and ignited the world's first gasified coal well.

With a bang, a huge pillar of fire leapt into the air, shooting up almost twenty meters. Closest to the mouth of the jet, the column was a clear, pure blue, but just above that it turned a blinding yellow before gradually turning red. It whistled in the air, and those closest to it could feel its surge of heat. Its radiance lit the surrounding hills, and from a distance it would look as if a sky lantern were shining over the plateau.

A white-haired man, the director, emerged from the crowd and shook Liu Xin's hand. He said, 'Please accept the congratulations of a closed-minded relic. You've succeeded! But I hope you'll extinguish it as soon as possible.'

'Even now you don't trust me? It won't be extinguished. I want it to keep burning, for the whole country and the whole world to see.'

'They've already seen it.' The director pointed to the throng of TV reporters behind him. 'But as you well know, the test seam is no more than two hundred meters from the surrounding main seam at its closest point.'

'But we've laid three firebreaks at those spots. And we have high-speed drills on standby. There won't be any problems.'

'You're engineers from the ministry, so I have no authority to interfere. But there's potential danger in any new technology, no matter how successful it may seem. I've seen my share of dangers in my decades in coal. Maybe that's the reason for my rigid thinking. I'm truly worried. . . . However,' and the director again extended a hand to Liu Xin, 'I'd still like to thank you. You've shown me hope for the coal industry.' He gazed at the pillar of fire again. 'Your father would be pleased.'

Two more jets were ignited in the next two days, so there were now three pillars of fire. The production volume of the test seam, calculated at a standard supply pressure, had reached five hundred thousand cubic meters per hour, equivalent to more than a hundred large coal gas furnaces.

The underground coal fire was moderated entirely by computer, with the scale controlled to a stable-bounded area no larger than two-thirds of the total area within the curtain. At the mine's request, multiple fire-control tests had been conducted. On the computer, Liu Xin described a ring around the fire with the mouse, and then clicked to constrict it. The whining of the high-pressure pumps outside changed, and within an hour the fire had been contained within that ring. Meanwhile, two more fire curtains, each two hundred meters long, had been added in the risky direction of the main seam.

There was little for him to do. Most of his time he devoted to taking media interviews. Major companies inside and outside of China, including the likes of DuPont and Exxon, were swarming to propose investment and collaboration projects.

On the third day, a coal-seam firefighter came to Liu Xin to say that their chief was about to collapse from fatigue. Aygul had for the past two days led the firefighting squad in a mad series of subterranean firefighting exercises. He had also, on his own initiative, rented satellite time from the National Remote Sensing Center to survey the region's crust temperature. He hadn't slept in three days, spending his time instead doing rounds outside the curtain ring, each circuit taking all night.

When Liu Xin found Aygul, he saw that the stocky man had gotten much thinner, and his eyes were red. 'I can't sleep,' he said. 'The nightmares start as soon as I shut my eyes. I see those fire columns erupting all around me, like a forest of fire . . .'

'Renting a sensor satellite is a huge expense,' Liu Xin said gently. 'And although I don't see the need, you've done it and I respect your decision. I'll be needing you in the future, Aygul. I don't think your firefighting squad will have much to do, but even the safest place still needs a fire team. You're exhausted. Go back to Beijing for a few days' rest.'

'Leave now? You're insane!'

'You grew up above ground fire. That's why your fear of it goes so deep. Right now we may not be able to control a massive fire like the one in the Xinjiang mines, but we soon will be. I want to set up the first gasified coalfield for commercial use in Xinjiang. When that time comes, the underground fires will be under our control, and the land of your hometown will be covered in glorious vineyards.'

'Dr. Liu, I respect you. That's why I'm working with you. But you overestimate yourself. Where ground fire is concerned, you're still just a child.' Aygul smiled bitterly and walked away shaking his head.

Disaster struck on the fifth day. The sun had just come up when Liu Xin was shaken awake by Aygul, who was out of breath, wild-eyed, and almost feverish. His trouser legs were soaked through with dew. He held a laser-printed photograph in front of Liu Xin's face, so close it blocked his vision entirely. It was a false-color infrared sensor image returned from the satellite, a vibrant abstract painting he couldn't understand, so he just stared in confusion. 'Come!' Aygul shouted, and dragged Liu Xin out of the tent by the hand.

Liu Xin followed him up a hill on the north side of the valley, his confusion growing all the while. First, this was the safest direction, separated from the main seam by more than a kilometer. Second, Aygul had led him nearly to the top of the hill, but the curtain ring was far, far beneath them. What was there to go wrong here? When they reached the top, Liu Xin was about to gasp out a question when Aygul pointed in a different direction, to a place even farther off. Liu Xin laughed in relief—there was no disaster. The mine was directly ahead of where Aygul pointed, and between that hill and the one beneath their feet was an even slope that led to a meadow at the bottom. That was Aygul's target. The mine and the meadow seemed peaceful at this distance, but after a longer look Liu Xin saw something strange about the meadow: in one circular spot, the grass appeared darker than the surrounding area, a difference only noticeable upon careful observation. He felt his heart seize, then he and Aygul raced down the hill to that patch of darker green.

When they got there, Liu Xin examined the round patch of grass, which had wilted to the ground as if it had been scalded. He put his hand on it and felt heat emanating from the ground. In the center of the circle a puff of steam rose in the light of the rising sun. . . .

After a morning of emergency drilling and the dispatch of another thousand-odd ground rats, Liu Xin confirmed the nightmarish fact: the main seam had caught fire. The scope of the fire was unknown for the time being, since the ground rats had a maximum below-ground speed of around ten meters per hour. However, with the fire so much deeper than the test seam, the fact that its heat was radiating above ground meant it had been burning for quite some time. It was a big fire.

The strange thing was that the thousand meters of earth and stone between the main seam and the test seam was whole and unbroken. The ground fire had ignited on either side of the thousand-meter buffer zone, leading someone to suggest that it was unrelated to the experiment. But that was no more than self-delusion; even the person who had said it didn't really believe the two weren't in some way connected. Deeper exploration cleared up the matter late that night.

Eight narrow coal belts extended from the test seam. Only half a meter at their narrowest point, they were hard to detect. Five of them were bisected by the fire curtain, but the other three led downward and just skirted the curtain's bottom edge. Two of these terminated, but the last one led directly to the main seam a kilometer away. All of them were actually ground fissures that had been filled up by coal; their connection to the surface provided them with an excellent supply of oxygen. The one linking the test seam and the main seam thus acted as a fuse.

None of the three was marked on the materials Li Minsheng had provided, and in fact, such long and narrow belts were extremely rare in the field of coal geology. Mother Nature had played a cruel joke.

'I had no choice. My kid's got uremia and needs continual dialysis. The money from this project was too important to me, so I didn't fight you as strongly as I could have. . . .' Li Minsheng's face was pale, and he avoided Liu Xin's eyes.

The three of them stood atop the hill between the two ground fires. It was another early morning. The entire meadow between the mine and the peak was now dark green, apart from the previous day's circular area, which was now a burnt yellow. Steam wafted from the ground, obscuring their view of the mine.

Aygul said to Liu Xin, 'My fire brigade from Xinjiang has landed in Taiyuan with equipment, and they'll be here soon. Teams from elsewhere in the country are headed here too. The fire looks to be spreading fast.'

Liu Xin looked silently at Aygul for a long moment before he asked in a low voice, 'Can you tame it?'

Aygul shook his head.

'Then tell me: How much hope is there? If we seal off the vents, or inject water to quell the fire . . .'

Again, Aygul shook his head. 'I've been doing this my whole life, but ground fire still consumed my hometown. I told you that where ground fire is concerned, you're still just a child. You don't know what it is. That far underground it's slipperier than a viper, wilier than a ghost. Mortals can't stop it from going where it wants. Under our feet is a huge quantity of high-quality anthracite, and this devil's been coveting it for millions of years. Now you've released it, and given it limitless energy and power. The ground fire here will be a hundred times worse than in Xinjiang.'

Liu Xin shook the Uighur man by the shoulders in desperation. 'Tell me how much hope we have! Tell me the truth, I beg you!'

'Zero,' Aygul said softly. 'Dr. Liu, you can't atone for your sins in this lifetime.'

An emergency meeting was held in the main bureau building attended by the bureau leadership and the heads of the five mines, as well as a group of alarmed officials from the city government, including the mayor. The meeting's first act was to establish an emergency command center headed up by the director, with Liu Xin and Li Minsheng as members of the leading group.

'Engineer Li and I will do our utmost, but I'd like to remind you all that we're now criminals,' Liu Xin said, as Li Minsheng sat silently, head bowed.

'Now's not the time for recrimination,' the director said. 'Act, and think of nothing else. Do you know who said that? Your father. Once, back when I was a technician on his squad, I ignored his warning and enlarged the extraction range so I could meet production targets. As a result, a huge quantity of water entered the works, trapping more than twenty squad members in the corner of a passageway. Our lamps had gone out, and we didn't dare strike a lighter, afraid of gas on the one hand and of using up the oxygen on the other, since the water had sealed us off completely. You couldn't see your hand in front of your face, it was so dark. Then your father told me he remembered there was another passageway above us, and our ceiling was probably not all that thick. Next thing I heard was him scratching at the ceiling with a pick. The rest of us felt around for our picks and joined him, digging in the darkness. As the oxygen level dropped, we began to feel woozy and tight-chested. And on top of that there was the darkness, an absolute blackness no one on the surface is able to imagine, but for the glint of picks striking the ceiling. Staying alive was sheer torture, but it was your father who kept me going. Over and over he said to me in the darkness, 'Act, and think of nothing else.' I don't know how long we dug, but just when I was about to faint from lack of breath, a chunk of the ceiling fell in and the glare of the explosion-proof lamps from the overhead passageway shone through the hole. . . . Later your father told me that he had no idea how thick the roof was, but it was the only thing we could do: act, and think of nothing else. Your father's words have been etched ever deeper on my brain over the years, and now I pass them on to you.'

Experts who had rushed from all over the country to attend the meeting soon drafted a plan for fighting the fire. The options at hand were limited to just three. First, cut off the underground fire's oxygen. Second, use a grout

133

curtain to cut the path of the fire. Third, inject massive quantities of water underground to quench the fire. These three techniques were to proceed simultaneously, but the first had been demonstrated ineffective long ago. Air vents supplying oxygen to the fire were difficult to pinpoint, and they would be hard to seal off even if located. The second method was effective only against shallow coal-seam fires and was much slower than the pace of the underground fire's advance. The third method was most promising.

News was still embargoed, and the firefighting proceeded quietly. High-power drilling rigs, emergency transfers from Renqiu Oil Field, passed through the mining city under the eyes of curious onlookers; the army entered the hills; whirling choppers appeared in the sky . . . a cloud of uncertainty descended over the mine, and rumors spread like wildfire.

The drills were lined up at the head of the subterranean fire, and once drilling was complete, more than a hundred high-pressure pumps began injecting water into the hot, smoking boreholes. The sheer quantity of water meant that the water supply to both the mine and the city was cut off, which only increased uncertainty and unrest among the public. But initial results were encouraging: On the big screen in the command center, dark spots appeared surrounding the position of the boreholes at the head of the red-colored fire, indicating that the water had dramatically dropped the fire temperature. If the line of dots connected, then there was hope for stopping the fire's spread.

But this slightly comforting situation did not last long. The leader of the oil field drilling crew found Liu Xin at the foot of the enormous rig.

'Dr. Liu, no more drilling can be done at two-thirds of the well positions!' he shouted over the roar of the drills and pumps.

'Are you joking? We've got to add more water-injection holes to the fire.'

'No. Well pressure at those positions is growing too quickly. Any more drilling and there'll be a blowout!'

'Bullshit. This isn't an oil field. There's no high-pressure gas reservoir. What's going to blow?'

'You know nothing! I'm shutting down the drills and pulling out.'

Enraged, Liu Xin grabbed his collar. 'You will not. I order you to continue drilling. There will not be a blowout. You hear me? There won't!'

Even before he finished speaking, they heard a loud crash from the direction of the rig, and they turned in time to witness the well's heavy seal fly off in two pieces as a yellowish-black mud spurted into the air together with pieces of broken drill pipe. Bystanders shouted in alarm, and the mud gradually lightened in color as its particulate content reduced. Then it turned snow-white, and they realized that the ground fire had heated the injected water into pressurized steam. High up on the rig they saw the body of the drill driver, suspended and twisting slowly in the roiling steam. There was no trace of the other three engineers who had been on the platform.

What happened next was even more terrifying. The head of the white dragon broke free from the ground and gradually took flight, until finally the white steam had risen above the rig like a white-haired demon in the sky. There was nothing in the space between the demon and the mouth of the well apart from the wreckage of the rig. Nothing but that terrifying hiss. A few young engineers, under the impression that the blowout had stopped, took hesitant steps forward, but Liu Xin grabbed two of them and shouted, 'That's suicide! It's superheated steam!'

They watched in terror as the damp headframe was blasted dry in the steam's heat, and the thick rubber pipes strung from it liquefied like wax. The infernal steam assaulted the frame with a hair-curling thunder. . . .

Further water injection was impossible, and even if it weren't, it would act more to combust than to quench the fire.

All emergency command center personnel assembled at the third mine, by Shaft No. 4, the nearest to the fire line.

'The fire is nearing the mine's extraction zone,' Aygul said. 'If it gets there, then the mine passages will supply it with oxygen and multiply its strength considerably. . . . That's the present situation.' He broke off, and glanced at the bureau director and the heads of the five mines uncomfortably, unwilling to violate the greatest taboo in mining.

'And conditions in the shafts?' the director asked without emotion.

'Excavation and extraction are proceeding as normal in eight shafts, primarily for stability's sake,' the head of one mine said.

'Shut down production altogether. Evacuate all staff in the shafts. Then . . .' The director paused and remained silent for a few seconds.

Those few seconds felt immeasurably long.

'Seal the shafts,' the director said at last, uttering the heartbreaking words.

'No! You can't!' The cry burst from Li Minsheng before he could stop himself. 'What I mean is . . . ' He grasped for counterlogic to present the director. 'Sealing the shafts . . . sealing the shafts . . . will throw everything into chaos. And . . .'

'Enough,' the director said with a gentle wave of his hand. His expression said everything: *I know how you feel. I feel the same way. We all do.*

Li Minsheng crouched on the ground, head in hands, shoulders shaking with silent sobs. The mining leadership and engineers stood silently before the shaft. The cavernous entrance stared back at them like a giant eye, just as Shaft No. 2 had stared at Liu Xin two decades before.

They shared a moment of silence for the century-old mine.

After a while, the bureau's chief engineer broke the silence with a low voice: 'Let's take up as much equipment as we can from down below.'

'Then,' the mine chief said, 'we ought to get together demolition squads.'

The director nodded. 'Time is of the essence. You get to work. I'll file a request with the ministry.'

The bureau party secretary said, 'Can't we use military engineers? If we use miners for the demolition squad, and anything happens . . .'

'I've considered it,' said the director. 'But we only have one detachment of military engineers at the moment, far too few even for one shaft. Besides, they're not familiar with subterranean demolitions.'

Shaft No. 4, closest to the fire, was the first to shut down. When the tramloads of miners reached the entrance, they found a hundred-strong demolition squad waiting around a pile of drills. They inquired, but the demolition squad members didn't know what they were expected to do; their orders were only to assemble beside the drilling equipment. Suddenly, their attention was seized by a convoy heading toward the entrance. The first truck bristled with armed police, who jumped down to secure a perimeter around a parking area for the vehicles that followed. When the eleven trucks stopped, the canvas was pulled back to reveal neat stacks of yellow wooden crates. The miners were stunned. They knew what was in these crates.

Each crate held twenty-four kilos of ammonium nitrate fuel oil, fifty tons of it altogether in the ten trucks. The final, somewhat smaller truck carried a few bundles of bamboo strips for lashing the explosives together, and a pile of black plastic bags, which the miners knew held electronic detonators.

Liu Xin and Li Minsheng hopped down from the cab of one of the trucks and saw the newly appointed captain of the demolition squad, a muscular, bearded man, coming their way with a roll of charts.

'What are you making us do, Engineer Li?' the captain asked as he unrolled the paper.

Li Minsheng pointed to a spot on the chart, his finger trembling slightly. 'Three blast lines, each thirty-five meters long. Detailed positions are on the chart underneath. One-hundred-fifty-millimeter and seventy-five-millimeter boreholes, filled with twenty-eight kilos and fourteen kilos of explosives, respectively, at a density of . . .'

'I'm asking, what are you trying to make us do?'

Li Minsheng went silent and bowed his head under the captain's fiery stare.

The captain turned toward the crowd. 'Brothers, they want us to blow up the tunnels!' he shouted. There was a moment of commotion among the miners, but a wall of armed police came forward in a semicircle to block the crowd from reaching the trucks. But the police line distorted under the pressure of the surging black human sea, until it was at the breaking point. All of this took place in a heavy silence, with the scuffle of footsteps and clack of gun bolts the only sounds. At the last moment, the crowd ceased its tumult as the director and mine head stepped up onto the bed of one of the trucks.

'I started work in this mine when I was fifteen. Are you just going to destroy it?' shouted one old miner. The wrinkles carved into his face were visible even beneath the thick cover of coal dust.

'What are we going to live on after it's closed?'

'Why are you blowing it up?'

'Life in the mine was difficult enough without you all messing around.'

The crowd exploded, waves of anger surging ever fiercer over the sea of coal-blackened faces flashing white teeth. The director waited silently until the crowd's anger turned to restless movement, then, when it was just about to get out of control, he spoke.

'Take a look in that direction,' he said, pointing to a small rise near the mine entrance. His voice was not loud, but it quieted the angry storm, and everyone looked where he was pointing.

'We all call that the old coal column, but do you realize that when it was erected, it wasn't a column, but a huge cube of coal? That was in the Qing Dynasty, more than a hundred years ago, when Governor Zhang Zhidong erected it at the founding of the mine. A century of wind and rain have weathered it into a column. Our mine has weathered so much wind and rain during that century, so many difficulties and disasters, more than anyone can remember. That's more than a brief moment, comrades. That's four or five generations! If there's nothing else we've learned or remembered over the past century, then we must remember this—'

The director raised his hands toward the sea of faces.

'The sky won't fall!'

The crowd stood frozen. It seemed as if even their breathing had ceased.

'Out of all of China's industrial workers, all of its proletariat, none has a longer history than us. None has a history with more hardship and tumult than ours. Has the sky fallen for miners? No! That all of us can stand here and look at that old coal column is proof of that. Our sky won't fall. It never did, and it never will!

'Hardship? There's nothing new about that, comrades. When have we miners ever had it easy? From the time of our ancestors, when have miners ever had an easy day in their lives? Rack your brains: Of all the industries and all the professions in China and the rest of the world, are any of them harder than ours? None. None at all. What's new about hardship? If it were easy, now that would be surprising. We're holding up both the sky and the earth! If we feared hardship, we'd have died out long ago.

'But talented people have been thinking of solutions for us as society and science have advanced. Now we have a solution, one that has the hope of totally transforming our lives, bringing us out of the dark mines and into the sun to mine coal beneath blue skies! Miners will have the world's most enviable job. This hope has now arrived. Don't take my word for it, but look at the pillars of fire shooting skyward in the south valley. But these efforts have caused a catastrophe. We will explain all of this in detail later. Right now all you need to understand is that this may be the very last hardship for miners. This is the price for our wonderful tomorrow. So let's stand together and face it. As so many generations have before—again, the sky hasn't fallen!'

The crowd dispersed in silence. Liu Xin said to the director, 'I've known you and my father, and I can die without regret.'

'Act, and think of nothing else,' the director said, clapping Liu Xin on the shoulder, then gripped him in an embrace.

The day after demolition work commenced on Shaft No. 4, Liu Xin and Li Minsheng walked side by side through the main tunnel, their footsteps echoing emptily. They were passing the first blast area, and in the dim light of their headlamps, they could see the boreholes densely distributed in the high ceiling, and the colorful waterfall of detonation wires streaming toward a pile on the floor.

Li Minsheng said, 'I used to hate the mine. Hate it, because it consumed my youth. But now I realize that I've become one with it. Hate it or love it, it's what my youth was.'

'We shouldn't torture ourselves,' Liu Xin said. 'We've done something with our lives, at least. If we're not heroes, then at least we've gone down fighting.'

They fell silent, realizing that they were talking about death.

Then Aygul ran up, breathing hard. 'Engineer Li, look at that,' he said, pointing at the ceiling. A few thick canvas hoses, used for ventilating the mine, were now limp and slack.

Li Minsheng blanched. 'Shit! When was ventilation cut off?'

'Two hours ago.'

Li Minsheng barked into his radio, and soon the chief of ventilation and two ventilation engineers showed up.

'There's no way to restore ventilation, Engineer Li. All of the equipment from down below—blowers, motors, anti-explosion switches, and even some pipes—have been taken out!' the ventilation chief said.

'You idiot! Who told you to take them out? Are you suicidal?' Li Minsheng shouted, far past caring about decorum or professionalism.

'Engineer Li, watch your language. Do you know who told us? The director expressly said for us to take out as much equipment as possible before the shaft is sealed. We all were at the meeting. We've been working day and night for two days and have taken out more than a million yuan worth of equipment. And now you're cursing at us? What's the point of ventilation anyway when the shaft's going to be sealed?'

Li Minsheng let out a long sigh. The truth of the situation had still not been disclosed, leading to this kind of coordination issue.

'What's the problem?' Liu Xin asked after the ventilation staff had left. 'Shouldn't the ventilation be stopped? Won't that reduce the supply of oxygen to the mine?'

'Dr. Liu, you're a theoretical giant but a practical dwarf. You're clueless in the face of reality. Like Engineer Li said, you only know how to dream!' Aygul said. He had not spoken courteously to Liu Xin since the fire had started.

Li Minsheng explained, 'This coal seam has a high incidence of gas. Once ventilation is shut off, the gas will quickly accumulate at the bottom of the shaft, and when the fire gets here, it may touch off an explosion powerful enough to blow out the seal. At the very least it will blow out new channels for oxygen. There's no choice but to add another blast area.'

'But Engineer Li, the two areas above us are only half done, and the third hasn't even started. The fire is nearing the southern mining zone; there might not even be enough time to complete three zones.'

'I . . .' Liu Xin said carefully. 'I have an idea that may or may not work.'

'Ha!' Aygul laughed coldly. 'This is unprecedented. When has Dr. Liu ever been uncertain? When has Dr. Liu ever had to ask someone else before making a decision?'

'What I mean is that we've got a blast zone already set up at this deep point. Can we detonate it first? That way, if there's an explosion farther down the shaft, there will be one obstacle, at least.'

'If that worked we would have done it already,' Li Minsheng said. 'The blast will be large enough to fill the tunnels with toxic gas and dust that won't disperse for a long time, impeding further work in the tunnels.'

The ground fire's advance was faster than anticipated. The construction group decided to detonate with only two blast zones in place, and ordered all personnel evacuated from the shaft as quickly as possible. It was near dark. They were standing around a chart in a production building not far off from the entrance, considering how to detonate at the shortest possible distance using a spur tunnel, when Li Minsheng suddenly said, 'Listen!'

A deep rumble was coming from somewhere below ground, as if the earth were belching. A few seconds later they heard it again.

'Methane explosions. The fire has reached the mine,' Aygul said nervously.

'Wasn't it supposed to still be farther away?'

No one answered. Liu Xin's ground rats had been used up, and with the only sensing techniques now at their disposal it was difficult to precisely determine the fire's position and speed.

'Evacuate at once!'

Li Minsheng snatched up his radio, but no matter how he shouted, there was no answer.

'Before I came up, Chief Zhang was worried he'd smash a radio while working,' a miner from the demolition squad told him. 'So he put them with the detonation wires. There are a dozen drills working simultaneously down there. It's pretty loud!'

Li Minsheng jumped up and dashed out of the building without even grabbing a helmet. He called a tram, then headed down the shaft at top speed. The moment the tram vanished into the shaft entrance, Liu Xin could see Li Minsheng waving at him, and there was a smile on his face. It had been a long time since he'd smiled.

The ground belched a few more times, but then silence descended.

'Did that series of explosions consume all of the methane in the mine?' Liu Xin asked an engineer standing beside him, who looked back at him in wonder.

'Consume it all? You've got to be kidding. It will just release more methane from the seam.'

A sky-spitting thunder rolled, as if the Earth itself were exploding under their feet. The mouth of the mine was engulfed in flames. The blast lifted Liu Xin up into the air, and the world spun madly about him. A mess of stones and crossties were thrown by the blast, and he saw a tramcar hurtle out of the flames, spit out of the entrance like an apple core. He landed heavily on the ground as rock rained down on him, and it felt as if each was coated in blood. He heard more deep rumbles, the sound of the explosives detonating in the mine. Before he lost consciousness, he saw the fire at the entrance disappear, replaced by thick clouds of smoke. . .

One Year Later

He walked as if through hell. Clouds of black smoke covered the sky, rendering the sun a barely visible disk of dark red. Static electricity from dust friction meant the smoke flickered with lightning, which lit up the hills above the ground fire with a blue light, exposing the image indelibly onto Liu Xin's mind. Smoke issued from shaft openings that dotted the hills, the bottom of each column glowing a savage dark red from the ground fire before gradually blackening farther up the columns that swirled snakelike into the heavens.

The road was bumpy, and the blacktop surface was melted enough that with every few steps it almost peeled the soles off his shoes. Refugees and their vehicles packed the roadway, all of them in masks against the stifling sulfurous air and the snowflake-like ash that fell endlessly and turned their bodies white. Fully-armed soldiers kept order on the crowded road, and a helicopter cut through the smoke overhead, calling through a loudspeaker for no one to panic. . . . The exodus had begun in the winter and was initially planned to be completed in one year, but a sudden intensification of the ground fire meant they had to proceed more urgently. Chaos reigned. The court had repeatedly delayed Liu Xin's hearing, but this morning he had been left unguarded in the detention center and had made his way uncertainly outside.

The land around the road was parched and fractured into fissures filled with the same thick dust that billowed around him. A small pond steamed, its surface crammed with floating corpses of fish and frogs. It was the height of summer, but no stitch of green was visible. Grass was withered yellow and buried under dust. The trees were dead as well, and some were even smoking, their charcoal branches reaching toward the evening sky like grotesque hands. Smoke wafted from some of the windows of the empty buildings. He saw an astonishing number of rats, driven from their nests by the fire's heat, crossing the road in waves.

As he went farther into the hills, the heat became even more palpable, rising up around his ankles, and the air more choked and dirty.

Even through his mask it was hard to breathe. The fire's heat was not evenly distributed, and he instinctively skirted the most scorching places. It left him few paths. Where the fire was particularly fierce, the buildings had caught flame, and there were periodic crashes as structures collapsed.

He had reached the mine entrances. He walked past a vertical shaft, now more of a chimney, its enormous rig red-hot under the heat and emitting a sharp hiss that made his skin crawl. He had to detour around its surging heat. The separator building was enveloped in smoke, and the piles of coal behind it had melted into a single enormous chunk of glowing coal flickering with flames. . . .

There was no one here. The soles of his feet were burning, the sweat had almost dried off his body, his difficulty breathing pushed him to the edge of shock, but his mind was clear. With his last ounce of strength he walked toward his destination. The mouth of the shaft, glowing red from the fire within, beckoned to him. He had made it. He smiled.

He turned in the direction of the production building. The roof might be smoking but it was not on fire, at least. He walked through the open door and entered the long changing room. Light from the shaft fire shining through the window filled the room with a hazy red glow and caused everything to shimmer, including the line of lockers. He walked along the long row, inspecting the numbers until he found the one he wanted.

He remembered it from his childhood: His father had just been appointed head of extraction, the wildest team, well-known for being hard to handle. Those rough young workers had been dismissive of his father at first, because of the way he had timidly asked for a detached locker door to be nailed back in place before their first prework meeting. The crew had mostly ignored him, apart from a few insults, but his father had said only, 'Then give me some nails and I'll put it up myself.' Someone tossed him a few nails, and he said, 'And a hammer too.' This time they really ignored him. But then they suddenly fell quiet, and watched in awe as his father pressed the nails into the wood with a bare thumb. At once the atmosphere changed, and the workers lined up and listened respectfully to his father's prework talk. . . .

The locker wasn't locked, and upon opening it, Liu Xin found it still contained clothes. He smiled again, at the thought of the miners who had used his father's locker over the past two decades. He took out the clothes and put them on, first the thick work trousers, then the equally thick jacket. The uniform smeared with layers of mud and coal dust had a sharp odor of sweat and oil that was surprisingly familiar, and a sense of peace came over him.

He put on the boots, picked up the helmet, took the lantern out of the locker, wiped the dust off it with his sleeve, and clipped it to the helmet. There were no batteries, so he looked in the next locker, which had one.

He strapped the bulky lantern battery to his waist, then realized that it was drained: work had been halted for a year, after all. But he remembered where the lamp shop was, directly opposite the changing room, where in his youth female workers would spray the batteries with smoking sulfuric acid to charge them. That was impossible now; the lamp shop was shrouded in yellow sulfuric acid smoke. He solemnly put on the lamp-equipped helmet and walked over to a dust-covered mirror. There, in the flickering red light, he saw his father.

'Dad, I'll go down below in your place,' he said with a smile, then strode out toward the smoking mouth of the shaft.

A helicopter pilot recalled later that during a low-altitude flyby of Shaft No. 2, a final sweep of the area, he thought he saw someone near the opening, a black silhouette against the red glow of the ground fire. The figure seemed to be heading down the shaft, but in the next instant there was only red light, and nothing else.

120 Years Later
(A middle-school student's journal)

People really were dumb in the past, and they really had a tough time.

Do you know how I know? Today we visited the Mining Museum. What impressed me the most was this:

They had solid coal!

First, we had to put on weird clothing: there was a helmet, which had a light on it, connected by a wire to a rectangular object that we hung at our waists. I thought it was a computer at first (even if it was a little large), but it turned out to be a battery for the light. A battery that big could power a racing car, but they used it for a tiny light. We also put on tall rain boots. The teacher told us this was the uniform that early coal miners used for going down the mines. Someone asked what 'down the mines' meant, and the teacher said we'd find out soon enough.

We boarded a metallic, small-gauge segmented vehicle, like an early train, only much smaller and powered by an overhead wire. The vehicle started up and soon we entered the black mouth of a cave. It was very dark inside, with only an occasional dim lamp above us. Our headlamps were weak as well, only enough to make out the faces right beside us. The wind was strong and whistled in our ears; it felt like we were dropping into an abyss. Annoyingly, Aina screamed. That was Aina being Aina.

'We're going down the mine now, students!' the teacher said.

After a long while, the vehicle stopped. We passed from this relatively wide tunnel into a considerably thinner and smaller spur, and if not for my helmet, I would have knocked a few lumps in my head. Our headlamps created small patches of light but we couldn't see anything clearly. Aina and a few other girls shouted that they were scared.

After a while, the space opened up in front of us. Here the ceiling was supported by lots of columns. Opposite us, there were many points of light shining from lamps like the ones on our helmets. As we drew closer, I saw lots of people were at work, some of them making holes in the cave wall with a long-bore drill. The drills were powered by some sort of engine whose sound made my skin crawl. Other people with metal shovels were shoveling some sort of black material into railcars and conveyor belts. Clouds of dust occasionally blocked them, and lanterns cast shafts of light through the dust.

'Students, we're now in what's called the ore zone. What you see is a scene of early mining work.'

A few miners came toward us. I knew they were holograms, so I didn't move out of the way. Some of them passed through me, so I could see them very clearly, and I was astonished.

'Did China hire black people to mine coal?'

'To answer that question,' the teacher said, 'we'll have a real experience of the air of the ore zone. Please take out your breathing masks from your bags.'

We put on our masks, and heard the teacher say, 'Please remember that this is real, not a hologram.'

A cloud of black dust came toward us. In the beams from our headlamps I was shocked to see the thick cloud of particles sparkling. Then Aina started to scream again, and like a chorus, a lot of other kids, girls and boys, screamed as well. I turned to laugh at them, but I, too, yelped when I got a look: Everyone was completely black, apart from the portion the masks covered. Then I heard another shout that turned my hair on end: It was the teacher's voice!

'My god, Seya! You don't have your mask on!'

Seya hadn't put on his mask, and now he was as completely black as the holographic miners. 'You said over and over in history class that the key goal was to get a feel for the past. I wanted a real feel!' he said, his teeth flashing white on his black face.

An alarm sounded somewhere, and within a minute, a teardrop-shaped micro-hovercar stopped soundlessly in front of us, an unpleasant intrusion of something modern. Two doctors got out. By now, all of the real coal dust had been sucked away, leaving only the holographic dust floating around us, so their white coats stayed spotless as they passed through it. They pulled Seya off to the car.

'Child,' one doctor said, looking straight into his eyes. 'Your lungs have been seriously harmed. You'll have to be hospitalized for at least a week. We'll notify your parents.'

'Wait!' Seya shouted, his hands fumbling with the rebreather. 'Did miners a hundred years ago wear these?'

'Shut your mouth and go to the hospital,' the teacher said. 'Why can't you ever just follow the rules?'

'We're human, just like our ancestors. Why . . .'

Seya was shoved into the car before he could finish. 'This is the first time the museum has had this kind of accident,' a doctor said severely, pointing at the teacher and adding, before getting into the hovercar, 'This falls on you!' The hovercar left as silently as it had come.

We continued our tour. The chastened teacher said, 'Every kind of work in the mine was fraught with danger, and required enormous physical energy.

For example, these iron supports had to be retrieved after extraction in this zone was completed, in a process called support removal.'

We saw a miner with an iron hammer striking an iron pin in one of the supports, buckling it in two. Then he carried it off. Me and a boy tried to pick up another support that was lying on the ground, but it was ridiculously heavy. 'Support removal was a dangerous job, since the roof overhead could collapse at any time . . .'

Above our heads came scraping sounds, and I looked up and saw, in the light of the mining lanterns, a fissure open up in the rock where the support had just been removed. Before I had time to react, it fell in, and huge chunks of holographic stone fell through me to the ground with a loud crash. Everything vanished in a cloud of dust.

'This accident is called a cave-in,' the teacher's voice sounded beside me. 'Be careful. Harmful stones don't always come from up above.'

Before she even finished, a section of rock wall next to us toppled over, falling a fair distance in a single piece, as if a giant hand from the ground had pushed it over, before finally breaking up and raining down as individual stones. We were buried under holographic rocks with a crash, and our headlamps went out. Through the darkness and screams, I heard the teacher's voice again.

'That was a methane outburst. Methane is a gas that builds to immense pressure when sealed in a coal seam. What we saw just now was what happens when the rock walls of the work zone can't hold back that pressure and are blown out.'

The lights came back on, and we all exhaled. Then I heard a strange sound, at times as loud as galloping horses, sometimes soft and deep, like giants whispering.

'Look out, children! A flood is coming!'

We were still processing what she said when a broad surge of water erupted from a tunnel not far away. It quickly swamped the entire work zone. The murky water reached our knees, and then was waist-high. It reflected the light of our headlamps to shine indistinct patterns on the rocky ceiling.

Wooden beams stained black with coal dust floated by, and miners' helmets and lunch boxes. . . . When the water reached my chin, I instinctively held my breath. Then I was entirely underwater, and all I could see was a murky brown where my headlamp shone, and air bubbles that sometimes floated up.

'Mine floods have many causes. Whether it's groundwater, or if the mine has dug into a surface water source, it's far more life-threatening than a flood above ground,' the teacher said over the sound of the water.

The holographic water vanished and our surroundings returned to normal. Then I noticed an odd-looking object, like a big metal toad puffing out its stomach. It was huge and heavy. I pointed it out to the teacher.

'That's an anti-explosion switch. Since methane is a highly flammable gas, the switch suppresses the electric sparks that ordinary switches create. That's related to what we'll see next, the most terrifying mining danger of all . . .'

There was another loud crash, but unlike the previous two times, it seemed to come from within us, bursting through our eardrums to the outside, as huge waves contracted our every cell, and in the searing waves of heat, we were plunged into a red glow emitted from the air around us that filled every inch of space in the mine. Then the glow disappeared, and everything plunged into darkness.

'Few people have actually seen a methane explosion, since it's hard to survive one in the mines.' The teacher's disembodied voice echoed in the darkness.

'Why did people used to come to such a terrible place?' Aina asked.

'For this,' the teacher said, holding a chunk of black rock into the light from our headlamps, where its innumerable facets sparkled. That was the first time I saw solid coal.

'Children, what we just saw was a mid-twentieth-century coal mine. There were a few new machines and technologies after that, such as hydraulic struts and huge shearers, which went into use in the last two decades of the century and improved conditions somewhat for the workers, but coal mines remained an incredibly dangerous, awful working environment. Until . . .'

It turned dull after that. The teacher lectured us on the history of gasified coal, which was put to use eighty years ago, when oil was nearly exhausted and major powers mobilized troops to seize the remaining oil fields. The Earth was on the brink of war, but it was gasified coal that saved the world. . . . We all knew this, so it was boring.

Then we toured a modern mine. Nothing special, just all those pipes we see every day, leading out from underground into the distance, although it was the first time I went inside a central control building and saw a hologram of the burn. It was huge. And we saw the neutrino sensors and gravity-wave radar monitoring the underground fire, and laser drills . . . all pretty boring, too.

The teacher recounted the history of the mine, and said that over a century ago, it had been destroyed in an uncontrolled fire that burned for eighteen years before going out. In those days our beautiful city was a wasteland where smoke blotted out the sky, and all the people had left. There were many stories of the cause of the fire; some people said it had been started by an underground weapons test, and others said it was connected to Greenpeace.

We don't have to be nostalgic for the so-called good old days. Life in those days was dangerous and confusing. But we shouldn't be depressed about today, either. Because today will one day be referred to as the good old days.

People really were stupid in the past, and they really had a tough time.

THE THINKER

思想者

TRANSLATED BY JOHN CHU

朱中宜 - 译

The Sun

He still remembered how he felt the first time he saw the Mount Siyun Astronomical Observatory thirty-four years ago. After his ambulance crossed the mountain ridge, Mount Siyun's highest peak emerged in the distance. Its observatories' spherical roofs reflected the golden light of the setting sun like pearls inlaid into the mountain peak.

At the time, he'd just graduated from medical school. A brain-surgery intern assisting the chief of surgery, he'd been rushed here to save a visiting research scholar from England who'd fallen on a hike. The scholar had injured his head too seriously to be moved. Once the ambulance arrived, they drilled a hole in the patient's skull, then drained some blood out to reduce brain swelling. Once the patient had been stabilized enough to move, the ambulance took him to the hospital for surgery.

It was late night by the time they could leave. Out of curiosity, while others carried the patient into the ambulance, he examined the several spherical observatories that surrounded him. How they were laid out seemed to imply some sort of hidden message, like a Stonehenge in the moonlight. Spurred on by some mystical force that he still didn't understand even after a lifetime of contemplation, he walked to the nearest observatory, opened its door, then walked inside.

The lights inside were off except for numerous small signal lamps. He felt as though he'd walked from a moonlit starry sky to a moonless starry sky. The only moonlight was a sliver that penetrated the crack in the spherical roof. It fell on the giant astronomical telescope, partially sketching out its contours in silver lines. The telescope looked like a piece of abstract art in a town square at night.

He stepped silently to the bottom of the telescope. In the weak light, he saw a large pile of machinery. It was more complex than he'd imagined. He searched for an eyepiece. A soft voice came from the door:

'This is a solar telescope. It doesn't have an eyepiece.'

A figure wearing white work clothes walked through the door, as though a feather had drifted in from the moonlight. The woman walked over to him, bringing a light breeze along with her.

'A traditional solar telescope casts an image onto a screen. Nowadays, we usually use a monitor. . . . Doctor, you seem to be very interested in this.'

He nodded. 'An observatory is such a sublime and rarefied place. I like how it makes me feel.'

'Then why did you go into medicine? Oh, that was very rude of me.'

'Medicine isn't just some trivial skill. Sometimes, it, too, is sublime, like my specialty of brain medicine, for example.'

'Oh? When you use a scalpel to open up the brain, you can see thoughts?' she said.

Her smiling face in the weak light made him think of something he'd never seen before, the sun cast onto a screen. Once the violent flares disappeared, the magnificence that remained couldn't help but make his heart skip a beat. He smiled, too, hoping she could see his smile.

'Oh, we can look at the brain all we want,' he said, 'but consider this: Say a mushroom-shaped thing you can hold in one hand turns out to be a rich and varied universe. From a certain philosophical viewpoint, this universe is even grander than the one you observe. Even though your universe is tens of billions of light-years wide, it's been established that it's finite. My universe is infinite because thought is infinite.'

'Ah, not everybody's thoughts are infinite but, Doctor, yours seem to be. As for astronomy, it's not as rarefied as you think. Several thousand years ago on the banks of the Nile and several hundred years ago on a long sea voyage, it was a practical skill. An astronomer of the time often spent years marking the positions of thousands of stars on star charts. A census of the stars consumed their lives. Nowadays, the actual work of astronomical research is dull and meaningless. For example, I study the twinkling of stars. I make endless observations, take notes, then make more observations and take more notes. It's definitely not sublime as well as not rarefied.'

His eyebrows rose in surprise. 'The twinkling of stars? Like the kind we can see?' When he saw her laugh, he laughed, too, shaking his head. 'Oh, I know, of course, that's atmospheric refraction.'

'However, as a visual metaphor, it's pretty accurate. Get rid of the constant terms, just show the fluctuations in their energy output, and stars really do look like they're twinkling.'

'Is it because of sunspots?'

She stopped smiling. 'No, this is the fluctuation of a star's total energy. It's like how when a lamp flickers, it's not because of the moths surrounding it, but because of fluctuations in voltage. Of course, the fluctuations of a twinkling star are minuscule, detectable only by the most precise measurements. Otherwise, we'd have been burned by the twinkling of the sun long ago. Researching this sort of twinkling is one way of understanding the deep structure of stars.'

'What have you discovered so far?'

'It'll be a while before we discover anything. For now, we've only observed the twinkling of the star that's the easiest to observe—the sun. We can do this for years while we gradually expand out to the rest of the stars. . . . You know, we could spend ten, twenty years taking measurements of the universe before we make any discoveries and come to some conclusion. This is my dissertation topic, but I think I'll be working on this for a long while, perhaps my whole life.'

'So you don't think astronomy is dull, after all.'

'I think what I'm working on is beautiful. Entering the world of stars is like entering an infinitely vast garden. No two flowers are alike. . . . You have to think that's a weird analogy, but it's how exactly I feel.'

As she spoke, seemingly without realizing it, she gestured at the wall. A painting hung there, very abstract, just a thick line undulating from one end to the other. When she noticed what he was looking at, she took it down, then handed it to him. The thick, undulating line was a mosaic of colorful pebbles from the area.

'It's lovely, but what does it represent? The local mountain range?'

'Our most recent measurements of the sun twinkling, it was so intense and we'd rarely ever seen it fluctuate like that this year. This is a picture of the curve of the energy radiated as it twinkled. Oh, when I hike, I like to collect pebbles, so . . .'

The scientist was only partially visible in the surrounding shadow. She looked like an elegant ink line a brilliant artist drew on a piece of fine, white calligraphy paper. The curve's intelligence of spirit filled that perfect white paper immediately with vitality and intention. . . . In the city he lived in outside the mountains, at any given moment, more than a million young women, like a large group of particles in Brownian motion, chased the showy and vain, without even a moment of reflection. But who could imagine that on this mountain in the middle of nowhere, there was a gentle and quiet woman who stared for long stretches at the stars. . . .

'You can reveal this kind of beauty from the universe. That's truly rare and also very fortunate.' He realized he was staring and looked away. He returned the painting to her but, lightly, she pushed it back to him.

'Keep it as a souvenir, Doctor. Professor Wilson is my advisor. Thank you for saving his life.'

After ten minutes, the ambulance left under the moonlight. Slowly, he realized what he'd left on the mountain.

First Time

Once he married, he abandoned his effort to fight against time. One day, he moved his things out of his apartment to the one he now shared with his wife. Those things that two people shouldn't share, he brought to his office at the hospital. As he riffled through them, he found a mosaic made of colorful pebbles. Seeing the multicolored curve, he suddenly realized that the trip to Mount Siyun was ten years ago.

Alpha Centauri A

The hospital's young employees' group had a spring outing. He cherished this outing particularly, because it was getting less and less likely they'd invite him again. This time, the trip organizer was deliberately mysterious, pulling down the blinds on all the coach windows and having everyone guess where they were once they arrived. The first one to guess correctly won a prize. He knew where they were the instant he stepped off the coach, but he kept quiet.

The highest peak of Mount Siyun stood before him. The pearl-like spherical roofs on its summit glittered in the sunlight.

After someone guessed where they were, he told the trip organizer that he wanted to go to the observatory to visit an acquaintance. He left on foot, following the meandering road up the mountain.

He hadn't lied, but the woman whose name he didn't even know wasn't part of the observatory staff. After ten years, she probably wasn't here anymore. He didn't actually want to go inside, just to look around at the place where, ten years ago, his soul, hot, dry, and as bright as the sun, spilled into a thread of moonlight.

One hour later, he reached the mountaintop and the observatory's white railings. Its paint had cracked and faded. Silently, he took in the individual observatories. The place hadn't changed much. He quickly located the domed building that he'd once entered. He sat on a stone block on the grass, lit a cigarette, then studied the building's iron door, spellbound. The scene he'd long cherished replayed from the depths of his memory: with the iron door half open, in the midst of a ray of moonlight like water, a feather drifted in. . . .

He was so completely steeped in that long-gone dream that when the miracle happened, he wasn't surprised: the observatory's iron door opened for real. The feather that once had emerged from the moonlight drifted into the sunlight. She left in a hurry to go into another observatory. This couldn't have taken more twenty seconds, but he knew he wasn't mistaken.

Five minutes later, they reunited.

This was the first time he'd seen her with adequate light. She was exactly as he'd imagined. He wasn't surprised. It'd been ten years, though. She shouldn't have looked exactly like the woman barely lit by a few signal lamps and the moon. He was puzzled.

She was pleasantly surprised to see him, but no more than that. 'Doctor, I make a round of every observatory for my project. In a given year, I'm only here for half a month. To run into you again, it must be fate!'

That last sentence, tossed off lightly, confirmed his initial impression: She didn't feel anything more about seeing him again besides surprise. However, she still recognized him after ten years. He took a shred of comfort in that.

They exchanged a few words about what had happened to the visiting English scholar who'd suffered the brain injury. Finally, he asked, 'Are you still researching the twinkling of stars?'

'Yes. After observing the sun's twinkling for two years, I moved on to other stars. As I'm sure you understand, the techniques necessary to observe other stars are completely different from those to observe the sun. The project didn't have new funding. It halted for many years. We just started it back up three years ago. Right now, we are only observing twenty-five stars. The number and scope are still growing.'

'Then you must have produced more mosaics.'

The moonlit smile that had surfaced so many times from the depths of memory over the past ten years now emerged in the sunlight. 'Ah, you still remember! Yes, every time I come to Mount Siyun, I collect pretty pebbles. Come, I'll show you!'

She took him into the observatory where they'd first met. A giant telescope confronted him. He didn't know whether it was the same telescope from ten years ago, but the computers that surrounded it were practically new. Familiar things hung on a tall curved wall: mosaics of all different sizes.

Each one was of an undulating curve. They were all of different lengths. Some were as gentle as the sea. Others were violent, like a row of tall towers strung together at random.

One by one, she told him which waves came from which stars. 'These twinklings, we call type A twinklings. They don't occur as much as other types. The difference between type A twinklings and those of other types, besides that their energy fluctuations are orders of magnitude larger, is that the mathematics of their curves is even more elegant.'

He shook his head, puzzled. 'You scientists doing basic research are always talking about the elegance of mathematics. I guess that's your prerogative. For example, you all think that Maxwell's equations are incredibly elegant. I understood them once, but I couldn't see where the elegance was. . . .'

Just like ten years ago, she suddenly grew serious. 'They're elegant like crystals, very hard, very pure, and very transparent.'

Unexpectedly, he recognized one of the mosaics. 'Oh, you re-created one?' Seeing her uncomprehending expression, he continued. 'That's the waveform of the sun twinkling in the mosaic you gave me ten years ago.'

'But . . . that's the waveform from a type A twinkling from Alpha Centauri A. We observed it, um, last October.'

He trusted that she was genuinely puzzled, but he trusted his own judgment as well. He knew that waveform too well. Moreover, he could even recall the color and shape of every stone that made up the curve. He didn't want her to know that, until he got married last year, that mosaic had always hung on his wall. There were a few nights every month when moonlight would seep in after he'd turned out the lights, and he could make out the mosaic from his bed. That was when he'd silently count the pebbles that made up the curve. His gaze crawled along the curve like a beetle. Usually, by the time he'd crawled along the entire curve and gone halfway back, he'd fallen asleep. In his dreams, he continued to stroll along this curve that came from the sun, like stepping from colorful stone to colorful stone to cross a river whose banks he'd never see. . . .

'Can you look up the curve of the sun twinkling from ten years ago? The date was April twenty-third.'

'Of course.'

She gave him an odd look, obviously startled that he remembered that date so easily. At the computer, she pulled up that waveform of the sun twinkling followed by the waveform of Alpha Centauri A twinkling that was on the wall. He stared at the screen, dumbfounded.

The two waveforms overlapped perfectly.

When her long silence grew unbearable, he suggested, 'Maybe these two stars have the same structure, so they also twinkle the same way. You said before that type A twinkling reflects the star's deep structure.'

'They are both on the main sequence and they both have spectral type G2, but their structures are not identical. The crux, though, is that even for two stars with the same structure, we still wouldn't see this. It's like banyan trees. Have you ever seen two that were absolutely identical? For such complex waveforms to actually overlap perfectly, that's like having two large banyan trees where even their outermost branches were exactly the same.'

'Perhaps there really are two large banyan trees that are exactly the same,' he consoled, knowing his words were meaningless.

She shook her head lightly. Suddenly, she thought of something and leapt to stand. Fear joined the surprise already in her gaze.

'My god,' she said.

'What?'

'You . . . Have you ever thought about time?'

He quickly caught on to what she was thinking. 'As far as I know, Alpha Centauri A is our closest star. It's only about . . . four light-years away.'

'1.3 parsecs is 4.25 light-years.' She was still in the grip of astonishment. It was as if she couldn't believe the things she herself was saying.

Now it was all clear: The two identical twinklings occurred eight years and six months apart, just long enough for light to make a round trip between the two stars. After 4.25 years, when the light of the sun's twinkling reached Alpha Centauri A, the latter twinkled in the same way, and after the same amount of time, the light of Alpha Centauri's twinkling was observed here.

She hunched over her computer, making calculations and talking to herself. 'Even if we take into account the several years where the two stars regressed from each other, the result still fits.'

'I hope what I said doesn't cause you too much worry. There's ultimately nothing we can do to confirm this, right? It's just a theory.'

'Nothing we can do to confirm this? Don't be so sure. That light from the sun twinkling was broadcast into space. Perhaps that'll lead to another star twinkling in the same way.'

'After Alpha Centauri, the next closest star is . . .'

'Barnard's Star, 1.81 parsecs away, but it's too dim. There's no way to measure it. The next star out, Wolf 359, 2.35 parsecs away, is just as dim. Can't measure it. Yet farther out, Lalande 21185, 2.52 parsecs away, is also too dim. . . . That leaves Sirius.'

'That seems like a star bright enough to see. How far is it?'

'2.65 parsecs away, just 8.6 light-years.'

'The light from the sun twinkling has already traveled for ten years. It's already reached there. Perhaps Sirius has already twinkled back.'

'But the light from it twinkling won't arrive for another seven years.' She seemed to wake all of a sudden from a dream, then laughed. 'Oh, dear, what am I thinking. It's too ridiculous!'

'So you're saying, as an astronomer, the idea is ridiculous?'

She studied him earnestly. 'What else can it be? As a brain surgeon, how do you feel when someone discusses with you where thought comes from, the brain or the heart?'

He had nothing to say. She glanced at her watch, so he started to leave. She didn't urge him to stay, but she accompanied him quite a distance along the road that led down the mountain. He stopped himself from asking for her number because he knew, in her eyes, he was just some stranger who bumped into her again by chance ten years later.

After they said goodbye, she walked up toward the observatory. Her white lab coat swayed in the mountain breeze. Unexpectedly, it stirred up in him how it had felt when they'd said goodbye ten years ago. The sunlight seemed to change into moonlight. That feather disappeared in the distance . . . like a straw of rice, sinking into the water, that someone desperately tries to grab. He decided he wanted to maintain that cobweb-like connection between them. Almost instinctively, he shouted at her back:

'If, seven years from now, you see Sirius actually twinkles like that . . .'

She stopped walking and turned toward him. With a smile, she answered, 'Then we'll meet here!'

Second Time

With marriage, he entered a completely different life, but what changed his life thoroughly was a child. After the child was born, the train of life suddenly changed from the local to the express. It rushed past stop after stop in its never-ending journey onward. He grew numb from the journey. His eyes shut, he no longer paid attention to the unchanging scenery. Weary, he went to sleep. However, as with so many others sleeping on the train, a tiny clock deep in his heart still ticked. He woke the minute he reached his destination.

One night, his wife and child slept soundly but he couldn't sleep. On some mysterious impulse, he threw on his clothes, then went to the balcony. Overhead, the fog of city lights dimmed the many stars in the sky. He was searching for something, but what? It was a good while before his heart answered him: He was looking for Sirius. He couldn't help but shiver at that.

Seven years had passed. The time left before the appointment he'd made with her: two days.

Sirius

The first snow of the year had fallen the day before, and the roads were slippery. The taxi couldn't make it up the last stretch to the mountain's peak.

He had to go, once again, on foot, clambering to the peak of Mount Siyun.

On the road, more than once, he wondered whether he was thinking straight. The probability she'd keep the appointment was zero. The reason was simple: Sirius couldn't twinkle like the sun had seventeen years earlier. In the past seven years, he had skimmed a lot of astronomy and astrophysics. That he'd said something so ridiculous seven years ago filled him with shame. He was grateful that she hadn't laughed at him there and then. Thinking about it now, he realized she had merely been polite when she seemed to take it seriously. In the intervening seven years, he'd pondered the promise she'd made as they left each other many, many times. The more he did, the more it seemed to take on a mocking tone. . . .

Astronomical observations had shifted to telescopes in Earth orbit. Mount Siyun Observatory had shut down four years ago. The buildings there became vacation villas. No one was around in the off-season. What was he going to do there? He stopped. The seven years that'd passed had taken their toll. He couldn't climb up the mountain as easily anymore. He hesitated for a moment, but ultimately abandoned the idea of turning back. He continued upward.

He'd waited so long, why not finally chase a dream just this once?

When he saw the white figure, he thought it was a hallucination. The figure wearing the white windbreaker in front of the former observatory blended into the backdrop of the snow-packed mountain. It was difficult to make out at first, but when she saw him, she ran to him. She looked like a feather flying over the snowfield. He could only stand dumbstruck, and wait for her to reach him. She gasped for air, unable to speak. Except that her long hair was now short, she hadn't changed much. Seven years wasn't long. Compared to the lifetimes of stars, it didn't even count as an instant, and she studied stars.

She looked him in the eyes. 'Doctor, at first, I didn't have much hope of seeing you. I came only to carry out a promise or perhaps to fulfill a wish.'

'Me too.' He nodded.

'I almost let the observation date slip by, but I never truly forgot it, just stowed it in the deepest recesses of my memory. A few nights ago, I suddenly thought of it. . . .'

'Me too.' He nodded again.

Neither of them spoke. They just listened to the gusts of wind that blew through the trees reverberate among the mountains.

'Did Sirius actually twinkle like that?' he asked finally, his voice trembling a little.

'The waveform of its twinkling overlaps precisely the sun's from seventeen years ago and Alpha Centauri A's from seven years ago. It also arrived exactly on time. The space telescope Confucius 3 observed it. There's no way it can be wrong.'

They fell again into another long stretch of silence. The rumble of wind through the trees rose and fell. The sound spiraled among the mountains, filling the space between earth and sky. It seemed as though some sort of force throughout the universe thrummed like a deep and mystical chorus. . . . He couldn't help but shiver. She, evidently feeling the same way, broke the silence, as though to cast off her fears.

'But this situation, this strange phenomenon, goes beyond our current theories. It requires many more observations and much more evidence in order for the scientific community to deal with it.'

'I know. The next possible observable star is . . .'

'It would have been Procyon, in Canis Minor, but five years ago, it rapidly grew too dark to be worth measuring. Maybe it drifted into a nearby cloud of interstellar dust. So, the next measurable star is Altair, in the constellation Aquila.'

'How far is it?'

'5.1 parsecs, 16.6 light-years. The sun's twinkling from seventeen years ago has just reached it.'

'So we have to wait another seventeen years?'

'People's lives are bitter and short.'

Her last sentence touched something deep in his heart. His eyes, blown dry by the winter wind, suddenly teared. 'Indeed. People's lives are bitter and short.'

'But at least we'll still be around to keep this sort of appointment again.'

He stared at her dumbly. Did she really want to part ways again for seventeen years?!

'Excuse me. This is all a bit overwhelming,' he said. 'I need some time to think.'

The wind had blown her hair onto her forehead. She brushed it away. She saw into his heart, then laughed sympathetically. 'Of course. I'll give you my number and email address. If you're willing, we'll keep in touch.'

He let out a long breath, as if a riverboat on the misty ocean finally saw the lighthouse on the shore. His heart filled with a happiness he was too embarrassed to admit to.

'But . . . Why don't I escort you down the mountain.'

Laughing, she shook her head and pointed to the domed vacation villa behind her. 'I'm going to stay here awhile. Don't worry. There's electricity and good company. They live here, forest rangers . . . I really need some peace and quiet, a long time of peace and quiet.'

They made their quick goodbyes. He followed the snow-packed road down the mountain. She stood at Mount Siyun's peak for a long while watching him leave. They both prepared for a seventeen-year wait.

Third Time

After the third time he returned from Mount Siyun, he was suddenly aware of the end of his life. Neither of them had more than seventeen years left. The vast and desolate universe made light as slow as a snail. Life was as worth mentioning as dirt.

They kept in touch for the first five of the seventeen years. They exchanged emails, occasionally called each other, but they never met. She lived in another city, far away. Later, they each walked toward the summit of their own lives. He became a celebrated brain-medicine expert and the head of a major hospital. She became a member of the National Academy of Science. They had more and more to worry about. At the same time, he understood that, with the most prominent astronomer in academic circles, it was inappropriate to discuss too much this myth-like thing that linked them together. So, they gradually grew further and further apart. Halfway through their seventeen years, they stopped contacting each other entirely.

However, he wasn't worried. He knew that, between them, they had an unbreakable bond, the light from Altair rushing through vast and desolate space to Earth. They both waited silently for it to arrive.

Altair

They met at the peak of Mount Siyun in the dark of night. Both of them wanted to show up early to avoid making the other wait. So around three in the morning, they both clambered up the mountain. Their flying cars could have easily reached the peak, but they both parked at the foot of the mountain and then walked up, as if they wanted to re-create the past.

Mount Siyun was designated as a nature preserve ten years ago, and it had become one of the few wild places left on Earth. The observatory and vacation villas of old became vine-covered ruins. It was among these ruins that they met under the starlight. He'd recently seen her on TV, so he knew the marks that time had left on her. Even though there was no moon tonight, no matter what he imagined, he felt that the woman before him was still the one who stood under the moonlight thirty-four years ago. Her eyes reflected starlight, making his heart melt in his feelings of the past.

She said, 'Let's not start by talking about Altair, okay? These past few years, I've been in charge of a research project, precisely to measure the transmission of type A twinkling between stars.'

'Oh, wow. I hadn't let myself hope that anything might actually come from all this.'

'How could it not? We have to face up to the truth that it exists. In the universe that classical relativity and quantum physics describes, its oddity is already inconceivable. . . . We discovered in these few years of observation that transmitting type A twinkling between stars is a universal phenomenon. At any given moment, innumerable stars are originating type A twinklings. Surrounding stars propagate them. Any star can initiate a twinkling or propagate the twinkling of other stars. The whole of space seems to be a pool flooded with ripples in the midst of rain. . . . What? Aren't you excited?'

'I guess I don't understand: Observing the transmission of twinkling through four stars took over thirty years. How can you . . .'

'You're a smart person. You ought to be able to think of a way.'

'I think . . . Is it like this: Search for some stars near each other to observe. For example, star A and star B, they're ten thousand light-years from Earth, but they're only five light-years from each other. This way, you only need five years to observe the twinkle they transmitted ten thousand years ago.'

'You really are a smart man! The Milky Way has hundreds of billions of stars. We can find plenty of stars like those.'

He laughed. Just like thirty-four years ago, he wished she could see him laugh in the night.

'I brought you a present.'

As he spoke, he opened a traveling bag, then took out an odd thing about the size of a soccer ball. At first glance, it seemed like a haphazardly balled-up fishing net. Bits of starlight pierced through its small holes. He turned on his flashlight. The thing was made of an uncountably large number of tiny globes, each about the size of a grain of rice. Attached to each globe was a different number of sticks so slender they were almost invisible. They connected one globe to another. Together, they formed an extremely complex netlike system.

He turned off the flashlight. In the dark, he pressed a switch at the base of the structure. A dazzling burst of quickly moving bright dots filled the structure, as though tens of thousands of fireflies had been loaded into the tiny, hollow, glass globes. One globe lit, then its light propagated to surrounding globes. At any given moment, some portion of the tiny globes produced an initial point of light or propagated the light another globe produced. Vividly, she saw her own analogy: a pond in the midst of rain.

'Is this a model of the propagation of twinkling among the stars? Oh, so beautiful. Can it be . . . you'd already predicted everything?!'

'I'd guessed that propagating the twinkling among the stars was a universal phenomenon. Of course, it was just intuition. However, this isn't a model of the propagation of stellar twinkling. Our campus has a brain-science research project that uses three-dimensional holographic-microscopy molecular-positioning technology to study the propagation of signals between neurons in the brain. This is just the model of signal propagation in the right brain cortex, albeit a really small part of it.'

She stared, captivated by the sphere with the dancing lights. 'Is this consciousness?'

'Yes. Just as a computer's ability to operate is a product of a tremendous amount of zeros and ones, consciousness is also just a product of a tremendous amount of simple connections between neurons. In other words, consciousness is what happens when there is a tremendous amount of signal propagation between nodes.'

Silently, they stared at this star-filled model of the brain. In the universal abyss that surrounded them, hundreds of billions of stars floating in the Milky Way and hundreds of billions of stars outside the Milky Way were propagating innumerable type A twinklings between each other.

She said lightly, 'It's almost light. Let's wait for sunrise.'

They sat together on a broken wall, looking at the model of the brain in front of them. The flickering light had a hypnotic effect. Gradually, she fell asleep.

Thinker

She flew against a great, boundless gray river. This was the river of time. She was flying toward time's source. Galaxies like frigid moraines floated in space. She flew fast. One flutter of her wings and she crossed over a hundred million years. The universe shrank. Galaxies clustered together. Background radiation shot up. After one billion years had passed, moraines of galaxies began to melt in a sea of energy, quickly scattering into unconstrained particles. Afterward, the particles transformed into pure energy. Space began to give off light, dark red at first. She seemed to slink in a bloodred energy sea. The light rapidly grew in intensity, changing from the dark red to orange, then again to an eye-piercing pure blue. She seemed to fly within a giant tube of neon light. Particles of matter had already melted in the energy sea. Shining through this dazzling space, she saw the borders of the universe bend into a spherical surface, like the closing of a giant palm. The universe shrank down to the size of a large parlor. She was suspended in its center waiting for singularity to arrive. Finally, everything fell into pitch darkness. She knew she was already within singularity.

After a blast of cold, she found herself standing on a broad white plain. Above her was a limitless black void. The ground was pure white, covered by a layer of smooth, transparent, sticky liquid. She walked ahead to the side of a bright red river. A transparent membrane covered the river surface. The red river water surged under the membrane. She left the ground, soaring into the sky. Not far away, the blood river branched into many tributaries, forming a complex network of waterways. She soared even higher. The blood rivers grew slender, mere traces against the white ground, which still stretched to the horizon. She flew forward. A black sea appeared. Once she flew over the sea, she realized it wasn't black. It seemed so because it was deep and completely transparent. The mountain ranges on the vast seafloor came into view. These crystalline mountain ranges stretched radially from the center of the sea to the shore. . . . She pushed herself up even higher and didn't look down again until who knows how long. Now, she saw the entire universe at once.

The universe was a giant eye calmly looking at her.

She woke suddenly. Her forehead was wet. She wasn't sure if it was sweat or dew. He hadn't slept, always at her side silently looking at her. Sitting on the grass in front of them, the model of the brain had exhausted its battery.

The starlight that pierced it had extinguished.

Above them, those stars hovered as before.

'What is "he" thinking?' she asked, breaking the silence.

'Now?'

'In these thirty-four years.'

'The twinkling the sun originated could just be a primitive neural impulse. Those happen all the time. Most of them are like mosquitoes causing tiny ripples on a pond, insubstantial. Only those impulses that spread through the whole universe can become an actual experience.'

'We used up a lifetime, and saw of "him" just one twinkling impulse that "he" couldn't even feel?' she said hazily, as though still in the middle of a dream.

'Use an entire human civilization's life span, and we still might not see one of "his" actual experiences.'

'People's lives are bitter and short.'

'Yes. People's lives are bitter and short. . . .'

'A truly insightful, solitary person.'

'What?' He looked at her, uncomprehending.

'Oh, I said "he," apart from completeness, is nothingness. "He" is everything. Still thinking, or maybe dreaming. But dreaming about what . . .'

'Let's not try to be philosophers!' He waved his hand as though he were shooing something away.

Out of the blue, something occurred to her. She got off the broken wall. 'According to the big bang theory of modern cosmology, while the universe is expanding, the light emitted from a given point can never spread widely across the universe.'

'In other words, "he" can never have even one actual experience.'

Her eyes focused infinitely far away. She stayed silent for a long time, before speaking. 'Do we?'

Her question sank him into his recollection of the past. Meanwhile, the woods of Mount Siyun heard its first birdcall. A ray of light appeared on the eastern horizon.

'I have,' he answered confidently.

Yes, he had. It was thirty-four years ago during a peaceful moonlit night on this mountain peak. A feather-like figure in the moonlight, a pair of eyes looking up at the stars . . . A twinkling in his brain quickly propagated through the entire universe of his mind. From then on, that twinkling never disappeared. That universe contained in his brain was more magnificent than the star-filled exterior universe that had already expanded for about fifteen billion years. Although the external universe was vast, the evidence ultimately showed it was finite. Thought, however, was infinite.

The eastern sky grew brighter and brighter, starting to hide its sea of stars. Mount Siyun revealed its rough contours. On its highest peak, at the vine-covered ruins of the observatory, these two nearly sixty-year-old people gazed eastward expectantly, waiting for that dazzling brain cell to rise over the horizon.

天口食者

DEVOURER

TRANSLATED BY HOLGER NAHM

霍尔格·南 译

Chapter I
The Crystal from Eridanus

It was right in front of him, but the Captain still could barely make out its translucent crystalline structure. Floating through the black void of space, it was hidden by the darkness, like a piece of glass sunken in the murky depths. Only the slight distortion of starlight its passage provoked allowed the Captain to make out its position. Soon it was lost again, disappearing in the space between the stars.

Suddenly, the Sun distorted, its distant, eternal light twisting and twinkling before their eyes. It gave the Captain a start, but he maintained his proverbial 'Asian cool'. Unlike the dozen soldiers floating beside him, he managed not to gasp in shock. The Captain immediately understood; the crystal, a mere thirty feet away, had moved in front of the Sun, shining sixty million miles in the distance. In the three centuries to come, this strange vista would play frequently across his mind, and he would wonder if this had been an omen of humanity's fate to come.

As the highest ranking officer of the United Nation's Earth Protection Force in space, the Captain commanded the force's interplanetary assets. It was a tiny unit, but it was equipped with the most powerful nuclear weapons humanity had ever devised. Its enemies were lifeless rocks hurtling through space: asteroids and meteorites that the early warning system had determined to be a threat to Earth. The mission of the Earth Protection Force was to redirect or to destroy these objects.

They had been on space patrol for more than two decades now, yet they had never had a chance to deploy their bombs. All rocks large enough to warrant their use seemed to avoid Earth, wilfully denying them their chance for glory.

Now, however, a sweep had discovered this crystal at a distance of two astronomical units. The crystal's trajectory was as precipitous as it was utterly unnatural, taking it straight toward Earth.

The Captain and his unit cautiously approached, their space suits' boosters spinning a web of trails around the strange object. Just as they closed to thirty feet, a misty light flashed to life inside the crystal, clearly revealing its prismatic outline about ten feet long. As the space patrol drew nearer, they could make out the intricate, crystalline pipes of its propulsion system. The Captain was now floating directly in front of it. Stretching his gloved right hand toward the crystal, he initiated humanity's first contact with an extra-terrestrial intelligence.

As he reached out, the crystal became transparent once more. A brilliantly coloured image now sprang to life inside it. It was a manga girl, with huge, rolling eyes and long hair that cascaded down to her feet. She was wearing a beautiful, flowing skirt, and she seemed to drift dreamily in invisible waters.

'Warning! Alert! Warning! The Devourer approaches!' she immediately shouted, stricken with obvious panic. Her large eyes stared at the Captain, a lithe arm pointing away from the Sun in unmistakable alarm. There could be little doubt the unseen pursuer was hot on her dainty heels.

'Where do you come from?' the Captain enquired, by all appearances unperturbed[1].

'Epsilon Eridani, as you apparently call it, and by your reckoning of time, I have travelled for sixty thousand years,' she replied, before again raising her cry. 'The Devourer approaches! The Devourer approaches!'

The Captain continued his enquiry. 'Are you alive?'

'Of course not. I am merely a message,' came the response. But it was only a short reprieve. 'The Devourer approaches! The Devourer approaches!'

'How is it that you can speak English?' the Captain continued.

---

1 后半句为译者润色添加，本版选择保留。后文不再标注。

The girl again replied without hesitation. 'I learned in transit,' she said, only to carry on: 'The Devourer approaches! The Devourer approaches!'

'And that you look as you do…?' The Captain let his question trail off.

'I saw it in transit,' she said, before continuing to shout with ever greater urgency. 'The Devourer approaches! The Devourer approaches! Oh, surely the Devourer must terrify you.'

'What is the Devourer?' the Captain finally asked.

'In appearance, it resembles a gigantic tyre. Hm, yes, that would be an analogy that works for you,' the girl from Eridanus began her explanation.

'You are very well acquainted with how things work on our world,' the Captain interrupted, raising an eyebrow behind his visor.

'I became acquainted in transit,' the girl replied, before again crying out: 'The Devourer approaches!' With that last cry, she flashed to one end of the crystal. Where she had been a second ago, an image of the 'tyre' appeared, and it indeed closely resembled a tyre, even though its surface glowed with phosphorescent light.

'How large is it?' one of the other officers queried.

'Thirty-one thousand miles in total diameter. The 'tyre's' body is six thousand miles wide, and the hole in the middle has a diameter of nineteen thousand miles.'

There was a long pause before someone asked the question now on everyone's mind. 'Are the miles you are talking about *our* miles?'

The girl answered immediately and calmly. 'Of course. It is so large that it can encircle an entire planet, just like one of your tyres might fit around a soccer ball. Once it has encased a world, it begins plundering the planet's natural resources, only to spit out the remains like a cherry pit when it is done!'

There was another pause before the officer spoke again, his voice quivering with trepidation. 'But we still do not understand what the Devourer really is.'

The girl in the crystal offered more information without hesitation. 'It is a generation ship, although we do not know where it came from or where it is going. In fact, even the giant lizards that pilot the Devourer surely do not know. Having wandered the Milky Way for tens of millions of years, they have certainly forgotten both their origin and their original purpose. But this much is certain: in the far past, when the Devourer was built, it was much smaller. It eats planets to grow, and it devoured our world!'

As she finished, the image of the Devourer in the crystal grew, gradually dominating its entire surface. It soon became apparent that it was slowly descending upon the unseen camera operator's world. Seen through the eyes of the planet's inhabitants, their world had become nothing more than the bottom of a slowly spinning, cosmic well. Complex structures were clearly visible, covering the walls of this titanic well. At first, they reminded the Captain of infinitely magnified microprocessor circuitry. Then, he realized that they were an endless string of cities, stretching the entire inner ring of the Devourer. Looking up, the image in the crystal revealed a circle of blue radiance emanating from the well's mouth. In the sky above, it formed a gigantic halo of fire, encircling the stars.

The girl from Eridanus told them that they were seeing the jets of the Devourer's aft ring engine. As she spoke, her entire body erupted into a flowing flourish, and even her cascading hair began to wave like countless twisting arms, with every last part of her expressing boundless terror.

'What you are seeing is the devouring of the third planet of Epsilon Eridani,' she told them. 'The first thing you would have noticed, had you been on our world then, was your body becoming lighter. You see, the Devourer's gravitational pull was powerful enough to counteract our planet's gravity. The destruction this wrought was devastating. First, our oceans surged to meet the Devourer as it passed over our planet's pole. Then, as the Devourer moved to fully encircle our world, the waters followed it to the equator. As the oceans swept the globe, the waves towered high enough to engulf the clouds.

'The incredible gravitational forces tore at our continents, ripping them apart as if they were nothing but tissue paper. Our sea floor and dry land were pockmarked by countless volcanic eruptions.' The girl paused in her narrative, only to pick it up with a flutter of her big eyes. 'Once it had encircled our equator, the Devourer stopped, perfectly matching our planet in its orbit around our Sun. Our world was right in its maw.

'When the plunder of a world commences, countless cables thousands of miles long are lowered from the Devourer's inside wall to the planet's surface below. An entire world is trapped, like a fly in the web of a cosmic spider. Giant transport modules are then sent back and forth between the planet and the Devourer, taking with them the planet's oceans and atmosphere. As they shuttle to and fro, other titanic machines begin to drill deep into the planet's crust, frenziedly extracting minerals to satisfy the Devourer's hunger.' The girl again paused, her eyes staring intensely into the distance. She resumed as abruptly as she had stopped. 'Devourer and planet cancel out each other's gravity, creating a low-gravity zone between this tyre-like entity and the planet. This zone makes it that much easier to bring the planet's resources to the Devourer. The epic plunder is extremely efficient.

'Expressed in Earth time, the Devourer only needs to *chew* on a world for a century or so. After it is done, all of the planet's water and atmosphere will have been picked to nothing. As the Devourer ravages, its gravity will also eventually deforms the planet, slowly stretching it along its equator. In the end, the planet will become...' the girl paused a third time, this time struggling for words rather than effect, 'how would you call it? Yes, discus-shaped. The Devourer, having sucked the planet completely dry, will move on, spitting out the planet. When it leaves, the planet will return to its spherical shape. As it re-forms, the entire world will suffer a final global catastrophe, its surface resembling the molten sea of magma that heralded its birth many billion years ago. Much like then, no trace of life will survive this inferno.'

'How far is the Devourer from our solar system?' the Captain asked as soon as she finished.

'It is just behind me!' she warned urgently. 'In your reckoning, it will arrive in a mere century! Alert! The Devourer approaches! The Devourer approaches!'

Chapter 2
Emissary Fangs[1]

Just as the debate over the crystal's credibility began to rage in earnest, the first small Devourer ship entered the solar system. It was heading straight toward Earth.

The first contact was again initiated by the space patrol led by the Captain. The mood of this contact could not have been more different than the last, and the mood was, by far, not the only contrast. The exquisitely wrought structure of the Eridanus Crystal bore all the hallmarks of the ethereal technology of a refined civilization. The Devourer's ship represented the polar opposite. Its exterior appeared exceedingly crude and ungainly, somewhat like a frying pan that had spent the better part of a century forgotten in the wilderness. It immediately reminded onlookers of a giant steampunk machine.

The envoy of the Devourer Empire matched his vehicle in appearance: a massive, awkward lizard covered in huge slabs of scales. Erect, he stood nearly thirty feet tall. He introduced himself as 'Faingsh', but his appearance and later behaviour quickly led to him being called 'Fangs' instead.

When Fangs landed at the feet of the United Nations Building, his craft's engines blasted a large crater, the splattering concrete leaving the surrounding buildings scarred and battered. Since the alien emissary's massive size prevented him from entering the Assembly Hall, the world's heads of state gathered on the United Nations Plaza in front of the UN Building to meet him. Some among them now covered their faces with bloody handkerchiefs, staunching foreheads gashed open by flying glass and concrete.

The ground shook with every step Fangs took toward them, and when the alien spoke, he roared. It was a sound like the screaming horns of a dozen train engines, and it made the hair stand on end of all who heard it. Although he had learned English in transit, Fangs spoke through an unwieldy translator

---

1　大牙，《诗云》中表述为 "Bigtooth"。本版无意取舍，保留原始译法。

hanging around his neck, the device repeating his words back in English. The rough male voice his translator produced, despite being much quieter than Fangs' real voice, nonetheless made his listeners' flesh crawl.

'Ha! Ha! You white and tender worms[1], you fascinating little worms,' Fangs jovially began.

All around, people covered their ears until the thunderous roar had ended, only removing their hands slightly to hear the translation.

'You and I will live together for a century, and I believe we shall come to like each other,' Fangs continued.

'Your honour, you must know that we are very concerned as to the purpose of your great mother ship's arrival in our solar system!' the Secretary General stated, raising his head to address Fangs. Even though he was shouting at the top of his lungs, he still managed to sound no louder than a mosquito's buzz.

Fangs adopted a human-like posture, raising himself on his hind legs. As he shifted his weight, the ground trembled. 'The great Devourer Empire will consume the Earth so that it may continue its epic journey!' he proclaimed. 'This is inevitable!'

'What, then, of humanity?' the Secretary General asked, his voice quivering ever so slightly.

'That is something I will determine today,' Fangs replied.

In the pause that followed, the heads of state exchanged meaningful glances. The Secretary General finally nodded and said, 'It is necessary that we discuss this fully between ourselves.'

Fangs shook his massive head, interrupting before they could speak further. 'It is a very simple matter: I merely need to have a taste...'

And with that, his giant claw reached into the gathered crowd and snatched up a European head of state. He gracefully tossed the man, a throw of twenty-odd feet, straight into his mouth. Then he carefully began to chew. From the first crunch to the last, his victim remained completely mute; it was

---

1　虫虫，《诗云》表述为"bug-bug"，本版无意取舍，保留原始译法。

impossible to tell whether it was dignity or terror that stayed his screams.

In the terrible moments that followed, the only sound was that of the man's skeleton snapping and cracking between Fangs' giant, dagger-like teeth. After about half a minute, Fangs spat out the man's suit and shoes, much as a human might spit out watermelon seeds. Even though the clothes were covered in oozing blood, they remained horrifyingly intact.

All the world seemed to have fallen completely silent, a deathly quiet seeming to be without beginning or end; without end, that is, until a human voice broke it.

'How, sir, could you just pick him up and eat him?' the Captain asked as he stood amongst the crowd.

Fangs walked toward him with colossal, thundering steps. The crowd scattered in his wake. He stood before the Captain and lowered his gaze of pitch black, basketball-sized eyes until he was staring right at him. He asked, 'I shouldn't have?'

'Sir, how could you have known that you can eat him?' the Captain asked flatly. 'From a biochemical perspective, it is almost impossible that a being from such a distant world should be edible.'

Fangs nodded, his large maw almost seeming to grin. 'I have had my eye on you. You watched me with cool detachment, lost in thought. What is it that you were contemplating?'

The Captain returned his smile and replied, 'Sir, you breathe our air and speak using sound waves. You have two eyes, a nose, and a mouth. You have four limbs arranged along a bilateral symmetry...' He let his thought drift off into silence.

'And you don't understand it?' Fangs asked, snaking his giant head right in front of the Captain's face. With a hiss, he exhaled a nauseating breath, reeking of blood and gore.

'That is correct. I do understand the principle of the matter well enough to find it incomprehensible that we should be so similar,' the Captain answered, showing no signs of revulsion or fear.

'There is something I do not understand. Why are you so calm? Are you a soldier?' Fangs asked in response.

'I am warrior in defence of Earth,' the Captain answered.

'Hm, but does pushing around small stones really make you a warrior?' Fangs countered with more than a hint of mockery.

'I am ready for greater tests,' the Captain solemnly stated, lifting his chin.

'You fascinating little worm.' Fangs laughed, nodding. Raising his body to its full height, he turned back to the heads of state. 'But let us return to the real topic at hand: humanity's fate. You are tasty. There is a smooth and mild quality about you that reminds me of certain blue berries we found on a planet in Eridanus. I therefore congratulate you. Your species will continue. We will raise you as livestock in the Devourer Empire. We will allow you to live a good sixty years before we bring you to market.'

'Sir, do you not think that our meat will be too tough at that age?' the Captain asked with a cold chuckle.

Fangs roared with laughter, his voice like an erupting volcano. 'Ha, ha, ha, ha! The Devourers like chewy snacks!'

Chapter 3

Ants

The United Nations engaged Fangs in several further meetings. Even though no one else was eaten, the verdict on humanity's fate remained unchanged.

A meeting was scheduled to take place at a meticulously prepared archaeological excavation site in Africa.

Fangs' ship landed right on schedule, about fifty feet away from the dig site. The deafening explosion and storm of debris that accompanied the craft's arrival had, by this point, become all too familiar.

The girl from Eridanus had advised them that the vessel's engine was powered by a miniature fusion reactor. The concept, like most of the information she had provided on the Devourers, was easy enough for the human scientists to understand; the things she told them about the technology of Eridanians, on the other hand, never failed to baffle the people of Earth. Her crystal, for example, began to melt in Earth's atmosphere. In the end, the entire section containing its propulsion system dissolved, leaving nothing but a thin slice of crystal floating gracefully through the air.

As Fangs arrived at the excavation site, two UN staffers presented him with a large album, a full square yard in size. It had been meticulously designed to accommodate the Devourer's huge stature. The album's hundreds of beautifully wrought pages revealed all aspects of human culture in brilliantly coloured detail. In some ways, it resembled an opulent primer for children.

Inside the large pit of the excavation site itself, an archaeologist vividly described the glorious history of Earth's civilizations. He threw all his passion into his desperate attempt to make this alien understand, to comprehend that there was so much on this blue planet worth cherishing. As he spoke, his fervour moved him to tears. It was a pitiable spectacle.

Finally, he pointed to the excavation and intoned: 'Honourable emissary, what you see here are the newly discovered remains of a town. This fifty-thousand-year-old site is the oldest human settlement discovered to date. Could the hearts of your people truly be hard enough to destroy this magnificent civilization of ours? A civilization that has developed, step by slow step, over fifty thousand years?'

While all this was going on, Fangs was leafing through the album with obvious, playful amusement. As the archaeologist finished, Fangs raised his head and glanced at the excavation pit. 'Hey, archaeologist worm, I care neither for your hole nor your old city in the hole. I would, however, very much want to see the earth you removed from the pit,' he said, pointing at a large pile of dirt.

The archaeologist went from baffled to completely stunned as the artificial voice of the translator finished relaying Fangs' request. 'The earth?' he asked, fumbling for words. 'But there's nothing in that pile of dirt.'

'That is your opinion,' Fangs said, approaching the mound of dirt.

Bending his gigantic body toward the ground, he reached into the pile with two of his huge claws, and began digging. A circle of onlookers quickly formed, many gasping at the deceptive deftness of Fangs' seemingly unwieldy claws. Prodding the soft earth, he repeatedly retrieved tiny specks from the soil, only to place them on the album. Fangs seemed completely engrossed in this strange labour for a good ten minutes. Having finished whatever he had been up to, he carefully lifted the album with both claws and straightened his body. Walking toward the gathered humans, he gave them a chance to see what it was that he had placed on the album.

Only by looking very carefully could those gathered make out that it was hundreds of ants. They were gathered in a tight bunch: some alive, others curled up in death.

'I want to tell you a story,' Fangs said as the humans studied the ants. 'It is the story of a kingdom. This kingdom was descended from a great empire, and it could trace its ancestry all the way back to the ends of Earth's Cretaceous period, during which its founders built a magnificent city in the shadow of the towering bones of a dinosaur.' Fangs paused, deep in thought, before continuing. 'But that is long-lost, ancient history, and when winter suddenly fell, the last in a long line of queens didn't even remember those glory days. It was a very long winter indeed, and the land was covered by glaciers. Tens of millions of years of vigorous life were lost as existence became ever more precarious.

'After waking from her last hibernation, the queen could not rouse even one out of every hundred of her subjects. The others had been entombed by the cold, some being frozen to nothing but transparent, empty shells. Feeling the walls of her city, the queen realized that they were as cold as ice and hard as steel. She understood that the Earth remained frozen. In this age of terrible cold, even summer brought no thaw. The queen decided it was time to leave the homeland of her ancestors and to seek out unfrozen earth to establish a new kingdom.

'And so the queen led her surviving subjects to the surface to begin their long and arduous journey in the shadow of looming glaciers,' Fangs said.

'Most of her remaining subjects perished during their protracted wanderings, consumed by the deadly cold. But the queen and a few straggling survivors finally found a patch of earth that remained untouched by frost. Overflowing geothermal energy warmed this sliver of land. The queen, of course, knew nothing of this. She did not understand why there should be moist and soft soil anywhere in this frozen world, but she was in no way surprised that she had found it: a race that persevered through sixty million long years could never suffer extinction!

'In the face of a glacier-covered Earth and a dim Sun, the queen proclaimed that it was here that they would found a new great kingdom, a kingdom that would endure for all eternity. Standing under the summit of a tall, white mountain, she declared that this new kingdom would be known as the 'Realm of the White Mountain',' he said grandly.

'In fact, the eponymous summit was the skull of a mammoth,' he continued. 'It was the zenith of the Late Pleistocene of the Quaternary Glaciation. In those days, you human worms were still dumb animals, shivering in your scattered caves. It would still be ninety thousand years before the first flicker of your civilization would appear a continent away on the plains of Mesopotamia.

'Living off the frozen remains of mammoths in the vicinity of the Realm of the White Mountain, the new settlement survived ten thousand hard years. Then, as the ice age ended, spring returned to Earth, and the land was again draped in green. In this great explosion of life, the Realm of the White Mountain quickly entered a golden age of prosperity. Its subjects were beyond number, and they ruled a vast domain. Over the next ten thousand years, the kingdom was ruled by countless dynasties, and countless epics told its stories.'

As he continued, Fangs pointed at the large pile of earth in front of them. 'That is the final resting place of the Realm of the White Mountain. As you archaeologist worms were preoccupied by your excavations of a lost and dead fifty-thousand-year-old city, you completely failed to realize that the soil above those ruins was teeming with a city that was very much alive. In scale it was easily comparable to New York, and the latter is a city on merely two dimensions. The city here was a grand three-dimensional metropolis with numerous layers. Every layer was densely packed with labyrinthine streets, spacious forums and magnificent palaces. The design of the city's drainage and fire prevention systems handily outshone those of New York.

'The city was home to a complex social structure and a strict division of labour,' he told his captive audience. 'Its entire society ran with machine-like precision and harmonious efficiency. The vices of drug use and crime did not exist here, and hence there was neither depravity nor confusion. But its inhabitants were by no means devoid of emotion, showing their abiding sorrow whenever a subject of the Realm passed away. They even had a cemetery on the surface at the edge of the city, and there they would bury their dead an inch under the ground.

'However, the greatest acclaim must be reserved for the grand library nestled in the lowest layer of this city. In this library, one could find a multitude of ovoid containers. Each container was a book filled with pheromones. The exceedingly complex chemistry of these pheromones stored the city's knowledge. Here the epics detailing the enduring history of the Realm of the White Mountain were recorded. Here you could have learned that in a great forest fire all the subjects of the kingdom embraced each other to form countless balls, and that, with heroic effort, they were able to escape a sea of fire by floating down a stream. You could have learned the history of the hundred-year war against the White Termite Empire; or of the first time that an expedition from the kingdom saw the great ocean...' Fangs let his translator's voice trail off.

Then his booming voice again rang out. 'But it was all destroyed in three short hours. Destroyed when, with an earth-shattering roar, the excavators came, blackening the sky. Then their giant steel claws came cutting down, grabbing the soil of the city, utterly destroying it and crushing all within. They even destroyed the layer where all the city's children and the tens of thousands of snow-white eggs, yet to become children, rested.'

All of the world again seemed to have fallen deathly quiet. This silence outlasted the quiet that had followed Fangs' horrible feast. Standing before the alien emissary, humanity was, for the first time, at a loss for words.

Finally Fangs said, 'We still have a very long time to get along and very many things to talk about, but let us not speak of morals. In the universe, such considerations are meaningless.'

Chapter 4
Acceleration

Fangs left the people at the dig site in a state of deep shock and despair. The Captain was again the first to break the silence. He turned to the surrounding dignitaries of all nations and said, 'I know that I am but a nobody and that the only reason I am fortunate enough to attend these occasions is because I was the first to come into contact with the two alien intelligent beings. Nonetheless, I want to say a couple of things: first, Fangs is right; second, humanity's only way out is to fight.'

'Fight? Oh, Captain, fight…' The Secretary-General shook his head with a bitter simile.

'Right! Fight! Fight! Fight!' the girl from Eridanus shouted from her crystal pane, as she flitted several feet above the heads of those assembled. In her sun-drenched crystal, the long-haired girl's entire body erupted into a flowing flourish.

'You people from Eridanus fought them. How did that end?' someone called out. 'Humanity must think of its survival as a species, not of satisfying your twisted desire for vengeance.'

'No, sir,' the Captain said, turning to face the assembled crowd. 'The Eridanians engaged an enemy they knew nothing about in a war of self-defence. Furthermore, they were a society that had historically not known war. Given the circumstances, it is hardly surprising that they were defeated. Nonetheless, in a century of bitter warfare, they meticulously acquired a deep understanding of the Devourer. We now have been handed that vast reservoir of knowledge by this spaceship. It will be our advantage.

'Judicious preliminary studies of the material have shown that the Devourer is by no means as terrible as we had first feared,' he told them. 'Foremost, beyond the fact that it is inconceivably large, there is little about the Devourer that exceeds our understanding. Its life forms, the ten billion-plus Devourers themselves, are carbon-based life forms, just like us. They even resemble us on a molecular level, and because we share a biological basis with the enemy, nothing about them will remain beyond our grasp. We should count our blessings; consider that we could just as well have been faced with invaders made of energy fields and the stuff of neutron stars.

'But there is even more cause for hope,' he said. 'The Devourer possesses very little, shall we say, 'super-technology'. The Devourer's technology is certainly very advanced when compared to humanity's, but that is primarily a question of scale, not of theoretical basis. The main energy source of the Devourer's propulsion system is nuclear fusion. In fact, the primary use for water plundered from planets – beyond providing basic life support – is fuel for this system. The Devourer's propulsion technology is based on the principle of recoil and the conservation of momentum; it is not some sort of strange, space-time bending MacGuffin.' The Captain paused, studying the faces before him. 'All of this may dismay our scientists; after all, the Devourer, with its tens of millions of years of continuous development, clearly shows us the limits of science and technology, but it also clearly shows us that our enemy is no invincible god.'

The Secretary-General mulled over the Captain's words, then asked, 'But is that enough to ensure humanity's victory?'

'Of course, we have more specific information. Information that should allow us to formulate a strategy that will give a good shot at victory. For example—'

'Acceleration! Acceleration!' the girl from Eridanus shouted over their heads, interrupting the Captain.

The Captain explained her outburst to the baffled faces around him. 'We have learned from the Eridanian data that the Devourer's ability to accelerate is limited. The Eridanians observed it for two long centuries, and they never once saw it exceed this specific limit. To confirm this, we used the data we received from the Eridanian spaceship to establish a mathematical model that accounts for the Devourer's architecture and the material strength of its structural components. Calculations using this model verify the Eridanians' observations. There is a firm limit to the speed at which the Devourer can accelerate, and this limit is determined by its structural integrity. Should it ever exceed this mark, the colossus will be torn to pieces.'

'So what?' the head of a great nation asked, underwhelmed.

'We should remain level-headed and carefully consider it,' the Captain answered with a laugh.

Chapter 5
The Lunar Refuge

Finally, humanity's negotiations with the alien emissary showed some small signs of progress. Fangs yielded to the demand for a lunar refuge.

'Humans are nostalgic creatures,' the Secretary-General had explained in one of their meetings, tears in his eyes.

'So are the Devourers, even though we no longer have a home,' Fangs had sympathetically answered, nodding his head.

'So, will you allow a few of us to stay behind? If you permit, they will wait for the great Devourer Empire to spit out the Earth after it has finished consuming the planet. After waiting for the planet's transformed geology to settle, they will return to rebuild our civilization.'

Fangs shook his gargantuan head. 'When the Devourer Empire consumes, it consumes completely. When we are done, the Earth will be as desolate as Mars. Your worm-technology will not be enough to rebuild a civilization.'

The Secretary-General would not be dissuaded. 'But we must try. It will assuage our souls, and it will be especially important for those of us in the Devourer Empire being raised as livestock. It will surely fatten them if they can think back on their distant home in this solar system, even if that home no longer necessarily exists.'

Fangs now nodded. 'But where will those people go while the Earth is being devoured? Besides Earth, we also will consume Venus. Jupiter and Neptune are too large for us to consume, but we will devour their satellites. The Devourer Empire is in need of their hydrocarbons and water. We will also take a bite out of the barren worlds of Mars and Mercury, as we are interested in their carbon dioxide and metals. The surfaces of all these worlds will become seas of fire.'

The Secretary-General had an answer ready. 'We can take refuge on the Moon. We understand that the Devourer Empire plans to push the Moon out of orbit before consuming the Earth.'

Fangs nodded. 'That is right. The combined gravitational forces of the Devourer and the Earth will be very powerful. They could crash the Moon into our ship. Such a collision would be enough to destroy our Empire.'

The Secretary-General smiled ever so slightly as he replied. 'All right then, let a few of us live up there. It will be no great loss to you.'

'How many do you plan to leave behind?' Fangs queried.

'The minimum to preserve our civilization, one hundred thousand,' the Secretary-General answered flatly.

'Well then, you should get to work,' Fangs concluded.

'Get to work? What work?' the Secretary-General asked, perplexed.

'Pushing the Moon out of its orbit. For us, that is always a great inconvenience,' Fangs answered dismissively.

'But,' said the Secretary-General, grasping his hair in despair, 'sir, that would be no different than denying humanity our meagre and pitiable request. Sir, you know that we do not possess such technological prowess!'

'Ha, worm, why should I care? And besides, don't you still have an entire century?' Fangs concluded with a chuckle.

Chapter 6
Planting the Bombs

On the gleaming white plains of the Moon, a spacesuit-clad contingent stood next to a tall drilling tower. The emissary of the Devourer Empire stood somewhat apart, his giant frame another towering silhouette against the horizon. All eyes were firmly focused on a metal cylinder being slowly lowered from the top of the drilling tower down into the drill well below. Soon the cable was speeding into the well. On Earth, two hundred and forty thousand miles away, an entire world was glued to the unfolding events. Then came the signal; the payload had reached the bottom of the well. All observers, including Fangs, broke into applause as they celebrated the arrival of this historic moment.

The last nuclear bomb that would propel the Moon out of orbit had been put in place. A century had passed since the Eridanus Crystal and the emissary of the Devourer Empire had arrived on Earth. For humanity, it had been a century of despair, a hundred years of bitter struggle.

In the first half of the century, the entire Earth had zealously thrown itself at the task of constructing an engine that could propel the Moon. The technology needed to build such an engine, however, utterly failed to materialize. All that was accomplished was that the Moon's surface had gained a few scrap metal mountains, the remains of failed prototypes. Then there were also the lakes of metal, formed where experimental engines had melted under the heat of nuclear fusion.

Humanity had asked the emissary of the Devourer Empire for technological assistance; after all, the lunar engines would not even have to be a tenth of the scale of the countless super-engines the Devourer possessed.

Fangs, however, refused and instead quipped, 'Don't assume that you can build a planetary engine just because you understand nuclear fusion. It's a long way from a firecracker to a rocket. Truth be told, there is no reason at all for you to work so hard at it. In the Milky Way, it is perfectly commonplace for a weaker civilization to become the livestock of a stronger civilization.

You will discover that being raised for food is a splendid life indeed. You will have no wants and will live happily to the end. Some civilizations have sought to become livestock, only to be turned down. That you should feel uncomfortable with the idea is entirely the fault of a most banal anthropocentrism.'

So humanity placed all their hopes in the Eridanus Crystal, but again they were disappointed. The technology of the Eridanian civilization had developed along completely different lines from Earth's or that of the Devourer. Their technology was wholly based on their planet's organisms. The crystal, for example, was a symbiont to a kind of plankton that floated in their world's oceans. The Eridanians merely synthesized and utilized the unusual abilities of their planet's life forms without ever truly understanding their secrets. And so, without Eridanian life forms, their technology remained completely unworkable.

After over fifty valuable years were wasted, despairing humanity suddenly produced an exceedingly eccentric scheme to propel the Moon. It was the Captain who first came up with this plan. At the time, he had a leading role in the Moon propulsion programme and had advanced to the rank of marshal. Even though his plan was unapologetically crazy, its technological demands were modest, and humanity's available technology was fully capable of making it work; so much so, in fact, that many were surprised why no one had come up with it earlier.

The new plan to propel the Moon was very simple. A large array of nuclear bombs would be installed on one side of the Moon. These bombs would, for the most part, be buried about two miles under the lunar surface. Their spacing would ensure that no bomb was destroyed by the blast of another. According to this plan, five million nuclear bombs were to be installed on the Moon's 'propulsion side'. Compared to these bombs, humanity's most powerful Cold War-era nuclear bombs were mere conventional weapons.

When the time came to detonate these super powerful nuclear bombs under the lunar surface, the force of their explosions would be wholly incomparable to the nuclear tests of earlier ages, suffocated deep

190

underground. These denotations would blow off a complete stratum of lunar matter. In the Moon's low gravity, the exploded strata's rocks and dust would reach escape velocity. As they were launched straight into space, they would exert an enormous propulsive force on the Moon itself.

If a certain number of bombs were detonated in rapid succession, this momentum could become a continual propelling force, just as if the Moon had been fitted with a powerful engine. By detonating nuclear bombs in different places it would be possible to control the Moon's flight path.

The plan would even go one step further, calling for not one but two layers of nuclear bombs within the lunar surface. The second layer would be installed at a depth of about four miles. After the top layer had been completely used up, two miles of lunar matter would be stripped from the propulsion side of the Moon. The unceasing denotations would then smoothly transition to the second layer. This would double the duration that the 'engine' could propel the Moon.

When the girl from Eridanus heard of this plan, she came to the conclusion that humanity was truly insane. 'Now I understand. If you had technology to match the Devourers, you might be even more savage than they are!' she exclaimed.

Fangs, on the other hand, was full of praise. 'Ha, ha! What a wonderful idea you worms managed to dream up. I love it. I love your vulgarity. Vulgarity is the highest form of beauty!' he commended humanity.

'Absurd! How can vulgarity be beautiful?' the girl from Eridanus retorted.

'The vulgar is naturally beautiful, and nothing is more vulgar than the universe! Stars burn manically in the pitch-black cold abyss of space. Isn't that vulgar? Do you understand that the universe is masculine? Feminine civilizations, like yours, are fragile, fine and delicate, a sickly abnormality in a tiny corner of the universe. And that is that!' Fangs replied.

A hundred years had passed, and Fangs' huge frame still brimmed with vitality. The girl from Eridanus was still vivid and bright, but the Marshal felt the weight of years. He was a hundred and thirty-five years old, an old man.

At the time, the Devourer had just passed the orbit of Pluto. It was awakening after its long, sixty-thousand-year journey from Epsilon Eridani. In the dark of space, its huge ring was lit up brilliantly, and its immense society set to work, preparing to plunder the solar system.

After the Devourer had passed the peripheral planets, it flung itself onto a precipitous trajectory toward Earth.

Chapter 7
Humanity's First and Last Space War

The acceleration of the Moon away from Earth had begun.

The Moon was hanging in the sky of Earth's day side when the first bombs were detonated. The flare from each explosion briefly lit up the Moon in the blue sky, giving it the appearance of a giant silver eye frantically blinking in the heavens. When night fell on Earth, the one-sided flashes of the Moon were bright enough to cast shadows on the surface twenty-five thousand miles below. A pale silver trail following the Moon's back side was now visible. It was composed of the rocks blasted into space from the Moon's surface. Cameras installed on the propulsion side of the Moon showed strata of rock being blasted into space like billowing floodwaters. The waves of rock quickly faded into the distance, becoming thin strands trailing the Moon. Turning toward the Earth's other side, the Moon circumscribed an accelerating orbit.

Humanity's attention, however, was now squarely focused on the great and terrible ring that had appeared in the sky: the Devourer's approach loomed over the Earth. The enormous tides its gravity caused had already destroyed Earth's coastal cities.

The Devourer's aft engines flashed in a circle of blue light as it engaged in final orbital adjustments on its approach. It eventually perfectly matched the Earth's orbit around the Sun, while at the same time it aligned its axis of rotation with Earth's. Having completed these adjustments, it ever so slowly began to move toward the Earth, ready to surround the planet with its huge ring body.

The Moon's acceleration continued for two months. During this time, a bomb had exploded within its surface every two or three seconds, resulting in an almost incomprehensible total of 2.5 million nuclear explosions. As it entered into its second orbit around the Earth, the Moon's acceleration had forced its once circular orbit into a distinctly elliptical shape. As the Moon moved to the far end of this ellipse, Fangs and the Marshal arrived on its forward-facing side, away from the exploding bombs. The Marshal had expressly invited the alien emissary for this occasion.

As they stood on the lunar plain surrounded by craters, they felt the tremors from the other side shake deep beneath their feet. It almost seemed as if they could sense the powerful heartbeat of Earth's satellite. In the pitch-black sky beyond, the Devourer's giant ring dazzled with its brilliant light, its huge shape consuming half the sky.

'Excellent, Marshal-worm, most excellent indeed!' Fangs applauded, his voice full of sincere praise. 'But,' he continued, 'you should hurry. You only have one more orbit to accelerate. The Devourer Empire is not accustomed to waiting for others. And I have another question: the cities you built below the surface a decade ago are still empty. When will their inhabitants arrive? How can your spaceships transport one hundred thousand humans here from Earth in only one month?'

'We will bring no one here,' the marshal calmly replied. 'We will be the last humans to stand on the Moon.'

Hearing this, Fangs twisted his body in surprise. The Marshal had said 'We', meaning the 5,000 officers and soldiers of Earth's space force. They formed a perfect phalanx on the crater-covered lunar plain. At the front of the phalanx a soldier brandished a blue flag.

'Look, this is our planet's banner. We declare war upon the Devourer Empire!' the Marshal announced defiantly.

Fangs stood dumbfounded, more confused than surprised. Immediately, his body began to reel as he was thrown onto his back by the Moon's sudden gravitational surge. Fangs was knocked prone to lunar ground, stunned beyond any thought of movement. All around him lunar dust kicked up by his massive fall slowly began to drift to the ground.

But the dust was quickly thrown up again, stirred by massive shock waves reverberating from the other side of the Moon. These shocks soon left the entire plain covered in a layer of white dust.

Fangs realized the frequency of nuclear explosions on the other side of the Moon had abruptly increased several times over. Judging by the sharp increase of gravity, he could infer that the Moon's acceleration must have increased several times as well. Rolling over, he retrieved a large handheld computer from a pocket in the front of his spacesuit. He brought up the Moon's current orbital trajectory on it. Immediately, he realized that this tremendous increase of acceleration would take the Moon out of orbit. The Moon would break free of Earth's gravity and shoot off into space. A flashing red line of dots showed its predicted course.

It was on a collision course with the Devourer.

Discarding his computer without a second thought, Fangs slowly rose to his feet. Straining his neck against the explosive increase in gravity, he peered through the billowing clouds of lunar dust. Standing in front of him was Earth's army, still upright, stalwart like standing stones.

'A century of conspiracy and deceit,' Fangs mumbled under his breath.

The Marshal just nodded in agreement. 'You now realize that it is too late,' he pointed out gravely.

Fangs spoke after a long sigh. 'I should have realized that the humans of Earth were a completely different breed from the Eridanians. Life on their world had evolved symbiotically, free of natural selection and the struggle for survival. They did not even know what war was.' He halted, digesting what had happened. 'We let that guide our assessment of Earth's people. You have ceaselessly butchered one another from the day that you climbed down from the trees. How could you be easily conquered? I…' Again he paused. 'It was an unforgivable dereliction of duty!'

When the Marshal spoke, his steady, level tone explained further what Fangs was realizing. 'The Eridanians brought us vast quantities of vital information. The information included the limits of the Devourer's ability to accelerate. It is this information that formed the basis of our battle plan. As we detonate the bombs that change the Moon's trajectory, its manoeuvring acceleration will come to exceed the Devourer's acceleration limit three-fold. In other words,' he said, 'it will be thrice as agile as the Devourer. There is no way you can avoid the coming collision.'

'Actually, we were not completely off guard,' Fangs said. 'When the Earth began producing large quantities of nuclear bombs, we began to monitor their whereabouts. We made sure that they were installed deep within the Moon, but we did not think...' Fangs trailed off.

Behind his visor, the Marshal smiled faintly. 'We aren't so stupid as to directly attack the Devourer with nuclear bombs,' he said. 'We know that the Devourer Empire has been steeled by hundreds of battles. Earth's simple and crude missiles would certainly have been intercepted and destroyed, one and all. But you cannot intercept something as large as the Moon. Perhaps the Devourer, with its immense power, could have eventually broken or diverted the Moon, but it is far too close for that now. You are out of time.'

Fangs snarled. 'Crafty worms. Treacherous worms, vicious worms... The Devourer Empire is an honest civilization. We put all things out in the open, yet we have been cheated by the deceitful treachery of the Earth worms.' He gnashed his huge teeth as he finished speaking, his fury almost goading him to lock his giant claws around the Marshal. The soldiers and their rifles aiming right at him, however, stayed his talons. Fangs had not forgotten that his body, too, was but flesh and blood. One burst of bullets would end him.

With his eyes firmly fixed on Fangs, the Marshal stated, 'We will leave, and you, too, should make your way off the Moon, otherwise you will surely be killed by the Devourer Empire's nuclear weapons.'

The Marshal was quite correct. Just as Fangs and the human space forces left the Moon's surface, the interceptor missiles of the Devourer struck. Both sides of the Moon now flashed with brilliant light. The forward facing side of the Moon exploded as huge waves of rocks were blasted into space. All around the Moon, lunar matter was violently scattered in all imaginable directions. Seen from the Earth, the Moon, on its collision course with the

Devourer, looked like a warrior, wild hair ablaze with rage. There was no force that could have stopped it now! Wherever on Earth this spectacle was visible, seas of people erupted into feverish cheers.

The Devourer's interception action did not continue for long and soon ceased. It realized that it had been completely meaningless. In the moments in which the Moon would close the short distance between them, there was no way to divert its course or to destroy it.

The explosions of the Moon's nuclear propulsion had also ceased. It was now fast enough, and Earth's defenders wanted to preserve enough nuclear bombs to carry out any last-minute manoeuvres. All was silent.

In the cold quiet of space, the Devourer and Earth's satellite floated toward each other in complete tranquillity. The distance between the two rapidly decreased. As it dwindled to thirty thousand miles, the control ship of Earth's Supreme Command could already see the Moon overlapping the giant ring of the Devourer. From there, it looked like a ball bearing in a track.

Up to this point, the Devourer had not made any changes to its trajectory. It was easy to understand why: the Moon could have easily matched any premature orbital manoeuvre. Any meaningful evasive action would have to be taken in the final moments before the Moon's impact. The two cosmic giants were almost like ancient knights in a joust. They were charging toward one another, galloping across the distance separating them, but the victor would only be decided in the blink of an eye before they made contact.

Two great civilizations of the Milky Way held their breath in rapt anticipation, awaiting that final moment.

At twenty thousand miles, both sides began their manoeuvres. The Devourer's engines were the first to flare, shooting blue flames more than five thousand miles out into space. It began its evasion. On the Moon, nuclear bombs were once again ignited, ferociously detonating with unprecedented intensity and frequency. It carried out its adjustments, matching its course to ensure a collision. Its arcing tail of debris clearly described its change of direction. The blue light of the Devourer's five-thousand-mile flames merged with the silver flashes of the Moon's nuclear blasts; it was the most magnificent vista ever to grace the solar system.

Both sides manoeuvred like this for three hours. The distance between them had already shrunk to three thousand miles when the computer displays showed what no one in the control ship ever would have believed to be possible: the Devourer was changing course with an acceleration speed four times greater than the limit the Eridanians had claimed possible!

All this time they had unreservedly believed in this limit. They had made it the foundation of Earth's victory. Now, the nuclear bombs remaining on the Moon no longer had the capacity to make the necessary adjustments to give chase. Calculations showed that in three short hours, even if they did all they could, the Moon would brush past the Devourer, falling short by two hundred and fifty miles.

One last burst of dizzying flashes washed over the control ship, exhausting all of the Earth's nuclear bombs. At almost exactly the same moment, the Devourer's engines fell silent. In a deathly quiet, the laws of inertia told the final verses of this magnificent epic: the Moon scraped past the Devourer's side, barely missing. Its velocity was so high that the Devourer's gravity could not catch it, only twisting its trajectory a little as it zoomed past. After the Moon had passed the Devourer, it silently sped away from the Sun.

On the control ship, the Supreme Command fell into a deathly silence. Minutes passed.

'The Eridanians betrayed us,' a commander finally whispered in shock.

'The crystal was probably just a trap set by the Devourer Empire!' a staff officer shouted.

In an instant, the Supreme Command fell into utter chaos. All but one began to scream and shout: some to vent their utter despair, others to conceal it. All were on the verge of hysteria. A few of the non-military personnel wept; others tore the hair from their heads. Spirits stood teetering on the verge of the abyss, ready to fall forever.

Only the Marshal remained serene, standing quietly in front of a large screen. He slowly turned and with one simple question calmed the chaos. 'I would ask all of you to pay attention to one detail: why did the Devourer cut its engine?'

Pandemonium was immediately replaced by deep thought. Indeed, after the Moon had used its last nuclear bomb, the enemy had no reason to shut down its engine. They had no way of knowing whether or not there were any bombs left on the Moon. Furthermore, there was the danger of the Devourer's gravity catching the Moon. Had the Devourer continued to accelerate, it could have easily extended the distance to the Moon's trajectory. It could have – should have – made it farther than those tiny, barely adequate two hundred fifty miles.

'Give me a close up of the Devourer's outer hull,' the Marshal commanded.

A holographic image was displayed on the screen. It was a picture being transmitted by a miniature, high-speed reconnaissance probe flying three hundred miles above the Devourer's surface. The splendidly illuminated surface of the Devourer came into clear view. In awe, they beheld the massive steel mountains and canyons of its giant ring body slowly turn past their view. A long black seam caught the Marshal's attention. In the past century, he had become very familiar with every detail of the Devourer's surface, but he was absolutely certain that *that* gap had not existed before. Others quickly noticed it, as well.

'What is that? Is it... a crack?' someone asked.

'It is. A crack. A three-thousand-mile-long crack,' the Marshal said, nodding. 'The Eridanians did not betray us. The data in the crystal was accurate. The acceleration limit is real, but as the Moon approached, the despairing Devourer decided to damn the consequences and to exceed it by four-fold, desperate to avoid the collision. This, however, had consequences: the Devourer has cracked.'

Then they found more cracks.

'Look, what's going on now?' someone shouted as its rotation brought another part of Devourer's surface into view. A dazzling bright light began glowing on the edge of its metal surface, as if dawn were creeping over its vast horizon.

'The rotational engine!' an officer called out.

'Indeed. It is the rarely used equatorial rotational engine!' the Marshal explained. 'It is firing at full power, trying to stop the Devourer's rotation!'

'Marshal, you were spot on, and this proves it!'

'We must act now and use all available means to gather detailed data so that we can run a simulation!' the Marshal commanded. Even as he spoke, the entire Supreme Command was already executing the task.

Over the past century, a mathematical model had been developed that precisely described the Devourer's physical structure. The required data was gathered and processed very efficiently, and so the results were quickly produced: it would take nearly forty hours for the rotational engine to reduce the Devourer's rotation to a speed at which it could avoid destruction. Yet in only eighteen hours the centrifugal forces would completely break the Devourer into pieces.

A cheer rose among the Supreme Command. The big screen shone with the holographic image of the Devourer's coming demise: the process of the break-up would be very slow, almost like a dream. Against the pitch blackness of space, this giant world would disperse like milk foam floating on coffee, its edges gradually breaking off, only to be swallowed by the darkness beyond. It looked like the Devourer was melting into space. Only the occasional flash of an explosion now revealed its disintegrating form.[1]

The Marshal did not join the others as they watched this soul-soothing display of destruction. He stood apart from the group, focused on another screen, carefully observing the real Devourer. His face betrayed no trace of triumph. As calm returned to the bridge, the others began to take notice of him. One after the other they joined him at the screen, where they discovered that the blue light at the Devourer's aft had reappeared.

The Devourer had restarted its engine.

Given the critical state the ring structure was already in, this seemed like

---

1 《诗云》引用了该段落，中文版无意在两个版本之间进行抉择，故两处均保留原译法。

an utterly unfathomable mistake. Any acceleration, no matter how minute, could cause a catastrophic break-up. But it was the Devourer's trajectory that truly baffled the onlookers: it was ever so slowly retracing its steps, returning to the position it had held before its evasive manoeuvres. It was carefully re-establishing its synchronous orbit and re-aligning its axis of rotation with Earth's.

'What? Does it still want to devour the Earth?' an officer exclaimed, both shocked and confused.

His question provoked a few scattered laughs. All laughter, however, soon fell silent as the others became aware of the look on the Marshal's face. He was no longer looking at the screen. His eyes were closed. His face was blank and drained of all colour. In the past hundred years, the officers and personnel who had made fending off the Devourer a pillar of their soul had become very familiar with the Marshal's countenance. They had never seen him like this. A calm fell over the gathered Supreme Command as they turned back to the screen. Finally, they understood the gravity of the situation.

The Devourer still had a way out.

The Devourer's flight toward the Earth had begun. It had already matched the Earth in both orbital speed and rotation, as it approached the planet's South Pole.

If it took too long, the Devourer's own centrifugal forces would tear it apart; if it went too fast, the power of its propulsion would rip it to pieces. The Devourer's survival was hanging on a thin thread. It had to hold to a perfect balance between timing and speed.

Before the Earth's South Pole was enveloped by the Devourer's giant ring, the Supreme Command could see the shape of the frozen continent change rapidly. Antarctica was shrinking, like butter in a hot frying pan. The world's oceans were being pulled toward the South Pole by the immense gravity of the Devourer, and now the Earth's white tip was being swallowed by their billowing waters.

As this happened, the Devourer, too, was changing. Countless new cracks began to cover its body, and all of them were growing longer and wider. The first few tears were now no longer black seams, but gaping chasms glowing with crimson light. They could easily have been mistaken for the portals to Hell, thousands of miles in length.

In the midst of all this destruction, a few fine white strands rose from the ring's massive body. Then, more and more of these filaments emerged, flowing from every part of the Devourer's body. It almost looked like the huge ship had sprouted a sparse head of white hair. In fact, they were the engine trails of ships being launched from the great ring. The Devourers were fleeing their doomed world.

Half of the Earth had already been encircled by the Devourer when things took a turn for the worse: The Earth's gravity was acting almost like the invisible spokes of a cosmic wheel, bearing the disintegrating Devourer. No new cracks were appearing on its surface and the already open rips had ceased growing. Fourteen hours later, the Earth was completely engulfed by the Devourer. The effect of the planet's gravity was stronger at this point, and the cracks on the Devourer's surface were beginning to close. Another five hours later, they had completely closed.

In the control ship, all the screens of the Supreme Command had gone black, and even the lights were now dark. The only remaining source of illumination was the deathly pale rays of the Sun piercing through the portholes. In order to generate artificial gravity, the mid-section of the ship was still slowly rotating. As it did, the Sun rose and fell, porthole to porthole. Light and shadow wandered, as if it were replaying humanity's forever bygone days and nights.

'Thank you for a century of dutiful service,' the Marshal said. 'Thank you all.' He saluted the Supreme Command. Under the gaze of the officers and personnel, he calmly straightened his uniform. The others followed his example.

Humanity had been defeated. The defenders of Earth had done their utmost to discharge their duties and, as soldiers, they had done their duty gloriously. In spirit, they all accepted their unseen medals with clear consciences. They were entitled to enjoy this moment.

Chapter 8
Epilogue: The Return

'There really is water!' a young lieutenant shouted with joyous surprise. It was true; a vast surface of water stretched out before them. Sparkling waves shimmered under the dusky heavens.

The Marshal removed the gloves of his spacesuit. With both hands, he scooped up some water. Opening his visor, he ventured a taste. As he quickly closed his visor again, he called, 'Hey, it's not too salty.' When he saw that the lieutenant was about to open his own visor, he stopped him. 'You'll suffer decompression sickness. The composition of the atmosphere is actually not the problem; the poisonous sulphuric components in the air have already thinned out. However, the atmospheric pressure is too low. It is like being at thirty thousand miles above the ground before the war.'

A general dug in the sand at his feet. 'Maybe there's some grass seeds,' he said, smiling as he raised his head to look at the Marshal.

The Marshal shook his head. 'Before the war, this was the bottom of the ocean.'

'We can go have a look at New Land Eleven. It's not far from here. Maybe we can find some there,' the lieutenant suggested.

'Any will have been burnt long ago,' someone commented with a sigh.

Each of them scanned the horizon in all directions. They were surrounded by an unbroken chain of mountains only recently born by the orogenic movements of the Earth. They were dark blue massifs made of bare rock. Rivers of magma[1] spilling from their peaks glowed crimson, like blood oozing from the body of a slain stone titan.

The magma rivers of the Earth below had burned out.

This was Earth, two hundred and thirty years after the war.

After the war had ended, the more than one hundred survivors aboard the control ship had entered the hibernation chambers. There they waited for

---

1 岩浆河，与原文略有出入，但符合逻辑，中文版未作调整。

the Devourer to spit out the Earth; then they would return home. During their wait, their ship had become a satellite, circling the new joint planet of Devourer and Earth in a wide orbit. In all that time, the Devourer Empire had done nothing to harass them.

One hundred and twenty-five years after the war, the command ship's sensors picked up that the Devourer was in the process of leaving the Earth. In response, it roused some of those in hibernation. By the time they woke, the Devourer had already left the Earth and flown on to Venus. The Earth had been transformed into a wholly alien world, a strange planet, perhaps best described as a lump of charcoal freshly out of the oven. The oceans had all disappeared, and the land was covered in a web of magma rivers.

The personnel of the control ship could only continue their hibernation. They reset their sensors and waited for the Earth to cool. This wait lasted another century.

*

When they again woke from hibernation, they found a cooled planet, its violent geology having subsided; but now the Earth was a desolate, yellow wasteland. Even though all life had disappeared, there was still a sparse atmosphere. They even discovered remnants of the oceans of old.

So they landed at the shore of such a remnant, barely the size of a pre-war continental lake.

A blast of thunder, deafening in this thin atmosphere, roared above them as the familiar, crude form of a Devourer Empire ship landed not far from their own vessel. Its gigantic doors opened, and Fangs took his first tottering steps out, leaning heavily on a walking stick the size of a power pole.

'Ah, you are still alive, sir!' the Marshal greeted him. 'You must be around five hundred now?'

'How could I live that long? I, too, went into hibernation, thirty years after the war. I hibernated just so I could see you again,' Fangs retorted.

'Where is the Devourer now?' the Marshal asked.

Fangs pointed into the sky above as he answered. 'You can still see it at night; it is but a dim star now, just having passed Jupiter's orbit.'

'It is leaving the solar system?' the Marshal queried.

Fangs nodded. 'I will set out today to follow it.'

The Marshal paused before speaking. 'We are both old now.'

Fangs sadly nodded his giant head. 'Old...' he said, his walking stick trembling in his hand. 'The world, now...' He continued pointing from heaven to Earth.

'A small amount of water and atmosphere remains. Should we consider this an act of mercy from the Devourer Empire?' the Marshal asked quietly.

Fangs shook his head. 'It has nothing to do with mercy; it is your doing.'

The Earth's soldiers looked at Fangs in puzzlement.

'Oh, in this war the Devourer Empire suffered an unprecedented wound. We lost hundreds of millions in those tears,' Fangs admitted. 'Our ecosystem, too, suffered critical damage. After the war, it took us fifty Earth years just to complete preliminary repairs, and only once that was done could we begin to chew the Earth. But we knew that our time in the solar system was limited. If we did not leave in time, a cloud of interstellar dust would float right into our flight path. And if we took the long way round, we would lose seventeen thousand years on our way to the next star. In that time, the star's state would have already changed, burning the planets that we wished to consume. Because of this we had to chew the planets of the Sun in great haste and could not pick them clean,' Fangs explained.

'That fills us with great comfort and honour,' the Marshal said, looking at the soldiers surrounding him.

'You are most worthy of it. It truly was a great interstellar war. In the lengthy annals of the Devourer's wars, you were among the most remarkable soldiers! To this day, all throughout our world, minstrels sing of the epic achievements of the Earth's soldiers,' Fangs stated.

'We would sooner hope that humanity would remember the war. So, how is humanity?' the Marshal queried.

'After the war, approximately two billion humans were migrated to the

Devourer Empire, about half of all of humanity,' Fangs answered, activating the large screen of his portable computer where pictures of life on the Devourer appeared. The screen revealed a beautiful grassland under blue skies. On the grass, a group of happy humans was singing and dancing, and at first it was difficult to distinguish the gender of these humans. Their skin was a soft, subtle white, and they were all dressed in fine, gauzy clothes with beautiful wreaths of flowers on their heads. In the distance, one could make out a magnificent castle, clearly modelled on something from an Earth fairy tale. Its vibrant colours made it look as if it were made of cream and chocolate.

The camera's lens drew closer, giving the Marshal a chance to study these people's countenances in detail. He was soon completely convinced that they were truly happy. It was an utterly carefree happiness, pure as crystal. It reminded him of the few short years of innocent childhood joy that pre-war humans had experienced.

'We must ensure their absolute happiness,' Fangs said. 'It is the minimum requirement for raising them. If we do not, we cannot guarantee the quality of their meat. And it must be said that Earth people are seen as food of the highest quality; only the upper class of the Devourer Empire society can afford to enjoy them. I myself cannot afford such delicacies.' Fangs paused for a moment. 'Oh, Marshal. We found your great-grandson, sir. We recorded something from him to you. Do you care to see it?'

The Marshal gazed at Fangs in surprise, then nodded his head.

A fair-skinned, beautiful boy appeared on the screen. Judging by his face he was only ten years old, but his stature was already that of a grown man. He held a flower wreath in his effeminate hands, having obviously just been called from a dance.

Blinking his large, shimmering eyes, he said, 'I hear that my great-grandfather still lives. I ask only one thing of you, sir. Never, ever come see me! I am nauseated! When we think of humanity's life before the war, we are all nauseated! What a barbaric life that was, the life of cockroaches! You and your soldiers of Earth wanted to preserve that life! You almost stopped humanity from entering this beautiful heaven! How perverse! Do you know how much shame, how much embarrassment you have caused me? Bah! Do not come looking for me! Bah! Go and die!' After he had finished, he skipped off to join the dancing on the grassland.

Fangs was first to break the awkward silence that followed. 'He will live past the age of sixty. He will have a long life and will not be slaughtered.'

'If it is because of me, then I am truly grateful,' the Marshal said, smiling miserably.

'It does not. After learning about his ancestry, he became very depressed and filled with feelings of hatred toward you. Such emotions prevented his meat from meeting our standards,' Fangs explained.

As Fangs looked at these last few humans before him, genuine emotions played across his massive eyes. Their spacesuits were extremely old and shabby, and the many years past were etched into their faces. In the pale yellow of the Sun, they looked like a group of rust-stained statues. Fangs closed his computer and, full of regret, said, 'At first, I did not want you to see this, but you are all true warriors, more than capable of dealing with the truth, ready to recognize,' he paused for a long moment before continuing, 'that human civilization has come to an end.'

'You certainly destroyed Earth's civilization,' the Marshal said, staring into the distance. 'You have committed a monstrous crime!'

'We finally have started to talk about morals again,' Fangs said with a laugh and a grin.

'After invading our home and brutally devouring everything in it, I would think that you had forfeited all right to talk about morals,' the Marshal said coldly.

The others had already stopped paying attention; the extreme, cold brutality of the Devourer civilization was just beyond human understanding. Nothing could have been less interesting to the others than a discussion with them about morals.

'No, we have the right. I now truly wish to talk about morals with humanity,' Fangs said before again pausing. ' 'How, sir, could you just pick him up and eat him?' ' he continued, quoting the then Captain. Those last words left nobody unshaken. They did not emanate from the translator, but came directly from Fangs' mouth. Even though his voice was deafening, Fangs somehow managed to imitate those three-hundred-year-old words with perfection.

Fangs continued, resuming his use of the translator. 'Marshal, three hundred years ago, your intuition did not mislead you: When two civilizations – separated by interstellar space – meet, any similarities should be far more shocking than their differences. It certainly shouldn't be as it is with our species.'

As all present focused their gaze on Fangs' frame, they were overcome with a sense of premonition that a world-shaking mystery was about to be revealed.

Fangs straightened himself on his walking-stick and, looking into the distance, said, 'Friends, we are both children of the Sun; and while the Earth is both our species' fraternal home, my people have the greater claim to her! Our claim is one hundred and forty million years older than yours. All those millennia ago, we were the first to live on this beautiful planet, and this is where we established our magnificent civilization.'

The Earth's soldiers stared blankly at Fangs. The waters of the remnant ocean rippled in the pale of the yellow sunlight. Red magma flowed from the distant new mountains. Sixty million years down the rivers of time, two species, each the ruler of this Earth in their own time, met in desolation on their plundered home world.

'Dino... saur!' someone exclaimed in a shocked whisper.

Fangs nodded. 'The Dinosaur Civilization arose one hundred million years ago on Earth, during what you call the Cretaceous period of the Mesozoic. At the end of the Cretaceous, our civilization reached its zenith, but we are a large species, and our biological needs were equally great. In the wake of our population increase, the ecosystem was stretched to its limit, and the Earth was pushed to its brink as it struggled to support our society. To survive, we completely consumed Mars' elementary ecosystem.

'The Dinosaur Civilization lasted twenty million years on Earth,' he continued, 'but its true expansion was a matter of a few thousand years. From a geological perspective, its effects are indistinguishable from those of an explosive catastrophe; what you call the Cretaceous–Tertiary extinction event.

'Finally, one day all the dinosaurs boarded ten giant generation ships and, with these ships, sailed into the vast sea of stars. In the end, all ten of these ships were joined together. Then, whenever this newly united ship reached another star's planet, it expanded. Now, sixty million years later, it has become the Devourer Empire you now know.'

'Why would you eat your own home world? Are dinosaurs bereft of all sentiment?' someone asked.

Fangs answered, lost in thought. 'It is a long story. Interstellar space is indeed vast and boundless, but it is also different than you would imagine. The places that truly suit us, as advanced carbon-based life forms, are few and far between. A dust cloud blocks the way to the centre of the Milky Way just two thousand light years from here. There is no way for us to pass through it, and no way for us to survive in it. And after that it becomes an area of powerful radiation and a large group of wandering black holes.' Fangs paused, before continuing, still speaking more to himself than to the humans before him. 'If we should travel in the opposite direction, we would just come to the end of the Milky Way's spiral arm and then, not far beyond, there is nothing but a limitless, desolate void. The Devourer Empire has already completely consumed almost all the planets that could be found in the habitable areas that exist between these two barriers. Now, the only way out is to fly to another arm of the Milky Way. We have no idea what awaits us there, but if we stay here we will certainly be doomed. It will be a journey of fifteen million years, taking us right through the void. To survive it, we must build large stocks of all possible expendables.

'Right now, the Devourer Empire is just like a fish in a drying stream. It must make a desperate leap before its water completely evaporates. It realizes that the most likely end is reaching dry land and succumbing to death under the scorching Sun; but there is the slight chance that it may fall into a neighbouring water hole and so survive.' Fangs lowered his gaze toward the humans, bending down to almost eye level. 'As far as sentiment is concerned, we have lived through tens of millions of arduous years and fought stellar wars beyond number. The hearts of the dinosaur race have long since hardened. Now the Devourer Empire must consume as much as it possibly can in preparation for our million-year journey.' Fangs again paused, deep in thought. 'What is civilization? Civilization is devouring, ceaselessly eating, endlessly expanding; everything else comes second.'

The Marshal, too, was deep in thought. Looking at Fangs, he asked, 'Can the struggle for existence be the universe's only law of biological and cultural evolution? Can we not establish a self-sufficient, introspective civilization where all life exists in symbiosis? A civilization like that of the Eridanians?'

Fangs answered without hesitation or pause. 'I am no philosopher; perhaps it can be done. The crux is, who will take the first step? If one's survival is based on the subjugation and consumption of others and if that should be the universe's iron law of life and civilization, then whoever first rejects it in favour of introspection will certainly perish.'

With that Fangs returned to his spaceship, but he re-emerged, now carrying a thin, flat box in both talons. The box was about ten feet square, and it would have easily taken four men to carry it. Fangs placed the box on the ground and opened its top. To the humans' surprise, the box was filled with dirt, and grass was growing on it. On this lifeless world, its green left no heart untouched.

As Fangs opened the box, he turned to the humans. 'This is pre-war soil. After the war, I put all of our planet's plants and all of its insects into suspended animation. Now, after more than two centuries, they have awoken. Originally, I wanted to take this soil with me as a memento. Alas, I have thought more about it, and I have changed my mind. I have decided to return it to where it truly belongs. We have taken more than enough from our home world.'

As they gazed upon this tiny piece of Earth, so full of life, the humans' eyes began to moisten. They now knew the dinosaurs' hearts had not turned to stone. Behind those scales, colder and crueller than steel and rock, beat hearts that longed for home.

Fangs rattled his claws, almost as if he wanted to cast off the emotions that had gripped him. Slightly shaken, he said, 'All right then, my friends, we will go together, back to the Devourer Empire.' Seeing the expression on the humans' faces, he raised a claw before continuing. 'You will, of course, not be food there. You are great warriors and you will be made citizens of the Empire. And there is still work that needs your attention. A museum to the human civilization needs to be built.'

The eyes of every single Earth soldier turned to the Marshal. He stood deep in thought, then slowly nodded.

One after the other, the Earth's soldiers boarded Fangs' spaceship. Because its ladder was intended for dinosaurs, they had to pull the full length of their bodies up each rung to climb inside. The Marshal was the last human to board the ship. Grasping the lowest rung of the ship's ladder, he pulled his body off the ground. Just at that moment, something in the ground beneath his feet caught his eye. He stopped in mid-pull, looking down. For a long time he hung there, motionless.

He had seen... an ant.

The ant had climbed out of that box of soil. Never losing sight of the tiny insect, the Marshal let go of the ladder and squatted down. Lowering his hand, he let the ant clamber onto his glove. Raising it to his face, he carefully studied the small creature, its obsidian body glinting in the sunlight. Holding it, the Marshal walked over to the box, where he cautiously returned the ant to the tiny blades of grass. As he lowered his hand, he noticed more ants climbing about the soil beneath the grass.

Raising himself, he turned to Fangs who was standing right by his side. 'When we leave, this grass and these ants will be the dominant species on Earth.'

Fangs was at a loss for words.

'Earth's civilized life seems to be getting smaller and smaller. Dinosaurs, humans and now probably ants,' the Marshal said, squatting back down. He looked on, his eyes deep with love and admiration as he watched these small beings live their lives in the grass. 'It is their turn.'

As he spoke, the Earth's soldiers re-emerged from the spaceship. Climbing down to Earth, they returned to the box of living soil. Standing around it they, too, were filled with deep love.

Fangs shook his head. 'The grass might survive. It might eventually rain here at the seaside, but it won't be enough for the ants.'

'Is the atmosphere too thin? They seem to being doing just fine at the moment,' someone noted.

'No, the air is not the problem. They are not like humans and can live well in this atmosphere. The real crux of the matter is that they will have nothing to eat,' Fangs replied.

'Can't they eat the grass?' another voice joined in.

'And then? How will they live on? In this thin air, the grass will grow very slowly. Once the ants have eaten all the blades, they will starve. In many ways, their situation mirrors the destiny of the Devourer civilization,' Fangs mused.

'Can you leave behind some food from your spaceship for them?' another soldier asked, almost pleaded.

Fangs again shook his massive head. 'There is nothing on my spaceship besides water and the hibernation system. On that note, we will hibernate until we catch up with the Devourer. But what about your spaceship, do you have any food on board?'

Now it was the Marshal's turn to shake his head. 'Nothing but a few injections of nourishment solution. Useless.'

Pointing to the spaceship, Fangs interrupted the discussion. 'We must hurry. The Empire is accelerating quickly. If we tarry, we will not catch up.'

Silence.

'Marshal, we will stay behind.' It was the young lieutenant who broke the silence.

The Marshal forcefully nodded.

'Stay behind? What are you up to?' Fangs asked in astonishment, turning from one to the other. 'The hibernation equipment on your spaceship is almost completely depleted and you have no food. Do you plan to stay and wait for death?'

'Staying will be the first step,' the Marshal calmly answered.

'What?' Fangs asked, ever more perplexed.

'You just mentioned the first step toward a new civilization,' the Marshal explained.

'You,' Fangs could hardly believe his own words, 'want to be the ants' food?'

Earth's soldiers all nodded. Without a word, Fangs gazed at them for what seemed like forever, before turning and slowly hobbling back to his spaceship, leaning heavily on his walking stick.

'Farewell, friend,' the Marshal shouted after Fangs.

Fangs replied with a long, drawn-out sigh. 'An interminable darkness lies before me and my descendants: the darkness of endless war and a vast universe. Oh, where in it could there be a home for us?'

As he spoke, the humans saw that the ground beneath his feet had grown damp, but they could not tell if he had, or even could, shed tears.

With a thunderous roar, the dinosaur's spaceship lifted off and quickly disappeared into the sky. Where it had vanished, the Sun was now setting.

The last warriors of Earth seated themselves around the living soil in silence. Then, beginning with the Marshal, they all, one by one, opened their visors and stretched out on the sandy earth.

As time passed, the Sun set. Its afterglow bathed the plundered Earth in a beautiful red. As it faded, a few stars began to twinkle in the sky. To his surprise, the Marshal saw that the dusky sky was a beautiful blue. Just as the thin atmosphere began to render him unconsciousness, the Marshal felt the tiny movements of an ant on his temple, filling him with a deep sense of contentment. As the ant climbed up to his forehead, he was transported back to his so very distant childhood. He was at the beach, lying in a small hammock that hung between two palm trees. Looking up to the splendid sea of stars above, he felt his mother's hand gently stroke his forehead...

Darkness fell. The remnant ocean lay flat as a mirror, pristinely reflecting the Milky Way above. It was the most tranquil night in the planet's history.

In this tranquillity, the Earth was reborn.

山

MOUNTAIN

霍尔格·南 —译

TRANSLATED BY HOLGER NAHM

Chapter 1
Where There's a Mountain

'Today is the day I'm finally going to get you to tell me why you never go on land,' the Captain declared, arching an eyebrow. 'It's been five years, and the *Bluewater* has docked in heaven knows how many ports in more countries than I can count, yet you have never gone ashore. Not even when we docked back in China. And not even last year, back in Qingdao when we were in for overhauls. You're the last person I'd need to tell that the ship was a complete mess, and noisy, and still you stayed put, holed up in your cabin for two months,' the Captain continued, eying Feng Fan intensely as he spoke[1].

'Do I remind you of that movie, *The Legend of 1900*?' Fan asked in return.

'Are you insinuating that if we ever scuttle the *Bluewater*, you plan on going down with the ship like the guy in the movie did?' the Captain countered, unsure if Fan was joking or not.

'I'll change ships. Oceanographic vessels always have a place for a geological engineer who'll never leave ship,' Fan replied.

The Captain returned to his original point. 'That naturally begs the question: is there something on land that keeps you away?'

'On the contrary,' Fan answered, 'there is something that I yearn for.'

'And what's that?' the Captain asked, curious and now a bit impatient.

'Mountains,' Fan uttered, his gaze dissolving into a thousand-mile stare.

They were standing portside on the geological oceanographic research vessel the *Bluewater*, looking out onto the equatorial waters of the Pacific.

The *Bluewater* had crossed the equator for the first time a mere year ago. Back then, they had given in to the whimsy of marking the occasion with the ancient rite of the line-crossing ceremony. Their discovery of a manganese nodule deposit in the seabed, however, had left them crisscrossing the equator more times than any of them could possibly remember. By this point, they had all but forgotten about the existence of that invisible divide.

As the Sun slowly set beyond the sea's western horizon, Fan noticed that the ocean was unusually calm. In fact, he had never seen it so quiet. It reminded him of the Himalayan lakes, perfectly still to the point of blackness, like the eyes of the Earth. One time, he and two of his team had sneaked a peek at a Tibetan girl bathing in one of those lakes. A group of shepherds had spotted them and given chase, blades drawn. When they had failed to catch them, the shepherds had resorted to slinging stones. The disconcertingly accurate bombardment had left Fan and his cohorts no other option than to surrender. The shepherds had sized them up and finally let them go.

Feng Fan recalled that one of them had muttered in Tibetan: they'd never seen any outsiders run so quickly up here.

'You like the mountains? So that's where you grew up then?' The Captain ended Fan's reminiscences.

'No, not at all,' Feng Fan explained. 'People who grew up surrounded by mountains usually care nothing for them. They end up seeing the mountains as the things that stand between them and the world. I knew a Sherpa who scaled Everest forty-one times, but every time his team would get close to the peak, he'd stop and watch the others climb the final stretch. He just couldn't be bothered to reach to the top. And make no mistake about it; he could have easily pulled off both the northern and southern ascent in ten hours.

'There are only two places where you can really feel the true magic of the mountains: on the plains from far away, or on a peak,' Feng Fan continued. 'My home was the vastness of the Hebei Plain. In the west, I could see the Taihang Mountains, but between them and my home lay an immense expanse of perfectly flat land, without obstructions or markers. Not long after I was born, my mother carried me outside the house for the first time.

My tiny neck could barely carry my head, but even then, I turned to the west and babbled my heart out. As soon as I learned to walk, I took my first tottering steps toward those mountains. When I was a bit older, I set out one early morning and walked along the Shijiazhuang-Taiyuan Railway. I walked until noon when my grumbling stomach made me turn back, yet the mountains still seemed endlessly far away. In school, I rode my bicycle toward the mountains, but no matter how fast I pedalled, the mountains seemed to withdraw just as quickly. In the end, it never felt as if I had gotten even an inch closer to them. Many years later, distant mountains would again become a symbol of my life. Like so many things in life that we can clearly see but never reach, a dream crystallized in the distance.'

'I visited there once, ' the Captain noted, shaking his head. 'The mountains are very barren, covered with nothing but scattered stones and wild grasses. You were doomed to be disappointed. '

'I wasn't. You and I feel very differently about these things. For me, all I saw was the mountain, and all I wanted was to climb it. I really wasn't looking for anything on the mountain. When I climbed those mountains for the first time and I saw the plain stretch out below me, I felt like I had been reborn.' As Feng Fan finished, he realized that the Captain was paying no heed to his words; instead, he was looking to the sky, staring at the scattered stars.

'There, ' the Captain said, pointing skyward with his pipe. 'There shouldn't be a star there. '

But there was a star. It was faint, barely visible.

'Are you sure? ' Fan turned his gaze from the sky to the Captain. 'Hasn't GPS done away with sextants? Do you really know your stars that well? '

'Of course I do, ' the Captain answered. 'It is a basic element in the craft of sailing.' Turning back to Fan, he returned to the topic at hand. 'But you were saying…'

Feng Fan nodded. 'Later at the university, I put together a mountaineering team, and we climbed a few mountains taller than twenty-three thousand feet. Our final climb was Everest. '

The Captain carefully studied Feng Fan before finally saying, 'I thought so! It really is you! I always thought you looked familiar. Did you change your name? '

'Yes, I used to be called Feng Huabei, ' he admitted.

'Some years ago, you caused quite a stir. Was what the media said about you true then? ' the Captain asked.

'The gist of it. In any case, those four climbers are certainly dead because of me, ' Fan said glumly.

Striking a match to relight his pipe, the Captain continued. 'I reckon that being the leader of a mountaineering team is not that different from being a captain: the hardest part is not learning when to fight on, but understanding when to back down. '

'But if I had backed down then, it would have been very hard to get another shot at it,' Fan immediately replied. 'Mountain climbing is a very costly undertaking, and we were just college students. It had not been easy for us to find sponsors.' He paused, taking a deep breath. 'The guides we hired had refused to go on, and so it took much longer than anticipated before we set up the first base camp. The forecast predicted a storm, but we studied the images and maps, and came to the conclusion that we still had at least twenty hours before it would hit. By then, our team had already set up the second camp at twenty-six thousand feet, and so we thought that we could make it to the peak if we set out immediately. You tell me, how could we have backed down then? I never even contemplated giving up, and so continued our ascent. '

'That star is getting brighter, ' the Captain said, looking up again.

'Of course it is. The sky is getting darker, ' Fan retorted dismissively.

'This seems different,' the Captain noted. 'But go on. '

'You probably know what happened next: when the storm hit, we were close to the so-called 'Chinese Ladder' of the Second Step on a vertical rock face that rises from twenty-eight thousand five hundred feet. The peak was almost within reach, and save for a strand of cloud rising from the other side of the summit, the sky was still perfectly blue. I can still clearly remember thinking that the peak of Everest looked like a knife's edge cutting open the sky, drawing forth its billowing, pale blood. ' Fan paused at the memory before returning to his tale. 'It only took a few moments before we lost all visibility; when the storm hit us out of nowhere, it whipped up the snow. Everything was shrouded in an impenetrable white that left behind only murky darkness. In a heart-stopping instant, I felt the other four members of my team blown off the cliff. They were hanging by my rope, and all I was clinging to was my ice axe wedged into a crack in the wall. It simply could not have held the weight of five people. I acted on instinct, cutting the buckle strap that held the rope. I let them fall. ' He paused again, swallowing hard. 'They still haven't found the remains of two of them. '

'So four died instead of all five, ' the Captain noted dryly.

'Yes, I acted according to the mountaineering safety guidelines. Even so, it remains my cross to bear.' Fan paused again, this time distracted by something other than his memories. 'You're right. There's something strange about that star. It's definitely getting brighter. '

'Never mind,' the Captain said. 'Does your current...' he paused, pursing his lips, '... shall we say condition, have anything to do with what happened then? '

'Do I have to spell it out? You must remember the overwhelming condemnations and the crushing contempt the media heaped on me back then, ' Fan reminded him. 'They said I acted irresponsibly, that I was a selfish coward, that I sacrificed my four companions for my own life. ' He was clearly still pained. 'I thought I could at least clear myself of that last accusation, so I donned my climbing gear and put on my mountain goggles. Ready for a climb, I went to my university's library and scaled a pipe straight up to its roof. I was just about to jump when I heard the voice of one of my teachers; I hadn't noticed him come up to the roof behind me. He asked me if I was really willing to let myself off the hook that easily, if I was just trying to avoid the much harsher punishment awaiting me. When I asked what he meant, he told me that would entail a life as far away as possible from mountains. To never again see a mountain – would that not be a harsher punishment?

'So I didn't jump. Of course, I attracted even more ridicule, but I knew that what my teacher had told me was right: this would be worse than death for me. To me, mountain climbing had been my life. It was the only reason I studied geology. To now live a life, eternally separated from the object of my passion, tormented by my own conscience – it felt just. That was the reason why I applied for this job after graduation, why I became the geological engineer of the *Bluewater*. On the ocean,' he said with a sigh, 'I'm as far as I can be from mountains. '

The Captain stared blankly for a long moment, at a loss for words. Finally, he came to the conclusion that it would probably be best to just leave it be. As if on cue, something in the sky above abruptly forced a change of topic. 'Take another look at that star, ' he said, an edge in his voice.

'Heavens! ' Fan exclaimed as he, too, looked up. 'It's turning into something! '

The star was no longer a dot but now a small, yet rapidly expanding, disc. In the blink of an eye, it turned into a striking sphere in the sky, glowing bluishly.

A flurry of rapidly approaching footsteps drew their gazes back down to deck. It was the First Mate, wearing his headpiece, running straight towards them.

He was barely within earshot when he breathlessly called to the Captain, 'We have just received message: an alien ship is approaching Earth! We can clearly see it from our position on the equator! Look, there it is! '

The three of them looked up, only to see that that small sphere had continued its rapid expansion. It had already ballooned to the size of the Moon.

'All stations have ceased their regular broadcasts and are now reporting on it! ' the First Mate rattled on. 'The object had been spotted earlier, but they have just now confirmed its true nature. It is not responding to any of our attempts to hail it, but its trajectory shows that it is being propelled by some immense force, and it is hurtling straight toward Earth! They say it is as big as the Moon!'

Above them, the alien sphere was no longer the size of the Moon; it was now easily ten times as big, looming large in the heavens. It appeared much closer than the Moon. With a finger firmly on his earpiece, the First Mate continued, 'They say that it has stopped. It is now in geosynchronous orbit twenty-two thousand miles above the Earth. It has become a geostationary satellite.'

'A geostationary satellite? Are you saying it is just going to hang above us?' the Captain shouted.

'It is! Over the equator, right above us!' the First Mate confirmed.

Feng Fan stared at this huge sphere in the sky; it seemed almost transparent, suffused with an unfathomable blue light. Looking at it left Fan with the strange impression of staring at the sea. A feeling of profound mystery, of intense anticipation, would grip him every time the sampling probe was raised from the seabed. Looking up now, he experienced a very similar sensation. It was as if some long-forgotten remnant of the Earth's oceans from time immemorial had returned to the surface.

'Look, the ocean!' the Captain shouted, wildly thrusting his pipe aftward. 'What is happening to the ocean?' He was the first to break free from the hypnotic power the giant sphere seemed to exert over all of them.

Where he pointed, the ocean's horizon had begun to bend, curving upward like a sine wave. This huge swell of rising water rapidly grew taller and taller. It was as if a titanic, albeit invisible hand was reaching down from space to scoop up the ocean.

'It's the spaceship's mass! Its gravity is pulling at the ocean!' Feng Fan exclaimed, rather surprised that he still had enough of his wits about him to understand what was happening. The ship's mass was probably equivalent to that of the Moon, but it was ten times closer! It was fortunate that the ship had entered a geosynchronous orbit. The water it was pulling would be held in one spot. If the spaceship moved, it would send a gravitational tidal wave across the world so large that it could easily ravage continents and destroy cities.

This colossal wave had by now swelled up to the heavens, rising as a flat-topped cone. Its mass shone with the blue glow of the ship above, even as its edges burned with the bright crimson fire of the setting Sun, now hidden behind the towering waves. The stark, cold air at the cone's summit chilled the froth, sending forth streams of misty clouds that quickly bled away in the night sky, as if the dark heavens had been cut open. Feng Fan felt his heart stir with memories as he took it all in. His mind drifted toward the day of the climb…

'Give me its height! ' the Captain shouted, jerking him back to the here and now.

A minute later, someone called out, 'Almost thirty thousand feet! '

Before them was the most terrifying, most awesome, and most magnificent sight humanity had ever faced. Everyone on deck stood transfixed by its spell.

'It must be destiny…' Feng Fan mumbled, mesmerized more than most by its grandeur.

'What did you say? ' the Captain demanded loudly, his eyes still fixed on the rising waters.

'I said that this must be destiny, ' Fan repeated.

It was – it had to be – destiny. He had gone to sea to avoid mountains, to put as much distance between them and him as humanly possible; and now he was in the shadow of a mountain that eclipsed even Everest by almost a thousand feet. It was the world's tallest mountain.

'Port five! Full ahead! We need to get out of here now! ' the Captain commanded the First Mate.

'Out of here? Is it dangerous? ' Feng Fan asked, confused.

'The alien spaceship has already created a huge area of low pressure. Right now a gigantic cyclone is taking form. I tell you, this could be the greatest tempest the world has ever seen. If it catches the *Bluewater*, we will be ripped straight out of the water and tossed about like a leaf in a storm. I just pray we will be able to outrun it,' the Captain explained, sweat clearly visible on his brow.

Just then the First Mate signalled them all to be quiet. Covering his earpiece with one hand, he listened intently, and then said, 'Captain, the situation is much worse than that! They are now saying that the aliens have come to destroy Earth! With nothing but its enormous mass, their ship is doing much, much worse than just raising a storm; it is about to gash a hole in Earth's atmosphere! '

'Hole? Hole to where? ' the Captain asked, his eyes wide.

The First Mate explained what he had just heard over the radio. 'The spaceship's gravity will puncture the upper layers of the atmosphere. Earth's atmosphere will be like a pricked balloon, its air escaping through that puncture, right into space! All of Earth's atmosphere will disappear! '

'How long do we have? ' the Captain asked, confronted with horror after horror.

'The experts say that it will only take a week or so for the atmospheric pressure to fall to a lethal level, ' the First Mate reported mechanically, but his wild eyes betrayed his panic. 'They say that when the pressure falls to a certain point, the oceans will begin to boil. ' He continued, his voice beginning to break. 'Heavens, that would be like...' His head trembled as he heard further news. 'All of Earth's major cities have fallen into chaos. Humanity has lost all semblance of sanity. Everywhere people are rushing into hospitals and factories, pillaging all the oxygen they can get their hands on. ' His eyes continued to widen. 'Wait, now they are saying that Cape Canaveral is being overrun by a crazed mob trying to get its hands on the liquid oxygen used in the rocket fuel. ' The First Mate's spirit appeared to slump along with his body. 'Oh, it's all over! '

'A week? That doesn't leave us enough time to make it home, ' the Captain said steadily. It seemed that his composure had returned. With a quick flick of his fingers, he re-lit his pipe.

'Right, there's no time to make it home...' the First Mate echoed, his voice now emotionless.

'If that is what it's going to be, we might as well get on with it and make the best of the time we have left, ' Feng Fan noted, a sudden edge of enthusiasm in his voice. His entire body was readying to the occasion, flushed with excitement.

'And what is it that you want to do? ' the Captain asked.

'Climb a mountain, ' Fan answered with a smile.

'Climb a mountain? Climb…?' The First Mate's face suddenly twisted from puzzlement to outright shock. 'That mountain? ' He gasped, pointing at the mountain of water looming above them.

'Yes. It's now the world's tallest peak. Where there's a mountain, there will always be someone to climb it, ' Fan replied calmly.

'And how do you plan to climb it?' the First Mate asked.

'Isn't it obvious? Mountain climbing is something one does with hands and feet, so I will swim, ' Fan said with a smile.

'Are you crazy?' the First Mate shouted. 'How are you going to swim up a thirty-thousand-foot slope of water? It looks like a forty-five degree incline to me! That is going to be very different from climbing a mountain. You'll have to swim nonstop; and if you stop, even for a moment, you'll slide down the side! '

'I want to try. ' Fan would not be dissuaded.

'Let him go then,' the Captain flatly stated. 'What better time than now to embrace our passions? How far is it to the foot of that mountain? '

'About a dozen miles, ' someone answered.

'Take one of the lifeboats, ' the Captain told Feng Fan. 'Remember to take enough food and water. '

'Thank you! ' Fan expressed his heartfelt gratitude.

'It looks like today fortune smiles upon you,' the Captain said with a wry smile, giving Feng Fan a slap on the shoulder.

'I believe so, ' Fan replied. 'Captain, there is one thing I haven't yet told you: one of the four climbers on Everest was my girlfriend. A single thought flashed through my mind when I cut that rope: I don't want to die. There's still another mountain to climb, ' he said, pain and bright enthusiasm merging in his eyes.

The captain nodded. 'Go. '

'And,' the First Mate said, looking lost, 'what do we do? '

'Full speed ahead away from the coming storm. One more day to live is one more day to live, ' the Captain answered thoughtfully.

Feng Fan stood in the lifeboat, his gaze following the *Bluewater* as it sailed into the distance. Soon, the ship he had once seen as his home for life was well and truly out of reach.

Behind him, the mountain of water towered serenely under the blue glow of the alien sphere. Had he not seen it form, he could have easily been tricked into thinking that it had been there for millions of years. The ocean was very calm, its flat surface unruffled by waves. Feng Fan, however, could feel a breeze brush his face; it was weak, but it was blowing toward the looming waters. Raising the lifeboat's sail, he began his journey to the mountain. The wind soon picked up, and his vessel's sail filled in its wake. The lifeboat's prow now cut the ocean's surface like a knife as it sped toward Fan's goal.

In the end, the twelve-mile journey took no longer than forty minutes. As soon as Feng Fan began to feel the hull of his boat climb the slope of water, he leapt off the side of his vessel into the shining blue waters that were aglow with the light of the alien vessel above.

A few strokes later, he became the first person to swim a mountainside.

From where he was now, he could no longer see the summit. Lifting his head out of the water, all he saw was an unending expanse of sloping water, a forty-five degree incline. He could almost imagine a titan beyond the horizon, lifting the ocean like a vast, watery blanket.

Feng Fan began to swim the breaststroke, conserving as much energy as possible. The First Mate's warning was still fresh in his mind. A quick calculation told him that it would be about eight miles to the summit. On level water, his endurance would have allowed him to easily cover the distance, but here he would have to deal with the slope. If he stopped moving upward, he would slip down. That alone would make reaching the summit almost impossible. It did not matter; the very act of even attempting to climb this watery Everest was a greater achievement than he had ever dared to hope for in all of his mountaineering dreams.

But then, Fan became aware of some odd sensations. He felt the angle of the slope increasing, his body gradually inclining more. However, swimming up seemed to demand no additional effort. Looking back, he could see the lifeboat that he had abandoned at the mountain's foot. Before leaving the vessel, he had lowered its sail, yet it remained floating on the slope, strangely stationary. Fan decided to try something.

He ceased his strokes and began to carefully observe his surroundings. He was not sliding. Quite to the contrary, he was floating on the slope as if it did not exist at all! Fan slapped his forehead as he cursed his and the First Mate's foolishness: if the ocean's water on the slope did not flow downward, why would a person? Or a boat, for that matter?

The gravitational pull down the incline was being neutralized by the giant sphere's mass. The further up he climbed, the less he would feel of Earth's gravity. This meant that the slope's angle would not matter one bit. As far as gravity was concerned, there was neither a watery slope nor a mountain in the ocean. The forces acting on him would be no different from those on the level ocean.

He knew now this mountain would be his.

He continued to swim upward. As he climbed, he felt his strokes gradually become less and less exerting. In large part, this was due to his body growing lighter, making it easier and easier to come up for air. Around him, Fan could see another sign of the reduced gravity: the higher he got, the slower the ocean's spray fell. This phenomenon was mirrored in the undulations and movements of the waves. They, too, grew ever slower the higher he swam. The harshness of the open sea had all but left them, leaving the waves softer and gentler than normal gravity would ever allow.

It was by no means calm, however. The wind was picking up, and bands of waves had begun to rise on the watery slope. Freed from much of Earth's gravity, these billows rose to considerable heights. However, they did not roll up the slope as full-bodied waves, but as thin slices of water that twisted in on themselves as they gently collapsed. In a strange way, they reminded

Fan of exquisitely thin wood shavings sliced from the ocean by an invisible planer. The waves did nothing to hinder his progress. In fact, it was quite the opposite; sweeping toward the summit, they actually pushed him along as he continued his climbing swim.

As the pull of gravity grew weaker, even stranger things happened: instead of pushing him, Fan was now being gently thrown along by the waves. In the blink of an eye, he felt himself leaving the water and flying over the ocean's surface, only to be caught by another wave a moment later, and then he was up in the air again. The gentle yet powerful hands of the ocean carried him along, rapidly passing him upward and onward. He soon discovered that under these strange conditions, the butterfly stroke was best suited to expediting his already rapid ascent.

Around him, the wind had picked up even more strength. Gravity's grip on Feng Fan, on the other hand, was becoming weaker and weaker. The waves up here easily reached thirty feet in height, before falling in slow motion. These huge billows were also gentler than they had ever been, softly rolling into one another; they did not even make a sound as they fell. The only remaining noise was the howling of winds.

Fan's ever-lighter body was leaping from wave crest to crest. As he jumped again, he suddenly realized that he was spending more time in midair than he was in the water. Up here, he could hardly tell if he was swimming or floating. Time and again, the thin waves would come to completely envelope him, rolling him into a tunnel formed by the slowly tumbling waters. The gently roiling roof of these tunnels glowed in a blue light. Through the thin, watery roof he could see the light's source – the giant alien sphere hanging in the sky. The wave tunnel distorted the ship's form; to Feng Fan, as though he was seeing it through teary eyes.

He glanced at the waterproof watch he wore on his left wrist. He had only been climbing for an hour, and at this hope-defying speed, it would only take another hour for him to reach the summit.

Fan thought of the *Bluewater*. Considering the current wind speeds, the tempest was only moments away from unleashing its fury. There was no way that the ship would be able to outrun the coming cyclone. In a flash, it occurred to Fan that the Captain had made a grave mistake: he should have turned the *Bluewater* straight toward the water mountain. Since gravity exerted no pull down the slope, the ship could have sailed up to the peak just as easily as it sailed the level ocean, and the peak would be at the eye of the storm – safe and calm! No sooner had he realized this than he pulled the walkie-talkie from his life jacket. He tried to reach her, but the *Bluewater* did not respond.

By now, Feng Fan had mastered the skill of leaping from wave crest to crest. He had been climbing like this for twenty minutes, making it two-thirds of the way to the top. From here, the perfectly round summit already seemed within reach. It glittered in the softly glowing light of the alien spaceship above. To Fan, the summit looked like an alien world, waiting for him. At that moment, the whistling of the wind suddenly turned into a sharp howl. This terrifying noise came from all directions, accompanied by a sudden increase in the wind's strength. Fifty-foot waves – even one hundred-foot waves – thin as sheets, rose high; but they never fell, torn apart by the cyclone's gale in midair. Looking up, Feng Fan could see that the slope above him was covered in the spray of broken wave crests dancing a crazed, wind-whipped dance over the ocean's surface. Illuminated by the glow of the alien sphere, the chaotic splashes shone with dazzling white light.

Finally, Feng Fan made his last leap. A thin, hundred-foot wave carried him into the air. It was torn to slivers by the powerful wind the moment he left its crest, and he found himself falling toward a band of waves slowly rolling in front of him. The waves looked like giant, transparent wings slowly unfurling to embrace him. Just as Fan's outstretched hands reached the waves, they shattered into white mist, their glittering crystal film ripped apart by the violent winds. A strange noise that sounded disturbingly like laughter accompanied the bizarre spectacle. It was also the very moment that Feng Fan stopped falling; his body was now light enough to float. The manically twisting ocean below slowly began to grow more distant as he was thrown into the air like a feather in a hurricane.

Almost weightless, Fan was turned and swirled in the twisting air. Dizzy, he felt as if the glowing alien sphere was spiraling around him. When he was finally able to steady himself, he realized with a start that he was actually swirling through the air above the summit of the water mountain!

From up here, the bands of giant waves rolling up the mountain looked like nothing more than long lines. Spiraling toward the peak, they made the mountain look like a titanic watery whirlwind. Feng Fan felt the circles he was making above the peak grow smaller and smaller, while his speed accelerated. He was being carried directly into the heart of the cyclone.

The moment Fan arrived at the exact eye of the storm, he felt the wind suddenly weaken. The invisible hand of air that had been holding him suddenly let go, and he fell toward the water mountain, straight into the faint blue glow of the summit.

He plummeted deep into the mountain before he felt himself floating upward again. He was surrounded by darkness, and in a matter of mere moments, the fear of drowning beset him. With mounting panic, Fan suddenly realized that he was in mortal peril: the last breath he had gulped before he fell had been at thirty thousand feet! At that height, he would have hardly breathed in any oxygen at all, and in the minimal gravity here, he would only rise very slowly. Even if he swam up with all his strength, he feared that the air in his lungs would not be enough to carry him back to the surface.

Feng Fan was gripped by an eerie sense of *deja vu*. He felt himself returned to Everest, completely in the dark, enshrouded by the swirling snow of the storm, utterly overwhelmed by mortal fear. Within this darkest moment, Fan found a light in the black; several silvery spheres were floating upward next to him. The largest of these spheres was about three feet in diameter. Looking at them, he suddenly realized that they were air bubbles! The weak gravity had allowed giant bubbles of oxygen to form in the ocean. With all the strength he could muster, he thrust himself at the largest bubble. No sooner had his head pierced the silvery shell than he was able to draw breath again. As he slowly recovered from the dizziness oxygen deprivation had induced, Fan found himself enveloped by the air bubble. He was in a space of air completely surrounded by water, and looking up, he could see the ripple of the surface shimmer through the top of his bubble. Floating upward, he noticed a sudden drop in the water pressure, causing his bubble to rapidly expand. As the bubble grew, Feng Fan could not shake the impression that he was caught in a crystalline party balloon, floating into the sky.

The blue shimmer of the waves above slowly grew brighter and brighter, until finally their glare was so strong that he was forced to avert his gaze. Just then, the bubble burst with a soft pop. Fan had reached the surface; and he was going further, the weak gravity launching him a good three feet into the air. His drop back to the surface was not a sudden but a gentle descent.

As he fell, Feng Fan noticed countless beautiful watery orbs gently dropping alongside him. These orbs greatly varied in size, the largest being roughly the size of a soccer ball. All of them shone and glittered with the blue light from the gigantic sphere above. As Fan looked more closely, he saw that they, in fact, contained layers upon layers, which made them sparkle with crystal light. These orbs were splashes of water that had been cast from the ocean as he had broken its surface. The low gravity had allowed their surface tension complete freedom to shape themselves like this. Reaching out, Fan touched one of the orbs. The sphere shattered with a strange metallic ring that was wholly unlike any sound he had ever imagined water producing.

Except for the orbs, the summit of the water mountain was altogether tranquil, the waves rushing in from all sides merging into nothing but broken swell. This was, beyond all doubt, the eye of the storm, the only place of quiet in a chaotic world. The calm was offset by a tremendous background howl – the screaming of the cyclone. Looking into the distance, Feng Fan found himself, along with the entire mountain of water, to be in a massive 'well'. The walls of this well were made of the swirling, frothing waters of the cyclone. These impenetrable masses of water and wind slowly turned around the water mountain. Looking upward, Fan saw that they appeared to reach straight into space. Shining through the mouth of the well was the alien sphere. Like a giant lamp hanging in space, its light illuminated all within the well. Gazing up, Fan could see strange clouds forming around it. They looked like fibers, trailing a loose net around the alien vessel. These strands of cloud shone brightly, appearing to glow from within. Fan could only guess that they were made of ice crystals formed by the Earth's atmosphere, escaping into space. Even though they appeared to surround the spaceship, there actually had to be a good twenty thousand miles between the web and the blue sphere. If his guess was right, the atmosphere had already begun to leak and the mouth of this giant, swirling well was nothing other than the fatal hole in Earth's shell.

It doesn't matter, Fan thought to himself. I have reached the summit.

Chapter 2
Words on the Mountaintop

Suddenly, the all-pervading, ambient light changed. Flickering, it began to dim. Looking up again, Feng Fan saw that the alien sphere's blue light had disappeared. It suddenly occurred to him what that light had been. It was the background light of an empty display; the entire body of that huge alien sphere was one gigantic screen. Just then, this massive screen began to display an image. It was a picture taken from a great height, and it revealed a person floating in the ocean, his face turned skyward. That person was Feng Fan. Thirty seconds ticked past, then the image disappeared. Fan had immediately understood its meaning; the aliens had shown that they could see him. It made Fan feel like he was truly standing on the roof of the world.

Two lines of text appeared on the screen. They contained all the alphabets and characters Fan had ever seen. Recognizing the words for 'English', 'Chinese' and 'Japanese', he surmised that they must spell out the names of all the world's languages. He also spotted a dark frame quickly moving between the different words. It all appeared rather familiar. His guess was soon proven right, as he discovered that this frame actually did follow his gaze! He fixed his eyes on the characters for 'Chinese', causing the dark frame to stop over them. He blinked once, but there was no response.

Maybe it needed a double-click, Fan thought, blinking twice. The dark frame flickered, and the giant sphere's language menu closed. In its stead, a huge word appeared in Chinese.

>> Hello!

'Hello!!' Fan shouted his response into the sky. 'Can you hear me?'

>> We can hear you; there is no need to shout. We could hear the wings of a mosquito anywhere on Earth. We picked up the electromagnetic waves leaking from your planet and so learned your languages. We want to have a little chat with you, the text on the sphere now read.

'Where do you come from?' Fan asked, his voice now considerably lower.

A picture appeared on the surface of the giant sphere, showing a dense cluster of black dots. These dots were connected by a complicated web of lines. The sheer intricacy of the picture made Fan's head swim. It obviously was some sort of star map. Sure enough, one of these dots began to glow in a silver light, growing brighter and brighter. Unfortunately, Feng Fan could not really make heads or tails of it, but he was confident that it had already been recorded elsewhere. Earth's astronomers would be able to understand it. The sphere soon displayed characters again, but the star map did not disappear. Instead, it remained in the background, almost like some sort of alien desktop.

>> We raised a mountain. You came and climbed it.

'Mountain climbing is my passion,' Fan answered.

>> It is not a question of passion; we must climb mountains.

'Why?' Fan asked. 'Does your world have many mountains?' He realized that this was hardly humanity's most pressing issue, but he wanted to know. Everyone he knew considered mountaineering an exercise in foolishness, so he might as well talk about it with aliens. After all, they had just professed that they were prone to climb; and after all, he had gotten this far all by himself.

>> There are mountains everywhere, but we do not climb as you do.

Feng Fan could not tell if this was meant as a concrete description or an abstract analogy. He had no choice but to express his ignorance. 'So you have lots of mountains where you come from?' It was more question than statement.

>> We were surrounded by a mountain. This mountain confined us, and we needed to dig to climb it.

This answer did nothing to alleviate Fan's confusion. For a long time he remained silent, contemplating what the aliens were trying to tell him.

Then they continued.

Chapter 3
Bubble World

>> Our world is a very simple place. It is a spherical space, somewhat more than three thousand five hundred miles in diameter, according to your units of measurement. This space is completely surrounded by layers of rock. No matter what direction one chooses to travel, the journey will always end with a solid wall of rock.

>> Naturally, this shaped our first model of the cosmos: we assumed that the universe was made of two parts. The first was the three-thousand-five-hundred-mile space in which we lived; the second was the surrounding layers of rock. We believed the rock stretched endlessly in all directions. Therefore, we saw our world as a hollow bubble in this solid universe, and so we gave our world the name 'Bubble World'. We call this cosmology the Solid Universe Theory. Of course, this theory did not deny the possibility of other bubbles existing in these infinite layers of rock. However, it gave no indication how close or far those other bubbles might be. That became the impetus for our later journeys of exploration.

'But, infinite layers of rock cannot possibly exist; they would collapse under their own gravity,' Feng Fan pointed out.

>> Back then we knew nothing of gravitational forces. There was no gravity inside the Bubble World, and so we lived our lives without ever

experiencing its pull. We only really came to understand the existence of gravity many thousands of years later.

'So these bubbles were the planets of your solid universe? Very interesting,' Fan commented. 'Density in our universe is entirely the inverse. Your universe must be an almost exact negative of the real universe.'

>> The real universe? You are ignorantly considering the universe only as you know it right now. You have no idea what the real universe is like, and neither do we.

Chastened, Fan decided to continue his line of enquiry. 'Was there light, air and water in your world?'

>> No, none, and we needed none of them. Our world was made entirely of solids. There were no gases or liquids.

'No gases or liquids. How did you survive?' Fan asked.

>> We are a mechanical life form. Our muscles and bones are made of metals; our brains are like highly integrated chips, and electricity and magnetism are our blood. We ate the radioactive rocks of our world's core, and they provided us with the energy we needed to survive. We were not created, but evolved naturally from extremely simple, single-celled mechanical life forms when – by pure chance – the radioactive energies formed P-N junctions in the rocks. Instead of your use of fire, our earliest ancestors discovered the use of electro-magnetism. In fact, we never found fire in our world.

'It must have been very dark there then,' Fan remarked.

>> Actually, there was some light. It was generated by the radioactive activity within our world's walls. Those walls were our sky. That 'sky's' light was very weak, and it constantly shifted as the radioactivity fluctuated. Yet it led us to evolve eyes.

>> Since our world's core lacked gravity, we did not build walls. Instead, our cities floated in the dim, empty space that was our world. They were about as big as your cities, and seen from afar, they would have looked to you like glowing clouds.

>> The evolutionary process of mechanical life is much slower than that

of carbon-based life, but in the end we reached the same ends by different means; and so one day we, too, came to contemplate our universe.

'That sounds like it must have felt cramped. Was it like that for you?' Fan asked, mulling over the sphere's strange revelations.

>> 'Cramped' ... ... That is a new word. We came to experience an intense desire for more space, much stronger than any similar longing that might affect your species. Our first journeys of exploration into the rock layers began in earliest antiquity. Exploration for us meant tunnelling into the walls in an attempt to find other bubbles in our solid universe. We had spun many fascinatingly alluring myths around these distant spaces, and almost all of our literature dealt with the fantasy of other bubbles. Soon, however, exploration was outlawed, forbidden on pain of death by short-circuiting.

'Outlawed? By your church?' Fan assumed.

>> No, we have no church. A civilization that cannot see the sun and stars will be without religion. There was a very practical reason for our Senate to forbid tunnelling: we were not blessed with the near infinite space you have at your disposal. Our existence was limited to that 3,500-mile bubble. All the debris that the tunnelling produced ended up within this space. As we believed in infinite layers of rock stretching in all directions, those tunnels could have become very long indeed, long enough even to fill the entire bubble space at the core of our world with rubble! To put it another way: we would have transformed the empty sphere in the core of our world into a very long tunnel.

'There could have been a solution to the problem; just move the newly mined rubble into the already excavated space behind the diggers,' Fan suggested. 'Then you would have only lost the space needed by the explorers to sustain themselves and dig.'

>>Indeed, later explorers used the very method you just described. In fact, the explorers would only use a small bubble with just enough space for them and their mission. We came to call these missions 'bubble ships'. But even so, every mission meant a bubble ship-sized pile of debris in our core space, and we would have to wait for the ship to return before we could return those

rocks into the wall. If the bubble ship failed to return, this small pile would mean another small piece of space lost to us forever. Back then we felt as if the bubble ship had stolen that piece of space. We therefore came to call our explorers by another name – Space Thieves.

>> In our claustrophobic world, every inch of space was treasured, and ages later an all-too-large area of our world had been lost in the wake of the far-too-many bubble ships that had failed to return. It was because of this loss of space that bubble ship exploration was outlawed in antiquity. Even without legal censure, life in the bubble ships was fraught with hardships and dangers beyond imagining. A bubble ship was usually made of a number of diggers and a navigator. At the time, we did not yet have mining machinery and so had to rely on manual excavation, comparable to rowing on your early vessels. These early explorers had to dig tirelessly with the simplest of tools, pushing their bubble ship through the layers of rock at a painfully slow pace. Working like machines in those tiny bubbles surrounded by solid rock – confined in every way, in search of an elusive dream – doubtlessly proves an incredible strength of spirit.

>> As the bubble ships tended to return along the way they had come, the journey back was usually a good deal easier. The rock in their path would have already been loosened. Even so, a gambler's hunger for discovery often led the ships to go well beyond the point of safe return. These unfortunate explorers would run out of strength and supplies, and remain stranded mid-return, their bubble ship becoming their tomb. Despite all of this, and even though the extent of our exploratory efforts was greatly scaled back, our Bubble World never gave up on the dream of finding other worlds.

Chapter 4
Redshift

>> One day, in the year 33,281 of the Bubble Era – this is expressed in your chronological terms, as our world's reckoning of time would be too alien

for you to understand – a tiny hole began to open in the rocky sky of our world. A small pile of rocks drifted out of this hole, their weak radioactive light sparkling like stars. A unit of soldiers was immediately dispatched to fly to this crack and investigate. Now keep in mind that there is no gravity in the Bubble World. They discovered an explorer's bubble ship that had returned. This ship had set out eight years ago, and the world had long given up hope that it would ever return. The ship's name was the *Needle's Point*, and it had dug one hundred and twenty-five miles deep into the rock. No other ship had ever made it as far and returned.

>> The *Needle's Point* had set out with a crew of twenty, but when it returned, only a single scientist remained. Let us call him Copernicus. He had eaten the rest of the crew, including the captain. In ancient times, this means of sustenance had, in fact, proven to be the most efficient method for explorers going into the deep layers of rock.

>> For breaking the strict laws against bubble ship exploration and for cannibalism, Copernicus was sentenced to death in the capital city. On the day the sentence was to be carried out, more than a hundred thousand gathered in the central square of the capital to witness his execution. Just as they were waiting for the awesome spectacle of Copernicus being short-circuited in a beautiful shower of sparks, a group of scientists floated onto the square. They were from the World Academy of Science, and they had come to announce a groundbreaking discovery: researchers had discovered something in the density of the rock samples the *Needle's Point* had retrieved. To their great surprise, the data indicated that the rock density had steadily decreased the further the ship had dug!

'Your world had no gravity. How did you ever measure density?' Fan interjected.

>> We used inertia; it's somewhat more complicated than your methods. No matter, in those early days our scientists thought that the *Needle's Point* had merely chanced upon an uneven layer of rock. However, in the following century, legions of bubble ships journeyed forth in all directions, penetrating deeper than the *Needle's Point* ever had, and they, too, returned with rock

samples. What they found was incredible: density decreased in all directions, and did so consistently! The Solid Universe Theory that had reigned supreme in the Bubble World for twenty millennia was shaken to its core. If the density of the Bubble World continually decreased as one dug outward, then it stood to reason that it would eventually reach zero. Using the gathered data, our scientists were easily able to calculate that this would happen at about twenty thousand miles.

'Oh, that sounds very much like how Hubble used the redshift!' Fan exclaimed, recognizing the concept.

>> It is indeed very similar. Since you could not conceive of the redshift velocity exceeding the speed of light, you concluded that it denoted the edge of the universe; and it was very easy for our ancestors to comprehend that an area with a density of zero is open space. Thus a new model of the universe was born. In this model, it was assumed that density decreased at increasing distances from the Bubble World, eventually declining to the point of opening into a space that would then continue into infinity. This is known as the Open Universe Theory.

>> The Solid Universe Theory, however, was deeply ingrained in our culture, and its supporters dominated the discourse. Soon they found a way to salvage the Solid Universe Theory, coming to the conclusion that all the decreasing density meant was that a spherical layer of looser rock encircled the Bubble World. Were anyone to pass through this layer, they theorized, they would find no further decrease. They calculated the thickness of this loose layer to be two hundred miles. Testing this theory was, of course, not difficult; one merely needed to dig through two hundred miles of rock. It did not take long for ships to reach this distance, but the decrease of density continued unabated. So the supporters of the Solid Universe Theory declared that their previous calculations had been mistaken and that the true thickness of the layer of loose rock was three hundred miles. Ten years later, a ship crossed this distance, and again the decrease in density was shown to continue beyond it. In fact, the speed of decrease increased. The Solid Universe purists then expanded the layer of loose rock to nine hundred miles...

>> In the end, an incredible, epochal discovery forever sealed the fate of the Solid Universe Theory.

Chapter 5
Gravity

>> The bubble ship that crossed the two hundred-mile mark was called the *Saw Blade*. It was the largest exploration vessel we had ever built, outfitted with an extremely powerful excavator and an advanced life-support system. Its cutting-edge equipment enabled the ship to travel farther than anyone had ever gone before, changing the course of our history.

>>As it passed a depth – or one might say height – of two hundred miles, the mission's chief scientist – we shall call him Newton – reported an utterly baffling observation to the ship's captain: whenever the crew went to sleep floating in the middle of the bubble ship, they would wake up lying on the tunnel wall closest to the Bubble World.

>> The captain did not think it meant anything; he concluded that it was the result of homesick sleep floating and nothing more. In his mind, the crew wanted to return to the Bubble World, and so they would always find themselves floating toward home in their sleep.

>> Consider, however, that there was no air in the Bubble World, and therefore no air in the bubble ship. This meant that there were only two ways to move: either by pushing off from the wall, something that could not possibly happen while the crew was floating in the middle of the ship; or by discharging their bodies' excrement to propel themselves. Newton, however, never found any trace of that happening.

>> Even so, the captain would not put stock in Newton's claims. He should have considered otherwise, as it was this indifference that would soon leave him buried alive. On the day it happened, the crew was particularly exhausted after having completed the latest stage of the dig, and so they did not immediately move the day's debris to the back of the ship. The plan was

to move the rocks first thing after they had rested. The ship's captain joined the diggers, and they went to sleep in the centre of the ship. They all woke with a start, buried alive! In their sleep, they and the rocks had all moved toward the rear of the bubble ship, closer to the Bubble World! Newton very quickly realized that all things in the ship had a certain tendency to move toward the Bubble World. This movement was very gradual and barely noticeable under normal conditions.

'So your Newton did not need an apple to discover gravity,' Fan quipped.

>> Do you really think it was that easy? For us, the discovery of gravitation was a much more involved process than it ever could have been for your kind; it had to be, considering the environment in which we lived. When Newton discovered the directionality of attraction, he had to assume that it originated from the 3,500-mile empty space of the Bubble World; and so our early theory of gravity was marred by a rather silly assumption. We had concluded that it was vacuums that produced gravity, not mass.

'I can see how that happened. In an environment as complex as yours, it would of course be much more difficult for your Newton to figure things out than it had been for ours,' Fan said, nodding.

>> Indeed. It took our scientists half a century before they began to unravel the mystery. Only then did we begin to truly understand the nature of gravity, and soon we were able – by using instruments not too different from those you used – to measure the gravitational constant. Even so, it was a painfully slow process before the theory of gravity found widespread acceptance in our world. As it spread, however, it became the final nail in the coffin of the Solid Universe Theory.

>> Gravity did not allow for the existence of an infinite, solid universe around our bubble. The Open Universe Theory had finally triumphed, and the cosmos it described soon came to exert a powerful attraction on the inhabitants of our world.

>> Beyond the conservation of energy and mass, Bubble World physics was also bound by the law of the conservation of space. Space in the Bubble World was a sphere roughly three thousand five hundred miles in diameter.

Digging tunnels into the layers of rock did nothing to increase the amount of available space; it merely changed the shape and location of the already existing space. Furthermore, we lived in a zero-gravity environment, and so our civilization floated in space at the core of our world. We affixed nothing to the walls of our world, which would have been comparable to the ground you live on. Because of this, space was the most treasured commodity of the Bubble World. The entire history of our civilization was one long and bloody struggle for space.

>> Now, we had suddenly learned that space was quite possibly infinite. How could it not have whipped us into a frenzy? We sent forth an unprecedented number of explorers, waves upon waves of bubble ships digging forward and outward. They all did their utmost to reach that paradise of zero density that the Open Universe Theory predicted could be found beyond 19,900 miles of rock.

Chapter 6
World's Core

>> From what has been said, you should now, if you are smart enough, be able infer the true nature of our Bubble World.

'Was your world the hollow centre of a planet?' Fan gave his best guess.

>> You are correct. Our planet is about the same size as Earth; its radius measures roughly five thousand miles. Our world's core, however, is hollow. This space at its centre is approximately three thousand five hundred miles in diameter. We are the life inside that core.

>> Even after the discovery of gravity, it still took us many centuries before we finally came to understand the true nature of our world.

Chapter 7
The War of the Strata

>> After the Open Universe Theory had fully established itself, the quest for the infinite space outside became our only real concern. We no longer cared about the consumption of space inside the Bubble World. Massive piles of rock, dug out by the fleets of bubble ships, soon came to fill the core space. This debris began to drift around our cities in vast, dense clouds. It got so bad that the cities, which had been moving about at ease, were forced to remain motionless. Because had they moved, the denizens of the core would have suffered devastating downpours of stone rain. Only half of the space these rocks stole was ever recovered.

>> At the time, a World Government had come to replace our Senate. Its politicians took on the responsibility of overseeing and safeguarding the core space. They attempted to crack down harshly on the frenetic explorers, but this had very little affect. Most of the explorers' bubble ships had already dug into the deep layers of our planet.

>> The World Government soon realized that the best way to stop bubble ships would be with bubble ships. Following this logic, the government began building an armada of gigantic ships designed to intercept, attack and destroy the explorers' vessels deep within the rock. The government's ships would then retrieve the space that had been stolen. This plan naturally met with the resistance from the explorers, and so the prolonged Strata War broke out, fought in the vast battlefield of layers of rock.

'That sounds like a very interesting way to fight a war!' Fan called up at the sphere, intrigued.

>> And very brutal, even though at first the pace of the fighting was languid, at best. The excavation technology of the time only allowed our bubble ships to move at a pace of less than two miles per hour through the rock.

>> Large ships were the most highly valued asset on both sides in the Strata War. There was a simple reason for this: the larger the bubble ship, the

longer it could go without refuelling; also, the ships' offensive capabilities were in direct proportion to their size.

>> Regardless of how big they were, the ships of the Strata War were all built to have the smallest bow width possible. Again, this had a very simple reason: the slenderer the bow, the smaller the area of rock that the ship would need to dig through and the faster the ship would be able to move. As a result, almost all of the warships looked very similar when seen from the front. On the other hand, their lengths varied widely. In extreme cases, our largest ships ended up looking like very long tunnels.

>> The battlefields of the Strata War were, of course, three-dimensional, and so the combat was fought somewhat like your forces engaging in aerial warfare, even if things were a good deal more complicated for us. When a ship encountered the enemy, its first course of action was to hastily broaden its bow width. The ships did so to bring the largest possible front of weaponry to bear; in this new configuration, a ship could transform into a shape similar to that of a nail.

>> When necessary, the bow of a bubble ship could also split into multiple sections, like a claw ready to strike. This configuration would allow the ship to attack from multiple directions at once. The raw complexity of the Strata War also revealed itself in another tactic: every warship could separate at will, transforming into multiple smaller ships. Ships could also band together, quickly combining to form a single, giant ship. Whenever opposing battle groups met, the question of whether to form up or split up was an object of profound tactical analysis.

>> Interestingly enough, hindering the drive for further exploration wasn't the only effect of the Strata War. In fact, the war also spurred a technological revolution that would play a critical part in our future endeavours. Not only did it bring about the development of extremely efficient excavators, but it also led to the invention of seismoscopes. This technology could be used to communicate through the layers of rock and could also be employed as a form of radar. Powerful seismic waves were also used as weapons. The most sophisticated seismic communication devices could even transmit pictures.

>> The largest bubble battleship we ever built was called the *World-of-the-Line*. It was commissioned by the World Government. In its standard configuration, the *World-of-the-Line* was more than ninety miles long. It was just as its name suggested: a small, very elongated world, all of its own. For its crew, serving on the *World* was much like it would be for you to stand in the English-French Channel Tunnel; every few minutes a high-speed train rushed by, delivering tunnelled debris to the aft of the ship. The *World-of-the-Line* could of course break up into an armada all by itself, but for the most part it operated as a single vessel of war. Naturally, it did not always remain in its 'tunnel' configuration. In motion, its stretched hull could be bent impressively, forming a closed loop or even crossing its own path to create intricate shapes. The *World-of-the-Line* was equipped with our most advanced excavators, allowing it to travel twice as fast as ordinary bubble ships, reaching a cruising speed of up to four miles per hour. In combat, it could even manoeuvre at speeds exceeding six miles per hour! Furthermore, an extremely powerful seismoscope was installed in its hull, allowing it to pinpoint bubble ships at ranges eclipsing three hundred miles. Its seismic wave weapon had an effective range of three thousand three hundred feet, and anything and anyone within a bubble ship it targeted would be shattered to pieces or crushed. So it swept through the massive strata without ever being challenged, and destroyed countless bubble ships. Every once in a while the *World-of-the-Line* returned to the Bubble World, carrying with it its booty of space recovered from the explorers.

>> It was the devastating blows struck by the *World-of-the-Line* that finally pushed the explorer movement to the brink. It seemed the age of exploration was about to come to a sudden end.

>> Throughout the duration of the Strata War, the explorers continually found themselves outmatched. Perhaps most importantly, they were prevented from building or forming a ship longer than five miles. Any ship larger than that would be quickly detected by the seismoscopes installed on the *World-of-the-Line* and the walls of the Bubble World. Once they were spotted, destruction would be swift. And so, if exploration was to continue in

earnest, it became imperative to destroy the *World-of-the-Line*.

>> After extensive planning and preparation, the Explorer Alliance encircled and attacked the *World-of-the-Line* with over a hundred warships. Not one of the explorers' ships was longer than three miles in length. The battle ensued a thousand miles outside the Bubble World and became known as the Thousand-Mile Battle.

>> The Alliance first assembled twenty ships, combining them to form a twenty-mile-long ship, one thousand miles outside the Bubble World, daring the *World-of-the-Line* to attack. The *World* took the bait, rushing in for the kill in its tunnel configuration. Just as it was speeding toward its prey, the Alliance sprang its ambush. Over a hundred ships dug forward, simultaneously attacking the flanks of the *World-of-the-Line* in the vertical direction. The mighty ninety-mile ship was split into fifty sections. Each of these sections, however, could carry on the fight as a powerful warship in its own right. Soon, more than two hundred ships from both sides were engaged in fierce battle, tunnelling through the rock in a brutal and chaotic melee. Warships were constantly combining and separating, eventually blurring into an amorphous cloud of vessels and violence. In the final phase of the battle, the one-hundred-and-fifty-mile battlefield became honeycombed beyond recognition by the loosened rock and empty space left behind by the destroyed ships. The Thousand-Mile Battle had created an intricate three-dimensional maze, two thousand two hundred and fifty miles beneath our planet's surface.

>> The jarring rumble of vicious, tight combat reverberated all throughout this bizarre battlefield for what seemed like an eternity. Located so far from the core of the planet, gravity produced very noticeable effects on the action – effects that the explorers were far more familiar with than the government forces. In this great maze battle, it was this difference that slowly swung the battle in favour of the Explorer Alliance. In the end, their victory was decisive.

Chapter 8

Under the Ocean

>> After the battle, the Explorer Alliance gathered all the space left over by the battle into a single sphere sixty miles in diameter. In this new space, the Alliance declared its independence from the Bubble World. Despite this declaration, the Explorer Alliance continued to coordinate its efforts with the explorer movement in the Bubble World from afar. A constant stream of explorer ships left the core to join the Alliance, bringing considerable amounts of space with them. In this way, the territory of the Explorer Alliance continually grew, in effect allowing them to turn their territory into a fully stocked and equipped forward-operating base. The World Government, exhausted by the long years of war, found itself unable to stop any of this. In the end, they were left with no other option than to acknowledge the legitimacy of the explorer movement.

>> As the explorers pierced higher altitudes, they came to dig through ever more porous rock. This was not the only benefit these heights offered; the strengthening gravity also made dealing with the excavated debris that much easier, and this newly discovered environment led to success after success. In the eighth year after the end of the war, the *Helix* became the first ship to cross the remaining two thousand two hundred and fifty miles, completing the five-thousand-mile journey from the planet's centre, three thousand two hundred and fifty miles from the edge of the Bubble World.

'Wow! That was all the way to the surface! It must have been so exciting for you to see the great plains and real mountains!' Fan exclaimed, fully absorbed in the visitors' story.

>> There was nothing to be excited about; the *Helix* reached the seabed.

Fan stared up at the alien sphere in shocked silence.

>> When it happened, the images from the seismic communicator began to shake and, in a flash, ended altogether. Communication had been lost. A bubble ship tunnelling through the rock beneath it could only catch one strange sound on its seismoscopes; a noise that in the open would have

sounded like something being peeled. It was the sound of tons upon tons of water bursting into the vacuum of the *Helix*. Neither the machine life forms nor the technology of the Bubble World had ever been designed to come into contact with water. The powerful electric current produced by short-circuiting life and equipment almost instantly vaporized everything the water embraced. In the rushing waves, the crew and instruments of the *Helix* exploded like a bomb.

>> Following this event, the Alliance sent more than a dozen bubble ships to fan out in various directions, but all met a similar fate when they reached that apparently impenetrable height. Not one crew was able to vindicate their sacrifice by sending back information that could have led us to understand that mysterious peeling sound. Twice a strange crystalline waveform could be seen on the monitors, but we were completely incapable of comprehending its nature. Subsequent bubble ships attempted to scan what lay above with their seismoscopes, but their instruments produced only mangled data; the returning seismic waves indicated that what lay above was neither space nor rock.

>> These discoveries shook the Open Universe Theory to its core and academic circles began discussing the possibility of a new model. This new model stipulated that the universe was bound to a five thousand-mile radius. They came to the conclusion that the lost explorer ships had come into contact with the edge of the universe and had been sucked into oblivion.

>> The explorer movement was faced with its greatest test yet. Before the *Helix* incident, the space taken by lost explorer ships had always remained, if only in theory, recoverable. Now, however, our people were faced with the edge of the universe. The space it eagerly devoured appeared to be lost forever. Considering this, even the most steadfast explorers were shaken. Remember that in our world, deep within layers of rock, space – once lost – could never be renewed. With this in mind, the Alliance decided to send a final group of five bubble ships. As they reached an altitude of three thousand miles, these ships proceeded with extreme caution. If they were to suffer the same fate as the previous missions, it would mean the end of the explorer movement.

>> Two bubble ships were lost. A third ship, the *Stone Cerebrum*, however, made groundbreaking progress. At an altitude of three thousand miles, the *Stone Cerebrum* was slowly digging upward, every foot of rock tunneled with the utmost caution. When the ship reached the seabed, the ocean's waters did not gush through the entire ship and so did not instantly collapse the vessel, as had happened in all previous attempts. Instead, the seawater spurted through a small crack, forced into a powerful but minute stream by the immense pressure above. The *Stone Cerebrum* had been designed with a beam width of 825 feet. By the standards of the explorer ships, this was considered large, yet it turned out to be an unbelievable stroke of luck. Because of the ship's size, the rising seawater took nearly an hour before it filled the ship's entire interior. Before coming into contact with the bursting water, the ship's seismoscope had recorded the morphology of the ocean above, and numerous data and images had been successfully transmitted back to the Alliance. It was on that day that the People of the Core saw a liquid for the first time.

>> It is quite imaginable that there might have been liquid in the Bubble World in ancient times, but it would have been nothing but searing magma. Once the violent geology of our planet's formation had finally come to rest, this magma must have completely solidified. In our planet's core, nothing remained but solid matter and empty space.

>> Even so, our scientists had long since predicted the theoretical possibility of liquids, but no one had really believed that this legendary substance could actually exist in the universe. Now, however, in those transmitted images, the scientists clearly saw it with their own eyes. And what they saw left all of them in shock: shocked at the white, bursting jet, shocked at the slow rise of the water's surface, and shocked at seeing that demonic substance warp itself into any form, clinging to every surface in complete defiance of all laws of nature. They saw it ooze into even the tiniest cracks, and they witnessed how it seemed to change the very nature of rock, darkening it with but a touch, even as it seemed to make it shimmer like metal. However, what fascinated them most was that while most things disappeared into this strange substance, some shattered remains of the crew

and machinery actually came to float on its surface! There was nothing that seemed to distinguish those things that floated from those that sank. The People of the Core gave this strange liquid substance a name; they called it 'amorphous rock'.

>> From that point on, the explorers could again celebrate a long string of successes. First, engineers of the Explorer Alliance designed a so-called drainpipe. In essence, it was a six-hundred-and-fifty-foot-long, hollow, drilling pole. After it had been drilled through the final layers of rock, the drill bit of this pole could be opened like a flap valve, drawing the ocean's waters down the pipe. Another valve was attached to the bottom of the drainpipe.

>> Another bubble ship rose to an altitude of three thousand miles. Then it began drilling the drainpipe through the final layers into the seabed. Nothing could have been easier; drilling was, after all, a technology with which the People of the Core were abundantly familiar. There was another piece to the puzzle, however, and that required technology of which we had never even conceived: sealing.

>> As the Bubble World had been completely devoid of liquids or gases, sealing technology had never been necessary, or even imaginable, to the People of the Core. As a result, the valve at the bottom of the drainpipe was far from watertight. Before it was even opened, it allowed water to leak out and into the ship. This accident, however, proved to be very fortunate indeed; had the valve ever been opened fully, the power of the onrushing water would have been much greater than the spray through the rock crack encountered by the *Stone Cerebrum*. It would have burst forth in a concentrated beam of water, powerful enough to cut through everything in its path like a laser. Now, instead, the water seeped through the porous valve at a much more controllable drip. You can imagine just how fascinating it was for the crew of the bubble ship to see that thin stream of water trickling before their very eyes. This liquid was completely unknown territory to them, much as electricity had been to early humanity.

>> After carefully filling a metal container with the strange liquid, the

bubble ship retreated to the lower layers, leaving the drainpipe buried in the rocks. As the ship descended, the explorers took great precautions, keeping their strange sample as still and safe as possible in its container. Carefully observing it, they soon made their first new discovery: the amorphous rock was actually transparent! When they had first seen the seawater shoot through the cracked rock, it had naturally been heavily laden with sediment and mud. The People of the Core had accepted this as the amorphous rock's natural state. Following this discovery, the ship continued to descend, and as it did, the temperature on board began to rise.

>> It was with a deep fear that the explorers suddenly came face to face with the most horrible realization yet: the amorphous rock was alive! Stirring, its surface had begun to roil with anger, its terrifying form now covered with countless bursting bubbles. But this monster's surging life force seemed to consume its very being, its body dissolving into a ghostly white shadow. Once all the amorphous rock in the container had transformed into this new phantasmal state, the explorers began to feel a strange sensation grip their bodies. Within moments, the sparks of shorting circuits erupted from within their bodies, ending their lives in agonizing fireworks.

>> Seismic waves transmitted this terrible spectacle live to the Explorer Alliance, right up until the monitors, too, fell silent. A quickly dispatched relief ship suffered the same fate. As soon as it made contact with the doomed vessels, its crew also erupted into terrible sparks, dying in pain. It seemed as if the amorphous rock had become a spectre of death, looming over all of space. The scientists, however, noticed that the second series of short circuits was nowhere as violent as the first spectacular displays of death. This led them to a conclusion: as the area of space increased, the density of that amorphous spectre of death decreased.

>> It took many lives and countless horrible deaths, but in the end the People of the Core finally discovered another state of being they had never encountered before: gas.

Chapter 9
To the Stars

>> These momentous discoveries even moved the World Government, and they reunited with their old enemies, the Explorer Alliance. The Bubble World now also committed its resources to the cause, heralding a period of intense exploration marked by rapid progress. The final breakthrough was within reach.

>> Even though we came to an ever greater understanding of water vapour, we still lacked the sealing technology that would have allowed the core's scientists to protect our people and machinery from harm. Nonetheless, we had come to learn that at an altitude above two thousand eight hundred miles, the amorphous rock remained dead and inert, unable to boil. To study the strange new states, the World Government and the Explorer Alliance constructed a laboratory at an altitude of two thousand nine hundred miles. They equipped this facility with a permanent drainpipe. Here experts began to study the amorphous rock in earnest.

'Only then could you begin to undertake the work of Archimedes,' Fan chimed in.

>> You are quite correct, but you should not forget that our earliest forbears had already done the work of Faraday.

>> As a byproduct of their work in the Laboratory for Amorphous Rock Research, our scientists came to discover water pressure and buoyancy. They also managed to develop and perfect the sealant technology necessary to deal with liquids. Now we finally understood that sealing the amorphous rock would be an incredibly simple undertaking, much simpler in fact than drilling through layers of rock. All that would be required was a sufficiently sealed and pressure-resistant vessel. Without excavators, this ship would be able to rise at speeds that seemed almost incomprehensible to the People of the Core.

'You built a Bubble World rocket,' Fan noted with a smile.

>> More of a torpedo, really. This torpedo was a metallic, pressure-

resistant, egg-shaped container with no drive or propeller whatsoever. It was designed for a crew of one. We shall call this pioneer 'Gagarin'. The torpedo's launch pad was set up in a spacious hall excavated at an altitude of three thousand miles. One hour before the launch, Gagarin entered the torpedo, and the entire vessel was hermetically sealed. After all instruments and life-support systems had been checked and determined to be functional, an automatic excavator began digging its way through the mere thirty feet of rock separating the launch hall from the seabed above. With a mighty roar, the ceiling collapsed under the pressure of the amorphous rock. The torpedo was immediately and completely submerged in a sea of liquid. As the chaos began to subside, Gagarin could finally catch a glimpse of the outside world through his transparent steel-rock porthole. With a start, he realized that the launch pad's two searchlights were casting beams of light through the amorphous rock. In the Bubble World, which lacked air, light could not scatter and emit beams. This was the first time any of us had ever seen light this way. Just then seismic waves communicated the launch order, and Gagarin pulled the release lever.

>> The anchor hinges holding the bottom of the torpedo to the rock sprang open, and the torpedo slowly began to rise from the seabed. Engulfed by the amorphous rock, it soon began to accelerate, floating upward.

>> Given the pressure at the seabed level, it was very easy for our scientists to calculate that roughly six miles of amorphous rock covered the ocean's floor. If nothing unexpected happened, the torpedo would float to the surface in roughly fifteen minutes. What it would encounter there, no one could know.

>> The torpedo shot up unimpeded. Through his porthole, Gagarin could see nothing but fathomless darkness. Only the occasional glimpse of dust zipping past in the lights outside his porthole gave him any indication of how rapidly he was ascending.

>> All too soon panic began to well in Gagarin's heart. He had lived all his life in a solid world. As he now entered, for the first time, a space filled with amorphous rock, a feeling of utterly helpless emptiness threatened to drown

the very core of his being. Fifteen minutes seemed to stretch into infinity as Gagarin did his best to focus on the hundred thousand years of exploration that had led to this moment...

>> And just as his spirit was about to break, his torpedo broke the surface of our planet's ocean.

>> The inertia of the ascent shot the torpedo a good thirty feet above the water's surface, before it came crashing back down toward the sea. Looking through his porthole as he fell, Gagarin could see the boundless amorphous rock, stretching into forever, shimmering with strange sparkles. But he had no time to see where the light was coming from; the torpedo slammed heavily into the ocean with a great splash, sending amorphous rock splattering in all directions.

>> The torpedo came to rest, floating on the ocean's surface like a boat, gently rocking with the waves.

>> Gagarin carefully opened the torpedo's hatch and slowly raised himself out of the vessel. He immediately felt the gust of the ocean breeze, and, after a few perplexed moments, he realized that it was gas. Trembles of fear shook his body as he recalled a flow of water vapour he had once seen through a steel-rock pipe in the laboratory. Who could have ever foreseen that there could be this much gas anywhere in the universe? Gagarin soon understood that this gas was very different from the gas produced by boiling amorphous rock. Unlike the latter, it did not cause his body to short circuit.

>> In his memoirs he later wrote the following description of these events:

>> I felt the gentle touch of a giant, invisible hand brush by my body. It seemed to have reached down from a vast, boundless, and completely unknown place; and that place was now before me, transforming me into something wholly new.

>> Gagarin lifted his head and then and there he finally embraced the reward of one hundred thousand years of our civilization's exploration: he saw the magnificent, sparkling wonder of the starlit sky.

Chapter 10
Of The Universality of Mountains

'It really wasn't easy for you. You had to explore for so many years, just to reach our starting point!' Fan exclaimed in admiration.

>> That is the reason why you should consider yourself a very lucky civilization.

Just then, the size of the ice crystal clouds formed by the escaping atmosphere dramatically increased. The heavens shone with a sparkling light, a brilliant rainbow wreath blooming as the alien vessel's glow scattered in the ice. Below, the titanic cyclonic well continued its rumbling turns. It made Fan think of an insanely massive machine pulverizing the planet bit by thundering bit. Here on top of the mountain, however, everything had become completely still. Even the tiny ripples had disappeared from the summit's surface. The ocean was mirror still. Again, Feng Fan was reminded of the mountain lakes of North Tibet…

With a jolt, he forced his mind back to reality.

'Why did you come here?' he asked the sphere above.

>> We are just passing by, and we wanted to see if there was intelligent life here with which we could have a chat. We talk to whoever first climbs this mountain.

'Where there's a mountain, there will always be someone to climb it,' Fan intoned, nodding.

>> Indeed, it is the nature of intelligent life to climb mountains, to strive to stand on ever higher ground to gaze farther into the distance. It is a drive completely divorced from the demands of survival. Had you, for example, only been concerned with staying alive, you would have fled from this mountain as fast and far as you could. Instead, you chose to come and climb it. The reason evolution bestows all intelligent life with a desire to climb higher is far more profound than mere base needs, even though we still do not understand its real purpose. Mountains are universal, and we are all standing at the foot of mountains.

'I am on the top of the mountain,' Feng Fan interjected. He would not stand for anyone, not even aliens, to challenge the glory of having climbed the world's tallest mountain.

>> You are standing at the foot of the mountain. We are all always at the foot. The speed of light is the foot of a mountain; the three dimensions of space are a foot of a mountain. You are imprisoned in the deep gorge of light-speed and three-dimensional space. Does it not feel... cramped?

'We were born this way. It is what we are familiar with,' Fan replied, clearly lost in thought.

>> Then the things that I will tell you next may be very unfamiliar. Look at the universe now. What do you feel?'

'It is vast, limitless, that kind of thing,' Fan answered.

>> Does it feel small to you?

'How could it? The universe stretches out endlessly before my eyes; scientists can even peer as far as twenty billion light years into space,' Fan explained.

>> Then I shall tell you: it is no more than a bubble world twenty billion light years in radius.

Fan had no words.

>> Our universe is an empty bubble, a bubble within something more solid.

'How could that possibly be? Would this larger solid not immediately collapse in under its own gravity?' Fan asked, bewildered.

>> No, at least not yet. Our bubble is still expanding in this super-universal solid. Gravitational collapse is only an issue for a bounded, solid space. If, however, the surrounding solid area is actually limitless, then gravitational collapse would be a non-issue. This of course is no more than a guess. Who could know whether this solid super-universe has its own limits?

>> There is so much space for speculation. For example, one could theorize that at its immense scale, gravity is offset by some other force, just like electromagnetism is largely offset by nuclear forces on the microscopic scale. We are not aware of such a force, but when we were inside the Bubble

World, we remained unaware of gravity. From the data we have gathered, we can see that the form of the universe's bubble is much like your scientists have surmised. It is just that you do not know what lies beyond it yet.

'What is this solid? Is it...?' Fan hesitated for a moment. 'Rock?' he finally asked.

\>> We do not know, but we will discover that in fifty thousand years, once we reach our destination.

'Where exactly are you going?' Fan asked.

\>> The edge of the universe. Our bubble ship is called the *Needle's Point*. Do you remember the name?

'I remember,' Fan answered. 'That was the ship that first discovered the law of decreasing density in the Bubble World.'

\>> Correct. We do not know what we will find.

'Does the super-universe have other bubbles in it?' Fan enquired.

\>> You are already thinking very far ahead, indeed.

'How could I not?' Fan responded.

\>> Think of the many small bubbles inside a very big rock. They are there, but they are very hard to find. Even so, we will go and look for them.

'You truly are amazing.' Fan smiled, holding a deep admiration for the adventurous aliens.

\>> Very well, our little chat was most delightful, but we must make haste; fifty thousand years is a very long time, and we are burning daylight, so to speak. It was a pleasure meeting you; and remember, mountains are universal.

The sheer density of the ice crystal clouds made the last few words indistinct, blurred behind the clouds. And with those final words, the giant sphere, too, began to slowly dim, its form fading smaller and smaller into the heavens. Soon it had shrunk to a mere dot, just another star in an endless sky. It left much faster than it had arrived, and within moments it had disappeared altogether across the western horizon.

Everything between heaven and ocean was returned to deep black. Ice crystal clouds and the cyclonic well were swallowed by the darkness, leaving only a trace of swirling black chaos, barely visible in the skies above. Feng Fan could hear the roar of the encircling tempest rapidly diminish. Soon, it was no more than a soft whimper, and before long, even that had died. All that remained was the sound of the waves.

Feng Fan suddenly became aware of the sensation of falling. Looking around, he could see the ocean slowly begin to change. The perfectly round summit of the water mountain had begun to flatten like a giant parasol being stretched open. He knew that the water mountain was dissolving, and that he was plummeting a good thirty thousand feet. Within minutes, the water he was floating on stopped falling, having reached sea level. The inertia of his fall carried him down deep below the surface.

Luckily, he did not sink too far this time and quickly bobbed up to the surface.

As he surfaced, he realized that the water mountain had completely disappeared into the ocean, leaving not even the slightest trace, appearing just as if it had never been there. The cyclone, too, had spun itself out of existence, even though he could still feel the hurricane force winds batter him as they whipped up large waves. Soon, the ocean's surface would be calm again.

As the ice crystal clouds scattered, the magnificent starry heavens again spanned the sky.

Feng Fan looked up at the stars, thinking of that distant world so very, very far away – so remote that even the light of that day must have been reeling from exhaustion before reaching Earth. There, in that ocean long ago, Gagarin of the Bubble World had raised his head to the stars as Fan did now; and through the vast barrenness of space and the desolation of time, he felt a deep bond of kinship unite their spirits.

In a sudden a burst of nausea, Feng Fan felt himself retch. He could tell from the taste it was blood. Miles above sea level, on the summit of the water mountain, he had suffered altitude sickness. A pulmonary oedema was hemorrhaging. He instantly realized the severity of the situation. The sudden increase of gravity had left him too exhausted to move. Only his life jacket was keeping him afloat. He had no inkling as to the fate of the *Bluewater*, but he was almost certain that there could be no boats within at least half a mile of him.

When he was atop the summit, Feng Fan had felt his life fulfilled. Up there, he could have died in peace. Now, suddenly, there was no one on the planet who could have been more afraid to die than he was. He had climbed to the rocky roof of our planet, and now he had also climbed the highest watery peak the world had ever known.

What kind of mountain was left for him to climb?

He would have to survive; he had to find out. The primal fear of the Himalayan blizzard returned. Once, this fear had made him cut the rope connecting him to his companions and his lover. He had sealed their fate, leaving them dead to the world. Now he knew that he had done the right thing. If there had been anything left for him to betray to save his life, he would have betrayed it.

He had to live. There was a universe of mountains out there.